I DARE YOU

Also by Murray Bailey

Singapore 52
Map of the Dead

I DARE YOU

Murray Bailey

Heritage Books

HB

First published in Great Britain in 2016 by Heritage Books

1

copyright © Murray Bailey 2016

Set in Plantin Light 11.5/18pt and Tahoma 11.5pt

ISBN 978-0-9955108-0-7
e-book ISBN 978-0-9955108-1-4

Printed and bound by Clays Ltd, St Ives plc

Cover design by James Deacon
Author photograph by Arthur Yeung

Heritage Books, Truro, Cornwall

For my wife, Kerry.
You are my North Star.

ONE

With the sea air in his nostrils and the sunrise turning the ocean to liquid gold, he considered it one of those good-to-be-alive days. Which he found ironic considering his old job.

The humidity was always a problem. Except for this morning. An unusual cool breeze aided his daily run along the coast. He vaulted the wall into his garden and began his routine of press-ups and burpees. Three sets of a hundred. He stretched and dived into the pool.

When he emerged, his careworn housekeeper was waving at him. He'd learned a while back that it was too dangerous to have an attractive maid. There were plenty of pretty young women in the city. Easy to pick up. Easy to leave.

"Señor que es urgente!"

He snatched up a towel and followed the housekeeper into the air-conditioned villa. She pointed at the study.

He could already hear the beep, and the signal was confirmed by a blinking red light on the console.

"Gracias, Cristina." He flicked the response switch that meant he was ready to take a call and asked Cristina for an espresso.

Five minutes later, dressed and espresso consumed, the phone rang. There were no introductions but he

1

knew the voice. Codename Mustang. He would never use that name even though they both knew the line was scrambled and untraceable.

"I may need you for a cleaning job."

"May?"

"Depends how the dice fall," Mustang said, trying to draw him in no doubt.

"I'm retired."

"Or in exile?"

Cristina bustled past the patio window and he realized he was looking out at the palms, the beach and blue ocean beyond. Yes, Panama had its downsides, which was mainly the humidity. But better hot than the cold. He didn't like cold weather. Nightly electrical storms provided an amazing light show which he figured was down to the humidity. And since the canal had been widened, Panama City had become Central America's version of Dubai. Maybe it wasn't nirvana, but as an escape it was pretty damn good.

Mustang continued: "Just this one and you'll have enough money to retire properly. I presume you have the same account?"

"Yes."

"Check it while I send you the details." The line abruptly ended.

The advance in his bank account was more than he was usually paid in total. The reference code was relevant. Intrigued, he connected to a secure site and used the code to download a file.

Cristina showed no surprise at his request for a pack of gum. He popped a stick in his mouth and unconsciously played with the paper, folding and refolding. It helped him think and at other times it filled long hours of waiting.

He read the file. Remove the guy now; that would seem the easiest option. Mustang didn't explain. There was no *why*, just the *who*. The guy was part of Mustang's plan, and once over, the best case was it'd clean itself up. No need for his services. But plan for the worst. That was why Mustang needed someone. Someone he could trust to do it thoroughly.

The file had scenarios. The job: to get people to make the best case happen. And if it didn't then any witnesses had to be dealt with.

The final payment didn't depend on the scenario. He could buy a small island plus change for that. No more living in Panama. Maybe he'd have a host of pretty girls around the place.

He would never speak directly to Mustang again. Unless something went wrong. But nothing would.

He sat by the pool and re-read the file. Swallows darted across the water and their dips for flies caused a myriad of small ripples. He looked at the papers he'd been unconsciously folding and saw that he'd made a horse.

Why was Mustang so concerned? What had triggered the actions? The main guy was already in play, but which scenario would occur?

A young bird misjudged and hit the water. It flapped and paddled frantically before taking to the air again. He kept his eye on it, watched it swoop around, dipping perfectly the next time. There would be no second shot for him. It had to be right first time, whichever scenario played out. That meant being in control. He needed someone in the States and, he realized, someone else. In that moment his plan began to form. Watch, track and, if necessary, take control. He knew who to use: an ex-lover. She'd be attracted by the money and intrigue and

3

maybe the promise. He needed her in England. In Windsor. That wouldn't be a problem.

Getting her close to the girl may prove more of a challenge.

Time for the Janitor to come out of retirement.

4

TWO

There are days when a moment, an action, a decision, can determine the course of the rest of our lives. Sometimes we have a premonition or we can look back and recognize a warning sign. For Kate, the change was heralded by a thought, a random thought, as she stood at the rear bedroom window: how much of another person can we really know? Do we only see what they want us to see?

After six months, she was pretty certain the guy who had just left her Windsor apartment was the one for her. *Mr Right*, as her sister would tease. Sure, Kate didn't know everything, but didn't she know enough? A lifetime together would provide plenty of time for all the little facts and details.

Joe appeared at the corner and walked past the garages to his old silver Audi parked along by the fence. Even though he called himself *just a salesman* for a mobile phone company, anyone could see he was much more than that: the way he held himself, the way he walked with strong, confident strides.

He glanced up as he opened the car door and flashed his perfect Hollywood smile.

"Get a new car," she mouthed, and he laughed.

Joe was generous with many things, although never to himself. He would happily treat her, but when it came to something for himself, he would make do. "Need versus want," he would say. "The auto works fine and I don't need a new one."

"What about wanting something?"

"How about: I want you—and you are all I need?"

She smiled at the memory of the conversation. It was a good line, a little corny perhaps, but it worked, just like the line he used when they first met. She checked her watch as the Audi pulled away: 8:05. Whenever she was working part-time as a physio at the private tennis and health club, she used the late start to prepare breakfast for them both. But Joe's schedule always seemed so precise, and there he was again driving off at the same time. That side of him confused her slightly. On the one hand he was relaxed and fun but on the other he liked his routine. A mild case of OCD, perhaps? She could live with his tidiness—so long as the tins in the cupboard weren't lined up with their labels facing the same way.

The thought of tidiness prompted Kate into action. It was her morning to clean the bathroom and she also needed to pop into town.

She was crouching by the bath when the home phone rang. Turning quickly made her heel knock into the bath panel. The panel popped out along part of the top edge. She tried to push it back but it immediately sprang away, only wider this time. Now she could see the dusty floor beneath the bath. In her opinion, no one should ever see the fragility of their home. Builders should make houses into secure cocoons, where bricks and dirt and spiders were on the outside. The thought of a giant house spider lurking under the bath made her neck prickle.

The phone stopped ringing.

Kate knelt beside the bath and, trying not to look into the dark space, gave the panel a solid push. It didn't go back. There was no escaping it: she had to look at what she was doing. After a moment's consideration, she decided the top and bottom would have to be manoeuvred into place. It would have to start with the whole panel coming away. Carefully, as though slow movement would be less likely to result in spiders running out, Kate pulled the panel free from the bath.

She took a breath and looked at the strip along the floor where the bottom edge slotted in. Something caught her eye. A blue bag, the size of a small handbag, nestled under the tub. Gritting her teeth she reached for the bag, pinched a corner between finger and thumb, and pulled it free. She stood, took a step backwards and stared at it.

The shrill ring of the phone snapped her attention away. The only people who rang the home number were cold callers and Kate's mother. A second attempt was sure to be her mother. Perhaps something was wrong. Kate scuttled to the nearest phone.

"Hello?"

"Kate, it's your mother." She always started like that although there was an edge of stress to her voice this morning.

"What's wrong, Mumsie?"

"I can't connect to the internet this morning."

Great! Kate the PC support person. "Check the lights on the router—you know, the black box that connects to the phone line?"

There was a scuffling sound and then: "The lights are all green."

"Yes, but look at the symbol that's like the world. Is that light on?"

"No. Oh God, what do I do?"

"It's all right. Nothing's wrong. Remember, you've had this problem before. All you need to do is reboot— switch the black box off at the wall. Wait a minute and then switch it on again." While Kate listened to silence she stared in the direction of the bathroom. What was in the bag? Had it been left there by mistake? Possibly plumber's tools?

"Are you there, love?"

"I'm still here, Mumsie."

"The internet light blinked for a while and is now lit."

"Great, that should have fixed it."

Kate's mother said she was on the PC, and after a few seconds she reported that her web page had opened. Immediately, she started to chat about other things.

"Mumsie, I'm sorry. I haven't time right now. I'll call you tonight or maybe tomorrow evening. I've things to do."

Kate ended the call abruptly, with her mother still talking, and returned to the bathroom. She stared at the bag. Navy blue, two leather-looking handles, a clasp on top. The material was thick, maybe canvass. There was no dust.

This hadn't been left by a plumber. The apartment was over ten years old and, as far as Kate knew, no plumbing work had been done since construction. No, this bag had been put there deliberately. It had been hidden and only one person could have done it.

The bag dominated the centre of the table. Kate sat, her hands together, her fingers pressed against her lips as though she were praying but preventing the words from coming out.

Her long-haired, chocolate-coloured Siamese cat jumped onto her lap. She pushed him away. "Not now, Tolkien."

Tolkien wound himself around the chair and her legs until she placed a hand out. He stopped and pushed his head against her fingers.

"OK, let's do it." She stood, reached for the clasp, flicked it apart and withdrew her hands. The bag didn't open. She reached forward again, gritted her teeth and pulled at the clasps. It opened like a doctor's bag with a hinged metal frame. Inside was something wrapped in black plastic.

Tip it out or take it out? She opted for tipping. The plastic-wrapped item clunked onto the table, followed by a bundle of money, a British passport and a mobile phone.

Kate sat down again, her hands trembling. Through the plastic it looked like a gun.

THREE

Joe came into the lounge and said, "You're home earlier than I expected." He bent down to kiss her as she lay sprawled on the sofa.

Kate held up a hand to stop him. "Better not—I'm not feeling well." She couldn't bring herself to make eye contact.

"Anything I can get you?"

Kate pulled Tolkien closer to her chest, felt her heartbeat against him. "Nothing at the moment."

"Let me get changed and I'll attend to your every wish, your every whim."

She listened to his footsteps on the stairs. This was the final scene she'd played over and over in her head after calling in sick for work. Her first thought was to leave the house and stay with her sister until he moved out. Then she had decided to stuff all his clothes in a bag and leave them outside. She had started by pulling his clothes from the wardrobe and then stopped. His favourite shirt—the one he had worn on the day they met—had brought the memories flooding back.

At Sarah and Peter's engagement party, she found herself watching from the sidelines. Sarah had once been Kate's best friend but she hardly knew anyone else there.

And then the man with the enigmatic eyes and perfect white smile leaned close and whispered, "I dare you."

"Excuse me?"

"I dare you to cut in and ask that guy for a dance."

Kate realized she'd been watching a mismatched couple—the guy tall and thin, the girl's head only coming up to his sternum. Both were dressed in browns and black—dowdy and almost severe—out of place at the party.

Joe said, "I reckon they're from opposing Mafia families and their union was supposed to bring the two together."

Oddly, she'd had a similar thought. "That would explain it," she said with a smile.

"So, I dare you to break it up—and see what happens."

She rose to the challenge, and when she returned, Joe introduced himself.

As they shook hands, he said, "So, what do you think?"

"That while I was watching them, Joe, you were watching me."

"Guilty as charged." His lovely teeth flashed in a smile. "But I meant, what do you think about the odd couple now?"

She stole a glance at the skinny man who was again dancing with his short partner. "He's a Russian spy," she said, "keeping an eye on American expats." Then, before he could respond: "OK, now it's my turn: I dare you to eat one of those disgusting pickled herrings—with a dollop of chocolate sauce."

The childish game of dare continued for over an hour. Between horror and stitches from laughter she learned that Joe was an Italian-American working with Peter at Oskar, a mobile phone company.

"How do you know Sarah?" he asked.

"My best friend from school." While Kate had gone on to study physiotherapy, Sarah had read Business Studies at university then travelled the world before finding she had a penchant for selling foreign houses and settled in the Czech Republic. However, Kate knew that Peter was largely the reason for choosing Prague.

Before the party was over, Joe called for a taxi. They slipped away and were driven out to the countryside to join a Witches' Night celebration. Bonfires pushed flames into the dark sky and the crackle of wood accompanied the cackle of people dressed as witches. Effigies burned on the fires to great cheers and howls of glee and, if not for the food and beer stalls, Kate would have believed they'd been transported back to the Middle Ages.

In the early hours, they drove back to the town square and, after a stroll, found a café where they watched the sun rise over the river.

Kate thought falling in love was for others—if it existed at all—but spending the last few hours with Joe was making her reconsider. Her flight home was booked for the afternoon and, just when she wondered about catching some shut-eye before she'd get ready, Joe asked if she could rollerblade.

"Not since I was a kid."

She laughed nervously and found herself agreeing when he said, "Then I dare you."

With the sun warming a broad azure sky, they hired skates and joined crowds of young people on the streets. Although Kate's balance was better than she'd feared, she accepted Joe's offered hand. She lost sense of how many miles they'd travelled and, when they reached Prague Zoo, they put their skates in a locker and went in.

Kate had been to London Zoo in Regent's Park but had never imagined a zoo as large as Prague's.

"It's over 100 acres with 4,800 animals," Joe said and then grinned. "I'm not the font of all knowledge—I just read it at the gate."

They spent a couple of hours jumping on and off the tram to travel around and see the enclosures. Joe's favourite was the Indonesian Jungle with its exotic animal cries and the humidity of a steam room. For Kate, the giraffe enclosure with its cute baby on long wobbly legs was the best, although Joe likened it to her on skates. A silverback gorilla reminded Kate of Andrew, a close friend and masseuse at the Royal Berkshire club.

Checking the time on her phone, she said, "I'd better get going, if I'm to catch my plane." When she saw what he was thinking, she quickly added, "And don't dare me to miss it. I have work to get to on Monday."

Joe accompanied her back to her hotel to get her things and then saw her off at the airport. She hoped for a farewell kiss and was not disappointed. He seemed to read her mind, leaned in and lightly brushed her lips with his. Then, instead of pulling back, he kissed her more strongly and, as she responded, he pulled her close.

"Where did you learn to kiss like that?" she asked with a Cheshire cat grin once it ended.

"It's the Italian in me." He hesitated, holding her gaze. "I'd like to see you again. How about next weekend? I'll come to you."

Of course, she accepted and could think of nothing else until he turned up at her apartment the following Friday. They toured Windsor Castle, visited her favourite cafés and took a boat out on the river. She discovered then that they not only shared friends and an interest in exercise but they had both lost someone close in the past few years. Her father had died and he'd lost

13

his twin brother. And that was another connection, because Kate's sister had twins.

A week later she returned to Prague and began a romance that alternated between countries each weekend. In between, he sent her silly poems and messages of love every day and, when they were together, the world became both exciting and interesting and her laughter came easily.

Then after three months he said, "I've been offered a job at O2 in the UK."

"You'll live near me?"

He grinned. "Not only that, but I dare you to let me live with you."

Six months she had known him. Six amazing months. And now this.

"Kate." Joe had come back into the lounge and stood in the corner. "Where's my bag?" His tone was calm and flat.

She looked at him.

"You've been crying." Now there was concern in his voice.

She said, "What's going on?" Tolkien squirmed in her grasp and managed to escape.

Joe said nothing, took a step towards her.

"Stop!"

He froze and held out his arms like he wanted to hug her.

Kate sat up and glared. Her chest was tight as she forced the words out. "How dare you use me! How dare you lie to me! And how dare you have a bloody gun in my house!"

"I can explain."

There was a long silence and Kate blinked tears from her eyes.

Eventually she said, "I'm waiting."

"It's difficult."

"Difficult to explain why you told me you were American when you have a British passport? I bet it is. And difficult to explain why there's a picture of you in the passport but it's not Joe Rossini. No, it's Joe Ranieri." She shook her head, wiped the tears from her cheeks and stood. She pointed to the stairs. "Get out!"

Joe didn't move. "I'm kind of in protection—witness protection."

"What?"

He sighed, pointed to a chair and sat in it. "You know I said I was in the army? I was. Something happened and... and I had to leave. You see, I know things..."

She waited, held her breath.

He shook his head, sadness in his eyes. "I'm not allowed to talk about it. I shouldn't even tell you this much."

"But... so what? You didn't just quit, you said protection."

"I had to get out and take an identity. For all intents and purposes I'm now Joe Rossini. The job with Oskar Mobile was a cover, part of my new life."

Kate sat down and held her head for a moment. "Are you telling me our relationship has been part of your cover, Joe?"

He moved over to the sofa, knelt and cupped her chin gently. "No! I love you, Kate. I'm telling you this precisely because I love you." He kissed her. After hesitating, she accepted and returned the affection.

When she pulled away, she said, "Why the British passport in the name of Ranieri?"

"That was in case I needed it. I should have changed my ID but you already knew me as Rossini. I shouldn't have gotten involved with anyone but I fell for you. I want to be with you but at the same time don't want you involved."

"And you can't tell me anything else?"

"Not yet. Not until I can."

"And how do I deal with it—knowing, but not really knowing?"

That's when he said, "Trust me. Please just trust me."

And within a month he was gone.

FOUR

Twelve months later

Shadowed and deserted, the outpatients department echoed with the last of the staff closing up for the evening. As the reception light went out, raindrops sparkled on the glass doors of the hospital like orange jewels in the dark. With her phone pressed to her ear, Kate wondered if the rain had stopped long enough to risk the short walk home.

"Kate?" Darcy prompted in her ear, and Kate realized she'd missed the end of her sister's monologue.

"Sorry, I'm just tired and was wondering whether the rain had stopped." It was a weak excuse and Darcy would know. Kate stepped out into the orange-lit car park, keeping the excuse going: "I've been on my feet all afternoon seeing patients. Most have bad backs. And now my back—"

"You work too hard. I've told you before, two jobs is one too many."

"I have two half-jobs. It's the modern way."

"You and I both know the hospital isn't half a job. Working at the club is extra. You're over-compensating." Darcy didn't say more, but Kate knew it was a bit of a dig.

17

Kate sensed her throat flush with annoyance. It was OK for Darcy, stay-at-home mother of two, husband with a good job in the City. Two years Kate's junior and as controlling as when they'd been kids.

Kate was about to say something she may have regretted but Darcy switched back to the reason she'd called.

"So, you'll give Terry a chance?"

Terry. Mum's first man-friend since Dad had died. It had been four years. Was that long enough to wait?

"She's entitled to some happiness. Just because you..." Darcy bit off the end of her sentence and then said, "I'm sorry."

Kate had stopped walking. How long had she been standing on the kerb beside the road? Cars came around the bend on the one-way system, lights briefly in her eyes, tyres hissing on the wet surface. There was no one else on the street except for someone about thirty yards behind, coming out of the hospital car park.

At a break in the traffic, Kate began to cross. "Darcy, look, I'll call you tomorrow." She ended the call, dropped the phone into her handbag and pulled her collar up against the chill damp air.

She always took the back way to her house because of the church, with its cherry trees a cloud of pink in the spring. Although it was the wrong time of year, and dark, she could still imagine its prettiness.

Footsteps behind made her glance back. A man in a hoodie hurried six paces or so behind, head down. She turned and he seemed to be right beside her. Her pulse crazy, she stopped, hand on the pepper spray in her bag. But he was there and then gone. Kate breathed and cursed herself for being so paranoid. He was just some guy rushing to get home after work. She shook her head, glad no one knew about this irrational fear.

She took the alleyway between the houses. There were no street lights here. The garage space beyond provided enough orange glow to see the path and the four steps at the end.

Kate sensed someone before she heard him. A sixth sense prickled in her neck and pulled on her jaw. Then footsteps were right behind her—someone running.

She leapt the steps into the garage area. A hand grabbed her shoulder. She twisted and spun, snatched the pepper spray and swung it towards the man. It was the same guy in the hoodie.

"Hey!" he shouted, letting go of her jacket and stumbling a pace beyond her. He stepped back, looking from her to the spray and back. He raised his hands, shook his head and said, "I was just running home— Sorry!" The words came out as staccato breaths.

She didn't believe him and there was something about his eyes, the way he looked at her.

"You grabbed me," she said.

"I tripped up the steps. I was going to fall. Sorry." He studied her for moment, his eyes narrow, as though thinking, and then he ran off.

Kate watched him round the corner of the car park before she could move again. When she reached her front door she looked up and down the road in case the man in the hoodie was still around. Seeing no one, she took out her key and a trembling hand finally got the door open.

Kate sat on the stairs with her head in her hands until the shaking stopped. The timer clicked on the upstairs' lights and, when she got up, Tolkien was sitting on the top step watching her with his intelligent blue eyes. She rubbed his head as she passed and stood by the mirror at the top of the stairs. With an ashen face and eyes wide and black, she thought she looked a decade older than her twenty-six years.

She continued to look at the shadow of herself as she phoned Darcy.

"You all right, sis?" Darcy asked, after Kate told her what had happened.

"I'll be OK." As Kate smeared the tears with the palm of her hand, she could hear her sister's twins in the background. One of them was calling, but Darcy wasn't giving up.

"Kate, you should—"

"OK, what if I tell the police? And what if they find him? What if he tells them I had pepper spray?"

"I don't see—"

"Joe gave it to me. It's the real stuff—the illegal stuff."

Darcy was quiet for a moment and Kate knew what was coming next. It had been almost a year since Joe had disappeared. Yes, he had fake identities, but he was no criminal. The Joe she knew was kind and loving and generous. Of course he had a past, but he'd confessed his secret and she believed him. Everyone else said she was crazy and told her to move on, and Darcy was the most critical.

"You know what may or may not have happened tonight has nothing to do with Joe, right?" Before Kate could respond, she heard a crash like broken pottery on the other end. Darcy said, "One second," shouted at the children and then smoothly resumed the conversation with Kate. "This is just a coincidence, sis. Tell me you know that."

Kate didn't say anything. On one level it didn't, but the awareness—the self-preservation—that was all about what Joe had told her.

Darcy said, "Run yourself a nice hot bath. Have a soak and I'll be over in forty minutes."

20

"No, you've got the girls and it's got to be their bedtime." Kate knew that Darcy's husband Tim wouldn't be home yet, so coming over would mean bringing the twins. "I'll be fine. I'll take your advice on a soak in the bath though."

Darcy put up a fight, but Kate repeated, "I'll be fine. Seriously, I'll be fine."

"OK, just promise me you'll call if you need me. I'll come over anytime. If Tim's not here, I'll get a neighbour to mind the girls."

"I love you, sis," Kate said and felt the tears return.

"Love you too, sis. And promise me you'll stop thinking about Joe."

Tolkien was looking expectant as Kate ended the call. She bent, ruffled his brown fur and he mewed something, probably about wanting food. Tolkien loved to talk, and on most evenings Kate would have accommodated but, after feeding him and running a bath, she put a chill-out album on the iPod, closed her eyes and let the past come back to life.

FIVE

The phone disturbed Kate's daydreams.

"Hi Mumsie."

"Are you all right, Pip dear?"

Pip had been Kate's father's pet name for her and her mother used it occasionally. Somehow, when she did, it helped. "I'm fine, Mumsie. I'm fine."

"Well, your sister just called and told me all about it. You really should call the police." Her mother continued for a while, but the subject never really changed.

When Kate could get a word in, she said, "Really, I'm fine. And the police won't take it seriously because he didn't actually attack me."

"But he probably would have."

"We don't know that for certain."

"Well at least get one of those personal alarms."

"I'll think about it."

"That's good, dear. Now do you have plans for a week on Sunday? Will you come over for lunch?"

Kate knew that Terry would be there. "Mumsie, I don't think—"

"Please, it would mean a lot—to both of us."

"I'll think about it." she said, but knew she'd make other plans.

"Like you'll think about calling the police?"

Kate knew she'd find it difficult to deal with the police. There was no point. They wouldn't do anything, just like they'd done nothing about Joe's disappearance.

That night, she found herself reliving the day it all happened. She recalled the cold crispness of the November air and the crunch of the leaves underfoot as they strolled on The Long Walk in Windsor's Great Park.

Joe had taken the day off so that they could spend time together and enjoy The Changing of the Guard. On the walk they hadn't spoken much, and Joe pulled at his right eyebrow, something he did when deep in thought. It'd been over two weeks since they had taken a kayak up to Henley. He'd told her stories of being in the army— and that he had a secret he couldn't share. He'd wanted to say more, she could tell, but each time managed to stop himself.

Perhaps that was why he was quiet now. Eventually he seemed to shake off the melancholy and said, "What a great day!" He placed an arm around her shoulders. "I love this country. Beautiful girl, beautiful colours. And look at those stags. They're awesome—I can just picture their heads on a trophy wall."

He winked and laughed as he ducked her playful swipe. Her Joe was back.

"It's not normally this pretty in the autumn," she said. "We've been lucky this year. It's usually wet and windy."

"Reminds me of Virginia in the fall." He ran a hand through her hair and then pulled her close into a long kiss. When they broke apart, she pointed out the green birds flying between the trees. "Look, parakeets! About ten years back, some pet birds escaped from West London," she explained. "They've made their home here. They seem to be thriving."

He raised his eyebrows and smiled. "Out of place—but happy. I know how they feel."

"You OK, Joe?"

A flash of concern, then a smile. "Sorry, hon. It's just work. You know how it is. Someone high up at O2 has been riding my ass. I'm fine. And I love you."

She held him tighter as they walked and continued towards the castle. As they approached, she pointed to the flag on the tower—the Queen's crest, her colours.

"The Queen's at home," she said. "You can always tell when the Queen's here. When she's not, they fly the Union Jack."

"That's crazy," Joe said. "So a terrorist would know when she's in the castle, know when to attack? And look here," he continued, grabbing her elbow and leading her to the right of the fence. "This side gate. Only a rusty padlock to stop a terrorist? What a joke."

She was impressed with the observation, but said, "There's never been any trouble." Then she thought about it and added, "Unless you count the idiot who climbed over the fence a few years ago dressed as Osama bin Laden."

"And I read that some lunatic climbed over a wall at Buckingham Palace and managed to get into the Queen's bedroom."

"That was ages ago," she said dismissively, but he was having none of it.

"You Brits are amazing. You think you're safe because there hasn't been a problem in the past. It's only a bloomin' lunatic, so that's awlright... mate!" he said in an attempt at Cockney.

She laughed. "That's a terrible impression!"

"Cor blimey, governor, it's proper brilliant," he said, mocking the excessive use of the words *proper* and *brilliant* by the British, although he didn't understand its use as sarcasm.

"No, stop!" Laughing, she doubled up in pain. "You're making my sides hurt."

At the castle's main gates, a uniformed policeman prevented unauthorized entry. Kate thought about commenting on the reliability of the British police, but decided against it. She could just imagine his cheeky response: *How reliable are these police who don't even carry guns?*

She checked her watch: 10:40. The Changing of the Guard would begin any second. Moments later, marching-band music struck up in the distance. They hurried to High Street just in time to see the men appear from Victoria Barracks, about two hundred yards along the road. Crowds of tourists lined the street all the way to the castle gates.

"You know it's officially called Mounting the Guards!" he said.

"Now that *would* be a sight to see," she said, laughing.

They pushed their way towards the castle, where the huge black statue of Queen Victoria glares down. Joe used his size to wriggle to a good vantage point so they would see the soldiers march up the hill to the statue before turning right, towards the castle and main gate.

Although he liked to deny it, Joe loved playing the tourist. It had attracted him to historic Prague and he had visited all the sights in London and Windsor. However, in reality "all the sights of Windsor" only meant they had been inside the castle twice and around the grounds of Eton College and a visit to the site where the Magna Carta had been signed.

The band, five lines of five, looked like the famous Coldstream Guards, with ceremonial red uniforms, gold buttons and enormous bearskin hats. They played so loud and with a marching rhythm that people in the crowd found themselves walking and nodding in time.

"The Irish Guard," she said.

Joe raised his eyebrows, impressed.

She grinned, held up a hand in confession. "I saw the name outside Victoria Barracks."

Behind the band filed the twelve young men of the Queen's Foot Guards—four lines of three—who would be exchanged in the ceremony. Three officers led the twelve and a sergeant major marched at the rear.

In the past, Joe had led the way ahead of the parade to stake out a prime spot by the gate and then peer through the bars as the ceremony unfolded. This time he held back.

As Kate moved to get ahead, Joe touched her arm and said, "Let's follow, for a change."

She didn't question it. They moved against the flow until they joined the crowd at the rear of the parade. This wasn't going to work well. She could see people already claiming the best positions at the gate. As the last soldier passed through the entrance, the crowd surged.

Someone pushed her.

"Hey!"

Bodies pressed all around. Then there was another surge and she felt a hand on her shoulder. For a moment she assumed it was Joe providing support. Then she stumbled and felt the person's weight lean into her, pressing down. A man's fat stomach pushed against her. She staggered and fell.

"Hey!"

No one helped her up. People were fixated on getting a good view. Joe didn't help her either. Where was he anyway? She elbowed her way between people and found a space on the path away from the shoving

26

tourists. She caught her breath and scanned the crowd for Joe, starting at the gates and working back. She couldn't see him. A small wall ran along the path and she stood on it.

"Joe?" she called. It was ridiculous to think he might hear above the noise.

Something prompted her to turn then, away from the main crowd.

A red tourist bus and a handful of taxis lined the road. People milled about, but three men caught her attention. Sixty yards or so away they moved together; the outer two had suits and hats. They were so close that the man in the middle looked like he was being guided.

They walked towards a nondescript maroon estate car parked between the taxis. As they turned to get in, she saw him clearly.

"Joe!"

Her shout was swallowed by the clamour, but he seemed to respond. He started to turn then hesitated. The two men grabbed him roughly. They shoved him into the back seat of the car. One of the men joined him in the back, the other walked to the driver's side.

What the hell? *Do something!*

Kate jumped from the wall and tried to hurry towards the road. People were in the way, jostling. She shoved one, then two, not caring about the protests. In less than a minute, she broke through the dense part of the crowd and began to run.

"Joe!" she shouted out again.

The car was so close, Kate saw him clearly as he leaned to the window. His eyes were wide with concern and his mouth moved. It looked like: "Trust me. I dare you."

As she neared the road, the car accelerated away around the bend.

And that was the last time she saw him.

SIX

Lisa looked around, checking no one could overhear. "You know Julian at the club?" she whispered.

Kate and her friend sat outside a café at the bottom of Peascod Street, waves of heat belting from a patio heater. It had changed its name, menu and décor, and would change again within a year, a constant rotation of independents trying to make it on an overcrowded stretch in a town driven by the tourist season and beyond sight of the castle. In the evening the cafés tried to be upmarket bars but there was still too much competition and the token heater did not make the outdoor eating experience remotely reminiscent of the Med.

"Of course I do." Kate played along and leaned in conspiratorially. "I may not be a member but I do know the other staff there."

"Well, he's my new personal trainer." Lisa grinned. "Dishy, don't you think?"

Kate had to agree, Julian was a good-looking guy, although too into his own body and looks. In his early twenties, he was at least ten years younger than Lisa. "Not my type," she said, "but I know quite a few of the girls fancy him."

Lisa worked for American Airlines and had been working out of Chicago O'Hare for the past two years but was now back at London Heathrow. They had met at Ceroc dance classes, and while Kate briefly tried it and attended for fun and dancing, Lisa's clear goal was to pick up guys. She'd also discovered that Lisa was a member of the Royal Berkshire club.

"What are you working on these days?" Kate asked, struggling to understand why Lisa's news should be interesting.

Lisa winked.

"No, I mean fitness-wise."

"Overall conditioning, but my thighs and bingo wings especially."

Kate nodded and took a sip of her Pinot Grigio.

Lisa leaned closer and dropped her voice. "We've been in the Lookout—Julian and I." The Lookout was the public expanse of Windsor Forest next to the club where trainers often took people jogging. "Power-walking," Lisa continued as if reading Kate's mind.

"Won't be long before you can come running with me then," Kate said.

Again, Lisa looked to check no one could overhear. "We went off the trail—you know, one of the secluded tracks." She winked and Kate wondered what the secret was.

Lisa leaned in even closer so that she could whisper into Kate's ear. "Well, when we were out of sight, he grabbed me and took me in the undergrowth..." She stopped and stared. "You all right? You've gone all pale."

Kate forced a smile. It'd been over a week since confronting the man in the hoodie. The mention of being grabbed brought back the sensation of the man's hand on her shoulder. "I haven't told you," she said, "but a guy recently tried to... I don't know."

"Attack you?"

"To be honest I don't know what would have happened, but he grabbed at me in the dark. I know it's silly but your story just brought it all back."

"Oh you poor love. You're shaking." Lisa held Kate's hand and gave her a hug. "I'm so sorry, I had no idea."

"Of course you didn't. It's not your fault."

Following Kate's story, Lisa asked, "Did you tell the police?"

"The Thames Valley Police are a waste of time. Community policing, fine, but anything serious and they're totally ineffectual." Kate felt her throat flush; the incident with Hoodie-man had been replaced by anger and frustration with the police.

Lisa frowned. She returned to her seat and ordered them both another drink before insisting on knowing what had happened. Kate didn't explain that Joe had warned her. Or about his secret. Andrew, the silverback gorilla of a masseuse, was the only person she shared that with. Now, as the anniversary of his disappearance loomed, she found herself remembering every detail of the day he'd told her. The day she called their *semi-versary*.

"I've known you for six months as of today," Kate said, luxuriating in the bed. The sunlight streamed through a gap in the bedroom curtains, forming a bright wedge from Joe's torso and up to his forehead. She placed a hand on his firm chest and pushed her fingers through the knot of dark hair.

"Is that some kind of record?" he said, laughing, and she responded with a playful push.

"Like an anniversary, only a six month one—a *semi-versary*." She paused, studying his face. "Is everything all right, Joe? Are we OK?"

"God, yes, we're fine." He kissed her. "And, Ms Blakemore, I love you."

She looked deep into his grey-brown eyes and believed him, but he had been troubled for over a week—ever since their conversation about his secret. She desperately wanted to ask for more detail but couldn't push it. She was certain he was the one and would just have to give him time.

"Great, then let's celebrate our *semi-versary*."

He grinned at her. "Oh, OK. So what would you like to do? Catch a movie? Go to the theatre? A candlelit dinner?"

"Surprise me," she said, and raised an eyebrow.

Joe rolled on his side, a sparkle of mischief in his eyes. He ran his hand lightly over her body, starting with a gentle caress of her face and finishing at her thigh.

"I said surprise me, Joe Rossini!"

He flashed his smile. "Maybe I can." He repeated the manoeuvre, only this time following the curve of her breast and ending further inside the thigh. Her body responded and she met his grey-brown eyes. Her breath juddered and she smiled.

"Oh boy, how do you do this to me? I'm putty in your hands." She stroked his side. "All right, I give in, but something special later to celebrate."

"Deal," he said, rolling over her. "I'll think of something." With tenderness, he kissed her neck.

Joe made a phone call and reported he'd arranged to borrow a kayak for the day. The plan was to paddle up the river Thames, from Marlow to Henley, find somewhere nice to eat and have a leisurely ride back with the current.

It was a perfect day, warm for late October. The sky was a washed-out blue with high strips of cloud like fine gauze.

After the first half an hour of paddling, Kate gave up and let Joe do the work in their two-man. She kept in rhythm with his strokes although her blades barely touched the surface.

He made it all the way to Henley without a rest—even carrying the kayak to bypass a lock.

Steering alongside boats moored by a bridge, they got out and Joe pulled the kayak onto the pavement. They joined the crowd on the patio of a pub called The Idle Hour and ate a hearty lunch.

The return, as predicted, was much easier. At the lock Joe carried the kayak onto the towpath and pulled out a blanket and a cool-bag he'd stowed in the prow. He spread the blanket on the grass, a weir splashing close by.

"I dare you to join me for a glass of champagne—" he said as he opened the bag, "hopefully still chilled—and strawberries."

He popped the cork and Kate held the two imitation glass flutes as he poured. They chinked plastic. "To us," he said.

"To many more semi-versaries," she said.

After the drink and strawberries, they lay on their backs and listened to the river and birds. Gilded by the last of the afternoon sun, the river added to the romance of the day and Kate felt herself drifting off to sleep.

"Hey, don't drop off!"

She opened her eyes and looked up into his face. She smiled, but for once it wasn't returned.

"Joe?"

"I need to tell you something," he said.

Kate's mind snapped awake.

"Last week—when I was late home—I met with my...
I guess you'd call him my handler. He said I can explain
the situation, but only a little—I can't tell you
everything."

She waited, held her breath and recalled that horrible
day waiting for Joe to come home, thinking about the
gun he'd hidden under the bath.

"I told you I'd been in the army. Well it was more
than just a short spell. I did two tours in Iraq and I'm
kinda connected to a Special Forces mission that went
wrong."

"What does Special Forces mean? Something like the
SAS?"

"Kind of. It's about a unit that was off the radar. You
know, the stuff the government doesn't admit to.
Plausible deniability—I'm sure you've heard the
expression."

"What, you mean stuff like rendition and torture?"

"Well it could, but I was never involved in any of
that."

"Did you kill anyone?"

"It was part of the territory. Soldiers have to be
prepared to kill."

"How many?"

He shrugged, shook his head.

Kate looked out across the water and then back. "You
said the mission went wrong."

"I can't talk about the details."

She saw the conflict in his eyes and stroked his head.
"What *can* you say, baby?"

"I can tell you about my history—about the army—
but nothing about Special Forces. Nothing about the
mission. I can't blow my cover—even to you. I know
that's hard, but there's a good reason. We believe that
there's someone who would like me dead. It's not really

witness protection. I'm kinda in hiding, though it's much more complicated than that." He sighed and held her close. "I love you, Kate, but I'm now worried that you may be in danger too. That's also why I can't tell you much really. The less you know, the better."

She wanted him to say he was joking then, but his face was deadly serious. "Should I be worried?"

"Not at the moment, hon. I'm going to do everything I can to make sure you're all right." He shook his head, sadness in his eyes. "If anything should happen, you need to believe that I love you and that I want to be with you. No matter what, I will put it right."

SEVEN

During Sunday lunch, Terry suddenly said, "There'll be a meteor shower at ten tonight."

Mumsie had introduced him as retired but a keen amateur astronomer. They'd made initial small talk and Kate had learned he'd worked at Bracknell Town Council for over thirty years, but after that he'd barely said a word. With short grey hair, hardly any neck and tired eyes—undoubtedly the result of three decades in the same role—Kate found something familiar about him but couldn't place it. He seemed inoffensive enough, if a little serious. However Kate felt her stomach tighten when he sat in her father's old carver at the dinner table.

As if it were a planned conversation, her mother said, "That's interesting, where in the sky will we be able to see it, Terry?"

Kate cringed, certain her mother didn't really know the difference between astronomy and astrology.

"If you look east you'll see Jupiter just below the constellation of Gemini..." Terry went on to talk about other planets and constellations and Kate found herself tuning him out. She could just picture Terry at his telescope, asking for instructions, and Mumsie reading out the latest horoscope. She stared at her cut-crystal wine glass on the mahogany table and tried to think of something other than there being a replacement for her father in the carving chair.

When she finished her meal she said, "Thanks for the dinner. It's been ages since I've had Sunday roast."

Her mum's eyebrows knitted together. "You need to look after yourself, sweetie."

Abruptly Terry piped up: "I hear you're a bit of a runner." Kate expected him to add something, but an awkward silence stretched between them until her mother broke it.

"Do you know Sheila Attwood, Kate, at the bottom of the road—number 18? Oh of course you do. You went to school with her son Gary."

Kate pulled a thin smile. "He was in the year above." In a few days it would be a year since Kate had lost Joe. That's why she'd finally accepted the invitation to lunch—as a distraction—but she had an inkling of what her mother was up to.

"That's right. Well, you might not know but Gary went to Cambridge to read Maths. Then he went into the City with some big firm. Anyway, he's moved back to the area, got a job in Reading. He's doing very well and..." Her mother stopped herself and had a mischievous sparkle in her eyes. "Well, Sheila is having a small get-together next week—for her sixtieth—and I wondered if you'd like to come along. Gary will be there."

Kate said nothing.

"Sounds like fun," Terry said, and Kate was sure he'd been prepped.

"I'm busy," Kate snapped back, and she saw her harshness made Terry blink.

He tried a smile. "You haven't been told which night it is yet, Pip."

Kate's blood boiled. She stood. "Firstly, my name is not Pip. It is Kate to you, Terry. And secondly I am busy all next week—though I don't see why I should justify myself to you." She realized it was an overreaction but couldn't stop herself. "Thanks again for Sunday lunch, Mum. It was appreciated, but I'd better be going."

As she drove home, Kate realized why Terry looked familiar: the hair, the tired eyes and, most of all, no neck. He was like the first policeman who had visited after Joe's disappearance, but that was where the similarity ended. No-neck, the policeman, could have been a bouncer with muscles like he could bench-press a truck. Terry on the other hand looked like he'd never lifted more than a pencil. She found herself thinking about the policeman and how lost and powerless she'd felt.

No-neck arrived to take a statement in the evening, a whole day after Joe's abduction. After seeing the car disappear, she'd run to the police station on Alma Road, an antiseptic room with white walls decorated by a handful of instructional posters. A policewoman sat distractedly behind a hatch and pointed to a phone on the wall as Kate began to speak.

"To report a crime, dial eight," she said.

A man immediately answered and listened patiently to her story, almost too patiently. She gave her details then Joe's name, date of birth, and description. Then the man asked for the make and registration number of the maroon car. Annoyed at herself, Kate admitted she hadn't noted it down.

"Are you all right? Do you need victim support?" he asked.

"No, I'm fine."

He gave her an incident report number and told her someone would be in touch.

"Is that it?" Her frustration boiled over.

"Not sure there's anything else we can do for now," he responded calmly. "Try and recall the details of the car."

Kate put the phone down and stared at it, willing the conversation to have been different. Eventually she tore herself away and staggered home.

The day went by and no one called. No Joe. No police. She telephoned the police station and was transferred to someone who, after patiently listening to her story and taking a note of her incident report number, confirmed that Joe was not a British national.

"American," Kate explained. "So someone is going to come round and help me?"

The man spoke in a collected manner and said a constable would visit to take a full statement.

There was something typically low ranking about No-neck: a middle-aged sergeant with the type of face that said both *don't mess with me* and *I don't care.*

"He was abducted," Kate said after the usual preliminaries.

No-neck sat opposite in the lounge and studied Kate as she drank tea and tried to choose her words carefully. She prayed there was no hysterical edge to her voice, although she thought No-neck was assessing whether she was a crank.

"So you say he was abducted." His voice showed no such consideration or emotion as he wrote in a notebook. "You're sure?"

Breathe. "Well, no—"

"Why would someone abduct him?"

What should she say? What could she say? Joe's secret was not one she was willing to disclose, even to a policeman. Perhaps the two were linked. Before she changed her mind, the policeman spoke again.

"Let's start at the beginning shall we, Ms Blakemore?"

"Kate."

"And your boyfriend's name?"

"Joe. Joe Rossini."

"Italian?"

"American. I explained on the phone."

The sergeant nodded as though this was significant. Maybe he was playing a game with her. Maybe this policeman knew something too.

"Appearance?"

"Six-one, short dark-brown hair, grey-brown eyes, sometimes look green." She stopped herself from adding: good-looking and has a nice smile. Instead, she handed the policeman a photograph.

"Walk me through the events of the day."

Kate gave him every detail she could recall, even down to the appearance of a lady who had helped calm her afterwards. No-neck wrote it down as though it were all important. Finally, he also asked for the car's registration number. Kate described the car, guessing the make wasn't top end. "Maybe a Vauxhall Vectra."

"Definitely a Vauxhall then?"

"No, but it was maroon."

"OK." He tucked his notebook into a breast pocket. "I'll see what I can find out." As Kate saw him to the door, he added, "Someone will be in touch."

That same easy phrase.

She doubted anyone would be in touch. She felt like she had just been through a process, a form-filling, target-meeting exercise. She let her irritation show: "What are you going to do about it?"

He tucked his notebook into his jacket pocket and smiled condescendingly. "If we hear anything, we'll call."

No one did call and, as the days became a week, the initial hysteria was replaced by a growing numbness. She called the police again, but couldn't get past a receptionist. She left a message and said if no update was forthcoming she would go to the press. After jabbing the *End Call* button like a slam of the phone, she wondered what she would say to a reporter. What could she say? Nothing about Joe's secret past, just the lack of action following the kidnapping. Would that be enough to get the media interested?

To clear her head she went out for fresh air and ambled around Windsor, stopped for a cup of tea at a café in the old station and then wandered through the arcade of boutiques, looking in shop windows. As she paused for a moment studying a quirky painting in an art gallery, she became aware of a man in a brown suit. He stood a little too close for comfort. She looked at his reflection. He was looking straight into her eyes.

Kate spun around. "Do you mind?" she said with a little more venom than intended. Then her eyes flicked from the man to another. The second man, in an identical brown suit, boxed her in. Was this what Joe had warned her about? Her mind screamed *run!*

"Kate Blakemore." The second man said—a statement not a question.

She weighed her options: dart left, right, push between, and then realized the man was holding out something for her to see.

His voice was hushed, the accent mild-American. "We're detectives, miss. Please come with us. We can talk." He turned and headed towards a café. The other man followed.

Threat gone, Kate stood still, adrenaline pumping through her veins. Then, as though pulled by an invisible string, she began to follow the brown-suited men.

Later it would register that the café they entered was empty. No staff even. But for now she had tunnel vision. The first suit sat at a table away from the door and she followed. He looked up and her eyes locked on his.

Her brain started to work. "Sorry, you said you were detectives?"

The first man nodded and introduced himself as Special Agent Woodall and his colleague as Hurwitz. He held up ID and said, "FBI to be precise. You reported the disappearance of Joe—"

"Rossini," she finished for him.

The man gave a slight nod, looked at her and said nothing for a while, thinking.

Kate's palms began to sweat, her heart suddenly drumming in her chest. She forced herself to speak. "Do you have news?" She swallowed hard and breathed. "I think he was kidnapped by the people after him."

Woodall nodded again. He paused as if assessing what to say, or maybe how to say it. As she waited for more of a response, she glanced from one to the other, thinking they seemed an uncomfortable pair. Woodall had pale skin and eyes, and sandy hair. He was clearly in charge. Hurwitz had warmer eyes and dark curly hair and acted like he was in the shadow of the sandy-haired agent or detective or whatever he was.

She said, "Sorry, but why are the FBI—?"

"Working with the British police?" Woodall said. "Joe wasn't kidnapped. He has been taken into custody." He looked at his partner, seemed to nod and then turned back to Kate. He said, "Only, Joe Rossini isn't his real name. It's Towers. His real name is Greg Towers."

"What?" was all she could mutter. The anxiety started to transform into a discomfort in her stomach—a rodent gnawing at her guts.

Hurwitz said, "He's British but passes himself off as an American. He was wanted for a number of ID thefts and impersonations both here and in the States." Again he hesitated and looked into Kate's eyes. "Mr Towers is also married. Married with two children in Charlottesville, Virginia."

Virginia? Yes, that fitted the comment on the walk through the leaves, but then what about his secret? She made a decision. "He told me he was something to do with Special Forces," she said quietly.

Hurwitz looked at her with pity.

"That's one of his covers, I'm afraid, Ms Blakemore. In addition to suspected fraud, there is a charge of impersonating an army officer." Woodall shook his head. "Apparently he bluffed his way in as a reservist."

Kate said nothing.

"The US equivalent of your TA," Hurwitz said.

Woodall studied her. "You look sceptical," he said. "May I suggest you look him up online."

It wasn't scepticism. She tasted bile and suppressed the urge to retch. When she stood, they didn't stop her, just impassively watched her walk out of the café.

She didn't recall walking home. She stood in front of her door and looked at her hand. It shook as she tried the key in the lock. Using the banister she walked slowly up one flight of stairs and then another. She staggered to her computer, switched on and googled "Greg Towers".

Kate read news articles that froze her to the chair for the rest of the day. Some focused on Towers' different identities, some on the plight of the women he had conned. There was no mention of the name Rossini.

For a time she felt a glimmer of hope. Could it be a coincidence? A mistake? She was grasping at straws until she read the most recent article, dated two years ago. Towers had been traced to the Czech Republic. As she read, she sensed a cold hand grip her heart and squeeze. Towers was believed to be working for a Czech mobile phone company. His live-in-girlfriend said he started to disappear for days at a time and then every weekend. He told her he was on covert missions in Iraq.

Three months earlier, the FBI with Interpol had closed in. Towers had fled.

That tallied with Joe coming to England and moving in with Kate.

EIGHT

Kate saw Lisa run along the corridor by the club lounge and waved. Lisa would be dashing to the boxercise class, Kate guessed, since Lisa had commented on how fit the instructor was. She'd already given up on personal trainer Julian, saying he was too demanding.

Lisa didn't see her, but as she looked back, Andrew scooted a chair next to Kate and plonked his bulk down heavily with a sigh. "How you doing, kiddo?"

Kate put the newspaper aside and smiled at her friend. "Long day," she said, and absently touched her right shoulder, thinking of the hours she'd worked—a day at King Edwards Hospital and a few hours in the evening at the Royal Berkshire club. "Naming no names, but my last patient is never happy. It's as though his sports injuries are my fault. He goes back to training hard before he's fully recovered and—"

"Katie!" Andrew was the only person who could get away with calling her that. Although he looked and had the posture of a silverback, he had the kindest heart she knew.

"Yes?"

Andrew creased his kind eyes. "I'm not talking about your work. I wondered how you're doing. I know what day it is today."

Kate shrugged. It had been a year to the day since Joe had gone. Andrew had been the only friend who had shown genuine sympathy. Unlike others, he never told her to get over her ex and he listened without judgement when she wanted to talk. He also had a knack of seeing right through her.

He reached forward and placed his paw of a hand on hers. "It's all right to miss him."

Kate turned so that no one else could see the tears that prickled her eyes. "I feel so stupid."

"To miss him? That's ridiculous. You were amazingly close. Some people go a whole lifetime without meeting a soulmate."

"But I feel stupid for believing him."

"You've been listening to your family again, Katie. Look, why don't you find out where they took him? You could even visit him in prison—hundreds of women do it."

Kate studied the concern on Andrew's face and slowly shook her head. She knew it was a massive contradiction, but part of her needed to believe in Joe. And confirming what the agents had told her—by tracking him down to a prison—would shatter the illusion that kept her going.

When she cleared out Joe's things, she'd asked Andrew to help. Everyone told her to dispose of them, but Andrew insisted they box it all up and he keep them in his attic. "Just in case," he'd said. And he'd been right. Somehow it helped—or did it just perpetuate the illusion? She didn't like to analyse too much.

She decided to change the subject. "How's the software programming going?" When he wasn't working as a masseuse, Andrew spent all his spare time either playing or writing computer games. A year ago he came up with what he said was a unique approach to encryption and was trying to sell the concept to the banks.

"Breakthrough!" Andrew beamed. "I didn't understand that banks will only deal with companies with a track record. So I've done a deal with an intermediary."

"That's great news. We should celebrate."

"Well, we're only at the preliminary stage—NDAs exchanged and talking about terms—but they have a number of small financial service companies who will jump at it. Mainly in the peer-to-peer sector, because regulations are tightening up—oh sorry, I'm being boring."

"Let's celebrate once you've signed the agreement then."

"Deal. It'll be my treat."

They talked about options and Andrew made her agree to a meal at the Delauney—his favourite London restaurant.

In the car park, as they were leaving, Andrew surprised her by saying, "Two things: firstly, you need to relax, so I insist on giving you a free massage. I'll email you my schedule for next week."

"That's kind. What's the other thing?"

"I'm going to dig out that cute photograph of you and Joe in Prague."

"I'm not sure it's a good idea," Kate said, fishing in her bag for her car keys.

Andrew gave her a hug. "Well, let's see, shall we?"

Kate knew there was no point in arguing with him, although all the talk of Joe made her think about her ex even more. The full moon hung low over the trees as she drove her red Mazda sports car home past Ascot race course and then Windsor Great Park. Since the night was so fresh and clear, she decided she'd go for a run through the park when she got home. That would empty her head of pointless memories.

She turned the key and began to open the front door. The door jammed half-open as post and a local free newspaper scuffed against the hallway matting. Tolkien padded down the stairs mewing as he went, a critical expression in his intense eyes.

She shrugged off her mood and smiled at him. "Well, good evening to you, my man. Let me sort out all this post and then I'll feed you."

Among the usual fliers for pizza takeaway and Indian restaurants was a collection bag from a charity, three letters—probably junk mail—and a small packet. Great! She had ordered a Pulsar heart monitor from eBay and here it was, already.

As Kate mounted the stairs, Tolkien skipped enthusiastically to the top, his criticism forgotten. She went to the dining table, put down the mail—except for the parcel—and tore it open. The monitor was in its original packaging and looked new—just as described in the listing.

Tolkien sat looking expectantly towards the kitchen. She pretended to carry on opening the packaging as she took a step towards the lounge. Tolkien dashed around her legs and complained loudly.

"Just teasing you!" she said, laughing.

Once he was fed and happy, she cut open the plastic packaging around the monitor, put on the watch and connected the heart monitor strap around her chest. She looked at the display to check her heartbeat.

Nothing.

"I'm dead!" she said to Tolkien, but he didn't find it funny. Instead, he jumped onto the table and studied her. The watch told the time but the little heart outline at the top of the display wasn't flashing. She pressed random buttons and changed the display, managed to mess up the date and time—but still no flashing heart. Inside the box she spotted a thick instruction booklet. "There's a gender stereotype that says men don't read instructions. Well I've got news for you," she said to her cat, "in my experience no one likes reading complicated instructions."

Disappointed and mentally preparing to return the monitor as faulty, she made herself some Earl Grey tea. In throwing away the tea bag she must have moved the watch close to the monitor and there was a beep. *Of course, the monitor needs to be initialized!*

Beep... beep... beep.

Sixty-one bpm. *Not bad at the end of a hard day.*

She jogged on the spot and felt a childish thrill as the beats per minute leapt up to one hundred. When she stopped she was pleased that it came down again fairly quickly: a sign of her fitness.

Tolkien wasn't impressed. He jumped off the table and onto the sofa's arm and implored her with his big blue eyes. "OK, Tolk," she said, "you can have a cuddle and then I'm going out for a short run."

Kate was about to sit when her phone rang. Andrew.

"Hey, Katie. Sorry to disturb you."

That made her smile—always so polite. "You know I've always time for you. You're practically one of the girls!" She expected a witty response, but instead there was a hesitation before he spoke cautiously.

"Kate?"

"What's up?"

"It's about Joe. I went up into the attic to get the box of his things."

Andrew hesitated, but Kate couldn't speak, her mouth was open, her short breaths amplified by the receiver.

"Well, something in the box... a little light is flashing." His tone was deadly serious. "Can you come over, right now? You need to see this."

NINE

The man calling himself Nanninga sat in a coffee bar in Las Ramblas, Barcelona, and waited for Christopher Martens to walk by. The man was easy to spot as he checked on his appearance in a window and then seemed to smile at himself.

Nanninga knew him well and had come to understand, even admire, the scams he'd pulled, recently netting himself over eight million dollars in a matter of months. Nanninga had investigated him and then tracked him down in Barcelona, moving from the Czech Republic and with plans to hit London next.

Martens' first fraud had been in the US, swindling a mortgage company: a federal offence which forced him to change his identity and move on. First he travelled through Europe before moving on to Asia, getting as far as Hong Kong. On his travels he must have discovered that the legal and valuation systems of Europe were more restrictive than the US, and then worked out a new scheme—one less likely to upset the criminal investigators. He had decided to target rich individuals rather than companies.

Nanninga put down his espresso and followed Martens, strolling towards Parc de la Ciutadella. This prime location, a stone's throw from the marina, abutted the old Olympic village, and Nanninga inhaled the warm air and a whiff of the ocean. He stopped fifty yards back when Martens mounted the steps to his latest development—four storeys, about three hundred years old with scaffolding outside. There was the name of a swanky construction company displayed on a sign. As expected, when Nanninga searched for the company on the internet, he was impressed by the portfolio of their totally fictitious upmarket developments.

Nanninga checked his watch: twelve minutes before his appointment. He hung back and then, on time to the second, rang the doorbell.

Martens opened the door with a smile, although Nanninga saw the confusion in his eyes. A racist, he expected a tall white Dutch diamond dealer and saw a smaller man of swarthy complexion.

"Mixed race," Nanninga said by way of explanation. He looked past the conman and saw some kind of light stone flooring, a large planter and giant fern, rich brown and dark grey walls, subtle down-lights. Nanninga stepped over the threshold and nodded. "Impressive."

"I use the best interior designers, so I hope you continue to be impressed when you see the apartment."

Nanninga had no doubt the interior designers had been easily duped by the lure of a big paycheque that would never arrive.

Martens led the way to a lift, all the time spinning a sales pitch as they travelled up a floor to a door marked "Three". Nanninga suspected that Martens had changed the number just before he arrived. It was called the "number and screwdriver scam". Martens finished one apartment to perfection and sold it ten times over. Each buyer bought one with a different number. The trick was to ensure all completions happened at the same time. Martens would take the money and run while his buyers discovered they were all trying to move into the same property.

The smell of fresh coffee and clean air washed out when Martens opened the door. The lights were already on and Martens walked straight into the kitchen.

"I prefer not to rush these things, Mr Nanninga—to give a sense of the place before we tour the property. So, can I suggest we sit and relax and review the details first?" He opened a refrigerator and removed plates of caviar, smoked salmon and paté de foie gras. "Now, Mr Nanninga, may I offer you a glass of champagne? Caviar and coffee perhaps?"

Nanninga looked directly at him, an expression of curiosity on his face, and for the first time Martens seemed to realize something wasn't right. His eyes went wide and he finally stopped talking.

Nanninga pulled a gun from beneath his jacket and shot Martens in each knee.

Phut. Phut.

The sound of the silenced gun contradicted the damage it caused. Small calibre meant the pain lasted longer.

Martens gasped and dropped to the floor clutching both knees. He tried to staunch the blood that seeped through his trousers and dripped onto the beautiful Italian floor tiles. A strange whine came from his throat as he looked up into Nanninga's cold dark eyes.

Nanninga now spoke in his natural Middle Eastern accent. "As you can guess, Mr Martens, I am not who I say I am. Oh, but then again neither are you! Now, you will answer my questions or you will die slowly and in extreme pain."

Martens dragged himself backwards and drew streaks of red on a plush white carpet. Nanninga casually stepped past him and closed the room's curtains. Now behind Martens, he said, "You are wondering what this is about, aren't you? Do you remember the name Riyad bin Shahd?"

Martens swivelled as Nanninga eased himself into an armchair, the gun on his lap no longer pointed at the bleeding conman. He watched the man's breathing change from panic to irrational hope—hope he could reason with his attacker or maybe buy him off.

Trying to sound calm, Martens said, "I don't recall a Ben Farhad. If there's any way—"

"Prince bin Shahd was one of the victims of your silly scam, Mr Martens. You sold him an apartment in the Czech Republic, but like these apartments, only one was finished and that one you sold many times over."

Martens nodded weakly. His hands trembled as he tried to hold himself up.

"You really should be more careful about who you decide to defraud."

Martens' eyes glazed briefly and Nanninga knew the man's vision was fading in and out.

"I'll give him the money back!" Martens said.

Nanninga flicked open the catches on Marten's briefcase and thumbed through the contents. When he looked back at Martens, the man's eyes were pleading. Nanninga shook his head. "My dear Mr Martens, this is not about money anymore."

While Martens lay dying, the Arab, who normally went by the name Amir, walked to the kitchen for a snack. He returned to the living room with biscuits and caviar on a napkin, and black coffee. He sat on the sofa and watched as he ate. When finished, he put the napkin and cup in his pocket. As he walked out of the apartment, Amir speed-dialled a number on his mobile phone.

"Speak," a voice said on the other end.

54

"It's done."

"Good."

"I've extracted information about associates." He paused. "And there's something else. There was information about that other matter."

"What other matter?"

"The problem with... with the missing friend from America." Amir hoped he'd be understood.

"You know where the man is?"

"No, but there is a trail. There's a link to someone called Sikorski, in Prague."

The voice on the line was silent for a while and Amir knew this was big.

Amir prompted, "Shall I take care of it?"

"Yes," the other man said with rare emotion in his tone. "Take care of it."

TEN

Kate put down the phone. There was a moment of hesitation as she wondered whether it would be more sensible to ignore the flashing thing in Joe's box. On the one hand, her mother and sister would disapprove, but on the other, Andrew's place was only ten minutes away and the intrigue was killing her. Seconds later she was in her Mazda driving to South Ascot.

Cars crammed along the dark narrow streets, half on, half off the pavement, and she had to pass Andrew's Victorian cottage looking for a space. Finally she found a gap big enough to squeeze into, parked and walked back.

She always had an odd feeling in his house. It was the polar opposite of hers. His home was chintzy and spotless with décor in keeping with the style of house, and if she didn't know better she'd assume there had been a woman's touch. Everything was ordered with nothing out of place, even temporarily.

Andrew was a hoarder by nature. His house was full of family antiques that overfilled the property but were too precious to be discarded. Kate knew he had a huge box of his father's camera slides. He would never view them, the technology was too passé, too old now, but he didn't have the heart to throw them away. He had his grandmother's crockery: fine china plates with gold leaf trim. Kate was amazed to see that each was unique in its pattern and totally over the top. It was probably worth something, but not a fortune because many items were missing. Andrew kept it all even though he would never use any of it.

Kate sat in the lounge waiting, as he went upstairs, located the box and returned carrying it like a trophy.

"You know, I half expected you to chuck it like my sister wanted," she said.

"You know me. I can't throw anything away. Anyway, I guess I wondered whether one day you might want some of these things back, if only to just confirm that you were over him."

Andrew placed the box in front of her and sat on the chair opposite. She stared at it for a while and then lifted the flaps.

The first thing she pulled out was a blue Cornish sweater, bought for Joe on a weekend break in Coverack, a tiny but quaint Cornish village. Kate had joked that he looked like a fisherman and could always catch lobsters and crabs if the mobile business didn't work out.

The next item was an electronic desk calendar he'd included in her pile of birthday presents. She'd never liked it and recalled now that he said something like, "Always think of me when you change the date." There was model of a British Beefeater that he'd bought at the Tower of London. Tacky. There were some medals from runs they had competed in and the London to Brighton cycle ride. There were piles of CDs—some containing photographs, others favourite music.

Under this was a pile of clothes, including the sexy underwear he had bought her when he first moved in. She felt a flush of embarrassment as she lifted them out one by one and quietly added them to the pile. Andrew didn't comment, but then again he didn't need to.

Under the clothes were three framed photographs of the two of them, a handsome couple, people said. Joe had framed her favourite: the one of the two of them on the Charles Bridge in Prague. Again, she remembered him saying something odd when he gave it to her, but she couldn't recall what it was. She held the photograph for a while, studying his face and his unusual grey-brown eyes that seemed so genuine.

She shook stray thoughts from her mind. "So what was so urgent that you get me to drive over here and spoil my evening run?"

"This," he said, picking up the desk calendar and handing it to her.

A grey plastic tube about five inches long, the calendar was electronic, changing the date automatically. So Joe's comment about her changing the date and thinking of him was nonsense.

A tiny light blinked at one end.

She turned it over in her hands and frowned. "I don't remember there being a light on this."

"It was beeping earlier. That's why I took a look and then called you."

"Batteries running out?"

"That's what I assumed." Andrew reached out and took the calendar. "The batteries go here," he said, indicating one end. "So what's this for?" As he spoke, he slid back a section on the back near the flashing light.

Expecting a display of the internal electronics, Kate was surprised to see a small empty compartment.

"Is that why you asked me over—to show me this?" she asked, suddenly deflated. "Is that it?"

"No." Andrew put his hand in his breast pocket and handed her something that looked like a tiny mobile phone memory card. "But this is."

"What is it?"

Andrew smiled. "Apart from the obvious—a memory card?" He raised an eyebrow. "I've already taken a look. Come on, let me show you."

He led the way into his study.

In contrast to the rest of the house, Andrew's study was not old-fashioned, but high tech. He loved the latest gadgets and had an impressive computer set-up, including two wide screens. She had seen him use the two screens on one PC and still didn't quite get how it worked. She didn't dare ask Andrew to explain because she doubted he could summarize it in less time than it would take to read the manual and, of course, she didn't read instructions.

Andrew took the card, slotted it into a larger card and inserted it into the pc. He opened Windows Explorer. There was a single file on the disk.

The file was named *Trust Me*.

ELEVEN

A vacuum sucked the air from Kate's lungs. The room spun.

Andrew gripped her shoulder. "You all right?"

She took deep breaths until she felt calmer. "It has to be from Joe. He wants to tell me the truth. What does it say?"

"There's the thing." Andrew double-clicked on the file and a window opened asking for a password. "Password protected." His fingers hovered over the keys. "Any ideas?"

"Try Joe."

No luck.

"Joe Rossini?"

Andrew tried it with and without a space. He also tried combinations of upper and lower case. Not right.

They tried versions of Kate's name. They tried *Tolkien.*

No.

Andrew used Windows Explorer to locate another file on his PC, clicked it open and set it running. "Password finder," he said. "It's infallible, providing it was encrypted with a Western keyboard and we have forever to decrypt it." He stood. "Come on, let's have a cup of tea while it's running."

Five minutes later, in the lounge, he handed her a cup of Earl Grey. "Talk to me," he said.

"I'm not sure what you want me to say."

"I know you don't want to believe it, but what if this message tells you that everything you heard from the agents—everything you read on the internet—was true?"

Kate sipped her tea and stared out of the window into the dark night.

Andrew said, "I guess we can at least rule out one option. He wasn't just an ordinary guy who worked for a mobile phone company."

She turned from the window and regarded her friend for a long time, couldn't read what he was thinking, but his eyes seemed unusually cold. "You were the only one who supported me about Joe," she said finally.

"You're assuming this is a positive message, aren't you?"

"I suppose I am."

"Katie, sweetie, I just want you to be prepared for the worst, that's all. Even though you've suppressed it, deep down you've held onto the dream that he was some kind of secret agent."

"There was the scar on his shin that he said was from shrapnel and the one on his side where a bullet had grazed him and broken a rib," she said, thinking back to when she'd probed him for details. "But it wasn't that, it was the silly stories of eating pasta between his knees while flying into Afghanistan; parachuting into enemy territory at night and landing on a chicken coop; playing American football with an ex-college player—across a minefield."

"For goodness sake. Would you have fallen for me if I had told you that I was a fireman and rescued six people from a burning office? My clothes caught fire and by the time I'd hauled out the last survivor, I was butt-naked."

"Be serious."

"OK. My point is that this stuff is easy to make up."

"I guess."

"Maybe he wasn't really a twin and just used that story because of your sister's twins. Conmen do that sort of thing to show you have something in common."

"He only told me about his twin later."

Andrew shrugged his big shoulders. "It was just an example. Maybe he wasn't deliberately conning you. Maybe he was a bit of a fantasist. People like that start believing their own stories, no matter how crazy. What did the US papers call him?"

"They likened him to the guy in *Catch Me If You Can*. The character Leonardo DiCaprio played."

Neither of them missed the irony of the Italian name.

Andrew said, "He was caught too."

Kate nodded, and before the tears burned her cheeks, Andrew was by her side, his big arms wrapped around her.

"Sorry, kiddo, I don't know what came over me." He gently eased her off his chest and she saw his eyes were softer now.

He said, "I'm just scared you're going to be hurt. There's just as much chance of the truth being a confession as an explanation."

She nodded.

"Don't get your hopes up, that's all I'm saying." He kissed her wet cheek, disappeared to his study and returned with disappointment etched on his face. "Program's still running. It could take a while."

"I should be going." Kate finished her tea. "Give me a call when you've cracked it?"

"As soon as."

Before she left she went back to the box, picked up the photograph of the Charles Bridge and put it in her

62

handbag. At the door she thanked him and he hugged her.

"Think about it," he said.

As she drove home she considered what Andrew had said and realized he'd played devil's advocate—preparing her for the worst—and, by the time she reached the Great Park, she knew she'd have to know the truth, no matter what. Her headlights picked out the thousand-year-old oak trees along the road, their gnarled outlines like giant old men reaching out into the night, and for the first time in a year she felt positive. She was wondering whether it was the prospect of closure when her phone rang. It was the wrong ringtone to be Andrew. She looked over to the passenger seat where her phone lay. The display said: *Sarah Mobile.* Kate snatched it up and pressed receive.

"Hi, Sarah. Look, I'm so sorry for not being in touch…"

There was no sound.

"Sarah?"

Dead air.

Kate glanced at the display. Number disconnected.

She pressed return call.

Voicemail.

"Hi, Sarah. It's Kate. You just called me. Call me back when you can."

Sarah didn't call back.

TWELVE

Amir found the address in a nice quiet suburb of Prague. Wearing generic workmen's blue overalls and carrying a canvas tool bag, he knocked on the door, layered thickly with years of black paint. He made a quick assessment: solid wood, old, single latch, easy. Opening his bag, he removed a flexible metal strip and was in the house within seconds.

"Hello," he called. "Gas engineer. The door was open."

Putting on his gloves, he walked along the hallway: high ceiling, herringbone parquet flooring, antique oak and yew furniture, oil paintings with ornate gilt frames. Old money, Amir decided.

He entered the first room. A dining room. Again, nice solid wood furniture: a table, eight chairs and a sideboard. He opened the drawers and cupboards and searched the contents. Finding nothing of interest, he checked behind the paintings. After replacing everything, he left the room as he'd found it.

The next room was a lounge or drawing room. Two leather sofas, a central low table and a long bookcase. An upright piano stood against the far wall. Amir had no doubt it was quality though well used. He searched it anyway, removing the backing felt to ensure nothing was hidden inside.

He searched the sofas carefully, without ripping them apart, and then turned his attention to the bookcase. Meticulously, one by one, he took the books out and flicked through them looking for loose pages. A few notes and receipts fell out and then a photograph. He examined it: three people and writing on the reverse. He placed it carefully in his bag.

When finished, he checked that the room looked undisturbed and went into the kitchen. He looked in the cupboards, apparently empty containers and anything that appeared unusual. A large pot containing white flour was out of place in a cupboard with non-baking items. Removing a glove, without touching the large pot, he delved into the flour, checking in case anything was hidden inside. Finding nothing, he shook the flour off his hand and replaced the glove. There was no disappointment, only patient searching.

From the kitchen he went upstairs. A toilet, another lounge and an office. There was nothing in the toilet cistern that shouldn't be there. The lounge was dominated by a 52-inch flat-screen TV. He shook his head. Out of place and inappropriate. The room felt lived-in, unlike the downstairs lounge. The furniture was more relaxed: a comfy sofa and two chairs. He searched them as he'd searched the leather sofas. Then he turned to the system beneath the TV: a computer-like box connected to a stereo system and a Blu-ray player. He switched off the power, opened the boxes and checked inside. Nothing unexpected.

A cupboard with DVDs, Blu-ray discs and CDs was next. Just like he had with the books, Amir checked the contents. Anything suspicious, such as a personally recorded disc or one in the wrong box that he didn't recognize, he placed in his bag.

The study was the least tidy room so far. Amir went first to the computer and switched it on. As anticipated, the sign-on screen required a password. Never mind, he could get that later. He checked the drives for discs and external memory. One flash drive was in a USB port and he put it in his bag. He also collected non-pre-recorded CDs and DVDs from a shelf and checked the contents of software boxes.

He searched the documents in the desk drawers and photographed anything that might be interesting. He flicked through the books on a bookshelf as he had done before, again keeping anything that fell out.

An address book lay open on a cabinet. A name and address on the page had a date written next to it. Not a birthdate, but this year and only two days ago. He photographed it and then photographed the whole book. He picked up a telephone and checked for messages— just one, a mother asking to be called back. He took a note of the recent calls held in the phone's memory.

When he was convinced he'd done all he could, he went up the second flight of stairs. A landing with a bureau, two large bedrooms—one clearly used, one not—a bathroom and a cupboard with a boiler. He took photographs of documents in the bureau but found nothing else of interest on this floor.

He moved a chair from the bathroom and stood on it to reach a hatch in the ceiling. Just able to reach the bolt, he slid it across and the hatch door swung open to reveal a folded wooden ladder. He pulled a rope and the ladder jerkily descended.

At the top, Amir threw a light switch and the attic space lit up brilliantly. It was mostly boxes, neatly arranged on boards and some other items that were probably antiques. Amir checked his watch. So far, the search had taken almost three hours. However it was still early afternoon and there was plenty of time. He began to search the boxes for anything of interest.

When he was finished, he returned everything as it had been, turned off the light and descended the ladder. Standing on the chair, he locked the hatch shut. Then, after dusting the cushioned seat, he returned the chair to the bathroom.

Amir went downstairs and sat in the lounge, facing the door. From beneath his overalls he took out his gun. He attached a silencer, laid the gun on his lap and waited for the homeowner to return.

THIRTEEN

After leaving the message for Sarah to call, Kate felt guilty. She hadn't spoken to her friend for at least three months.

Peter and Sarah's engagement hadn't lasted long. A whirlwind romance and an equally fast break-up. Ironic, when she thought about it. Joe had discussed Peter and Sarah's pending nuptials when all the time he was married. If the internet stories were true.

After splitting from Peter, Sarah had stayed in Prague and thrown herself into her work selling homes. The relationship had been passionate and fiery. Only it turned out to be a little too fiery. The fun had gone, and they had argued. The couple that had seemed in love and perfect found out that they couldn't get along.

Sarah hadn't understood why Kate was distraught about losing Joe. She tarred Joe and Peter with the same brush. "Men are bastards!" she had said. "From now on I use and abuse. I certainly don't plan to marry them."

Kate wondered how many women of her age were like Lisa and Sarah. Would she turn out the same once she knew Joe's truth? Kate hoped not and wondered how much the manner of Joe's disappearance—the suddenness of it—determined her outlook. Sarah's bitterness had grown over time while losing Joe had been a shock. Or maybe it's simply because we are different people, she thought.

After the initial call to comfort Kate, Sarah didn't want to talk about Joe. In Andrew's opinion, deep down, Sarah still had feelings for Peter. He said that talking about Joe would make her think about her ex. Maybe.

Back home, Kate poured herself a glass of Chardonnay and put the TV on—muted. As soon as she sat down, Tolkien leapt onto her lap and quickly settled. She took a sip and was just about to try Sarah again when the iPhone rang with a song called "Poker Face", which her sister Darcy had chosen for herself.

That would be it for the evening. When Darcy needed to talk, it would be for hours, although Kate couldn't tell her the about the message Joe had left.

"Hey, Darce."

"Hi, have you spoken to Mum lately?"

Darcy surely knew about the Sunday dinner with Terry and her outburst. Kate said, "Not since I went over. What's up?"

"Oh, just that she seems a bit down at the moment. Kate, I think you should cut her a bit more slack. She's had it hard, you know. It can't have been easy raising the two of us with Dad hardly around and then to lose him—"

"I have been supportive. I'm just finding it difficult to accept Dad's replacement so—"

"I think if you had kids of your own, you'd be much more sympathetic about what Mum went through."

Kate didn't bite. Instead she said, "So how are your two angels?"

As her sister got into the swing of her update on the three-year-old twins, Kate stuck a ready meal in the microwave and ate it. While she said the odd word, Darcy flitted between concern for their mother, what she'd been doing, and the challenges of bringing up her kids. Eventually Darcy said she was thinking about going back to work. Not her previous job at the mortgage company, because her old boss had never forgiven her for not returning from maternity leave. The man hadn't even sent a congratulations gift when the girls were born, and Darcy knew he wouldn't be flexible or sympathetic if she needed time off when the girls were sick. She also needed a job with hours that allowed for the picking up and dropping off of the girls when they started school.

After Darcy had stopped griping about her old boss and company, they spent another thirty minutes discussing her criteria and her options and Kate managed to get her sister to spell out a plan of action.

They didn't talk about Darcy's husband Tim, but at the end of the call Darcy said, "Tim sends his love."

Kate figured this meant everything was all right on the marital front. At least someone's relationship is fine, she thought. When she put her phone down, her ear was warm from having it pressed to the phone for so long. Not good.

Remembering it was recycling day in the morning, Kate collected a pile of papers and plastic from a cupboard in the kitchen. She was just about to take it downstairs to the outside bin cupboard when she remembered the junk mail and fliers in the kitchen. She'd abandoned them after opening the heart monitor packet.

Just in case, she looked at the three letters. One stood out. Looked like junk, but the stamp wasn't British.

She looked more closely. The Czech Republic.

Maybe a letter from Sarah. The address was handwritten although Kate didn't recognize it.

She tore open the envelope. It was a photograph. There was no letter, just the photograph of two young

70

men in army desert fatigues. They had beards and Arab scarves around their heads. Her first thought was that Sarah had sent her a photograph of her latest beau. Kate flipped the photo over to see what Sarah had written on the reverse.

A name that Kate had heard a year ago: Boomer. The second name was Mirrorman. And underneath, the words: *Find me.*

FOURTEEN

Peter Sikorski tidied his desk and logged off his laptop. He disconnected the machine, put it in his bag and added confidential papers to file securely at home. A good day, he told himself. The relaunched phone packages were starting to take-off. The bait-and-switch telephone campaign showed exceptional response rates and churn rates were marginally down. It all pointed to real growth rather than recycling existing customer performance.

Before he left his office, he did what he always did. He wrote on his whiteboard by the door. It was a message to himself for the morning. Tonight he wrote: *Compete on VOIP handsets.* Oskar Mobile was behind the competition on handsets. They'd missed a trick with the iPhone and had been slow to promote the BlackBerry. They were coming back, of course, but history showed that the first in the market won the prize. And the prize, as always, was sales.

As he walked the short distance to the metro station he tightened his coat. The dark sky was clear, the temperature was dropping quickly and he was relieved to get into the warm carriage for the journey home.

Relaxing in the seat, he wondered whether it was time to move on, whether he would be allowed, or was this it:

head of sales at Oskar Mobile. He earned more money than he'd ever dreamt he would, lived in an exclusive area of the city, had everything he wanted. Almost. In the past he hadn't thought to challenge his position, but surely now was a good time. Maybe he could have a relationship that wouldn't collapse under the stress. Maybe he could make a go of it again with Sarah. In the short time they'd been together, they had shared a great deal. She would understand—if she would have him back that is.

He continued to dwell on the past as he walked from the Střížkov metro station to his home. He wondered where Joe was now and how he was getting on. Peter had done his job, everything he needed to. He'd even followed the unexpected instruction he'd received. How had his last conversation with Joe gone?

Over a beer one evening Joe had said, "We've become good friends, Peter."

"Yes. I suppose it was unexpected, but we have."

"I need you to do something for me."

Peter had agreed.

"Even if it's against the rules?"

That caused him to hesitate, but a frisson of fear was immediately dispelled from his mind. Joe was a good man, a close friend. "Even then," he had said.

"Something may still happen."

"You must have mixed feelings about it."

He had been surprised when Joe had said, "Not really. I've met a wonderful girl and life's too short."

Peter had nodded, guessing what Joe was about to say. "So you are worried our guy will find the trail and it'll lead to Kate."

"There might be no warning, but if something happens to me, would you keep track of Kate, please?" He had shrugged. "You know, make sure she's all right."

In the hall, Peter took off his coat and shoes and slipped into comfortable house shoes. Without Sarah, the house always felt empty. His promise to Joe seemed hollow now. Sarah had been Kate's best friend and he couldn't even keep her. The heating clicked on and he noted absently that the house felt different—not just missing his girlfriend. The cleaner hadn't been in, had she? It wasn't her day.

He walked to the stairs and up to the first floor. In his office he took out the papers and put down the laptop bag.

A noise behind him! He swivelled. As he turned, he saw something flash close to his face. The pain in his head was bright but brief. He blacked out.

From the darkness, the recollection of someone knocking him out avalanched into his consciousness. He jolted awake. His neck felt like he'd been bulldozed. He tried to move, couldn't. He was bound to the office chair. A man stood impassively over him with a silenced gun pointing at his head.

A cruel smile cracked a swarthy face. "Tell me what you know," the Arab said.

"I don't know what you are talking about," Peter said weakly.

"Tut-tut." The man slapped Peter on both ears, producing the effect of an explosion in his head.

Peter's eyes rolled, unfocused for a minute.

When Peter breathed normally again, the Arab said, "That was just for fun. Now tell me everything you know."

Peter shook his head.

The Arab smiled, as though he preferred his victim to resist. "Peter... Peter, not only will you tell me the password to your computer and laptop, you will tell me

74

the combination to the safe behind the oil painting in the dining room. By the time I am finished with you, you will be desperate to tell me anything at all. You will tell me your girlfriend's birthday, how many times you have had sex with her and which position she prefers." He placed his thumbs on Peter's temples and applied enough pressure to threaten severe pain.

The Arab's face was close and Peter could smell the man's breath. He tried to blank out the image, think of happier moments, of the good times with Sarah, of hopes and dreams. The pressure across his forehead intensified. He looked into the man's eyes.

The Arab said, "Now, tell me about Joe Rossini."

FIFTEEN

Kate slept badly, with disjointed images that left her wishing she didn't have to get up when the alarm sounded. It was Saturday and she'd agreed to work half a day at the health club.

She was distracted all morning. She had three patients but her mind kept flipping between the mysterious data card and the photograph from Prague. Between patients, she dialled Sarah's phone, each time getting voicemail.

Her final patient suffered from tendonitis in his Achilles. On his previous appointment she had tried acupuncture into and around the painful areas. It seemed to work, and against her advice, the man went on to compete in a ten kilometre road race at the weekend. However, the tendons were inflamed more than ever and he asked for the needles again.

The poor chap howled with pain as she knocked one of the needles. She covered her clumsiness, claiming it was due to his weekend run, but her distraction was the true cause. The poor man was probably put off acupuncture for life.

Andrew was waiting for her at lunchtime. She greeted him with a smile. "What's the news about the document?"

"Still trundling on I'm afraid. But I have some news of my own... about work." He grinned like an excited child.

"Techion, the company I've signed an NDA with, are finalizing the contracts." He then spent twenty minutes giving her a progress update. It was always so positive and she loved him for his optimism.

Kate had Earl Grey and Andrew ordered a large black Americano. They ate paninis while he talked and she tried hard to follow his report. After five minutes her eyes glazed over as names and seemingly irrelevant detail were thrown at her. There was never a short version from Andrew. "It's too complicated to summarize," he would often say when she complained at being lost.

"So is that the news?" she asked when she could eventually get a word in.

He looked a little crestfallen before brightening again. "No! No! It's more than that. I just needed to give you the context," he said. "Well, the connection with Luigi led to meeting Paolo at Rialto. They are interested in the software. They have been planning to enter the peer-to-peer lending market, and my solution offers them a shortcut."

"Wow! That *is* great news. Make sure you get contracts and discuss the financial deal early on this time."

He said he would, but Andrew had avoided the commercial side of negotiations before.

"Make sure you do," she said. "You're too trusting for your own good."

He looked at her out of one eye. "Rearrange this sentence: black calling kettle pot the?"

"Maybe. Maybe not."

"What does that mean?"

She said, "I received a photograph in the post. I think Sarah might have sent it."

"And?"

"The photo is of a couple of soldiers."

Andrew raised an eyebrow, waited.

"Not just any old soldiers. There are names on the back. One of them is *Boomer*."

"Boomer?" Andrew looked thoughtful for a moment. "One of the characters from Joe's stories?"

"Exactly!"

"Why would Sarah have a photo of one of Joe's friends?"

"You're missing the point. Why would there be a photo of Boomer at all? If you recall, Joe's army experiences were part of his fantasy world. Boomer was the one who used to have a bowl of rigatoni pasta between his knees as a snack when they were off on a mission."

Andrew squinted, trying hard to recall. "Wasn't there a story about this guy picking up a grenade and throwing it back at the enemy?"

"That's the one. He was a college quarterback, allegedly. He could throw an American football eighty yards with ease. Joe said he could throw a grenade further than any other man he knew. And then there's the other name."

"Other name?"

"Mirrorman—it was the name of his made-up superhero as a kid. I think it's..." Kate shook her head, hardly able to say the words, to get her head around it. "I'm sure it's Joe. He's got a beard and most of his face is covered but I can see his eyes. It's Joe, I'm sure of it."

"Wow!" Andrew seemed to ponder this for a while before saying, "So what does all this mean?"

She smiled, knowing that Andrew was deliberately prompting her to get there ahead of him, to make her spell it out.

She obliged. "If—and I know it's still a big if—but if Boomer is real, then there's a possibility that the stories are real. And if the stories are real—"

"Then Joe didn't make it up," Andrew finished for her.

Joe may not have been a fantasist. And if that was true then why was he taken away like that? And why the hell did those agents lie?

SIXTEEN

Act One of *The Mikado* was coming to a close. It was a private gathering of Riyad bin Shahd's closest friends and business associates—forty men, all dressed in traditional Arab robes. There were women laid on for the evening but they waited in an adjoining room—the entertainment during the interval and aftershow party.

To the outside world, Prince bin Shahd was a traditionalist. He was not in the Saudi government but everyone knew he was powerful. He was a global kingmaker who worked behind the scenes and got what he wanted. One of his contradictory predilections was for the work of Gilbert and Sullivan. *The Mikado* was both ridiculously puerile and fascinating at the same time. And the silly operettas of Gilbert and Sullivan were the only thing that made him laugh.

He suspected that most of his guests didn't understand the Western humour, but it was important to appreciate how other people thought, and humour was one of the great avenues of insight. As the chorus completed their end of act song, bin Shahd applauded and his guests followed his lead. The curtain fell and he stood, nodding to the servants to open the doors to the antechamber where the girls waited patiently.

"Your Highness," a man called Hamasalih said, moving in from the side. He was dressed Western-style in a suit and everyone knew he was security. He leaned in close, conspiratorially. "Your Highness, I have news from Spain."

"Has Amir done his work?" the prince said without looking at the security man.

"He has."

"Did he make the crook suffer?"

"Undoubtedly. You know Amir enjoys his work."

It hadn't been about the money. It was the principle. Riyad bin Shahd was investing in property around the world. He knew how fragile the Middle East was and his investment in apartments was just one of his alternative strategies. The loss of a few hundred thousand dollars was nothing. The loss of pride was everything. No one scammed bin Shahd and lived to tell the tale.

He waved for a pretty girl to bring him a glass of champagne. She scurried over and he looked at her lasciviously as he took the proffered flute from her. Later, he thought, and then, after a sip of the Krug 1990, he looked into the eyes of his security man. "His tastes are perhaps his weakness."

Hamasalih inclined his head in agreement. "But he is also the best," he said. "He traced the fraudster even though the man was in a different country using a different identity. He has also made a remarkable discovery. He has found the fraudster has a connection to the other man."

"Mirrorman?"

"There's a link to the Czech Republic."

Bin Shahd nodded slowly. He took a long drink of the champagne and luxuriated in the sensation as it ran down his throat. He had been waiting for the news that Mirrorman had been traced, and here it was. He looked askance at his aide but the man had no idea and continued to explain.

"A fortuitous coincidence or perhaps a logical connection," Hamasalih said with a smile. "Whichever it is, I have had our men working in Prague."

As bin Shahd walked his security man into a private room, he decided it was time to explain the strategy. The hunt had been started and it was better everyone behaved as expected, but the prince himself could not be involved.

He closed the door, locked it and waved Hamasalih to a map on the wall. He said, "Tell me what you know."

Hamasalih provided an update on the investigation and ended by saying, "We traced him to a man called Petr Sikorski."

"No, tell me what you know—about why we are doing this."

"This is about the death of your son at the hands of the Americans."

The prince inclined his head.

Hamasalih continued: "Mirrorman has information that is harmful to your Highness."

The prince waited. The pause caused a flicker of doubt on his security aide's face. Yes it was time to explain.

Prince bin Shahd said, "The Americans play a foolish game. They think they make the rules and yet they don't. They think they understand the rules and yet they don't. They have foolish notions of right and wrong, white and black, good versus bad. And yet they play both sides, they give money and they take money. They give arms and they fight those same people they previously armed—and behind it there is always the money. They claim to trust God's will while all the time they pray to the god Mammon. Do you understand, Fouad?"

Hamasalih nodded and was honoured at the prince's use of his given name.

"Sit," the prince said. "I will tell you what happened and what you will make happen."

Awe lit Hamasalih's face when bin Shahd finished. "Masterful," he said.

The prince pointed to the map. "So the first connection was to Prague and we have traced Mirrorman's movements since? Is he in America?"

"He left Prague a year ago." Hamasalih stood and tapped on a small island to the west. "He went to England to be with a new woman."

"Do we have a name?"

"Yes, and an address."

"Any other details?"

"No. Our man, Amir, says the connection didn't know. There is a slight complication that the police have become involved. But as you know, the police are often unwittingly helpful."

The two minute bell rang to announce the imminent start of the second half of the operetta, but bin Shahd was too preoccupied to enjoy his favourite show.

"Amir has done a good job so far," he said. "Get him to the UK and locate the woman."

SEVENTEEN

Lisa had met her in Windsor for a glass of wine and a chat. Although Kate had worked a late shift at the club after a full day at the hospital, she felt uplifted by Lisa's enthusiasm for her story about the photograph.

She walked Kate home, insisting on seeing the intriguing picture. "So that one's Joe," she said, handing her the photo. "Dishy."

After Kate said goodbye and returned upstairs, she looked into Tolkien's intelligent eyes. "What do I do now, Tolk?"

Tolkien said something that was probably amazingly insightful but totally incomprehensible to human ears. However there was also a strong chance it included the phrase: *pick me up and stroke me.*

Her mobile rang. It was a number she didn't recognize but when she heard the voice Kate realized it was about time she programmed it in.

"Hello, dear. It's Ann from downstairs." That's how she always began when calling. "I took my net curtains down and can't put them back up. Would you be a dear and give me a hand?"

Ann: American, kindly, and in her seventies. Kate felt guilty that the only time she saw her was when Ann called and asked for help. She needed two replacement hips and had a six month wait. Kate didn't dare tell her that she worked at the hospital where Ann was on the waiting list. Kate couldn't have done anything about the waiting list but guilt by association is a terrible thing.

She was about to knock on her neighbour's door when Ann appeared, eager and enthusiastic.

Her cornflower blue eyes flashed. "I always know when you're leaving," she said. "I hear you run down the stairs."

She had said this before and Kate apologized for the noise.

"Oh no," Ann said with a smile, "I love to know that other people can run." And she sounded sincere.

Perhaps I should spend more time with Ann, Kate thought. Ann was one of those people who see the good in everything and everyone.

The elderly lady waved Kate into the lounge and insisted that she didn't need to take her shoes off. The room, like the whole apartment, was pristine.

Kate decided it was a good job Ann couldn't climb her stairs and see the state of her own home. Darcy criticized Kate's lack of domesticity. "Looks like I got Mum's housework genes," she would say. Kate's response was that she cleaned the house weekly but within a day the carpet looked grubby. She blamed the combination of a beige carpet and a hairy cat. However, the truth was she suspected Tolkien contributed very little.

Ann pointed to the windows. "I washed my nets," she explained. "You know, in the States I wouldn't dream of having net curtains. But they are so handy, and I am on the ground floor. Can I get you a cup of coffee? I've just made some fresh."

Not really a coffee drinker, Kate accepted the offer out of politeness.

As Ann walked painfully slowly into the kitchen, hobbling on a stick, Kate looked around the room and focused on the photographs on the sideboard. A family history. She knew Ann had a daughter about Kate's age—Brie. Kate had met her once and knew she worked for a foreign bank and lived thirty-odd miles away.

Ann's husband had died six years earlier and she had moved to be near her daughter, who had married an Englishman.

At least twenty photographs of the family adorned the sideboard. No one else, just the three of them in the pictures. In studying the pictures Kate wondered whether she would have similar family photographs one day. Her own sideboard just had a stereo, stacks of CDs and paperwork that needed to be dealt with.

Ann appeared in the kitchen doorway carrying a tray with two cups and a plate of biscuits. She balanced it in one hand, struggling in silence as she used the stick with the other.

Kate rushed over and took the tray from her. "You shouldn't have," she said, carrying it to the coffee table in the centre of the lounge floor.

"Before I sit down," Kate said, "what do you want me to do with the net curtain?"

"It's there, on the windowsill."

It was a simple matter for Kate to stretch the fitting over the retaining hooks either side of the window. Ann was smaller and must have struggled to remove it in the first place. Returning it would have been impossible.

Kate was convinced that most people with net curtains had never considered washing them but Ann's home was too pristine for that.

"Thank you so much, dear," she said easing herself into an armchair. "I normally have my daughter do it but she's not here until the weekend and the curtains did so need a wash."

Kate sat on the sofa and took a sip of coffee. It was very weak, which was fine given her preference for Earl Grey tea.

"You really should get an answering machine," Ann said after offering a biscuit that Kate refused.

"Oh?"

"Your telephone has been ringing all day."

She clearly meant Kate's home phone. Kate rarely used it these days due to the package she had with her iPhone. In fact, the only reason she had it at all was because it came as a bundle with the broadband.

"Sorry," Kate said, thinking the noise had disturbed her neighbour. "I really should unplug it. Apart from my mum, the only calls I get are people trying to sell me something or BT trying to get me to upgrade."

"Please don't think I'm complaining, dear. I just thought it must be something important, the way it kept ringing. It must have rung fifteen times... yes, at least fifteen."

That did surprise Kate. If it had been her mother, she would have eventually tried the mobile number. Kate pulled her phone from a pocket to check it was switched on. Annoyingly it had recently started to turn itself off occasionally. The phone was on, and there were no missed calls.

At that moment a muffled phone rang.

"There you go," Ann said raising her eyebrows conspiratorially.

God! Is it that loud? Kate had no idea it could be heard so clearly downstairs. She made a mental note to see if she could turn the volume down.

"You should go and answer it," Ann said.

"I'll just check." Kate dialled her mum's home on her mobile. Terry answered.

"Oh. Terry. Errr... Hi, is anything wrong?"

Hesitation and then: "I'd like you to give me more of a chance."

"Right. I mean with Mum. Is anything wrong? Has she been trying to get hold of me?"

"No. Would you like to talk to her?"

Kate said she'd call again to chat when she had more time and ended the call. She smiled at her neighbour. "Not my mum calling."

"You should complain to the telephone company, dear—if you are getting nuisance calls."

Taking another sip of the brown liquid that vaguely passed for coffee, Kate nodded. "I'll do that. Does my TV bother you? If my phone is that loud, my TV must be awful."

"Oh no, dear"—Ann gave her a kindly smile—"it's nice to know people are in and enjoying themselves."

Kate asked about her appointment and Ann said there was now a date for the first operation. One hip at a time. She said she was keen to get out and about and walk again. Her favourite walk was along the Thames, across the bridge to Eton, through the fields as far as the Windsor Racecourse. "Fewer tourists on that side of the river," Ann said. "Except for when the sun is out and the field fills up with all sorts—if you know what I mean."

Kate said her favourite walk was up through the deer park to the statue.

"George the Third," Ann said. "Most people have no idea who the man on the horse is because it looks like a Roman emperor, but it is the Queen's great, great, great-grandfather."

The upstairs home phone rang again, and Kate had a strange tingling sensation in her neck. *Who's calling? What's the urgency?*

Ann looked at her expectantly but Kate just shrugged and asked how Ann knew who the man on the horse was.

"I used to be an art-history teacher, you know. A long time ago now." The elderly lady suddenly had a wistful look in her eyes, as if remembering good old times. "When I first came to Windsor I walked everywhere, including up to the statue. I'm no great font of knowledge or sleuth, dear. You'll find there's an inscription around the back. Did you know that Windsor's guildhall was designed by Sir Christopher Wren?"

Kate pretended she didn't. But she hadn't heard the rest of Ann's story, which followed.

"Well the person commissioning it insisted that four columns were required to support the broad overhanging section. Wren said they weren't needed, so to prove a point he put them in for show only. Don't believe everything you see."

Kate laughed.

"Was that funny?" Ann asked, uncertain.

"Just similar to what someone once said to me."

Ann nodded. "I don't know about that, dear. Anyway, at some point someone didn't trust that the floor didn't need supporting. So the council had wooden blocks inserted above the columns—just in case!"

Kate found herself thinking about Joe: about not believing what she read, not believing what people said about him. Ann was still talking about Windsor and then about her daughter's job at the bank. Kate found she wasn't really listening. She heard her landline ring again. Would it ring again in another ten minutes?

89

Kate excused herself: "Thank you for the coffee and biscuits."

"Oh no, thank you once again for putting up my nets, dear." Ann levered herself to her feet, expertly using the stick, and hobbled to the door.

Kate said, "Anytime. And when you are up to it, let's do your favourite walk along the river."

Ann's cornflower blues twinkled with expectation and Kate left her on the doorstep feeling that she had doubled her good deed for the day.

At her door, she kicked off her shoes and climbed the stairs. This time she padded quietly, very conscious of any noise Ann would hear. In the lounge Kate glanced at the telephone as though she could will it to talk. She stood over it and checked her watch: thirty seconds to go. The ten minute break came and went. She picked up the receiver and dialled 1471 to check the last number to ring.

Number withheld.

She watched the phone for a few more minutes and the phrase *a watched kettle never boils* went through her head. She laughed at herself for such a stupid thought.

Still no call.

She went into the kitchen to prepare penne pasta with chopped vegetables and green pesto. She poured a glass of Chardonnay.

The phone rang and her heart missed a beat before it raced to make up for it. Kate gulped at the wine and walked to the phone. She imagined Ann standing downstairs willing her to answer it. Kate reached for the handset and hesitated.

She picked it up.

"Who is this prosim... please?" a man's voice said on the line, his voice heavily foreign.

Kate swallowed. It was an unusual way to start a conversation, and her heart continued to race. She felt a surge of discomfort, an overwhelming urge to put the phone down. Eventually she spoke. "Tell me who you are."

There was a hesitation and then: "My name is Inspector Cerny," he said, and this time Kate detected a familiar accent. "I am from the České policie. Please, what is your name?"

Kate's mind spun. *Czech police?* "What's this about?"

"Before I speak, what is your name?"

"Oh yes, sorry." She tried to compose herself, focus on the call, stop her mind racing through possibilities. She said her name.

"Prosím… please your address."

"I'm not happy—"

Before she finished, he interrupted. "You are in Wind-sore?" The policeman struggled with the name of the town. "—England? Yes?"

"Yes."

He asked for the full address and this time she gave it. "What's this about, officer?"

"You know Pan Sikorski, Petr?" Mr Peter Sikorski.

"Yes. Peter. He is—was engaged to my friend."

"Was? You know that he is dead."

"What?" She was thrown. *What is this policeman talking about? Peter dead? How could I know?* Then she realized the confusion. "I meant was engaged," she explained. "They are not together anymore."

"Ah, now I understand."

"You say he's dead?"

"You did not know?"

"No, I didn't know. How could I have known?"

"You do not sound sad your friend is a victim."

91

She sat down on the window ledge and shook her head at her reflection in the window. "Look, I'm sorry, I'm confused. It's late, and I've had a hard day. Yes, I'm saddened, but he wasn't a close friend. Dead you say? How did he—"

Inspector Cerny ignored the question. "You were not friends? Why your address was on open page in his address book then?"

"I don't know," she said. "I have no idea." But in that instance she did have an idea. In the reflection she could see the photograph of the soldiers—Boomer and Mirrorman—on the table. Now she wondered about the handwriting on the envelope. It wasn't Sarah's but it could be Peter's.

"Slečna Blakemorova?" Miss Blakemore. He used the usual Czech female version of a name.

"Yes?"

He waited as if hoping she would say something unprompted.

Should she mention the photograph? She decided it was better to wait. She didn't know for sure Peter had sent it. She would speak to Sarah first, and getting the Czech police involved seemed a complication too far.

Eventually he said, "You say he was to be married. You have her contact?"

"Yes, she's still in the Czech Republic." She picked up her mobile phone and reeled off Sarah's address and phone number. As she finished she had a horrible sick feeling in her stomach. "You don't think she's involved do you?"

"Thank you, Slečna Blakemorova. I will talk to police in England." He thanked her again and clicked off.

Kate stood by the window with the receiver still pressed to her ear, staring at her reflection. Then the realization struck her: Inspector Cerny had called Peter *the victim.*

Peter wasn't just dead. He'd been murdered!

EIGHTEEN

Voicemail.

"Hi, Sarah. It's me again. I heard the awful news about Peter. Are you OK? I know you're not together anymore but it must still be a shock." Kate paused. What else should she say? She decided to keep the call brief. "Hey, just give me a call. I'm here if you need to talk to anyone. Take care."

When she disconnected, Kate needed to speak to someone. She rang Andrew.

"Great news, Katie!" he said without introduction. "I can't talk long I need to be up early in the morning. I'm flying to Bologna."

Kate was a little thrown. "What? Oh, the Italian lead—the company interested in your software?"

"Yes. I'm just packing. What do they wear in Italy? Should I wear a suit?"

"I don't know. I'm sorry." And then she blurted it. "Peter's dead."

There was a hollow silence before Andrew spoke. "Sarah's Peter?"

"Yes."

"Oh my God, that's terrible. Is Sarah OK? How's she coping?"

94

Kate explained that she'd tried but hadn't managed to get through to Sarah.

"Maybe it's a problem with her phone."

"Maybe. I also had a phone call from the Czech police." Kate relayed the earlier conversation with Inspector Cerny.

Andrew choked. "You gave him your address?"

"He already knew it."

"Are you sure? It sounded like he just knew you were in Windsor. You don't know who he was. Grief, he could have been anybody!"

Kate was silent.

Andrew said, "Sorry. I've worried you haven't I?"

"Just a bit."

"Look. He had your number, knew your name and knew you were in Windsor. Thinking about it, if he knew that much he could have tracked you down."

"I guess."

"Tell you what—report the call to the police just so they know."

Kate made a noise reflecting her opinion of the police. "After my experience a year ago, I would predict their assistance will amount to a big zero."

"I almost forgot!" Andrew suddenly sounded more upbeat. "I've found something on the data card."

"Opened the file?"

"No. No. Found something else. I didn't think to look before. There was a hidden file, not password protected. There were just three words: *The Laughing Train*. Does that mean anything to you?"

"Yes," Kate said. "I know what The Laughing Train is."

NINETEEN

The Laughing Train.

It was a joke, a humorous reference. Close to the old station in Windsor there was a bar-restaurant that used to be called *Ha Ha*. Between the bar and a single platform stood a steam train, majestic in green, black and gold—a major tourist attraction on the route from the coach park, beyond the station, up to the castle.

Joe found it hilarious that people, particularly Japanese tourists, wanted their photograph taken next to Queen Victoria's personal locomotive. Hilarious because it was a replica—a *faux-loco* and a *crypto-tram*, as Joe called it.

Kate didn't know how this would help, but she felt a sense of optimism and was sure everything would be explained once Andrew opened the file.

When she got up, Kate sent Sarah an email:

I've tried calling. Perhaps your phone isn't working. Are you OK? Let me know. Kate

She had heard nothing from either Andrew or Sarah by the time she left for work, nor during the day. When she arrived home, Kate spotted an envelope poking out of the letterbox. Sometimes mail got stuck if it wasn't rigid enough to push through. She eased it out and saw her name scrawled on the front. Something from Andrew. She opened the envelope.

It said:

Dropped off on way to Heathrow. Software can't crack it. But did manage to find something that wasn't encrypted. Does First Words mean anything to you? I tried "Let there be light", but that didn't work!

Inside the envelope he had included a card reader with a USB connection. She rushed upstairs to her PC, ignoring Tolkien's plea for attention.

First words was easy. She switched on and plugged in the USB stick. When the window opened she clicked on the file. The password box popped up and she typed: **I dare you**

Ping.

Password correct, said a pop-up.

But nothing else happened.

Kate tabbed through the open windows. There was no document open.

She texted Andrew.

Have pword! But nothing opened. Have searched. Nothing.

Seconds later her phone rang. "Buon giorno from Italia!" Andrew said.

"That's good morning. It's evening."

"Hey, I only know a handful of Italian words, don't be so fussy. Anyway, stop the chit-chat. You cracked the code then?"

"Yes, it said I got the password correct, but no file opened."

"It could be hidden. Do *Ctrl-Alt-Delete* and you'll get the Task Manager." He waited.

"Done."

He asked what files were listed and she reeled them off. Nothing was a document program.

"OK," he said, "Now close everything except Windows Explorer, double-click on the file and then close Explorer and call up Task Manager and tell me what you see."

Kate did as instructed and told him that only the password program was running.

"OK, now type in the password and check Task Manager."

She complied. "Still only the password program."

"That's odd," he said, "I would expect that to at least close down once you have the password. Let's take a look at the processes that are running." He instructed her to click on the Processes tab and she talked him through the list of Image Names on the left hand side.

"Sorry, signorina, I haven't a clue. Look, when I get back I'll come over and run a diagnostic on it. But you might have to accept that there is no file. It could just be a joke, a fault, or perhaps the file was never created." He signed off with: "Ciao!"

Kate sighed and put her head in her hands for a moment.

Then a thought struck her. She double-clicked on the file again and the password window popped into the centre of her screen. No! She said to herself. Someone doesn't go to the extent of hiding a file in a desk calendar with encryption and password protection if there is nothing to see.

She glared at the screen, willing it to say something. It didn't and her eyes started to feel uncomfortable, constantly staring. She left the password window on the screen and went down to the kitchen, made a ham sandwich and poured a glass of Pinot Grigio. As she picked up the glass she wondered if the wine selection was subliminal. Andrew in Italy attempting Italian, ergo Italian wine.

She went back to staring at the screen, looking for inspiration.

What are you telling me, Joe?

It was a typical window: grey box with blue header. The writing was in black, the box for the password was white. The writing said, "Enter Password". The header was typical too. On the right were the *Minimize, Restore Down* and *Close* icons. On the left was an icon that looked like crossed keys, presumably representing the password software. The software name was *Runtime—* bold white letters.

Subliminal? Could it be?

She texted Andrew.

Is it possible that the password has to be entered at a specific time?

Possible. Ax, was the immediate reply.

Runtime.

Joe had been careful to hide the card. The password was one that only Kate would know, so it made sense that if time were important, it would be something that would be relevant to her.

The home telephone rang. She drummed her fingers and considered not answering. She didn't. It stopped ringing and Kate picked up, dialled 1471. It was a Reading number. Unlikely to be someone she knew? If it was Darcy, she'd ring the mobile.

Kate went back to thinking about times.

The Laughing Train.

Could it be that easy?

The phone rang and she snatched it up. It felt like her eureka moment was linked to the phone call—as though it would be Joe on the phone. Of course, it wasn't.

A man's voice, official-sounding, asked her to confirm her name. After the previous experience with the Czech policeman, she refused.

"I would like to speak to Kate Blakemore. Is that who I'm speaking to?"

"Yes."

"Is everything all right, Miss?" he asked, and she realized she must have sounded distracted. Her mind was on *Runtime*.

"Sorry who is this?" She tried to focus.

"Detective Inspector Mather from Thames Valley," he said. "It's about Peter Sikorski. I understand you spoke to the Prague police. I would like to come round and take a statement, Miss Blakemore."

"Yes, fine," she said. "When?"

"Is tomorrow afternoon all right?"

She was about to confirm when a thought crossed her mind. No-neck had not only seemed incompetent, he had made her feel uncomfortable. "Will it just be you, Detective?"

"Oh no, Miss. Don't worry, there will be a female detective accompanying me."

"Fine," she said, and agreed a time. She couldn't wait to get off the phone. She had to go.

She had to go to *The Laughing Train*.

TWENTY

Amir pulled into the square and parked. His van had a satellite TV and electrical company logo—Satcom—on the side and a ladder on the roof. The block of flats formed three-sides of the square with the girl's flat directly behind him. He got out and pulled a short ladder from the roof, left it propped at the rear and crossed to the opposite side of the square. As he approached, he noted the door to number eight was mainly frosted glass. There were two locks and a cat flap. Next to number eight's door was its twin. Number nine. No cat flap. He looked up and noted three floors. No open windows, but it was unclear which belonged to number eight.

Casually, he strolled around the rear. Along the side, cars were parked in a bay marked "residents only" with a warning from the management company that non-residents would be clamped. Beyond this was a row of garages all painted blue with padlocks in addition to locked door handles. All identical. A few cars were parked along the fence that bordered the short backyards of the properties. Again he glanced up at the building. It was possible that the flats were one floor each, but there was a symmetry that implied vertical.

A car pulled into the garaged area and Amir casually moved to a parked vehicle and examined a tyre. When the coast was clear he stepped onto the wheel and levered himself up, gaining a good view over the fence. The yards were wider than would be appropriate for a vertical arrangement of flats. There was definitely a ground floor flat, which meant he was no clearer about which windows belonged to the girl. He would have to watch before he broke in.

Two men in blue uniforms stood by his van. Police? How could they know? He had been assured the plates of the vehicle were clean, the documents in order. If they weren't, the supplier was going to pay with his life.

Amir walked away from the parked cars and headed for the main road as though just passing by. From St Leonard's Road, an arterial road that ran into the centre, he could no longer see the square or his van. He leaned against the wall of an Indian restaurant and, though not a smoker, lit a cigarette.

After finishing most of it, Amir decided to casually make his way back and identify the degree of threat. He put his hand on the gun in his pocket, wondering if things could really have deteriorated so quickly. His mind processed the options, considering who could have given him away. Rounding the bend to the square, he saw the uniformed men. They were no longer by the van, but almost at the other end, close to the target property. However, they showed no interest in the building but were studying each of the cars.

Amir walked around the side of the block as before, this time taking a closer look at the men.

Traffic wardens, just fucking wardens.

He took no chances, waited until the two men left, then returned to the van. There was a yellow and black plastic wallet stuck to his windscreen. He peeled it off, climbed in and flung the parking ticket on the floor.

Through the rear-view mirror he could clearly see the door marked "8". He took out his phone and pretended to be on a call, sat and watched.

At four thirty the light was fading and a fine drizzle had peppered the windscreen. It was a miserable, damp country, Amir decided, but, during his intensive surveillance, the rain went unnoticed. A handful of people had come and gone. A pilot and a couple of air stewardesses were the only people below geriatric age. He saw no movement in any of the windows above the door he watched. A light came on in one of the rooms and he figured this was on a timer. Then moments later a blonde girl on a mobile phone rounded the bend. He tracked her as she headed across the road. She put the phone in her purse. Amir judged her facial expression to be disappointment. Not bad-looking—fit body, possibly worked out. He smiled as she stopped at the door to number eight. This was the girl.

When she opened the door Amir saw an immediate flight of stairs. He also noted she'd used two keys.

Stepping out of the van, he busied himself with the ladder as though preparing to work. He saw the girl appear at the first-floor window. Another light went on and she drew the curtains. Seconds later a light went on upstairs. Second floor. So the flats were structured with one on the ground floor and two above, each set on two floors.

The curtains upstairs didn't close, which, he judged, meant she was at the rear of the property. To confirm this he walked swiftly around the back and glanced up. The blonde girl sat, side on to a window, looking at a computer. As he watched, she picked up her phone and began texting. After a while she got up and left the room.

He returned to the van and put on an engineer's jacket and picked up a steel case. It looked like it might contain equipment appropriate for his cover, but the tools were for a different task. With confidence now, he walked to the door of number eight and rang the buzzer.

No response.

After a couple of minutes, he pressed the doorbell once more—this time for longer.

Noise inside. The stairs light went on and he saw the girl trot down the stairs.

"Sorry if you've been waiting." She was flustered but had a disarming smile. "I was upstairs and wasn't sure the doorbell was sounding. What can I do for you?"

Amir raised his case. "ComSat engineer. I'm here to connect the satellite TV. The landlord ordered it." This last comment was a gamble, but Amir guessed her to be a tenant. Something about the flats, the pilot, the air stewardesses, all said: *rented.*

Her face showed confusion but no suspicion. "Oh? I thought there was something in the deeds that prohibited a satellite dish." Then she shook her head. "Actually, it's not convenient now. I'm just off out. Could you schedule something tomorrow?"

He placed his hand on the door and pulled a face that he hoped was friendly, unthreatening. "Sure. Of course. I was just passing. Wondered if I could get the job done early. I'll have the office call you to arrange a proper appointment." He took a step backwards.

The girl grabbed a coat by the door and stepped after him. Something crossed her face before Amir smiled, said good evening and turned. He heard her close the door and insert the deadlock key. As he reached the van he looked in the side mirror. She was already hurrying towards the main road. There was still no sign of suspicion.

She had locked her front door.

Or so she thought.

TWENTY-ONE

As Kate headed down to the lounge, she heard the buzzer. *Damn! I must do something about the sound.* It really didn't carry all the way to the top floor. Someone may have been waiting a while.

She opened the door to a man in grey overalls. An engineer. He talked about fitting a satellite TV. Have the residents resolved that issue?

Kate said, "I thought there was something in the deeds that prohibited a satellite dish." She wanted Sky, but now wasn't convenient. The priority was to check out the train, so she told him to make an appointment.

He said something about rescheduling as she grabbed her coat. For a moment Kate thought he was coming in, but it was just her imagination because he backed away from the door. She pulled on her coat as she stepped through the door. *Creep!* He was staring at her.

The man wished her a *good evening* and headed across the square to a van. She switched off the light, closed the door, and locked it.

She jogged lightly to the road and continued into town. It was the strange time of day between the shops locking up for the night and the restaurants opening. Later, St Leonard's Road would come alive, but now, the only people she passed were workers trudging home.

Within five minutes she reached the shopping area and practically skipped up the steps to the station's concourse. In front of her, Windsor's Victorian central station loomed like a relic from yesteryear. Outside the bar that had once been called *Ha Ha*, a few early birds sat at tables and nursed bottles of beer. She walked past to the steam train set at the end of the platform. A group of late tourists received the usual nonsense lecture about it being the Queen's train.

Kate chuckled to herself as she squeezed through the crowd to find the plate on the side of the engine.

1401.

Swindon Works.

Oct 1898.

1401. What was it? It wasn't a date. There was no explanation for the number.

1401.

Joe had once said, "Maybe it's the time the train runs."

Now there was no doubt: this was the *Runtime*. Joe was telling her to enter the password at 14:01.

Excited, Kate headed back home. The grey streets suddenly seemed happy and full of the evening's promise. People walking home from work now had purpose and pleasure at returning to their families. The only frustration was she had to wait. Kate couldn't do anything until tomorrow afternoon.

When she got home she put the deadbolt key in the lock and tried to turn it. Strange. It didn't rotate. She put the Yale key in the upper lock and it turned easily. She was surprised when the door opened. *Mustn't have deadlocked my door properly. Oh well.*

Tolkien was in the lounge. He stood in a corner, his tail bushy, his eyes wide.

106

"Hey, it's only me, Tolk!" she said. "No need to be scared of me, old boy." As she took a step towards him he bolted, shot down the stairs and clattered through the flap.

Crazy scaredy-cat.

Kate spent the evening on the phone, first to her mother and then her sister, Darcy. They had the usual conversation about Kate's jobs and Darcy said she was considering going back to work. She had brushed up her CV and sent it to a handful of recruitment agents.

Darcy switched to the subject of the twins. "India has cut her knee and Emmy has been vomiting. Norovirus, what else? Give it a couple of days and we'll all have the bug she's caught now."

"Sorry to hear it. Is India's knee bad?"

"Oh she'll survive, but Tim had to take her to A&E. Did you know they've closed our local? Good job it wasn't a real emergency. It took Tim half an hour to get there. They just taped it up and gave her a tetanus jab."

"Poor love." Kate hesitated then said, "Darce?"

"Yes."

"Something has happened."

"What?" Real concern.

"Nothing to worry about. I know you don't like me to talk about Joe, but—"

"Oh, Kate! Will you move on for Christ's sake? I know you loved him, but he was no good. The man you loved wasn't real. He was a fantasy."

"He's left me a coded message."

"What sort of message?"

"God! Darce, he's left me a document telling me the truth."

Her sister groaned. "Don't let him play with your head like this. You're a smart girl and I love you. I can't bear to see you played like this. Joe was no good. A secret message won't change that. Yes, it probably gives you an explanation. He will have answers for everything. Think of all those other women that fell for him. And, if it's not bad enough that he was still married, think about those children he abandoned."

Kate had been thinking. "Remember the detectives, the ones in the brown suits?" Something Andrew had said triggered the thought. "They pointed me to crimes in the US and said the FBI were after him. But the FBI doesn't operate outside the US and don't have jurisdiction in the UK. If they wanted someone, they would have to apply for extradition. That's how it works. And you arrest them at work or home, not just pick them up off the streets and shove them in a car!"

"You're grasping at straws. Maybe they thought it was safer to pick him up in the open. Maybe they knew he had a gun."

"OK, but then why didn't the police tell me straight off when I tried to find out what was happening? Why the cloak-and-dagger routine?"

Darcy sighed, exasperated. "Oh I don't know. Maybe it was too politically sensitive. Who knows how things work now, post nine-eleven?"

Kate had further thoughts. If the people who picked Joe up weren't the police then it was unlikely that the brown-suited men were FBI or detectives or whatever they had said. The story they told could have been a lie. As an extension to this logic, Kate wondered if this meant the internet articles could have been faked in some way. Maybe Joe didn't have a string of identities and women. Then what did he have? Why was he picked up, and who were they?

She didn't say any of this to Darcy. There was no point. She felt truly optimistic for the first time in a year.

Once she read Joe's secret message, she was sure all would be clear. Then Darcy would believe her.

Darcy said, "I love you. I don't like to think you're still being hurt by this."

"I'm fine. Honest, I feel fine."

"All right. Promise me you'll not keep dwelling on this. It's also high time you came over to visit. The girls will be excited to see you."

Kate promised to visit soon. She went to bed, still filled with anticipation. Thoughts were going round and round searching for answers that she didn't have. Knowing that she would be able to open the document at one minute past two tomorrow didn't help. She couldn't sleep.

In the still of the night, noises seem amplified. She thought she could hear a neighbour walking around.

A light switch clicked somewhere.

A car door slammed in the square.

There was the sound of someone moving about. A creak on the stairs. Must be the next-door neighbour, she told herself.

It sounded close.

She realized she was holding her breath, straining to hear. Her bedroom door was slightly ajar and she stared at it, suddenly petrified that someone was in the apartment. Another noise, closer. She gripped the covers, squinting her eyes to see.

The door moved.

TWENTY-TWO

Tolkien leapt onto the end of the bed and Kate jolted with shock and then relief. "Good grief, Tolk, I thought you were an intruder!"

He padded towards her and snuggled his body under her exposed arm. She immediately forgave him, relieved that he seemed more himself rather than the skittish cat that had dashed out when she'd come back. He began to purr and the comforting sound must have sent her to sleep, because the next thing she knew it was morning.

The excitement of the secret message immediately filled her head. How was she going to cope, waiting for 14:01?

When she saw the weather was fine she decided to go for a run, looping around Windsor Great Park for about six miles. After a shower she felt ready for the day, full of anticipation and hope. The run had also cleared her head a bit.

Boomer.

If Joe had been telling the truth and Boomer existed, then she would surely find something on the internet about him.

It took a matter of minutes to find the relevant information. Boomer was the nickname of Danny Guice, college quarterback and All Star. He had played for

Virginia Tech and was destined for the NFL. She read a few articles about how great he was, yard records and percentages that meant nothing to Kate but tallied with what Joe had said about Boomer's high promise at college. But he didn't make it as a pro. He had joined the army.

Kate discovered that the reason for him failing as a pro was a broken leg. Six months out and couldn't cut it when he returned. His new contract with The Pittsburgh Steelers was terminated. Some pieces alluded to an attitude change, as though the injury had affected his outlook. Unkindly, one suggested he was afraid. Maybe that was what prompted him to join the army.

Kate searched for the name Mirrorman but found nothing relevant to Joe. She tried combinations of Boomer and Danny Guice with Joe's various names. Nothing came up. Then she studied all the photos of Boomer.

Joe didn't appear in any of them.

So Boomer was real, Joe's story about him was true, but that didn't mean they were really friends. She shook the cynical thought from her head. She suspected that if anyone searched for her and a college friend they'd be hard-pressed to find a picture on the internet unless... she tried Facebook and similar social sites. No sign of Boomer on those. She tried searching in professional sites like LinkedIn and Naymz. Nothing. She had drawn a blank.

Amazed at how long she'd spent searching, she took a break and made a sandwich.

Thirty minutes to *Runtime*.

The doorbell rang as she finished her sandwich. A man and a woman stood on her doorstep. *Oh God!* She'd completely forgotten about the police.

"Kate Blakemore?" It was the voice of the man on the phone: Inspector Mather. The other person was a woman. She had red hair tied back in a severe ponytail.

"I haven't got long," Kate said.

Mather frowned at her.

Realizing the greeting appeared a little strange, Kate apologized and invited them in. Up the stairs she pointed to the dining table. They sat and looked like they expected to be offered tea. They didn't get it.

"This is Detective Sergeant Littlewood," Mather said. Then, as Littlewood smiled and nodded, Mather continued and asked about Sarah Wishart.

"Sarah? I thought this was about her ex-partner, Peter."

"Maybe it is. We are liaising with Czech police, but our principle concern is with the disappearance of Sarah. When was the last time you had contact with Sarah?"

"I, uh... Sarah's disappeared?"

The policewoman spoke. She had a nice face, although her thin lips and downturned mouth gave her a critical look. There was also a hard, unfriendly edge to her voice. "Please, Miss Blakemore, answer the question. When did you last have contact with Sarah?"

Kate was flustered, and this woman, with her tone, put her on edge. "I... I don't know."

Inspector Mather again: "But you recently left her a message and you have been sending her texts."

"That's true. But I haven't spoken to her." Suddenly, with everything that was going on, Kate's mind was blank about the order for things. However she felt a strong compulsion to try and justify herself. "The Czech police told me Peter had been murdered. I got a letter... a photograph in the post. I thought it might have been from Sarah. I wondered how Sarah was after Peter's death. Maybe she would need support, come and stay? Oh... and she called me."

Surprise lit up the inspector's face. "She called you? When was this?"

"Friday evening. Only we didn't speak. I didn't pick up in time and she didn't leave a message."

The police officers studied her face impassively. They waited as if the silence would prompt a confession. Littlewood took some notes.

"Can I see the photograph you received?" Mather eventually asked, when it was clear Kate wouldn't start speaking again.

Kate hesitated, checked her watch, then stood up and retrieved the photograph of Boomer and Mirrorman from the sideboard.

Mather looked at the photograph, flipped it over, handed it to Littlewood and said, "Who are they?"

Maybe it was the tension of the situation, but Kate told them she didn't know.

Littlewood's expression spoke of disbelief. "Boomer and Mirrorman—are they names? Who wants you to find them?"

Again she said she didn't know. "It was posted in the Czech Republic. I assume either Peter or Sarah. I don't know why."

"You think it might be Sarah Wishart asking you to find her?"

That made Kate blink. She hadn't considered that possibility. Could it be Sarah rather than Joe?

"Ms Blakemore?" Littlewood interrupted her thoughts.

"Sorry—what?"

"You seem distracted." Littlewood's eyes narrowed. "And you keep looking at your watch"

"I'm sorry, I really don't have the time for this right now."

"Why?"

"There's something I need to do." There were five minutes to *Runtime* and Kate was becoming more and more distracted. She had to end this now. "If you've no more questions..."

Annoyance fleetingly passed across the inspector's eyes, but he masked it well. "We do have more questions. If you don't mind, we will wait."

Kate stood up too quickly and felt a rush to the head. "I'm sorry. I'm sorry. We'll have to continue this another time. I really must go. I would like you to leave."

The police stood, their eyes fixed on Kate, hard and calculating. "All right," Mather said, his voice flat.

Littlewood placed the photograph of the soldiers in her notebook. "If you don't mind," she said, "we'll keep this." It wasn't a question.

Kate saw them to the door.

Littlewood prompted, "You're sure you don't know the men in the photograph?"

Kate held the door, willing them to go. "No idea," she said and read the immediate look on their faces: total disbelief. They were probably thinking, *She is lying about this, so she has probably lied about everything else.* Kate didn't care. She needed them out now. She needed to get to her computer.

Mather asked for a date to reschedule. "Call me," Kate said rather too abruptly and shut the door. She ran up the stairs, two at a time. As she reached the lounge she glanced through the window and saw the police standing outside, talking, probably evaluating.

It was 2pm. Kate needed to get on the computer and read Joe's message.

TWENTY-THREE

Kate had left the password window of the file open. As her computer clock changed to 14:01 she typed *I dare you* and hit *Enter*.

File path not found.

What? A Windows error message.

Kate quickly tried again. Same result. The digital display ticked over to 14:02. *Shit!* She had missed her minute's opportunity. She didn't get it. Was the *Runtime* wrong? There were other numbers on the train. There was 3904, the large serial number on the side of the cab. There was also the date—October 1898, representing when the train was supposedly built. *Could that be the time, 1898?* She admonished herself for not realizing that 98 couldn't be minutes. No, the Runtime joke was definitely 14:01, one minute past two.

File path not found.

She opened Windows Explorer and looked at the drives. There was nothing in the USB drives! Perhaps the card had worked loose, she thought. She reached down to push the card reader firmly into the slot. She'd call in sick and try again tomorrow.

The card reader was in place. It didn't move when she pushed. She pulled it out and pushed it firmly back in. Windows Explorer continued to register nothing in the drive.

Kate pulled the card reader out and looked at the slot where Joe's small card was inserted. The slot was empty. She searched the desk, all the time telling herself that it couldn't be there. Then she realized it could have fallen out, so she searched the carpet around the PC. There was a jumble of wires and cables at the back and she moved these aside.

Nothing.

She lifted the PC to check under it then sat back perplexed. What had she done? She distractedly glanced around the floor of the whole room until she snapped back into focus. *Runtime*. She had been in a hurry to get to the train. She had texted and been on the phone. The doorbell had sounded. That weird satellite guy was at the door. Her mind had been all over the place.

Could I have unconsciously removed the memory card and taken it with me?

She found the jeans she'd been wearing and checked the pockets. She went through her purse. She went to the coats at the front door and checked the pockets. She was totally stumped. Yes, it was a tiny memory card, but how could she have lost it?

Kate slumped on the sofa in the lounge and the tears came. A wave of tiredness and all the emotional turmoil of the past days flooded out. The card was her connection to Joe and she had lost it.

Amir sat in a nondescript blue van in the garage area behind the apartments. The girl had been singing to herself and spent most of the morning on the computer. He took note of her internet searches, his laptop mimicking her every keystroke. Why was she searching for someone called Boomer? Like her, he read Boomer's real name. There was no link between this man and her boyfriend, unless she believed Boomer was another alias. From the pictures it was clear that it was not. Then she looked for the name Mirrorman and tried different aliases for Joe. So she knew his codename. Perhaps this was going to be easier than he had anticipated.

She had the security window for the file open and he held his breath with anticipation each time she looked at it. But she keyed nothing in and continued to search. At lunchtime she went to the kitchen and prepared some food. Would she notice anything missing? He doubted it; the girl didn't strike him as the most organized. If she noticed it wasn't in its place, he guessed she'd assume it was in a drawer or somewhere else.

Voices. Two people, a man and a woman, rang the doorbell of number eight. Amir was pleased with himself for including a microphone in the doorbell. The sound wasn't ideal, but he could make out what they said. The girl cursed as she hurried to the front door. The man introduced himself. They were cops. Amir took notes as the cops asked the girl questions. She was tense and flustered, which suited his plans. The man and woman almost played the roles of good cop, bad cop, but it was subtle and they learned little. The girl handed them a photograph. So that is what she received from the Czech Republic: a photograph of someone called Boomer. Now it made sense.

She got more anxious and asked them to leave. Amir checked his watch. Almost 2pm. So he had been right, she was waiting for a specific time. *Runtime.* She needed to get rid of the cops and onto the computer.

When the girl showed them out, the police hadn't immediately left. For a short time they continued to stand near the front door, although it sounded like they may have taken a step back to look up at the apartment.

"What do you think?" the man asked.

"She's lying."

"I don't think she knew Sarah had disappeared. That seemed genuine. She probably has just been trying to make contact because of the ex-husband's death."

"I think you're right, but she lied about the photo. She knows who this Boomer character is. Why was she so agitated? She said she had something to do. Do you think it's related?"

The man paused as though considering. "It's related."

"We should bring her in—formally."

"Not yet. We are just looking into a missing woman in the Czech Republic. All right, this Peter Sikorski, her ex, has been murdered but we don't know that's linked." He said something else, but the cops were moving away and it became too faint for Amir to hear what they were saying.

Almost instantaneously the cursor on the laptop began to move across the password box. She typed, I dare you. She didn't click *Enter*, but the arrow hovered over the button. When the clock changed to 2:01 she clicked. Nothing happened for the girl, but on Amir's computer a text file opened. He flipped control back to his machine to see the file.

When he had finished reading, he picked up his phone.

Hamasalih answered on the first ring. "Speak," he said.

"I have the evidence that we have the right man."

"Good. Now find him. You know where he is?"

"No, but I have a plan."

Amir ended the call, turned off the phone and switched control back to the girl's PC. She wasn't there; he could hear sobbing and it disgusted him. Western

118

women were so weak. If she could cry at the loss of the disk, what state would she be in when he killed her fat effeminate friend?

TWENTY-FOUR

The next afternoon, Andrew called. "It's going really well," he said. "They've invited me to stay for the weekend."

"Sounds very promising," Kate responded, but her voice was flat and she immediately regretted not sounding more enthusiastic for him. "No really, that's good news."

"You sound despondent. What did the document tell you? I thought you'd be happier now."

She told him what had happened, that she'd lost the data card.

"Oh, Katie!"

"I'll find it," she said, trying to sound convincing.

"What about Boomer? Have you made any progress finding him?"

"I found some stuff on the internet." Realization struck her. "Oh, you mean try to trace him through the army. Is that possible? How would I do that?"

"No idea. I'd start with the internet, try the army websites. Anyway, got to love ya and leave ya. Finance people to see."

"Don't forget to hammer out those commercials... and get the agreement in writing."

"Yes, Mother," he said, and was gone.

Kate's spirits lifted after the call. She had something to focus on again and immediately began trawling the internet. She went on a number of general question-and-answer sites, registered and posted the question:

Hello! I'm trying to trace a friend in the US Army. How do I go about finding them?

She found an army forum, again registered and posted the question. Then she sat back and waited. After two cups of Earl Grey and no response, she pulled out a pad of paper. In pencil she wrote anything and everything she knew—everything Joe had told her—on the paper. She spaced the words out, putting Joe in the middle and placing the names Boomer, Sarah and Peter randomly on the page. Then she added *me* and drew lines from Joe to the others. She rubbed out Joe to Sarah. From Peter to *me* she wrote:

Photo of Boomer?

She drew a dotted line from Peter to Boomer. Were they connected? She'd start with assuming that Peter had sent the photograph on Joe's behalf.

She drew a connecting line between Sarah and Peter. Under Sarah's name she wrote:

What did she know?

Next to *Boomer* she wrote:

Danny Guice
Which army unit?

Under Joe's name she listed his aliases and the nickname *Mirrorman*.

She turned over the page and wrote:

Questions—Actions

and underneath that:

What was in the file named Trust Me? Can I trace Boomer? Is Joe really American?

It felt like there were more questions, but for the moment her mind was a blank.

She turned to the previous page, sipped the tea and stared at the mind map. No inspiration came for a while although something niggled at the back of her brain. Something she couldn't quite reach. Was it Joe's aliases that bothered her? She wrote:

FBI?

and drew an arrow to the aliases.

She had spoken to a British policeman before Woodall and the other one... what was his name? Woodall and... Hurwitz, the nicer one. What was No-neck's proper name? Drawing a blank, she moved on and wrote:

British police

then added the names *Mather* and *Littlewood* to her list.

She flipped over to the questions.

What do the British police know about Joe's arrest? How come the FBI could do that? Find who the other policeman—No-neck—was and speak to him.

Her thoughts were interrupted by her iPhone. Lisa.

"Fancy joining me and a bunch of others at a wine bar tomorrow evening?" Lisa sounded as bubbly as ever.

"Sounds perfect. I could do with something to take my mind off things."

"Oh, what things?"

Kate gave her a quick update on losing the data card with Joe's document on and trying to locate Boomer. Her friend listened intently.

"I have a boyfriend—well I guess he's an ex by now—in the States. Anyway, he used to be in the US Army. I could ask him if he knows how you could find Joe's friend."

"Wow, yes! Yes please. That'd be great."

122

"OK, consider it done... assuming he responds to me, that is. Must have been three years now. Anyway..." She hesitated. "Just another thought..."

"Yes?"

"Why don't you find out what happened to Joe?"

Silence.

Lisa said, "Kate? I said why not find out where Joe is?"

Kate realized she was pacing the room. That was *the* burning question she had avoided. What had happened to Joe since he was arrested? When she had searched for details about him all the newspaper reports were prior to him coming to England. Why had there been nothing since.

Her pulse quickened. "Oh my God, Lisa. I could kiss you. I've just had an idea." She quickly ended the call, with a promise to see her friend tomorrow, and dialled Thames Valley police. Her hands were shaking as she picked up Inspector Mather's business card and gave the receptionist his extension number. Mather answered on the second ring. There was no surprise in his voice when she introduced herself.

"I'd like to speak to you," Kate said. His long silence prompted her to continue. "I'm sorry I was rude yesterday, but I really did have something urgent to do. I was preoccupied."

Mather said, "I'd like you to come down to the station."

God, why do they say it like that? Something about the phrase made her feel guilty. Her nervousness made her laugh and then say something she immediately regretted. "Anything I should confess to?"

Fortunately, he didn't respond to the question. Instead, he said, "When can you make it?"

Kate suggested some times and he said he was based in the head office in Reading. They agreed on 4:30 tomorrow, Friday.

"I have a favour to ask." A little awkwardness edged Kate's voice.

"Favour?" Mather was curious.

"A year ago, my boyfriend was picked up by the police or secret service or maybe even the FBI—I'm unclear who." She could hear Mather writing notes. "It seemed to make sense at the time but now I'm not sure it does."

"What was his name—your boyfriend?"

"Joe Rossini." She spelt it out.

"I'll see what I can find."

A thought struck her. "Could you check the name Greg Towers as well?" She explained that this was supposedly his real name.

"Supposedly?"

Did she sound like some crazy woman? She wondered what to say. Over the telephone it was so difficult to judge whether the other person was interested or following. "The two men—they said they were detectives—told me Joe Rossini was a fake identity, that he was British and his real name was Greg Towers. He had used other IDs before too."

Inspector Mather's next words answered her fears. "I understand," he said. "Give me the exact date this happened and I'll pull the files."

When she put the phone down, a wave of calm came over her. Taking positive action, with the promise of some answers, brought a smile back to her face.

She spent the evening curled on the sofa with Tolkien, half watching an old Hitchcock movie. Just before half past nine she received an email response from one of the general question-and-answer websites.

Someone called *Scram79* wrote:

If you know your friend's unit, you will be able to find out where they are posted. Then contact the base.

Just as she read the email, her mobile rang. Queen ringtone. Andrew.

"Buona sera!" Andrew said.

"I see your Italian's improving."

He laughed. "My memory is too! I forgot to tell you something earlier, but before I say, how's the searching going?"

"Some progress, I think. I need to find out which unit Boomer was in."

"Great!"

"So what did you forget to tell me?"

Andrew paused, teasing. Finally, he said, "If you can't find the data card, no worries. We'll take a look on Monday when I get back."

Kate didn't get it. "What are you saying?"

"I copied the file onto my hard drive. We'll be able to read the *Trust Me* document."

TWENTY-FIVE

Amir learned two things that changed his plans: the girl's friend in Italy wasn't returning until Monday, but more importantly there was another copy of the document. There was information in that document that must never be made public. With so much at stake, it was clear that Amir needed to deal with the risk.

From Kate's PC, Amir easily obtained the address in South Ascot. Driving the Satcom van past the house, he noted that the door opened onto the street. Too exposed. He parked the van and found an alley which ran behind the row of Victorian houses. The narrow path provided access to the rear of the properties—small walled yards. Dressed in the blue overalls and carrying his small bag, Amir located Andrew's house and tried the gate. Locked, but a simple bolt could be reached over the top. He slid the bolt and entered the yard.

The rear door was a modern, five-lever affair. The downstairs windows were UPVC and had security bars. A room beside the kitchen appeared to be a study with computer equipment. The upstairs windows appeared to be sash-style and wooden—less secure. An alarm box on the rear was real, the one on the front a fake. He quickly returned to his van and removed a folding ladder and a lightweight satellite dish.

Erecting the ladder beside the alarm, he filled the box with *No More Gaps*. The foam quickly solidified and would prevent the bell from ringing. He stuck the satellite dish on the wall and, while looking as though he was fixing the cables, he was in fact beginning to cut through the glass.

He made a hole big enough to insert his arm and release a catch. He opened the window and stepped into a bedroom.

Without a moment's hesitation, he hurried to the landing and down the stairs. There was no doubt in his mind that the alarm would have been triggered and a monitoring company would get the automatic call. The police could be notified within minutes.

Amir located Andrew's study. There were three desktop computers, one of which looked as though it was being rebuilt. One PC was clearly the main one, so he disconnected it. He found flash drives and an external backup and put these in his bag. Then he picked up the PC and walked out of the back door. In total, he had been in the house for less than five minutes.

He left the ladder and fake dish on the wall and walked calmly to the van. He was long gone by the time the police arrived.

The first time he stopped, he went into the back and removed the hard drive from the PC, opened it and destroyed the disk. He did the same for the backup disk and crushed the flash drives. As he drove to his next destination in the countryside he tossed the components from the window into the ditches. He passed a lay-by containing a parked grey family saloon and continued on until he reached a tubular metal five-bar gate. On the other side of the gate was a short track through a copse to a field. He stopped under the cover of trees and began to pour petrol inside the cab and then the rear. After setting the van alight, he threw his overalls into the flames. Then he returned to the road, walked to the grey saloon, got in and drove away.

He picked up his phone and dialled.

"Speak," a man immediately answered.

"I had a problem. It looked as though there was another copy of the document."

"Had anybody read it?" Hamasalih asked, his voice showing no emotion.

"No. It's been dealt with it."

"And progress on finding our man?"

"The girl doesn't know, but she will find him. She is already making progress."

"Good."

"And if I need to help?"

"Do what you need to. You know what's at risk. We trust your judgement."

Amir switched off the phone. He hadn't mentioned the involvement of the British police. Their interest hadn't been expected so early. She had asked the inspector to find out what happened, which was good. However, they clearly wanted something. They wanted her at the police station.

TWENTY-SIX

Inspector Mather said, "Start from the beginning, Kate."

They sat in Interview Room Three in an intimidating building in an old section of Reading. Kate had never noticed it before today. Behind it, an imposing red-brick Victorian prison loomed, somehow threatening. The old prisons seemed a greater deterrent to crime, not that Kate considered herself a criminal. She could imagine a dingy interior with cast-iron stairs and balconies, and heavy doors that clanged shut, entombing the inmates in their six by eight cells.

Mather sat across from her, a desk between them. DS Littlewood sat to her left, at an angle, studying her side on. A tape recorder was whirring on the table. Kate had thought through everything she was going to say. After the phone conversation with Mather she realized that, unless the story was told logically, it could sound mad—as it had a year ago. And she didn't want to be treated like that again.

After a calming breath she began by explaining how she and Sarah had met at university. She told them what she knew about Peter, when they had met and about going to the engagement party. She progressed to meeting Joe—a friend and work colleague of Peter's. Kate felt no embarrassment at saying she and Joe had become lovers. After about three months he had managed to get a job in the UK and, shortly after that, had moved in to her apartment in Windsor. Then she described the shock of watching Joe being bundled into a car a few months after that.

"About a year ago?" Littlewood checked.

"Right. I thought it might have been a kidnapping and reported it to the police. Finally someone came and took a statement. I heard nothing until two detectives stopped me in the street."

"They said they were detectives?" Littlewood again.

"I'm pretty sure that's what they said. I didn't look at their badges. They told me that Joe was a conman and wanted on a number of charges. I checked on the internet, like they suggested, and found news articles about him, although his name wasn't mentioned."

"How did you know it was your boyfriend?"

"The dates tallied. Joe had been in the Czech Republic and left at the same time as the wanted man." Kate's voice trailed off. She took a sip of water and looked into Mather's face. The inspector remained impassive.

Kate began again: "A year to the day of his disappearance, my friend found something."

Littlewood asked who the friend was and wrote Andrew's name in her notebook. "Go on, please."

"There was a data card with an encrypted file. There was a password that only I would know. It was a message for me from Joe."

Littlewood leaned forward slightly. "What did it say?"

Kate studied the wall opposite. She felt her throat flush with embarrassment. "I don't know. I seem to have lost it. I was in a flap when you came round. I needed to key the password in at a certain time."

For the first time Mather's eyes registered something. Understanding, perhaps?

Littlewood said, "So you lost the file." Her tone suggested incredulity.

Kate was uncertain. "Yes... well... but my friend, Andrew, copied it. So on Monday I'll be able to try again."

"Monday?"

"When Andrew gets back from Italy."

Mather said, "Will you let us know what the document says?"

Kate hesitated. What if there was something Joe didn't want to be disclosed? That would explain the encryption. Eventually she said, "I'll tell you what I can."

Littlewood frowned but Mather nodded. "Tell us about the photograph," he said.

"I realized the envelope was posted in the Czech Republic. It contained the photograph."

Littlewood slid the photograph across the desk. "You know who Boomer and Mirrorman are, don't you?" An accusatory statement rather than a question.

Kate looked at it. "Yes," she said quietly. "I'm sorry I didn't explain before, but I was in a hurry and you would have wanted more. You'd have asked about Joe and you know how long that has taken to talk through."

"Who are they?" Littlewood prompted.

Kate kept her eyes on Mather. "Boomer is the name of Joe's buddy who used to play American football. Joe told me some stories about being in the army with him. I checked the internet and Boomer's real name is Danny Guice. The stories Joe told me about Boomer check out."

"You think Peter Sikorski sent you the photograph of Boomer and the other soldier?" Mather said. He shifted in his chair, his body language now more inclusive of the sergeant.

"I don't know. Maybe he did or maybe it was Sarah. I thought Sarah initially, but now it seems more likely to have been Peter—because of the connection with Joe. He was Joe's boss in Prague."

"What did you do with the envelope?" Mather asked.

"Threw it away."

"Could you get it?"

"It will have gone to recycling."

Littlewood leaned forward again. "Convenient."

The woman was beginning to annoy Kate. What did she think? That Kate had deliberately disposed of the envelope so they couldn't check? Kate bit her tongue and said, "No. Sorry, I didn't imagine it would be important. I guess I didn't think."

Mather again: "Could it have been Sarah's handwriting? After all, you said you hadn't seen her for a while."

"I'd have recognized Sarah's writing. Thinking about it now, I can say it didn't look remotely like hers."

Littlewood said, "Sarah and Peter—what was their relationship like after they split up?"

"What do you mean?"

"Did they stay in touch?"

Kate rubbed her forehead, thinking. "I guess. There was no chance of her getting back with him, but I think they were cordial. They had many friends in common, so they would have seen each other around."

"When did you last speak to her?"

"About three months ago, I think. Maybe more"

"But you earlier told us you were good friends. Her parents said you were best friends." Littlewood's voice changed pitch as though challenging Kate's response.

"People lose touch for a while."

"But before that you were regularly in touch?"

"Yes."

"So you are saying that you don't know whether Sarah and Peter fell out?"

"That's right," Kate said with exasperation. "I hadn't spoken to her for over three months." She read something in Littlewood's face and beat her to the next question. "And no, I hadn't been in touch with Peter either."

"When did she call you?"

"She rang last Friday—in the evening. I've told you that already."

"Why did she call you?" Littlewood said quickly.

Kate shook her head. "I told you—I didn't speak to her." A long pause followed and Kate started to think about the questions she had asked Mather, the real reason she had agreed to visit the police station.

Then it blurted out. Kate looked at Mather and said, "I've answered your questions. You've told me nothing. What do your reports show about Joe, about the detectives—or FBI or whatever they were—picking him up?"

Mather looked thoughtful, ran his tongue over his upper molars.

Littlewood seemed to sense her boss was about to disclose something. "Sir?"

Ignoring his sergeant, Mather gave a slight nod. "The report showed that everything you said about the arrest happened. But it was Special Branch—a joint operation with the FBI. Greg Towers was wanted for financial crimes linked to multiple identity thefts." He stopped.

There was more. Kate could see it in those dark eyes. "And?" she prompted.

Littlewood gave her a smile like the corners of her mouth were pulled by strictures. "Since nine-eleven in the States and then seven-seven here, things have become a lot easier. We work more closely now."

Kate searched Mather's face. She wanted honesty—after all, she'd willingly come to the station. In theory it could have taken a chunk out of her work day. She had made a commitment and she suddenly felt emboldened. "This is bullshit," she said under her breath to Littlewood but kept looking at Mather. "What happened next?"

Mather didn't hesitate. Afterwards she wished she'd let him drip feed the news, to lessen the shock. He said, "Towers is still in the UK."

Silence.

When was the last time she'd had a drink of water? Kate's tongue stuck to the roof of her mouth.

Mather must have realized she was struggling so he eventually continued. "The FBI applied for extradition, but Towers was found to be mentally unstable. We don't extradite the mentally ill, or at least the process is more difficult. The FBI seemed satisfied with the British solution and agreed to wait until his condition improved—if ever. So he's still here."

Kate found her voice. "British solution?"

Littlewood seemed to delight in what she said next: "A mentally ill criminal. There's only one place for the criminally insane in this country: Broadmoor."

Whoa! The room spun. Kate could only see the plastic cup of water in her hand and a white blur beyond. The water boiled in the cup. Her hand trembled. She tried to calm the hand, forced herself to sip and heard Inspector Mather say something about breathing. Gradually things came back into focus and her brain seemed to switch on again. She looked into Mather's eyes and saw concern, but now she also read something like cunning. Had this whole interview been planned? She'll say this, we'll say that. Probably.

Kate calmed herself. "Broadmoor?" It seemed so logical. Should she have worked it out? Could she have found out? There must have been court records. Broadmoor. Now that's a weird coincidence, she realized. Broadmoor Hospital was in a village called Crowthorne. Not many people know this, because even in the village the hospital is invisible, hidden in part of Windsor Forest. It wasn't far from Windsor.

Joe was close by.

TWENTY-SEVEN

Joe is in Broadmoor! "Thank you," Kate said weakly. The water had calmed her but she doubted she could stand without falling over. *God! He's so close. And has been for twelve months.*

I could have visited him—talked to him, she thought. Then the realization struck her that he was classed as criminally insane. What was she thinking? He's crazy! Did she really want to go and see him? And yet, there was this other story—Boomer and the army.

Mather was talking again. Kate tuned out her own thoughts and homed in on his voice. "We need to talk about Sarah," he said.

"You think something has happened to her?"

"Her ex has been murdered and no one has seen or heard from Sarah in a week."

"But you don't think she did it. Surely?"

"Well, we can't rule anything out as she is wanted for questioning by the Czech police. But at this point we are more concerned for her wellbeing. A missing person rather than a suspect."

Kate struggled with this. Her brain was functioning again, having forced thoughts of Joe to the back of her mind. "I'm sorry," she said, "but why would the British police be involved so early in a missing person case?"

"Politics," Littlewood muttered.

"More like high profile," Mather explained. "In the last couple of years we've had disappearances of British women around the world."

"The air stewardess found in the bathtub of sand in Japan," Kate said, remembering the news.

Mather agreed. "That and one in France and one in Kenya. A drop in the ocean in terms of world murders, but all of them pretty blonde British girls with high media coverage. In each case the force has been vilified for not doing something sooner. Maybe there's nothing to this one, but just in case…"

"And Peter's murder might be linked?"

"Maybe," Littlewood chipped in. "But Sarah is blonde, beautiful and met a lot of men through her work. What do you know about her job?"

Kate shrugged. Not much really. She told them about Sarah's background and that she was successful selling apartments to expats.

"Was there anyone in particular? A client or a boyfriend? Any name she might have mentioned in passing?" Littlewood asked.

"We weren't that close anymore," Kate explained. "I should have been there for her when she split with Peter, but first I had Joe and, after he left, I guess I didn't want the reminder. I was poor at staying in touch. But then, so was she. It wasn't all my fault."

"Of course not," Mather said before switching track. "When was the last time you saw Sarah's parents?"

"The engagement party. To be honest, I don't really know them."

"They will be going to Peter Sikorski's funeral on Wednesday." Mather paused as if prompting a response. When none came, he said, "Will you be going to the funeral?"

"I hadn't thought…"

"Kate…" Mather looked serious. "I would like you to go to Peter's funeral."

Kate was surprised. "Because?"

"In case you notice something, something we would miss. *Someone* we would miss."

"I don't know…"

Mather said, "It may help us. More importantly, it may help Sarah."

Kate chewed her lip. She was thinking about Joe in Broadmoor again. That's what mattered most to her at this moment.

As though the inspector could read her mind he said, "I'll do you a deal."

Kate looked at him quizzically.

"You're thinking of visiting Joe. But you won't get in. Since 2001 things have tightened up. They don't allow day visitors anymore, unless there's a very good reason. You aren't family and you aren't his solicitor."

Kate waited.

"Here's the deal," Mather said. "You agree to go to the funeral and I'll get you into the prison."

Kate's heart thumped in her chest. She took a sip of water, calculating. Then she said, "When would I need to fly to Prague?"

"Next Tuesday. And you won't be alone. There will be a plain-clothed policewoman accompanying you. When you get back I want an immediate debrief."

Kate nodded. "I'll do it," she said. "Providing I get into Broadmoor on Monday."

Mather pursed his lips, nodded. "All right, you have a deal," he said.

TWENTY-EIGHT

Mather called later and confirmed an unaccompanied visit to see Greg Towers at Broadmoor on Monday at 10:30.

Kate's mind flipped between excitement and trepidation for the rest of the day until she joined Lisa in an Ascot wine bar.

"Just enjoy the evening," Lisa said as they met up. "Switch off from this whole affair and enjoy yourself for a few hours. Whatever is on your mind can wait."

Kate managed pretty well, although later she couldn't help but ask whether Lisa had been in touch with her ex.

"I've sent a message. Don't you worry. As soon as I hear back, I'll let you know. Now, no more talk of Joe and his friend."

The weekend dragged by. She didn't get an update from Lisa but she received another response from a question-and-answer site. This was a message from someone calling himself *Pogostick*:

If they are enlisted you write to the EPMD (Enlisted Personnel Management Directorate) with as much information as you can. US Army Human Resources Command, 2461 Eisenhower Avenue, Alexandria, Virginia, 22331. If they are an officer contact the OPMD (Officer Personnel Management Directorate) via

US Army Human Resources Command, 200 Stovall Street, Alexandria, Virginia, 22332.

Kate didn't know Boomer's rank, but even if she did, these were postal addresses. She needed an answer quickly—phone numbers or email. There wasn't time to wait for snail mail!

Kate drove up a hill in Crowthorne, her Mazda jolting over the frequent speed bumps. The sky was lead-grey and, when the dark-red brick prison wall appeared between the trees, Kate had the sense of something out of a bad horror movie. At the top of the hill, she followed the giant wall to the left and towards a visitor's car park. A barrier was automatically raised as she approached. No real security. She was still outside the prison, a wall on one side, a fence on the other with part of Windsor Forest beyond. No residential houses or people anywhere to be seen. There was a real sense of isolation here.

She parked and walked to a security gate in the wall. Having been instructed to take nothing with her into the prison, she left everything in the car.

The gate was in fact two gates, one after the other. She noted a security camera and an intercom. Pressing the intercom button, she said her name and the first gate clanged to one side. Kate took two steps forward and the gate clanged shut behind her. Again, a camera, and she looked up into it. A pause and then the second gate slid noisily open.

Inside, Kate was surprised that the buildings looked more like a hospital than a prison. A building to the left had a sign: "Visitors' Reception". She opened a 1970s'-looking red door with a small wire-reinforced glass window and stepped into a waiting room. Orange plastic chairs in four lines faced a reception desk. The room was empty except for a security man standing behind the desk. She walked towards him and tried a smile.

At that instant there was an ear-splitting screech—a siren. The silence rushed back in moments later.

The guard grinned at Kate's shock. "Just a test, love," he said. "Who are you and who are you here to see?"

"Kate Blakemore to see Greg Towers."

He looked at a computer screen. About to speak, he reconsidered and raised a hand. Immediately, a second siren whooped, briefly deafening them. A very different siren, she noted.

The guard must have read her mind. "The first is to test the *Prisoner Escaped* alarm. The second is the *All-Clear*."

"You have a twenty-eight minute wait, I'm afraid." He handed her a security badge. "Help yourself to a free cup of coffee from the machine and take a seat."

She took a glance at the vending machine and thought better of it. She sat and watched the security man. He stood impassively, occasionally glancing at the computer screen, a little bored.

To kill the time, she said, "Am I the only visitor today?"

"There's a solicitor in the afternoon but that's it."

She nodded, thinking. "It just struck me that during the test would be the time to escape," she said, "Has anyone ever escaped as it's being tested?"

"No one has escaped for a long time." He winked knowingly. "Not since the changes."

"Changes?"

He smiled. "Used to be more like an open prison. The inmates used to be able to have parties. We even let the men and women mix once a month. Not now though."

"Because of trouble?"

141

"No, no. Politically sensitive. Oddly coincided with Peter Sutcliffe being interred."

"The Yorkshire Ripper?"

"The very same. Now the prisoners are kept to their rooms. When they are allowed out for an hour a day, it is on their own. No socializing anymore."

"Sounds sad," she said.

He shrugged, "Not for me to judge."

"When was the last escape?"

He brightened and then squinted at her. "Not a reporter are you?"

She laughed and told him she was a physiotherapist.

He nodded. "The Wolfman went on the run in 1991—that was the last time. He escaped twice! He sawed through a one-inch-thick steel bar and squeezed out of the window of a shower room on the third floor. It took two days to recapture him. Funny thing was, he was found hiding in a garden shed close by. In the old days people used to escape all the time. Usually they would get picked up trying to hitch rides or just walking out of town wearing nothing but dressing gowns and slippers. We had a knifing in—"

A buzzer made him look at an internal door to his right. It was another identical red 1970s' door with a small window. A face peered through the glass. A second buzz, this time caused by the desk guard pressing a button, and the door opened.

"Blakemore for Towers," the desk guard said.

The second guard nodded to Kate as she stood and walked towards him. "Follow me," he said.

The door closed with a solid clunk behind them and they walked the length of a corridor, brick-red tiles clickety-clacking under her feet.

The guard stopped at a door. "Have you done this before?" he asked.

"No." Kate's pulse began to quicken.

"You will enter the room and I will lock the door," he recited like a recording. "You will see a chair and a window. The window is security glass and cannot be broken. Beside the window is a telephone. You may talk to the prisoner using the telephone. He will enter from the other side of the window into a similar room. He will be accompanied by a prison officer. You have ten minutes. I will open the door when the time is up and you will leave at that time. Is that understood?"

"Yes." Her heart was now pounding high in her chest.

"If you wish to leave the room before the end of your allotted time, simply turn to me and signal."

"Understood," she said, her voice trembling slightly.

"Ready?" For a moment a touch of kindness entered his otherwise officious tone.

"Yes," she said, and smiled weakly.

He opened the door and she stepped inside the ten-by-eight room. Barely aware of the door shutting behind her, she sat in the chair and stared at the door through the glass partition. Her hands were slick with sweat.

The opposite door handle moved. The door opened outwards and a guard looked in as if checking the room. He stepped forward. Behind him, a second officer helped a man in a white straightjacket into the room.

Kate stared. Her chest constricted and her vision blurred. She pushed herself to her feet and swivelled, waved to signal the officious guard.

Quickly in the room, the man placed a hand under her elbow, providing support.

"Got to get out," she said quietly.

The guard guided her into the corridor.

"Miss? Are you all right, Miss?"

The clamp around her chest eased and she sucked in air. The guard held her and looked into her eyes, concern etched on his face. "Miss?"

"It's not him," Kate spluttered. "It's not Joe!"

TWENTY-NINE

Snapping out of her trance, Kate said, "Can I go back in?"

The guard opened the door and waved to the other room. The prisoner had been rising out of the chair but now sat down.

Kate re-entered the room, sat in the chair by the dividing panel and picked up the phone. The man opposite grinned wolfishly at her.

"Pick up the phone!" she mouthed.

He complied.

"Who are you?" she asked.

"Who are you?" he asked, voice slurred.

"I'm Kate Blakemore. Who are you?"

Confusion played in a wave across his brow. "Do I know you, Kate Blakemore?"

"No, you don't," she said, gaining in confidence and frustration. "Who are you?"

This time her tone compelled the man to answer. "Greg Towers," he said. "I don't think I've seen you before, Kate Blakemore." Each time he said her name he appeared to taste it.

She forced herself to stay calm, sound collected. "Do you know anyone called Joe Rossini?" She thought about the British passport she'd found. "Or maybe Joe Ranieri?"

He tapped his forehead rapidly with a finger then said, "I don't think I know either of them." He turned briefly to the guard, "Do I know anyone called Joe, Dave?" The guard ignored the question. Towers didn't seem to notice, his eyes swinging back to Kate's. "But I would like to know you better... Kate Blakemore."

She stood and signalled that the interview was over.

Towers called into the handset, "Will you come and visit me again, Kate Blakemore?" But Kate had left hers on the table.

In the corridor she waited for the guard to lock the door behind her and together they walked to the waiting area. She handed in her ID pass and exited the prison-hospital, reversing the process through the double security gate.

When she got into her car she sat for a moment composing herself. She took her phone out of her handbag and called Inspector Mather.

When Mather answered, Kate said, "The deal's off. I'm not going to Prague tomorrow."

Mather sounded surprised. "What's wrong? Tell me what's happened."

"You know what happened," Kate said belligerently. "I've just come out of Broadmoor and the man I've seen is not my boyfriend."

"What? They didn't let you see Greg Towers?"

"Oh yes," she said. "I saw Mr Towers all right, but he is not my boyfriend."

At the other end of the phone there was a long silence. Eventually Mather said, "I don't understand. The file says that Greg Towers was arrested twelve months ago for identity fraud and wanted for other potential US federal offences. He was retained at

Broadmoor because of his mental health. The Feds dropped a request for extradition. The file lists Joe Rossini as one of his aliases. It must be him."

Kate sighed. "And I'm telling you it's not. I know what my boyfriend looks like."

"There must have been a mistake somewhere. I can't believe it's a deliberate attempt to deceive. Frankly, it would be too big and too likely to fail."

"Well it worked for twelve months. Perhaps no one expected me to find him—or gain access."

"All right, I'll look into it, find out what really happened." He sounded convincing. "Meanwhile, I do want you to go to Prague. Remember you're also doing this for your friend."

"Am I?"

"Yes!"

She looked at herself in the rear-view mirror. "I'll think about it," she said.

Amir walked past the entrance to Broadmoor and headed for the woods opposite. He spotted Kate walking towards a building with a red door within the walls. When the siren sounded, Amir shrank further back into the woods, wondering what had happened. About a minute later an air raid-type "All-Clear" told him that it had probably been a test. There was no one around. Six cars in the car park. He walked to the red Mazda and, within seconds, had the door open using a device which found the frequency of her remote. Her handbag and phone were hidden from view behind her seat. He quickly went through her bag then took out the phone. When he had finished he replaced everything, relocked the car and slipped back to the vantage point in the woods.

After thirty-nine minutes, Kate reappeared at the door and headed for the double security gates. Amir couldn't quite make out the expression on her face but something about her demeanour suggested anger.

He slipped back to the wall and crossed in front of the barrier. Kate climbed into her car and sat immobile for a few minutes. Amir took out what looked like a mobile phone with an aerial. He listened. The girl was talking. He'd inserted a bug into her iPhone. Although there was interference, it was clear enough for Amir to understand.

Joe Rossini was not Greg Towers. The man in prison was not who she expected to meet.

Amir smiled. He'd read the encrypted document. There was no way on Earth that the girl's boyfriend had been arrested and interred in a prison for the criminally insane. But it was good to have it confirmed. He was pleased he had learned something else. The girl was supposed to go to Prague. It could only mean the police wanted her to go to the funeral.

He also liked the feisty way she'd spoken to the person on the other end of the line. She was tougher than he had first thought. The red sports car appeared at the barrier. Amir turned his back to the car, heard the barrier raise and the car drive away. He turned and ran to his own wheels, parked just before the turning into the prison. He turned on his satnav and a blue blip began to pulse on the screen. The girl's car.

As he drove down the hill he thought about her soft white skin. He pictured her jogging, her body not fat, not too hard. His loins stirred. Yes, he would have some fun with this girl before she died.

THIRTY

Kate got out of her Mazda as someone said, "Hello dear."

"Oh... hello, Ann." Kate shook distracted thoughts from her head. Worryingly, she realized she couldn't remember the drive back from Crowthorne.

"Are you feeling all right, dear?"

Kate smiled weakly. "Mind on other things I'm afraid."

Ann stepped carefully up the kerb and began to walk the short distance to her door. Kate walked in step.

"Come in for a *cuppa*," Ann said. It wasn't a question.

Kate chuckled. "You sound so very English. How can I refuse?" Then, recalling Ann's weak coffee, she added, "Do you have any Earl Grey tea?"

Ann opened the door and waved at the sofa for Kate to sit. There was a long delay before she said anything as she busied herself with the kettle. "I've been in England for so long, I do like to make an effort, dear," she eventually said. Noises of rooting in a cupboard, then: "I have Lady Grey. Will that be all right?"

"Yes, please."

"Slice of lemon?"

"Perfect."

Kate waited on the sofa and studied the photographs again. She was about to say something when Ann appeared with a tray: a mug of coffee for her and a fine bone china cup of black tea with lemon for Kate.

"I've been meaning to say something," Ann began. "There was a strange man around last week. He seemed to be outside your apartment."

"Yes, he was a bit odd. Some satellite company connecting Sky to the block."

"Good, good," Ann said, thoughtfully. "Only, I was a little concerned because I heard you go out." She smiled at the recollection. "Seemed in a bit of a rush, I would say. Anyway, straight afterwards I then thought I heard you go up your stairs. But then I heard you come in again a short time later. It couldn't have been you, could it?"

Kate frowned. "No, I went out for fifteen minutes or so. Perhaps Simon let him in." Simon lived in number seven, the mirror of Kate's apartment. "You probably heard the man in Simon's flat."

Ann didn't look convinced, but she said, "Yes, that must have been it. Simon wasn't home that day, but he will have arranged for access. Yes, that will be right."

Kate looked back at the photographs. She was still thinking about them. "Your husband was in the army— US Army, I mean."

"Yes, he was. Reached the heady heights of colonel. He was a good man, and I miss his company." Ann said this without a hint of sadness. "It was interesting to travel with him all over the world, and a colonel's wife is a full-time job, you know. I had duties to perform and there were certain expectations. Many of the wives find it difficult, but I enjoyed being an officer's wife. After all, I had plenty of time to study my art history, and the free travel was a bonus."

"You remember my boyfriend, Joe?"

"Of course, dear."

"He has a friend in the US Army—Danny Guice. I need to contact Danny. I don't really know where to start. How would I locate him?"

"Well, let's see..." Ann tapped her bottom lip in thought. "Do you know his rank and which unit he's in?"

"No, I've not been able to find anything that's less than about six years old. I think he was in some sort of secret unit. Does that make sense?"

"Not to me, dear," Ann smiled, "but I know someone who may be able to help. Let me make some telephone calls and see what I can find."

Before Kate left, she wrote Danny's name on a piece of paper and thanked Ann for the tea. She returned to her apartment exhausted from a rollercoaster of emotions: Joe's encrypted message to her; losing it and finding Andrew had a copy; getting nowhere with a search for Boomer; being told Joe was close by; then discovering it wasn't Joe in Broadmoor; and now a kind of hope again from Ann.

Realizing how exhausted she was, Kate closed her bedroom curtains and lay on her bed.

She must have fallen asleep because she was roused by her mobile phone ringing beside her head.

"Hello?" Her voice was just-woken-up rough.

"Can I come over?"

"Andrew! Hi—sorry, I was just having a nap. Still half asleep. You're back from Italy? Great. Of course you can come over."

"Be there within half an hour."

It dawned on her that he sounded sad, but he'd clicked off before she could question him.

★

Dying to ask about the *Trust Me* document, Kate held back, waiting for Andrew to speak. Her friend's eyes were red-rimmed from what she was sure were tears.

"I'm ruined," he eventually sighed. "More than ten years of work and it's gone."

"What's gone?"

"My PC with all my software has been stolen."

Kate's jaw dropped open. "Stolen?"

"While I was away, someone broke into my house and took the computer." Kate shook her head in disbelief. Andrew continued, guessing her next question. "And my backup. The police say it was a professional job. Came in through the least secure access and only stole the computer and drives. It can only mean one thing."

She waited, unclear what the *one thing* would be.

He put his head in his hands. "It was stolen to order! And it is too much of a coincidence that the Italians wanted me to stay for a few more days."

Kate shook her head again. "Surely not?"

He nodded. "It's all they needed. I probably told them too much as it was. You know me! With the software they can save themselves months, maybe years, of development."

She felt terrible raising it but had to. "And Joe's document... has that gone too?"

Andrew dropped his head. "I'm sorry..."

She put her arms around him and his tears flowed freely. She said, "It's all right. It's all right. I'm more worried about your work than the document." And it was true.

Later, she brought Andrew up to date regarding her investigations and the police interview.

He said, "I don't like the sound of the sergeant. What's her name—Littlewood?" Andrew smiled for the

152

first time that day. "Little wood, big chip on the shoulder! That's what I say."

"Clever." Kate laughed. "Maybe she does have a bit of a chip on her shoulder. Must be tough being a woman detective. It seems such a man's world."

"So, are you going to the funeral?"

"Yes. I've nothing to lose while I'm waiting for Ann to come up with something."

Andrew looked awkward but then said what was on his mind. "Can I stay here tonight?"

"Of course."

"Only I'll be uncomfortable in my house... and I need to get the window fixed and the security alarm sorted out."

"Stay a few nights. You can feed Tolkien while I'm in Prague."

He grinned. "Thanks, kiddo."

THIRTY-ONE

Littlewood was waiting at Heathrow Terminal 3.

Kate showed no surprise. "So you're the plain-clothed policeman Inspector Mather said was coming with me?"

Littlewood nodded without a smile. Her red hair was still tied back. She was dressed in what Kate assumed were her usual work clothes: blue trousers, jacket, flat sensible shoes.

Kate said, "You still look like a copper."

Littlewood ignored her. "Let's go," she said, and directed Kate to BA's check-in.

On the flight, Kate attempted to make conversation and learned Littlewood's first name was Sam. However, Sam's terse replies to any questions soon stopped Kate making an effort at friendship. So they travelled most of the way in silence, except for when necessary.

When they arrived at Prague airport, Kate expected they would get a taxi. Instead, a policeman met them. He too said very few words apart from introducing himself. His English was difficult to follow, but Kate surmised he told them they would be staying at the Hilton hotel in Prague's Old Town.

*

At the hotel, Kate declined Littlewood's dinner invitation with the excuse of a headache and chose from the limited room service menu. While she waited for the food, she called Andrew.

"How are you?" she said.

"Much better, thanks." He sounded his usual, optimistic self once more. "Techion emailed me the agreement. They want to proceed because it looks like Rialto will buy!"

"But your software was stolen."

"I can rebuild it more quickly than I thought. I forgot I had copies of old versions. Those discs weren't taken and, to be honest, I've only been tinkering these past few years. The fundamental mechanics are all there."

"That *is* good news. How's Tolkien?"

"Missing you, of course, but he's on my lap now and seems happy enough. Oh, and Lisa from the club is coming round later for a chinwag and a glass of vino. You know how she likes to talk."

"Sounds like you really are settled in! Are you still OK to feed Tolkien tomorrow and Thursday morning?"

"I'm not checking out from your place just yet, if that's all right," he said. "My house still has to be sorted—and I have my laptop, so I can work from anywhere."

Kate's food arrived and she ended the call, promising to provide an update about the funeral tomorrow. After dinner she chatted with her mother and then Darcy. She soaked for over an hour in the bath, regularly topping up the heat. When she climbed into bed, she expected to fall asleep immediately. Instead, she lay awake listening to the late-night street noise. Something was troubling her. Something about Andrew, or what he'd said. She eventually gave up, switched on a light and found a documentary in English on the History Channel.

Almost six thousand miles west, the Janator sat by his pool, chewing gum and reading the latest status reports. A critical juncture approached.

When he had finished he realised he'd made an origami cat from the paper wrapper. He scrunched it up. His subconscious mind gave away too much. It was a good job no one else would guess the meaning.

Kate had no idea what time she fell asleep, but the sun streamed through gaping curtains when she awoke and the TV burbled quietly with a grainy history programme from the 1960s—British prime minister Harold Macmillan giving his "winds of change" speech about South Africa.

After a simple breakfast of tea, toast and fresh fruit, Kate strolled outside. Bright sunshine filled the sky with the illusion of warmth, while a chill breeze tugged at the spaces in her coat and bit at exposed skin.

She wandered around the centre looking at the old buildings and sensing their character almost as though it were her first time in Prague. The city never ceased to impress her with its unique personality. Eventually, cold and thirsty, she crossed the Charles Bridge and, on the other side, dropped down stone steps to the island. Here she walked along the cobbled street and found an old pub where she'd come with Joe. This was where they had met on her first visit after the engagement party.

As she had eighteen months earlier, she ordered a small beer and sat in silence on a wooden bench that could have been a hundred years old. The room was poorly lit and clearly not really a daytime venue.

Her watch said a little after 10am—forty minutes before meeting up with Littlewood in the hotel reception. Together they would go to the Prague police station for a meeting with Inspector Cerny. The funeral was not to be at Slavia Cemetery as she had expected, but close by. Littlewood explained that the police hadn't released the body, so it wasn't a funeral at all, but a ceremony.

Kate sipped her beer and thought about Joe and the fun they'd had.

"Penny for them," the barman said with a friendly smile, his accent obviously Australian.

She smiled back but declined to say.

"It's a great day out. Shame to be in here on your own." He put down a glass he'd been drying and picked up another. She doubted they needed to be wiped so thoroughly. He winked and the smile stayed in place. The guy was flirting.

"Aussies! You are incorrigible," she said with laugh. "Definitely the worst, I should say."

"Oh, mate, surely the Italians are worse than Australians. Only just, mind!"

She finished her beer and stood. "How much?"

"For the beer? Nothing. On me. Perhaps you'll come back this evening and then share those deep thoughts?"

She shook her head. "Thanks for the beer though."

She stepped out into the sunlight and headed back to the bridge. It felt uplifting to be flirted with, even though it meant nothing. However, as she mounted the steps, her mood changed. It was the mention of Italians. She recalled the conversation with Andrew last night. He was convinced the Italians still wanted to do business. So if the Italians didn't break into Andrew's house, who the hell did?

THIRTY-TWO

The Městská police station smells of ancient dust, Kate thought. It looked like something out of the 1960s' documentary that had been on the TV, with metal-framed windows overlooking the street below. Stark and perfunctory, the interior had all the charm of a public lavatory.

Inspector Cerny was older than she'd expected from his voice. Either that or he was going prematurely bald. Rather than shave his head, he attempted to cover the patches with swept back, thinning hair. Apart from the hair, Kate assessed him as pleasant and gentlemanly as he tried hard to be understood.

Littlewood had her notebook out. There was a handheld tape machine on the table to record the conversation. The inspector asked if the interview could also be videoed. He pointed to a camera on the ceiling.

Littlewood looked at Kate for approval.

Kate said, "Not a problem."

"Good then..." The inspector cited case details and the people present for the purposes of the recording. Then he spoke to Kate: "Slečna Blakemore—you called him Peter rather than Petr?"

"I think that's how he preferred it pronounced." Kate nodded, guessing the inspector had practised saying her name rather than use the Czech version.

"Then I will call him Peter." He had a thick lever-arch file by his side and Kate wondered whether it was all the case notes.

Cerny saw her look. "There are some photographs I would like you to look at," he said. "There are a good number but, before we look at them, please tell me what you know."

Kate was unsure how much or what he wanted, so she repeated the information she'd shared with the Thames Valley police, starting with the first time she had met Peter through her friend Sarah and up to the phone call from the inspector informing her of his death.

"Sorry, I misunderstood you on the telephone," he said. "It must have been a shock."

She nodded, accepting the inspector's apology. "It was. Of course it was a shock. It's not every day you hear a friend is dead, let alone murdered."

"And your friend, Sarah, is missing."

Kate was asked to repeat what she had told Thames Valley police about the phone call and then having no response to calls, texts or emails. "Do you think she is dead?" Kate asked, and she looked closely to read the inspector's reaction.

"We do not think so," Cerny said, and she assessed this as genuine. "Now I would like—"

A knock on the door interrupted him, and a young policeman entered with a tray of sandwiches and apples. After placing them on the table, he returned with orange juice. Each time, the inspector announced the man's entrance and departure for the recording.

They took a break and Kate ate a prawn and lettuce sandwich and washed it down with the orange juice.

Cerny opened the lever-arch file and slid it over to Kate. Inside were photographs in plastic wallets, two per wallet. "Please take your time, look through them carefully," he said. "These are from Peter's computer memory. I would like you to take out any photographs of people that you recognize, even if they are..." he struggled for a moment.

Littlewood helped: "Even if they are incidental, like in the background."

"But there is no need to pull out those with Peter or Sarah, or either of their parents," Cerny continued. "We know who they are."

Kate began. At first she studied each picture slowly. A few hundred photographs later, and pulling out occasional pages, Kate asked for a rest. She took a ten minute comfort break and resumed the process until every picture had been reviewed.

Cerny removed the file and neatened the pile of pages she'd taken out. Then he asked her to talk through each one she recognized, noting the number of the page and placing a sticky yellow dot on the photograph. Approximately eighty sheets in total, most were people she vaguely recognized. Some she knew were friends, some work colleagues. One photograph was of Peter, Joe and a woman. Kate reported that she recognized Joe, but not the woman.

When she had finished, Cerny said, "Thank you." He had glanced at the wall clock. "We have good time for you to make it to the ceremony. The house is in Vyšehrad. You know it?"

Kate said she did. Cerny didn't immediately close the interview. There was a moment of uncomfortable silence and Kate looked at Littlewood for guidance. Littlewood was watching her intently.

The inspector said, "Before we end, Slečna Blakemore, who is WO?"

"I'm sorry?"

Littlewood said, "Do the initials WO mean anything to you?"

Kate thought for a moment. "No," she said with a categorical shake of the head.

Littlewood's eyes narrowed. "The photograph of your boyfriend with the victim—with Peter—had a title. The others did not." She paused for a heartbeat, two, three. "Did Peter or Joe shoot someone with the initials WO or called Wo?"

THIRTY-THREE

The service of remembrance was in a building opposite the Gothic Vyšehrad cathedral. Kate had attended a few registry office weddings and her initial impression of the service was the same. The only difference being a sombre atmosphere, created by sad music, white lilies and subdued lighting. Kate and Littlewood both wore black, having changed after the Czech police interview.

Peter's parents shook her hand at the door, their haunted eyes smiling briefly as they recognized her. She and Littlewood sat in the back row and studied people as they filed in. Kate immediately noted that most of the crowd were smartly dressed, the men in suits, the women in business attire—work colleagues, she assumed. Littlewood had asked her to point out any close friends of Sarah's and to watch out in case Sarah herself showed up. Kate agreed to do her best.

They sat on the back row. A kindly faced middle-aged woman introduced herself in English and then sat beside Kate. "You don't speak Czech?" she said.

Kate and Littlewood shook their heads.

"I can translate for you," the woman said. "Petr's mother has asked me." When Kate protested that she would be fine, the woman said, "Please, I've been told I must insist." She indicated that Kate should swap places with her so that she was between the two English ladies.

The room quickly filled to its capacity of up to a hundred people, the doors were closed, and at 4pm precisely, the service began. When the music stopped, the lights came up, and in an instant the room seemed less depressing. A man in a suit stood at a lectern and welcomed everyone on this solemn occasion, which should be a reflection and celebration of Petr Sikorski's life. As he spoke, the woman translated quietly.

The man then introduced Peter's father, who took his place at the lectern. He gripped the edges as though without them he might be unable to stand. He waited a moment, gathering his thoughts and strength. When he spoke, he told a long story of when Peter was a young boy, how proud they were when he rescued a friend from a river, putting another's safety above his own. He sat down and an uncle stood and told a story of Peter's sporting achievements, particularly swimming and football. A third family member talked of Peter's academic achievements. Then, one by one, friends and work colleagues went to the lectern and told stories, some of which seemed to have meaning, others merely anecdotes from a friend's life.

Two hours passed quickly, and finally the leader of the service returned and spoke at length about love. It was not a Bible reading, because this was not a religious ceremony, but by inserting references to God or Heaven, Kate thought, it could have been.

At the end, the man asked everyone to clap in appreciation of Peter's life. A few people cheered and Kate noticed tears cascade down Peter's mother's cheeks. Her husband held her close and forced a happy smile for everyone. Kate fought back tears of her own.

People turned and shook one another's hands warmly, and Kate found herself shaking hands with Littlewood who seemed totally unmoved by the proceedings. Kate shook hands with others before the translator said, "We will now go to the Sikorski household where they will serve food for everyone." She handed over a slip of paper with an address on it and Kate thanked her.

During the cab ride to Peter's parents' house, Littlewood said, "Was Sarah there?"

"I didn't see her."

"She could have been in disguise."

"I didn't see her. But then most of the time people had their backs to us."

Kate mentioned that she'd seen the very tall man with the short woman—the Mafia son and his partner, as she'd previously imagined them. "They were at Peter and Sarah's engagement party," she explained. "I noted they are now married. They weren't eighteen months ago."

"It happens," Littlewood said.

Kate looked at her expecting a grin, but nothing. The policewoman wasn't attempting humour. Kate said, "Were you ever married?"

Littlewood went to respond, hesitated and said, "Let's keep this on a formal basis. Anyone else you recognized?"

"Quite a few looked familiar but, like the photographs, I can't give you names. And I didn't see anyone I would class as a close friend of Sarah's—not from the time I knew her best."

Kate took a long breath. For a moment her sight blurred and her skin prickled.

"Are you OK? You look pale."

Kate held her stomach. "Feeling a bit dodgy. I'm sure it'll pass."

They arrived at the large house on the outskirts of Prague. Kate blinked a few times trying hard to focus and get her bearings. Stepping out of the cab, she sucked in the cold air and rubbed her face.

Littlewood asked the taxi driver to wait and stood at her side. "You don't look good," she said.

"I'll splash my face with water. I'll be fine."

They walked into the house, already crowded with people from the service. People continued to arrive to pay their respects. Kate found a toilet and locked herself in. She splashed water on her face and ran her wrists under the cold tap. She took a deep breath and felt a jolt in her abdomen. Just in time, she lifted the lid and emptied the contents of her stomach into the toilet. She knelt, gripping the toilet bowl for a while until the nausea passed.

After cleaning herself up, and putting some tissues in her pocket just in case, Kate emerged from the room. Littlewood waited outside, concern on her face. "Been sick?"

Kate nodded. "I think it must have been the prawns."

"Let's get you back to the hotel."

"Not straight away. I'll circulate for a few minutes, just in case I recognize someone here who wasn't at the service."

Littlewood agreed and waited by the front door as Kate weaved her way through the rooms bursting to overflowing with mourners. A few people nodded or spoke to her, but little registered. She avoided the room laid out with trays of sandwiches and picked up a bottle of mineral water from the kitchen.

"Anything?" Littlewood asked as Kate reappeared in the hallway.

"Apart from being bumped and squeezed to death in there, you mean? No. There was no one new I recognized."

They travelled back to the hotel in silence. Kate sipped on her water; Littlewood stared out of the window.

As the taxi bounced over an uneven section of road, Kate dribbled the water on her chin. She put her hand in a pocket to get the tissue. When she retrieved it, she realized there was more than tissue in her pocket, there was a piece of paper.

Casually, and careful not to attract attention, Kate unfolded the paper. On it was written:

Kino L 12 tonight. Tell no one! Be careful!

She recognized the handwriting immediately.

Sarah's.

THIRTY-FOUR

With the words *Be careful* playing over and over in her head, Kate stole from her room and took the emergency stairs. What did Sarah mean? Keep the appointment secret so that the police didn't know? Or was there something more sinister?

At 11:45 she emerged at the rear of the hotel. *Kino L* stood for Kino Lucerna, a cinema which was about ten minutes' brisk walk from the hotel. Kate wore black jeans and a jumper under her dark coat. Pulling up the collar to hide her face as much as possible, she kept to the shadows.

Slightly out of breath, she arrived at the cinema just before midnight. Her throat burned from the exertion following its date with stomach acid in the afternoon. The lights were on inside the cinema and people milled about. She walked under the glass dome from which hung an upside down horse with a man sitting on its underside. It never ceased to astound.

Upstairs, voices could be heard coming from the café-bar and, after a glance around downstairs, she decided to head for that. There were fifteen people at tables in the café-bar, mostly in pairs, but no one remotely like Sarah. She sat at a table overlooking the ground floor and ordered a mineral water from the waiter.

She drank the water and checked her watch. Almost 12:30. Where was Sarah? Was something wrong?

Ten minutes later she had just decided to give up when a familiar, hushed voice said, "Don't turn round."

"Sarah!"

"Try and look as though you aren't talking to me."

"What's going on?"

"Peter was murdered."

"I know. Look, the police don't think you did it, if that's what's frightening you. Your parent's are worried about you. Even the UK police are looking for you. There's even one—a woman detective—with me."

"You didn't..." Panic edged Sarah's whispered voice.

"No. No one knows I'm here."

"He's going to kill me too."

"Who?"

"I think he's the man who killed Peter. He came after me first. He was in my apartment, went through my things, my documents, my address book. I was hiding. He must have thought I was out. I heard him talking on the phone. When he came upstairs I hit him with a baseball bat, knocked him down the stairs. But he wasn't knocked out, just stunned. I ran past him. He grabbed me and then chased me outside and through the neighbourhood. When I thought it was all clear I tried to ring you. But he was there. I think he was able to track my phone. I switched it off and dumped it. I've been in hiding for two weeks."

"Where?"

"One of the empty properties I'm showing."

"And you're OK?"

"As long as he doesn't find me, I'll be fine."

"You can't keep hiding for ever."

"Kate, listen to me. You aren't getting it. You're in danger. There's a killer and he's tracking down anyone connected to Joe. Don't you get it? He used my information to find Peter. Equally, he could trace you from me or Peter."

"Oh God! Did you send me a photograph?"

"No. What photograph?"

Kate ignored the question. "So it must have been Peter who sent it. God! This man who you hit will know of my connection through Peter."

Kate recalled the break-in at Andrew's house.

The computer.

The computer had a copy of the *Trust Me* document.

The document on the memory card—she hadn't lost it!

The man had been in her house. Ann had heard him go in after Kate left to check the *Runtime* on the train. "He's already found me," Kate said, her mouth tasting bile for the second time that day. "He's been in my home. He looks Arabic, right?"

"Yes! You need to hide. You need to go into hiding right now!"

THIRTY-FIVE

The small sensor in Amir's hand vibrated, waking him up. The girl had opened her hotel room door. He checked his watch: 11:45. What was she up to?

Within minutes he was outside the Hilton, watching the road. He had timed the journey from her room to the front. She should be here by now. Movement further up the road caught his eye—somebody moving furtively, collar up to hide the face, keeping close to the wall and hurrying. It had to be the girl. Amir followed.

He saw her arrive at the arts cinema, briefly look around the ground floor and then head upstairs for the café-bar. She sat by the railings so that she could see the stairs. She was definitely meeting someone here. His pulse quickened, sure he knew who it was. He stood beneath the balcony, his back to her, studying a poster. In the reflection of the glass, dominated by the upside down horse, he could just make her out.

Amir's appearance was different. His hair long and bleached, his clothes casual under a loose-fitting parka. With his back to her, he was confident she wouldn't recognize him, possibly not even if she saw his face. With the blonde hair he looked more like a tanned surfer than an Arab.

He varied his position, moving out of view and changing his attention to a telephone, pretending to text someone. Glancing up at the reflection, he thought she looked like she was talking but couldn't see anyone else. He put the phone away and walked out of the cinema. A few minutes later he walked back in and glanced up as he passed under the balcony. A woman sat with her back to the girl from Windsor. From her profile, he could see her talking rapidly. He had to be sure it was the real-estate woman. Her hair was mid brown but something about the style said it was a wig. He casually mounted the stairs, picked up a magazine from a bench at the top and took a table in the café-bar. He ordered an espresso from the waiter and pretended to read the magazine.

Definitely a wig. Definitely the real-estate woman who had eluded him. He smiled as he became aware of his elevated pulse. He didn't need this other woman anymore. Christopher Martens had led him to Sarah Wishart and from her he had traced Peter Sikorski. But she had eluded him and was a worthy adversary.

The Blakemore girl stood, put money on the table and hurried out. He needn't follow her; she was going to the Hilton. The woman in the brown wig finished her drink and paid the waiter. She got up and headed to a door beside the bar. Toilets perhaps.

Amir waited a minute then reacted with a startling realization. He hadn't seen the woman enter. There's another way out! He pushed open the door and immediately saw a staircase go straight down to a fire exit. The door clicked shut.

He charged down the stairs to the door and looked out. She had about sixty metres head start. He slipped into the shadows and began to follow.

The walk was long and circuitous as she avoided main roads and zigzagged to the river and then followed it to a small development of executive apartments. As she reached the front door, she glanced up and down the street. He was close, hiding behind a brick pillar. He heard the key click open the door and began to move. Swiftly and silently, he walked up steps to within touching distance as she stepped over the threshold. She didn't know what hit her.

Sarah's eyes fluttered. Things blinked into focus like old celluloid film, dim and dark at the edges. She was lying on the floor in the bedroom. How had she got there? Then the pain in the back of her head kicked in and she winced, tried to touch the wound.

Her arms were restricted! She tried to stretch from her cramped position and immediately stopped. Something gripped her throat. She tilted her head slightly and saw she was bound. If she moved her legs, tried to straighten, it tightened a band around her neck.

Helpless, tied up on the floor of the apartment, she gingerly squirmed to look around. The hall light was on, but otherwise the apartment seemed dark and quiet. Carefully, she rolled the other way and then choked as fright made her reflexively jerk her legs.

"So you are awake," a man said from the bed. He sat up.

"Who?" she started to say but her throat was raw and her voice weak.

He climbed off the bed and the light caught his face.

She trembled. *Him!* Her breathing came in shallow puffs. She forced out a painful whisper. "You killed Peter, didn't you?"

The man smiled, and his eyes glinted in the light.

She tried again. "Why? I don't know anything."

He knelt down, his face now close to hers. "I know," he said, almost kindly. He poured some water into her mouth. "I know that's what you think. But you'll be surprised at what you do know—what information I'll find useful. Everybody knows things they think are unimportant or maybe forgot. You'd be surprised at how often people don't realize they even knew it."

She licked her lips and swallowed painfully. "You're going to kill me, aren't you?"

"That depends."

"Depends?"

"On you." Something flashed in his hand, and as he slashed down she realized with horror that it was a blade.

"Hold still," he said. "If you move too much I might cut you by mistake." He slashed some more but her brief hope, that the bindings would be cut, vanished as he pulled away shards of material. He cut and slashed until she was naked. The trembling began again.

"No. Please no!" She began to wail.

He slapped her face. "Oh dear. Now I can't let you talk for a while." He pushed something into her mouth, not a gag, but a device that wedged between the molars preventing her from fully closing it.

She started as cold metal touched her flesh. He ran the blade around her left nipple.

Her head shook, eyes wide with panic. His eyes locked onto hers. She saw his mouth twitch in a slight smile as his hand moved. There was a second of nothing and then excruciating pain wracked her body. As it subsided, her body twitched with shock.

"I'm sorry about that," he said coldly. "Just a demonstration of how much pain you can feel. It's just a nipple after all. Now you will answer my questions or we will discover how much pain you can withstand. And in the end you will tell me everything I want to know."

*

First he broke her strong spirit and then he used her. When he stood up from her body she was unconscious but still moving, silently rocking in the tide of her shallow breaths. He went into the bathroom and washed, pleased that there was very little blood on him. He wiped down the surfaces as a matter of habit, then returned to the bedroom and tucked the bedspread around her as though she were a sleeping child. From an inside pocket of the coat he pulled a small box and placed it beside her.

He walked out of the apartment and closed the door. He strolled along the river and breathed in deeply. It felt good, almost as good as he'd anticipated. She was bigger than the Blakemore girl, less fit. She had passed out too soon really. He hoped the other blonde one would put up a fight for longer. From his pocket he pulled out his phone and dialled a number. Behind him an explosion shattered the quiet of the upmarket neighbourhood.

He didn't look back.

THITY-SIX

Kate had heard the sirens in the night and, as their BA flight took off, she thought she saw a finger of black smoke on the bank of the river.

Last night, when she returned to the hotel, she had immediately called her sister.

"Do you know what time it is?" Darcy's voice had been thick with sleep. "It's tough having young kids. I don't get enough sleep as it is, without you calling at some crazy hour."

"Darce, listen. Pick me up from the airport." Her voice had quavered with nerves but she'd felt better talking and gave Darcy the terminal and arrival time.

"What's this about?"

"I need to stay with you for a while. I'm scared. I need to keep away from my Windsor place."

Darcy had wanted to know what was going on but Kate just promised to explain all when she was safe. "Don't tell anyone, not even Mum. OK?"

After Darcy had agreed, Kate called Andrew and told him to get out.

"I've a sister in Yorkshire," he'd said.

"I don't want to know. Just go and ... Andrew..."

"Yes?"

"Can you take Tolkien? I don't know how long I'm going to have to hide."

Andrew had agreed and promised to leave immediately.

Kate then lay on the bed, but there was no way she could sleep. She had picked up the hotel pen and notepad and written what Inspector Cerny had said. The title of the photograph with Peter, Joe and a woman.

"Shot WO," was what Cerny had said. Kate wrote SHOTWO. Then under this she had written SH O TWO and smiled at the misunderstanding. It was another message. O TWO was simple. It was the mobile operator O2. SH was less obvious. They were the initials. Kate didn't know if the woman in the picture was SH, but SH stood for Stephanie Harper.

THIRTY-SEVEN

What did Stephanie Harper know?

"Auntie Kate, look at my poorly knee." Three-year-old India disturbed Kate's thoughts. She jumped onto the sofa beside Kate and held up her leg. There was a white patch over the knee.

"India, do not touch that plaster!" Darcy's voice boomed from the kitchen.

India looked at her aunt with an air of conspiracy and then lifted the corner of the white plaster. She made big eyes, suggesting her aunt would be impressed. There was a cut about three centimetres long with strips of tape holding it together.

"Wow!" Kate whispered. "You are brave." She stuck the plaster back down and then pulled up the left leg of her jeans. In the soft skin between the shin and patella was a scar. India touched it. A gash like hers, but with light dots above and below.

India's face exaggerated concern. "Will my scar look like that?"

Kate shook her head. "In the olden days, doctors used to stitch cuts like this to hold them together." She pointed to the dots. "This is where the stitches went through. Nowadays they just use tape so your scar will almost disappear."

India thought for a moment. "Stitches—you mean like Mummy does with mending?"

"Yes, a bit like sewing."

"Ooo!" India jumped off the sofa, disappeared for a moment and returned with a sewing pack. She smiled sweetly. "Auntie Kate... please stitch my cut."

Kate laughed and tickled her niece. She had only been in Tim and Darcy's home for a few hours and the strain of the past few days had just melted away. A long soak in an aromatherapy bath had helped, even if she did have to remove the bath toys that kept falling in, disturbing the tranquillity. In the end she stopped fishing them out and watched the duck, frog, scuba diver and a submarine as they slowly completed circuits of the tub.

Darcy had taken Kate's suitcase from the Prague trip and added the clothes to the laundry. "Sort yourself something from my wardrobe," she said, realizing Kate had no other clothes to wear. "Make sure you wear your hair different to me though. Since we look similar, with my clothes on I don't want Tim mistaking you for me!" She had laughed.

Emma ran into the lounge, jumped and sat next to her twin. Identical. Joe and his brother had been twins—at first inseparable but later more like rivals. It must be difficult if you feel you have to compete with someone identical. Kate wondered whether her nieces would always be close or whether they would find it difficult when they were teenagers.

She stroked Emma's hair and kissed her head. Kate could tell them apart but knew others had difficulty. India had a mischievous look, possibly due to the slight off-position of one eye, although Emma was the more cheeky of the two.

Kate said, "It's a good job Emma has cut her knee, otherwise I'd never tell you apart!"

Emma laughed uncertainly, "No, Auntie Kate, I am Emma!"

"But your knee isn't cut!" Kate said with mock seriousness.

India laughed now. "No, Auntie Kate, my knee is cut. I am India!"

Kate grabbed them both and the three of them rolled on the floor, tickled and giggled.

When they stopped, India looked at Kate and said, "Are you wearing Mummy's top?"

"Yes, do you think we look alike—the same?"

Emma giggled. "Are you twins too?"

"No, unfortunately your mummy is two years younger than me."

India said, "But you look younger than Mummy, Auntie Kate!"

Kate pulled a face. "Whatever you do, don't tell your mummy that!"

Without hesitation, India jumped up and ran to the kitchen to tell her mummy.

"Oh dear," Kate said to Emma. The other girl shrugged as if to say, *what-can-you-do?* Kate shrugged back then and said, "Go and set up the Magic Ponies' castle. I need to make a phone call then I'll come and play with you."

After Emma had raced off to the playroom, Kate took out her iPhone. There was a voicemail; she'd probably missed the call while she took the bath. Kate decided to place the call to Stephanie Harper first.

Joe had worked at O2 in Slough. Stephanie Harper was a senior manager at O2. Kate didn't have the woman's number so she rang the head office and asked to be put through.

Reception transferred the call to an extension which immediately switched to voicemail. It announced that

Stephanie Harper wasn't at her desk and gave the option of leaving a message or speaking to a PA.

"Stephanie Harper's office, Kimberley speaking," the PA introduced herself.

Kim. Kate recalled Joe mentioning Kim the secretary. Not the fastest key on the keyboard, but Joe always spoke of her as reliable and friendly.

Kate said, "Oh hi, Kim. We've never met, but I'm Joe Rossini's girlfriend... ex-girlfriend. He used to work there."

"How can I help you today?" There was no recognition in her voice, none of the alleged friendliness.

"I would like to speak to Stephanie, if that's possible."

"Stephanie isn't in today. Can I take a message?"

"I really need to speak to her. It's urgent. The police..." Kate could hear the tension in her voice so she cut herself off. The silence from the other end of the line suggested Kimberley was thinking.

"You say it's about someone who used to work here?"

Kate snatched at the opening. "Yes. Yes, Joe Rossini."

"The name doesn't ring any bells, I'm afraid. Of course if he's left then he won't be on the system."

What? Kim doesn't know about Joe? It could be a different Kim, I guess. Kate persevered: "He worked with or for Stephanie, I think. It's a personal matter and it really is important. And Stephanie will know me." This last line seemed to clinch it.

"Look, I normally wouldn't do this, so you better be telling me the truth, otherwise Stephanie is going to be mad at me." Kimberley paused again as though confirming to herself what she was about to do was all right. "Here's her mobile phone number." She reeled off the number and Kate keyed it into her phone.

"Thank you, Kimberley. Thank you so much. I'm sure it'll be fine." She ended the call and immediately dialled the mobile number.

"Steph Harper."

"Stephanie, it's Kate Blakemore. Joe Rossini's girl... ex."

Dead air.

"Stephanie?"

"Meet me." Her tone was as clipped as her words. She gave Kate the name of a café at the Oracle shopping area in Reading. At 6pm. There was nothing else, just the formality of making a business-type appointment.

Kate replaced the handset, feeling a little odd. Stephanie hadn't asked her what it was about. Therefore she already knew.

THIRTY-EIGHT

The voicemail on Kate's phone was from Inspector Mather. "Please call me when you get this message." His voice had a hard edge to it that Kate hadn't heard previously.

She dialled the inspector's number.

"Where are you?" Mather snapped.

She hesitated then something made her say, "At home. Why?"

"The deal was that you would come straight in for a debrief. DS Littlewood said you disappeared when she went to the toilet. Do I need to send a patrol car round to pick you up?"

"No! No!" Kate realized her hands were shaking. How did she not understand that they wanted her to go straight to the police station? Her mind had been on meeting Darcy and following Sarah's instruction to go into hiding. For a moment, she thought about disputing the arrangement but then decided better of it. "I'm really sorry, it was a misunderstanding. My... someone picked me up at the airport. I'm happy to come in for a debrief. Anything to help." She checked her watch. "I can be there by 4:30. Is that all right, Inspector?"

*

Kate sat with the twins and their pony castle that played music as the ponies stood in certain places. The girls insisted that she make up a story and Kate duly complied. It wouldn't have won any prizes but the girls seemed enthralled and, since they also took part, the story morphed as it progressed. Eventually Kate stopped talking and the girls carried on with their own developments.

Kate slipped away and let her sister know she was going to Reading to see the police.

Darcy said, "Tim and I have plans tonight. The babysitter has called sick—probably caught the Norovirus off Emmy. Will you be back by eight?" When Kate said she would, Darcy continued, "Great! And perhaps tomorrow you'll finally tell me exactly what's going on. I want to understand what's so bad that you're afraid to go home."

Kate promised to explain and borrowed Darcy's SUV. The two car seats in the rear, the sun screens at the girls' windows, the toys on the floor and wearing her clothes felt like she had suddenly swapped lives with her sister. One moment the sporty single girl, the next a mum of two. It wasn't the sort of thing she normally thought about but as she drove to Reading she wondered whether she would ever settle down, whether she would ever have children.

Kate was led to Interview Room One at the Thames Valley Police office in central Reading. The clock on the wall blinked a minute to 16:28. Beside the door there was a large window-like mirror. One-way, Kate assumed.

Mather and Littlewood came in at 16:45. Their faces were impassive. No smiles, no handshakes. They sat opposite. Littlewood started a tape recorder and Mather

183

did the introduction to the interview, looking at Kate's face the whole time.

Then he said, "Why did you run?"

"Sorry?"

"From the airport. You'd arrived at the airport with Sergeant Littlewood. Why didn't you return with her? Why didn't you come straight back here for this interview?"

"You said debrief... I guess I didn't appreciate the urgency."

Mather said, "So if I had made it clear I wanted you to come straight back for further questioning about the disappearance of Sarah Wishart, you would have come?"

"Yes!"

"In Prague, you and DS Littlewood met Inspector Cerny and you reviewed photographs taken from Peter Sikorski's computer."

"Yes."

"You identified forty-eight photographs with people who you had seen before."

"I didn't count them, but it sounds about right."

"Did you know the names of any of the people in the photographs except for Peter, Sarah and their parents?"

"Yes. I recognized my ex-boyfriend, Joe Rossini."

Mather said, "And where is your ex-boyfriend?"

Kate sighed involuntarily. "I don't know. You told me he was at Broadmoor Hospital. It wasn't him. Do you know where he is?"

Mather ignored the question. "Who was the Chinese woman in the photograph with your ex-boyfriend and Peter Sikorski?"

People who lie, look away, don't they? Kate gave the inspector a cold look and said, "I don't know."

Mather held her stare, neither blinking. "Was the photograph the only one with a title?"

"I don't know that. The Czech inspector said as much."

"What does Shot WO mean?"

"I don't know."

"You seem defensive, Miss Blakemore."

"I am! I feel like this is an interrogation, like you don't believe me."

"Well let's see," Littlewood said.

Mather leaned in. "You recognized none of Sarah Wishart's friends at the funeral service or the Sikorski house?"

"No."

"You didn't see Sarah at the service or the house?"

"No. I was sick."

"So I heard. I'm sorry. What did you do after you got back to the hotel?"

"I had a bath and went to bed early."

"You went to bed early, and yet you look like someone who hasn't slept."

"I didn't sleep well. This whole thing has been very stressful."

"Where did you go during the night?"

"What do you mean?"

Mather looked down at Kate's hands on the table. She glanced too and saw a damp patch under each of them.

He said, "Are you denying that you went out during the night?"

She hesitated, her mind whirring. Sarah had made her promise not to say anything. Kate knew she could not betray that trust. "No. I needed air. I went for a walk." Damn! She realized she'd glanced away as she'd spoken.

"The night porter saw you come back, but not leave. You left via the fire escape didn't you?"

"Yes. I don't know why. Impulse. The stairs were closer to my room. Perhaps I thought I would just walk down the stairs. It was fresher there, but I went all the way and walked outside."

Kate looked at the clock. She needed to get going. Amazingly, she'd been there for two hours. She guessed long accusatory silences had filled the time and made it fly.

"Somewhere else you need to dash off to?" Littlewood asked.

"Excuse me?"

"You keep glancing at the clock. That's three times in a matter of minutes."

Kate thought quickly, fixed her eyes on Mather's forehead. "Yeah, well I took time off work to go to Prague and to come here now. I need to get back to work, do the late shift."

They seemed to buy it. Mather ended the interview and switched off the recorder.

He stood and walked around the desk. He waved in the direction of the door. "Thank you for coming in. It might not seem it but I think we are making progress."

Kate nodded uncertainly.

Mather led her out with Littlewood trailing her. Kate had a funny image of the sergeant stooped over her invisible footprints with a magnifying glass. Maybe it was her relief at getting away from the interrogation.

"You're smiling," Mather said as he extended his hand to say goodbye.

"Am I? Just something that amused me I guess," Kate said.

As they shook, he placed his left hand on her shoulder and looked deep into her eyes. "Think about helping Sarah," he said—the nice inspector was back. "Please think more about SHOTWO. Maybe it's not Shot WO. Maybe it's something else entirely."

Kate swallowed, broke the eye contact.

He continued: "Maybe it's a code. Maybe it's SH OT WO. Maybe it's the SH that are initials." He let go of her shoulder with a final pat. "Please think about it."

"I will," she said.

Kate turned and fled. She had to hurry. She had an appointment with Stephanie Harper.

THIRTY-NINE

The walk to the Oracle shopping centre was shorter than Kate had anticipated and she arrived early. A long queue at the coffee shop was a prelude to a crowded seating area. Teenagers from school, mums with kids, and office workers chilling out after a hard day perhaps. She scanned the tables. No one looked like Stephanie. No one looked like they might be waiting for her. Kate realized that Stephanie Harper might not be the woman in the photograph, although it seemed unlikely.

After selecting a cup of herbal tea and a blueberry muffin, Kate hovered over a table by the window and finally got a seat.

She sipped and nibbled. From her vantage point she could see over an entrance to the centre as well as to the coffee shop. She got into a kind of rhythm, glancing outside and then towards the queue. First, she checked for someone looking like the woman in the photograph and then anyone who also appeared to be looking for someone.

Fifteen minutes to go, her mobile rang. Lisa.

"I have news," Lisa began, excitedly. "My ex from the States says you can search army bases to find where someone is posted. I've just forwarded you his email."

As Lisa ended the call, Kate's phone buzzed with an incoming email. She opened it. After some personal stuff she skimmed over, there was a preliminary chat about the problems of finding someone in the British Army. The Ministry of Defence were highly protective of the location of British service personnel. The US Department of Defense was remarkably open about such information—despite 9/11.

He went on to recommend that she go to a US site called army.com/resources/find_buddies.html. This enabled the public to search directly for anyone and find where they were posted. If that failed then he recommended posting on the message boards of any bases where he might be or might have been located.

Kate clicked on the link. It took a long time to load onto her screen and didn't provide full HTML display. It appeared to be more of an army recruitment site and didn't seem to be official. She decided to view it properly on a computer when she got back to her sister's house.

She checked her watch. Less than five minutes to go. She resumed her routine of checking the coffee shop and entrance. A woman stood in the mall just outside the coffee shop. This lady wasn't Oriental; she also appeared to be early twenties, which was probably too young. She gave the impression of agitation, looking up and down the mall. Kate tried to make eye contact but it wasn't met. Kate resumed her scanning. The woman at the entrance met a man; they argued and walked away.

Kate glanced at her watch. Three minutes past.

At 6:10pm, a woman walked confidently past the queue at the entrance. She didn't look like the woman in the photograph but appeared about the right age and was wearing a business suit. Kate sat up. The woman was coming directly towards her.

Kate started to stand but as she moved she realized the woman was speaking to someone behind her. Kate turned to see a table with two ladies ready to greet their friend.

Kate finished her tea. A waitress began to wipe the table next to her just as her phone rang.

"Hi, Mumsie."

Kate's mother began to speak. It seemed that Darcy had told her about the situation. She was concerned and wanted to know what was going on.

The waitress came to Kate's table and bent over, cloth in hand.

"I'm sorry?" Kate said. Was the waitress rudely hurrying her to clear the table? "I've not finished here, thank you."

"We are very busy," the girl said awkwardly but straightened. As she started to turn away she dropped a napkin and shrugged.

Kate stared at the napkin. Something had been written on it, hurriedly scrawled in black pen. "Sorry, Mumsie. I'll have to call you back," she said, and put the phone away. Her mother immediately called back and Kate hit the red *End Call* button.

She opened the napkin so she could read the writing.

The first word she recognized was Stephanie.

Amir followed the blonde girl from the police station. He had bugged her house, her car and her iPhone. He knew she had met the detective inspector and was now on her way to meet the woman from the mobile phone company. She also seemed to text quite a bit and those records would be useful to monitor as well.

She looked amused as she left the police station and glanced in his direction but there was no sign of recognition. His disguise was good: nondescript, casual, unattractive, but she was too distracted anyway. She walked briskly without a backwards glance.

At the coffee shop he watched her sit down by the window overlooking the canal and entrance. He backed off. No need to watch Ms Blakemore here. Instead, he casually strolled to and fro in front of the shops on the first floor. Here he could watch the people ascend the escalator from the entrance and approach from the shopping arcade. He knew what Stephanie Harper looked like. Her company's website had social pictures as well as those of senior employees. Medium height and possibly of Chinese origin with bright brown eyes and full lips.

At five minutes to 6pm, Ms Harper appeared in the entrance to the main department store in the centre. Amir moved into a shop called Early Learning and watched. She checked out the café but hung back. There was another woman at the front agitatedly waiting for someone. Perhaps that made the Harper woman nervous.

After a moment, Stephanie Harper took her phone from a purse and looked at the screen, shook her head. After putting the phone away she seemed uncertain, and Amir thought she would leave. Then she seemed to make up her mind. She walked towards the coffee shop, but instead of going in she picked something up from the nearest table. Stopping beyond the sight of Ms Blakemore, the Oriental woman leaned against a wall and appeared to be writing. Moments later she moved to the rear of the queue, ensuring she was masked by the people in front. An assistant was clearing tables and when she neared the queue Stephanie spoke to her and placed something in her hand. A napkin. A nod towards Ms Blakemore at the window was a clear indication.

Amir understood and he made a swift decision. Follow Stephanie Harper.

Stephanie slunk away from the queue and hurried along the concourse, away from the coffee shop. This was not a direct route but Kate Blakemore might see her if she went another way. When she could, Stephanie cut through a store and took an escalator to the ground level called Riverside. There she crossed the canal and hurried into an NCP car park. She didn't look back.

She found her car and headed out of town to a suburb of Reading. The houses were in a Georgian terrace and hers was the last one. She had chosen it for the cherry tree outside on the verge. She reckoned it counted as a leafy suburb, although in autumn the tree looked cold and forlorn. Parking was never easy, but she found a residents' spot and returned to the front of her house.

As she walked up the path, a man's voice stopped her in her tracks.

"Ms Harper?"

She turned to see a reasonably handsome man approach. He reached the end of her path and raised a hand as though in greeting. He smiled with his mouth but not his eyes. At that moment Stephanie Harper knew her worst nightmare had arrived.

FORTY

The man on the phone said, "Speak."

"It is as we thought," Amir said. "The man is in protective custody. I found the operative in Prague. I have now found the operative in the UK."

"Is he a problem?"

"She," Amir corrected. "No, but not before confirming that the man is now in the United States."

Hamasalih said, "How will you track him there?"

"I am still using the English girl—the girlfriend."

"Will she find him?"

"I think so. If not..." Amir didn't need to complete the sentence. He said, "But I may need to help her. There was information in the document he left for her."

"Do it."

"One thing."

"Yes?"

"I may need help getting into the US. Should I hand over?"

"No, His Highness has confidence in you. It won't be a problem. When do you think you will travel?"

Amir said, "Very soon."

Kate read the scribbled note.

Not allowed to meet you. Too dangerous. If things change I'll be in touch

Too dangerous! Kate knew just how dangerous it was. Peter was dead. Sarah was in hiding, Andrew's house had been broken into—her apartment had probably been broken into. Hell, Kate herself was effectively in hiding!

What did Stephanie mean she wasn't allowed to meet? Who wouldn't let her?

Kate dialled Stephanie's number. It went straight to voicemail. She felt anger bubble up in her throat. "Stephanie, it's Kate Blakemore. Look, what the hell do you mean? You can't do this!" Her voice sounded more abrupt and desperate than she intended. Kate tried to calm herself before she said, "If you don't come straight back, then I'm going to go to your house. I know where you live." She ended the call. She didn't know where Stephanie lived but how hard could it be to find out?

She left her things at the table and queued for another tea.

When she sat down again, she had a plan. She searched for sites that provided electoral roll and phone details. She searched for Stephanie Harper in Reading and got hits on S Harper but not Stephanie. Some also provided births, deaths and marriages but required membership. She decided to go back to these if her fallback plan didn't work.

She called Ann.

"Hello, dear." Ann's tone was cheerful. "I haven't seen you for a few days. Your friend has been staying and looking after Tolkien. I've just seen him leave with Tolkien in a carrier. Is he all right?"

"My friend Andrew?"

"Tolkien."

"Oh, Tolkien's fine. I've just asked Andrew to take him somewhere safe." Kate had resisted saying anything to Ann but now she thought she had better warn her. "That man you saw outside—the satellite company man—he was in my apartment! I think he also broke into Andrew's."

"Oh my goodness. Are you all right, dear?"

"Yes, I'm fine. I just won't be coming home for a while. I really need to find that friend of Joe's in the US Army. Do you have any news?"

"Not yet, dear. I will try again on Monday if I don't hear over the weekend."

"That's very good of you." Kate hesitated, a little awkward about asking her next question. "Could I have your daughter's—Brie's—phone number?"

Ann provided it without question. She said, "Look after yourself, dear."

Kate thanked her and ended the call. She immediately called Brie.

"Oh, hi, Brie, it's Kate. I live above your mum's flat in Windsor."

"Sure. I remember. We met. Is something wrong with Mom?"

"No! No! You're mum's fine. I feel really terrible asking you this but I need an urgent favour."

After a pause, Brie said, "Oh?"

"I remember you told me about your job at the bank. You do credit searches to approve mortgages."

"Yes. Well I don't do the approvals myself but I do have a lot to do with the vetting." She sounded cautious.

"I need to find someone's address. I know it's probably not allowed but I really need help. I need to find the address for Stephanie Harper in Reading. I think she's mid-thirties, if that helps."

"It might but I can't do it. You need permission to search someone's credit file."

"I don't need to know anything about her credit, just her address."

"Have you tried 192.com?"

"Yes and others. I don't think she's registered on the electoral register or has a listed telephone."

"I can't help you. I could lose my job."

Kate must have sounded desperate. She said, "I might be in danger. I think she is too."

"What?" Brie said, incredulous. "You need to go to the police."

"The police can't help. I know this sounds crazy but someone broke into a friend's house and has been in mine. Another friend has been murdered."

"It does sound a little crazy, Kate."

"I know, I know. I'm sorry. I just hoped you might be able to help."

"I can't I'm afraid."

Kate ended the call and went back to the website, registered and paid the subscription. Just as she had anticipated, there was no one who matched Stephanie's full name. There were five female S. Harpers with about the right birth dates and Kate noted them down.

She checked her watch. She'd been in the coffee shop for forty-five minutes. The queue was down to a couple of people and the tables had thinned. No sign of Stephanie. Kate tried her number again but didn't leave a message.

She decided to give it another hour. While she waited she went back to the US Army website. Again it took a long time to load and was difficult to interpret. She found a search box and entered "Danny Guice" and hit *Enter*. After a long few minutes, a message told her that the name wasn't found. She tried "Daniel Guice" and then "Dan Guice". Same result.

Her phone rang.

"Where the hell are you?" Darcy. And very cross.

Oh God! She'd promised to be back by eight. It was already two minutes past. "Sorry. I totally forgot you needed me to babysit." She was up and heading for the exit.

"Are you on your way?"

"Yes! Yes. The traffic shouldn't be bad. I won't be long."

As she drove back to her sister's, Kate's phone vibrated with an SMS. As she ran into the house, she checked the text message. A short message from Brie:

Confirmed trouble with Mom. There was only one match. Hope this helps

Then an address in Reading.

Stephanie Harper's address.

FORTY-ONE

The girls were watching cartoons. Darcy and Tim were still in bed after a late night.

Kate knew her sister would still be cross. She might be even more cross when she read the note Kate left on the kitchen worktop:

Just popped out. Won't be long. Hope you had a nice evening and don't mind me borrowing the car again. Sorry about last night. Will explain all when I get back—K

Kate checked on the girls and slipped out. In the glovebox she found Darcy's satnav, plugged it into the cigarette lighter socket, and programmed it for Stephanie Harper's address.

The street was north-west of the town, an old part. Cars lined all the roads and traffic was heavier than she expected. The area appeared to be a special route into Reading for white vans—especially ones that wanted to hog the road so that oncoming cars needed to pull in. A blockage forced her to turn off the main drag and try and cut through. Not an expert at requesting an alternative route on the satnav, she ignored the machine's complaints and insistence that she turn around when possible.

Finally, Kate turned the SUV into Stephanie's road. Speed bumps deterred the white van drivers from this side street, which appeared to be a long sweeping curve. The satnav indicated that Stephanie's house was at the far end. As she passed the apex, Kate saw another blockage. Only this time the obstruction was caused by police vehicles and an ambulance.

With her heart in her mouth, Kate stopped in the road and looked ahead at the active crime scene. She had to get out. Scanning the road she saw no spaces, so she reversed to the first side street and turned down it. Finding a parking space, even though it was "Residents Parking Permits Only", she took it and switched off the engine. She got out, went back to Stephanie's road and then turned towards the activity.

She walked robotically, taking in the scene: blue and white police tape strung across the road on either side of the property; a temporary white tent over the front door; the ambulance starting to move.

A policeman removed the cordon and waved it through. As the ambulance passed her, she noted the siren and lights weren't on. It could mean one of two things but Kate wouldn't allow herself to think about them.

A crowd gathered by her side of the tape. Fifteen or so people standing, looking on. Police stood outside and people in white protective suits entered and left the building. Kate had seen enough TV crime shows to realize these were forensic investigators.

She reached the crowd and stood behind them. There was a lot of whispering between them and she leaned in to listen. Most of it was speculation, but someone confirmed it was a lady called Harper. Another said she had met Ms Harper who seemed like a nice girl. Chinese. Quiet. Kept herself to herself.

At the far side of the cordon, a car pulled up. A silver-grey BMW estate. The ribbon was raised so that it could enter. It rolled forward and stopped. Two people got out.

Kate moved back a pace.

Mather and Littlewood!

She was partially hidden behind a large man and watched the two detectives. Littlewood was on the telephone. Mather headed for another man without a uniform—possibly another detective. Mather spoke with the man and then indicated that he and Littlewood would go into the house. Littlewood ended the call and then began to talk animatedly to her boss. Mather shook his head. They stopped at the tent before the front door. Littlewood said something and Kate managed to read her lips—some of the words. At the same time, almost as though something caught his attention, Mather swivelled and scanned the onlookers.

Kate shrank back, causing the large man to turn and look at her. He said something, but Kate wasn't listening. She walked away from the scene, her heart hammering a hole in her chest.

The words she'd read on Littlewood's lips were: "...is dead... last night... it's definitely murder."

FORTY-TWO

An hour earlier, Mather had called Littlewood into his office. His scowl spoke volumes.

"She's been lying to us. You were right."

Littlewood allowed herself a slight smile. "You're talking about Kate Blakemore. What have you found out?"

Mather rose from his chair. "Let's go, we're going for a drive."

"Come on boss! What has happened? What did she lie about?"

"SHOTWO," Mather said and handed the sergeant a slip of paper with an address on it. He didn't say anything more until they were in the car and heading out of the centre.

Mather said, "There's been an incident. Last night a Reading woman was murdered. Her name... Stephanie Harper. SH."

Littlewood frowned. "So how does that make Ms Blakemore a liar?"

"OTWO means O2. Stephanie Harper at O2. It's where she worked. It's where Ms Blakemore's missing boyfriend worked. She must have realized."

As they neared the address, the roads became clogged with diverted traffic. "We're going the long way round,"

Mather explained. "Harper lived at a junction. The whole section has been cordoned off."

When they arrived at the street, Littlewood held up her warrant card and the ribbon was raised. Mather parked. "Quick word with the OIC," he said. "Then we'll go and take a look around."

Littlewood's phone rang. As she took it, Mather strode over to the officer in charge and introduced himself. The man said, "SOCO is still in there. If you want to go in, sir, you'll obviously have to suit up."

Mather nodded and waved for Littlewood to join him. They walked to the gate and when she ended the call he said, "Problem?"

"You could say that. The call was from the Prague police. It's not good news I'm afraid. Sarah Wishart is dead, identified from remains in a burnt-out building. Time of death sometime in the early hours of Wednesday night. About the time Blakemore was missing. And, Boss, it's definitely murder."

Mather shook his head. "Surely you don't think Ms Blakemore killed her friend?"

"Surely you don't think it's a coincidence?"

They stood in front of the tent by the door. Mather was deep in thought, and he looked up and down the street for inspiration. None came. Ms Blakemore had lied about going out in Prague. She must have visited Sarah Wishart. She had lied about knowing what SHOTWO meant, about knowing that SH stood for Stephanie Harper. What else was the woman covering up?

He was about to step into the tent, when something made him look down the road again.

"Shit, it's her, Sam!" He pointed and grabbed Littlewood's arm. "It's Kate Blakemore!"

They spun around, ran to the gate and began to run towards the cordon and crowd.

"Kate! Stop!"

The command made Kate turn and look. Mather and Littlewood were pushing through the crowd, then running in her direction.

Something snapped in her mind. The police would guess SHOTWO referred to Stephanie Harper and now she was dead. They'd soon realize Kate knew. Why else would she be here? She began to run. Turning the corner, she swung open the SUV's door and jumped in. The keys were a jumble in her clumsy hand. *Why did Darcy have so many damn keys?* As she fumbled, she glanced in the rear-view mirror. No one coming around the corner—yet. She found the ignition key, and turned.

Nothing.

Littlewood appeared, breathless, searching the street for a sign of Kate.

It's an automatic. Foot on brake first. Turn. The engine fired.

Kate knocked it into *Drive*, turned the wheel and the car lurched into the road just as Littlewood reached the door.

The detective banged on the window. "Stop!"

Kate didn't stop. She accelerated along the short street. As she turned right at the bottom, she glanced in the rear-view and saw Littlewood standing in the middle of the road, phone to her ear.

Although there was a thirty mile an hour speed limit, Kate floored it and hit the first speed bump at sixty. The SUV bounced up and crashed down, Kate fighting for control. As she approached the next speed bump she braked hard but still bounced over it.

Then she heard the siren.

Behind her, the BMW estate turned into the road and began to race after her. Kate's iPhone rang. She ignored it.

At the next junction she turned. And then turned again. After five more turns she hit an arterial road and took it, heading away from town and away from the traffic.

Again and again she looked in the rear-view for the pursuing police, but there was no sign of Mather's BMW.

Kate drove for twenty minutes through the Berkshire countryside, avoiding towns. Gradually the panic faded and, at a quiet lay-by hidden from the road, she stopped. She sat for a while just staring at trees. She had the window wound down and rested with her head in her hands.

What was she doing?

She looked at her phone. Five missed calls and a message. Nervous with anticipation she listened to the message.

It was clearly left during the chase; Kate could hear the siren, the engine acceleration and the crashes as the BMW bounced over the speed bumps. Sergeant Littlewood sounded breathless as she said, "Running from the police only makes things worse, Ms Blakemore. Call me now on this number. If you don't call within the hour, you will be arrested for obstructing the course of justice. This is serious, Ms Blakemore. We now know that you lied to us about knowing what the title meant, that you pretended not to know that SH was Stephanie Harper's initials. Did you have anything to do with her death? Did you have anything to do with Sarah Wishart's death? Fleeing the scene like this doesn't look good. If you are innocent then you should call me back."

Kate's chest constricted. Sarah's death? Sarah was dead too? Tears came then, streaming from her eyes, and great sobs wracked her body.

What was she going to do?

FORTY-THREE

Breathing in the cool earthy air, Kate felt herself relax a little, her mind clear. She thought through what had happened and the options. Her options were zero—or close to. Boomer was her only lead. Get hold of Boomer. That's what Joe wanted her to do. But how? Presumably the *Trust Me* document told her what to do. Now she needed Ann to get information from her contact. That seemed the only way.

She restarted the engine and took a deep breath. Tim and Darcy needed to know what was going on. They wouldn't be happy. Was Kate putting their family at risk? Her ringing phone snapped her back.

Darcy spoke, her voice quiet and restrained. "The police have been here looking for you."

"That was quick!"

"You're driving my car. Didn't take them long to work out where you were staying." Darcy's pitch changed. "What the hell were you thinking, running away from a scene of a crime?"

"I... I don't know. I guess I panicked."

Darcy took two deep breaths. "Tell me what's going on."

Kate explained as much as she could. As she spoke, she could sense Darcy's exasperation.

When she finished bringing her sister right up to date, Darcy said, "This is crazy! It's all based on Joe's lies..."

"It's not crazy, because there's someone out there—the Arab—who's killing people I know!"

"You need to hand yourself in to the police, Kate."

"I don't trust them."

"You need to trust somebody!"

There was a long pause before Darcy prompted, "Kate?"

"Yeah, I'm still here."

"Please call Inspector Mather. Running makes you seem guilty." Again a heavy pause. "Kate?"

"I'll think about it."

Darcy sighed. "What are you going to do? If you come back here the police will arrest you before you step through the door."

"I'll find a B&B. I need to think things through, consider my options. Maybe I just need some time to myself. My friends are dead, Darce!"

"All right, all right. Hopefully you'll work out what you need to do by Monday. I could do with my car back ... and I left my laptop in it."

"I'll just stay somewhere tonight and do something by Sunday evening. You'll have your car and laptop back in time for work."

"OK. Have a rest. Clear your head and then do the right thing." Then, in a more caring tone, she added, "Let me know when you are checked in, so I know you're safe. Also, if you need anything... And I'm here if you need to talk."

"Sure... and thanks, sis." Kate switched off the phone and pulled out of the lay-by. She headed back to a village she'd driven through; there was bound to be a pub with a room.

★

As she drove, random thoughts filtered through her brain. Then she replayed one that took prominence. Joe said he was Special Forces. Boomer was his buddy. Presumably Boomer was also Special Forces then. What was US Special Forces anyway? And maybe she could whittle down the number of bases. How many Special Forces units could there be?

She stopped at an inn advertising B&B, free Wi-Fi and parking. With the SUV out of sight of the road, she located Darcy's laptop and checked in under an assumed name.

In the room, she rang her sister, told her where she was and asked for the password to get into the computer. Within minutes she was online and googled *US Special Forces.*

The term appeared to be interchangeable with Special Operations, of which there were four: US Marine Corps Forces Special Operations, Army Special Operations, US Navy Special Warfare, and US Air Force Special Operations. These were all linked under a single command with the acronym USSOCOM.

Kate followed links starting with the Marines to a MARSOC website. Here there was no way to search for people or email addresses. There were contact phone numbers but they started with *com.* and she had no idea how to dial that. She then turned to the army site. Again no email addresses and confusing phone numbers, but two things caught her eye. Firstly, the name Fort Bragg, which she recalled seeing on the Army.com site. Secondly, the term Delta Force.

She googled *Delta Force* and read it was the term given to the US Army's 1st Special Forces Operational Detachment, a unit of the Joint Special Operations Command and located at Pope Air Force Base and Fort

Bragg, both in North Carolina. Joe had mentioned Virginia. Virginia—North Carolina, reasonably close?

Again she found no obvious means of contact. She went back to the Army.com site. There was no listing of Pope Air Force Base, but of the 128 camps listed, two said Special Operations Forces: Fort Bragg and Camp Mackall. She clicked on the link to Fort Bragg and again searched for a means of contact. Finally she spotted it: a link to a forum. Clicking on this she found herself redirected to Facebook. On the wall she posted the message that she needed to contact Danny Guice, believed to be in Special Ops.

She went to the Camp Mackall site and searched until she found a similar forum link. Again she posted her message on a wall.

Four thousand miles away, an algorithm, scanning electronic traffic, picked up the forum posts and fired off an automatic email.

FORTY-FOUR

Prince bin Shahd watched as Hamasalih dialled a number. It was an encrypted line and, should anyone try to trace it, they would eventually find a dead end in Belarus. He could hear the ringing but suspected there was no sound at the other end and visualized a red light frantically blinking in an office in America. Eventually it connected and the aide passed him the handset.

The call was answered with a gravel-filled Southern American drawl. "I was in a meeting." There was traffic noise in the background.

Hamasalih didn't bother questioning whether the line was secure. He knew it would be. He said, "Of course, I understand. The prince has a message. He says: it has been a long time, Mustang."

"Too long," Mustang said, walking.

Bin Shahd, listening in to the conversation, knew this was insincere, but it didn't matter.

Mustang said, "Where is His Highness?"

Hamasalih glanced at the prince. When bin Shahd shook his head, the aide responded, "You are dealing with me now."

Mustang didn't respond.

After two seconds, Hamasalih said, "It seems Mirrorman has been found."

"That is good news." Genuine interest from the other end of the line. "I trust he will be dealt with."

"He is in the United States."

A long pause, then: "Yes?"

"We need your assistance."

Another pause. Bin Shahd wondered if he could hear bird song in the background. Finally the American said, "That would be most difficult."

"However, as a favour to the prince, you will do it." Hamasalih's tone suggested anything but a favour. This was an obligation. "Remember, this may well be a personal issue for the prince, but if Mirrorman has information, there would be serious implications for you... my dear Mustang."

"But if such information did exist then it would surely have materialized by now. It's been—what—two years?"

"Perhaps. Perhaps you are right, my dear. But information may come from many sources."

The American bristled. "I don't respond well to threats."

"Oh you misunderstand me. Perhaps my English... We are friends, are we not?"

"The prince and I have been friends for a long time."

"Then we are friends also."

Mustang said nothing.

Listening to the other man's breathing, Hamasalih said, "And that friendship has been most beneficial, has it not?"

"I will do what I can," Mustang said, and bin Shahd wondered if the American was speaking through clenched teeth.

"I think that is the right decision. As I said, it really is your problem as much as ours."

"When?"

"Very soon—a matter of days."

They ended the call and bin Shahd turned to Hamasalih. "Make sure Amir is informed. Send our American friend the details of Amir's identity as soon as you know."

Hamasalih's face showed concern that he failed to hide quickly enough.

Bin Shahd read it. He said, "Mustang is a serpent, but even a serpent does not bite its own head off. There is too much at stake for the American to use the information against us. However, you should ensure Amir is fully prepared. I have no doubt that the American will involve his own resources. In fact, I count on it."

Hamasalih inclined his head. "He hasn't hesitated to do this in the past."

"No. And it is best that we know what and who." He ended the conversation with a wave of the hand and Hamasalih left. Bin Shahd stepped through the patio doors and watched the two young women swimming in the pool. As he admired their brown bodies glistening with oil and water, he felt something stir. Anticipation made his blood rise. He smiled. Was it desire for the nubile young things? Perhaps. But equally it was the expectancy—retribution for the death of his son.

FORTY-FIVE

Kate didn't sleep. All night she tossed and turned wondering if going to the police was the right thing to do. Would Sarah still be alive if she had gone to the police? She replayed the events of Prague and meeting Sarah at the arts cinema café. How much did the police know about that? Was Kate the last person to see Sarah alive? That made her wonder whether the Arab was there, trailing her. Had Kate led him to Sarah?

She also thought about Stephanie. If only she hadn't originally lied about recognizing the code. If she'd been open about it, they wouldn't now be looking at Stephanie's phone records to realize Kate was probably the last person to be in touch with her too. Because of the message she'd left it would also look like she'd been to Stephanie's house. Of course, one good thing about being arrested would be safety. The police might not be very helpful but, if she was in a cell, then the Arab couldn't get her. On the other hand, if she was in custody, she couldn't make progress finding Joe.

Kate must have cycled through these thoughts about ten times when her mobile phone buzzed. She looked at the clock. It was 3:17. She groaned. It was probably junk mail, and she wished she'd turned her phone off.

She picked it up to check the message before switching off. Yes, it looked like spam. The address was just a series of numbers. In fact, it didn't look like a proper email address because even the domain was a series of digits.

She was about to delete it when the subject made her stop. It said:

Re ur D Force inquiry

Delta Force.

Kate clicked on the message and read it.

Who are you and why are you looking for me? Danny

She immediately responded with:

I'm Kate Blakemore. I'm trying to find Joe Rossini. I think he wanted me to contact you to find him.

Danny replied:

If you are genuine, you will be able to access the following webmail. There was then a secure web address, again all digits. **Use this email address. The password is a twelve-digit number you should know. Enter this and check the Draft email folder.**

Barely containing her excitement, Kate booted up Darcy's laptop and connected to the internet. She typed in the domain and a sign-in box appeared asking for a Domain\Username and Password. In the first box she typed the strange email address, but when she got to the second she realized there were no twelve digits that seemed special. She tried her six-digit birthday followed by Joe's and then reversed it. She tried his birthday as eight digits followed by his credit card PIN, then reversed it. Then she stared at the screen, eyes glazed trying to think of numbers that Joe might have mentioned. "No!" she shouted and slapped the bed with frustration. Then she held her breath realizing it was the middle of the night and there were other people staying at the inn. She breathed again—no shouts of complaint.

There was only one thing to do. She emailed Danny back.

Help! I am genuine! I have no idea what the numbers are. I've tried all I can think of. Can you help at all?

The reply:

Maybe he gave you a locket or ring with the numbers engraved?

Joe had never given her any jewellery.

No

After a few minutes another email popped up.

On something else. A dog tag maybe?

Not a dog tag!

She called Andrew.

He answered after four rings, worried. "Are you all right?"

"I'm fine. Sorry to disturb you but I need your help. I need to know what Tolkien's name tag has engraved on it. I'm specifically after a twelve-digit code."

Andrew grunted. She heard what sounded like him getting out of bed. "I'll text you back with what's on there. If you don't get anything within thirty minutes, call me back, because I'll have fallen asleep. Let's hope he's not out!"

Less than ten minutes later, Andrew's text arrived.

611089680119. Hope this is it. Tell me about it tomorrow. Now go to sleep! Ax

Kate keyed the number into the password field and was immediately rewarded by access to a mail server. She clicked on the Drafts folder. There was a single email.

To communicate, type an email and then save it to Drafts. When you have read an email, delete it from

this and the Deleted Items folder so there is no record. Are you in danger?

She deleted the email from the folder and Deleted Items. She typed an email.

I found the code. Yes, I'm in danger. My friend is dead. So are two others. The killer is an Arab. Should I let the police arrest me? I think I'm safe at the moment but for how long I don't know. What should I do?

She saved it and waited. Moments later the email disappeared and a few minutes after that a new one replaced it.

Do not go home. Do not use your computer. If you can, use one in an internet café and never the same one twice. Do not use your cell. Take what cash you need then stop using your credit card or accessing your bank account. Can you get an airline ticket and fly to the US?

She replied:

I think so. Where and when?

Washington, Dulles International as soon as possible. Let me know the flight and I'll meet you at the airport. Another thing. Was there a photograph of you and Joe with writing on the back?

She looked in her bag. The three photos were still there. She removed each one from its frame and checked the reverse. Her favourite one, of the two of them on the bridge, had an odd phrase. She replied:

Yes there is

What are the words?

Dare or truth

He wrote:

That's it. Bring it with

Thanks. Very relieved!

It felt a little foolish but she saved the final message to the Drafts folder anyway.

Why did he want the photograph? Did he not know what Joe looked like? Thank goodness she had salvaged the photos from the box at Andrew's. Why was it important that there was writing on it?

She fell asleep. When she opened her eyes, she was surprised to see the time was after 10am. She called Darcy straight away.

"I need you to do something for me. I need you to get a flight to Washington, Dulles."

"Why would I...?"

"Sorry. I want you to buy the ticket in your name, for me." She paused to let it sink in and then added, "And let me have your passport." She held her breath.

"So you aren't going to the police?"

"No. Boomer—Danny Guice—has been in touch. He's going to help me find Joe. I think he knows where he is."

"Oh, Kate." Real concern.

"Please. I have to do this."

A long painful silence, then: "OK, I'll do it. I hope you know what you are doing. I should tell you there's a police car parked up the road. I'm sure they're waiting for you."

Not far away, Amir was listening. The girl had used the hotel phone but the bug in her iPhone had picked up her conversation. So she had been in touch with someone in

America and would fly out as soon as possible. She would be travelling under her sister's name.

Heathrow was the closest UK airport. It made sense for her to fly from there. He checked the internet for flights to Dulles. From her excitement, Amir predicted she would get a ticket on the earliest flight. He also predicted she would fly BA. Given time, Brits shopped for the best price. Under time pressure, he judged the girl's sister would automatically choose British Airways. The next realistic flight for her to catch was at 10:50 the next morning.

He bought a ticket for the flight using the name Emile Brassante, a businessman who worked for Mastercard in Brussels.

Once confirmed, he dialled the usual number.

"Speak."

Amir provided a brief update. He added, "I presume there will be no problems."

"No. Our friend will provide assistance."

"You mean with access and goods." By *goods* he meant a weapon.

"Also manpower."

"I work alone."

"Not this time you don't," the other man said and ended the call.

FORTY-SIX

Three hours later a knock on Kate's door made her jump.

"It's me—Tim," a voice called from the other side.

Kate opened the door and was surprised to see Tim in his cycling gear. His face was flushed red, his hair flattened. He slung a rucksack onto the bed and asked for a glass of water.

"You cycled," Kate said, stating the obvious.

After a few gulps, Tim said, "Twenty-five miles in under an hour." He grinned. "Not as bad as I thought I'd be. Yes, I cycled. Not much option really, since I couldn't see Darcy doing the ride."

"But—"

"The police. Didn't seem a good idea to lead them to you, so we needed to distract them. Darcy took my car with the girls. The police followed them." He opened the rucksack. "Here's her passport and driving licence."

As he handed the items over, there was a look on his face that Kate read. "I'll take good care of them."

"And a credit card," he said, handing over a Visa card.

Kate shook her head. "No, you can't give me a credit card too!"

"You'll need ID—and who travels without a credit card these days? And you certainly can't carry anything with your real name."

"All right. Thank you—both of you. I won't use the card."

"There's also two hundred pounds in cash. That's all I could take out at short notice. Seriously, if you need more, do use the credit card. Anyway, you'll probably spend less than Darcy, so it'll be a saving!"

Tim's feeble attempt at humour made her smile and then cry.

He hugged her. After a moment she pulled away and brushed tears from her cheeks. "Phew, you smell of sweat!"

He laughed. "That's more like it. So... there are a couple of changes of clothes in the rucksack. Hope you're not staying more than a couple of days!"

"I'll get some clothes out there... and pay you back."

From a side pocket he pulled a piece of paper. "Here's the e-ticket in the name Darcy Roberts. One-way, 10:50 tomorrow morning. You'll get in at 13:40, same day. Are you OK getting a taxi to the airport? Darcy really needs the car tomorrow. We need to get the girls to—"

"Yes. Yes, not a problem. Take the car now. A taxi won't be a problem." She handed him the car keys. Then she put the laptop in the case and gave him that too.

"Ring when you get there so we know you're OK," he said.

She shook her head. "I can't use my phone." She explained what Danny had said.

Tim frowned then said, "Just take the SIM card out. Get a SIM-only account in the US. Send us a cryptic text... you know, something like spam. We'll guess it's from you." He thought for a moment, running his hands through his hair as he did. Then he raised his eyebrows, an impish look on his face. "Tell you what, if everything is going well, use one of the twins' names in the text. If there's a problem put my name in the message. If there was a problem, but it's now all right, use Darcy's."

Kate shook her head. Tim seemed to be enjoying the cloak-and-dagger side of this. She knew she couldn't send a message that hinted at something being wrong. Imagine the worry! She'd find a better way to communicate. Danny was sure to know what to do. She said, "OK, that's a plan. Now get going before I change my mind and make you cycle home!"

Tim gave her a kiss and said, "Take care of yourself."

After he left, Kate realized she could only access the internet using her iPhone. Would that be all right? She decided not to risk it. She went down to the bar and chatted to the landlady over a glass of lager-shandy. She casually asked whether there was an internet café locally.

The lady thought it amusing that Kate would expect a small village to have an internet café. "You're not in Reading, you know, pet," she chuckled.

It was a long day for Kate. Waiting, watching TV, wondering what Danny Guice would tell her, whether he knew where Joe was. She decided against using the mobile phone to email Danny the flight details. Instead, she decided there must be internet access at Heathrow. She'd do it from there.

In the evening she ordered ham and cheese sandwiches in the room. The landlady brought them up. "Do you still need to send an email, pet?" she asked. "Because I have a computer in the office. You can use that if it's not for long, mind."

Kate thanked her and ate the sandwiches in the office—a small room cluttered with half-completed paperwork and unfiled invoices. Kate signed into the secure site and left a message for Danny. Along with the flight number and arrival time, she told him her sister's name—the name she was travelling under.

Minutes later, another message appeared in the Drafts folder:

Excellent. Remember, ditch the credit cards and cell. Bring the photo. Have a good flight. Danny

FORTY-SEVEN

Kate sat in Economy and looked out of the window as the plane climbed over Windsor.

When the stewardess offered drinks, she took two gin and tonics. She knocked them back hoping they would calm her trembling heart and shaking hands.

"Nervous flier?" the young man in the middle seat next to her asked.

She smiled weakly. "Something like that."

The scariest moment had been going through passport control although checking in had been awkward. The lady at the check-in desk had asked Kate a series of questions. They were innocent questions, but under the circumstances it seemed like an interrogation to Kate.

"How many bags are you checking in today?"

"None." Kate held up the rucksack.

"There's only one piece of cabin luggage allowed." The woman indicated Kate's handbag slung on her shoulder. She smiled. "Can you put it inside your rucksack?"

Kate nodded.

"I see this is a one-way ticket. When will you be returning?"

"I'm not sure yet."

"Do you hold a US entry visa?"

Kate was surprised. "We don't need a visa for the US, do we? I thought..." A lump caught in her throat.

"It's OK. There's the DS 160 Visa Waiver Form. You haven't applied then?"

"No. I, er..."

The check-in lady said, "Oh dear." She glanced at the queue. It was short. "I can do it now for you." She asked a bunch of questions and Kate had to keep reminding herself that she should answer as Darcy, a married woman, two years younger and with two kids. The questions were all fine, until she was asked: "Where will you be staying."

"Er... I don't know."

Wrong answer. Alarm briefly flashed on the lady's face.

"You need an address otherwise immigration won't let you in."

Kate felt the need to explain. "I'm meeting someone at the airport. I'm staying with him. I don't know his address." She stopped herself abruptly. Guilty people say too much don't they? She smiled her best what-can-I-do? smile at the check-in lady.

"Unusual," the woman said.

Kate's head momentarily cleared. "I'm staying the first night at the Radisson," she said trying to sound convincing.

The check-in woman searched on her computer. "Let's see. Radisson, Washington. Which one?"

"The airport?" Too much like a question.

"OK, I've got it. If immigration ask you, make sure this is the address you give them." She wrote it on a piece of paper. Underneath she wrote a code. "Your visa waiver has been accepted. You shouldn't need this reference, but just in case..." She handed the paper to Kate and then printed the boarding card.

Kate thanked the lady—a little too profusely—and headed for the washrooms. She splashed her face with cold water, dried and applied her make-up in Darcy's style. She retied her hair in a severe pony tail and looked at herself. Not bad. Surely she looked similar enough to pass for her sister. OK, so she was almost two inches taller, but the thought of a passport control officer measuring her made her smile.

She was ready.

The passport control queue moved tortuously slowly. Kate's momentary relaxation in the washroom had evaporated. Sweat prickled her clammy skin. She became aware of excessive blinking, tried to stop it, but only exacerbated the problem.

At the front of the queue the passport control man looked at her impassively. Looked at the boarding card. Looked at her. Looked at the boarding card. He turned to the man on the stool next to him. They both looked at the boarding card.

An eternity passed. Kate noted two heavily armed policemen to her right. She rotated her body away from them. How guilty did she look? What was wrong?

Then the second man said, "It's fine."

The first man turned back to her with a shrug. "Your boarding card isn't complete. Just go to the desk when your gate is announced and have them check your seat allocation." He smiled, handed the boarding card and passport back.

Kate staggered forward, unsure that her legs would keep her up. Mistake on the boarding card. So much for the efficient check-in woman—she must have been distracted by the visa problem.

The young man beside her on the plane had attempted other questions but soon got the message. She wasn't in the mood to talk. Kate put headphones on and found a classical music channel. The gin kicked in and within thirty minutes she was asleep.

In Business Class, a Belgian she would have recognized as the Arab, sipped Harrogate Spring Water. He also listened to a music channel, but wouldn't sleep; he rarely slept. Relaxation, switching off his mind, was just as effective. He was confident that there would be no problems at the other end. He would pass through immigration without suspicion and he would find the washroom in the arrivals lounge and locate the hidden package. An untraceable gun.

The steward didn't disturb Mr Brassante. The man looked asleep, a hint of a smile on his lips.

In the evening, Kate's phone would have rung if she had not removed the SIM. Instead, it went straight to voicemail.

"Hello, dear. It's Ann from downstairs. My contact has found the information you wanted. You wanted to know which base Danny Guice was at. Well, he was a Master Sergeant at Fort Bragg. Special Forces Operational Detachment 391." There was a pause. "I have some bad news I'm afraid. Mr Guice was in Iraq. He was killed in action two years ago. I'm sorry to tell you, dear, but your friend is dead."

FORTY-EIGHT

Thirty-one months earlier

The command sergeant whispered, "Tinman, how's my exit looking?"

Three men edged along a corridor, night-vision goggles on, assault rifles slung across their fronts, silenced pistols at the ready.

"Four guards. Looking good," Tinman's voice whispered back.

Another voice came on the comm. "Coming your way in five." Dogtag.

The command sergeant raised a hand. They stopped and he looked around a corner. Beyond, a door was edged with light. The comms room. He waved the two other men ahead and signalled: "Take it out—minimum force."

Boomer and Mirrorman removed their night vision and stepped either side of the door. Mirrorman crouched as Boomer slowly turned the handle then jerked the door open. Three men inside spun in alarm and all died instantly. Three clean shots.

While Mirrorman checked the surveillance equipment, Boomer signalled to Command Sergeant Topcat and stayed by the door watching the corridor.

Topcat stepped inside the room and pointed to a screen. It showed a lounge area in which two men sat on sofas. One looked asleep with what appeared to be an AK47 leaning against the sofa. The second sat opposite, his weapon propped by his side. Beyond was a double door.

Through the headset Dogtag said, "With you in one. Clear?"

Boomer responded, "All clear."

Moments later the fourth man stepped into the comms room. He nodded to Topcat. "Problem eliminated."

The command sergeant pointed to the door on the screen. *The package is in there.* Dogtag moved a body from the chair in front of the screen and sat down. Then to the others Topcat said, "Boomer, Mirrorman with me."

The three men crept through the house until they came to the lounge area. They didn't hesitate. The command sergeant walked in and shot the guard who was awake. Boomer took out the other man, who never woke up. The first man toppled sideways, his gun clattering to the ground.

The three soldiers moved to the double doors and waited, listening.

"Clear," Dogtag said over the headset.

Topcat nodded and Boomer opened the door to a room otherwise in darkness—a bedroom. Mirrorman ran to the bed and clamped his hand over the mouth of the man who started to sit up. He pulled him out, twisted him around and pressed him, face down into the mattress. Boomer taped the man's mouth and then took a black gown from Topcat.

"Put this on him," Topcat said.

Boomer dressed the man and then fastened his wrists together. They moved back to the doors.

"How's my exit?" Topcat whispered, but the response from Tinman in the compound was swallowed by alarm from Dogtag watching the CCTV. "Another hostile. Repeat, another hostile."

A guard had been in the lavatory. He opened the door to the lounge, saw his dead comrades and an armed man in black just inside the bedroom. He let off a short burst of gunfire.

The soldiers ducked out of the way just in time, but the syncopated splatter rang in their ears for a moment. Topcat signalled to Mirrorman where the hostile was. "On my mark. One... two... three."

Mirrorman rolled into the room and rapid-fired his Glock as Topcat stepped from behind the door and fired his assault rifle at the far sofa. They saw the guard hit the ground and, through the cloud of stuffing, Mirrorman stepped round the sofa and made sure the assailant was dead.

"Let's go! Plan B," Topcat said, no longer needing to whisper. "Dogtag, pull back from your position."

"Roger that. They heard you. All hell breaking loose."

Topcat: "Gopher, how you fixed?"

Over the sound of a diesel engine, Gopher responded, "On your mark."

With their prisoner, the three men moved rapidly into the corridor. Clear.

A rapid burst of gunfire. Topcat held up his hand. "Dogtag, report."

No response.

Topcat waved them forward. Boomer kept the rear, holding the prisoner and turning every few seconds to check behind. After a few paces they were at a junction.

They could hear running feet. Topcat held up two fingers and pointed. Two men.

Mirrorman and Topcat swung round the corner and each fired rapidly. One guard responded with a short burst from his own weapon but it was wild and he and his partner quickly died. Without hesitation, the soldiers moved swiftly along the corridor, past the dead guards, and worked their way back to the comms room.

The room was sprayed with bullets. Topcat entered, stepped over another body and went to Dogtag, who lay on the floor in a pool of blood. He checked for a pulse. "Man down," he said with a shake of the head.

More gunfire, outside this time.

Topcat said, "Tinman?"

"Holding them," a voice crackled back.

"We're going now. Cover yourself. Get to the alternate exit."

"Roger that," Tinman said.

Topcat picked up the dead soldier. Mirrorman took the other side and they dragged the body into the hall.

Topcat said, "I need that diversion, Gopher. Fire at will."

A few seconds later there was an explosion. From outside a mortar had been fired into the compound by the gate. A second mortar landed on the guard house.

The soldiers hurried to the rear. Topcat front-kicked an external door and they hurried into a yard. Gunfire drew attention to their left. Tinman crouched at a side wall and returned fire. "Help him," Topcat said to Mirrorman. Then to Gopher he said, "I'll have that exit now!"

Moments later, an explosion ripped a hole in the concrete outer wall. Through the dust, a truck reversed, crashing the remaining rubble out of the way. As the prisoner and dead soldier were put on the flatbed,

Mirrorman and Tinman provided cover, moving backwards towards the truck.

They jumped in and Topcat banged the cab. "Go!"

Gopher pulled the truck forward thirty yards and stopped. While the others continued to fire through the hole in the wall, Gopher took out a small remote control. He looked for Topcat's nod and pressed *Send.* Fifteen incendiary devices went off simultaneously, the one attached to the propane tanks sending a tower of flame high into the night sky. The complex became a huge roiling inferno.

The truck jolted into first and pulled away, bumping across the rough terrain. The men in the rear watched the town for signs of pursuit. None came.

Mirrorman put down his gun and slumped on the floor. He took a ragged breath and placed a hand inside his protective vest.

"I'm hit," he said.

FORTY-NINE

Present day

Kate stepped forward at immigration.

"Place your right hand on the pad and look into the camera, ma'am," the immigration man said. His tone was as if he'd said it twice. Maybe he had.

She responded and placed her hand on the black fingerprint reader. Her sweaty palm was immediately obvious.

"Are you all right, ma'am?"

She smiled wanly. "Think I'm coming down with something, that's all."

The man checked her immigration card and the passport on a computer. "Is this your final destination?"

"Yes."

"Travelling alone?"

"Yes."

"Business or pleasure today?"

"Pleasure."

"Where are you staying?"

She reeled off the address of the Dulles Radisson hotel.

He gave her a look as if to say, "Really?" Instead, he said, "On your own?"

"I'm meeting someone." That seemed to do it. Something akin to understanding crossed his face. She added, "My boyfriend."

He smiled then checked that she wouldn't be trying to find work and wouldn't overstay. Satisfied, he handed back the passport. "Hope you feel better soon, Mrs Roberts," he said, and raised a single eyebrow.

Oops! A married woman meeting a boyfriend. No wonder he had smiled. Embarrassed, she pulled the rucksack over one shoulder and headed for Customs, handing over the card that affirmed she didn't have any dairy products or nuclear missiles. She walked to the frosted glass exit doors expecting a shout at any moment. Fifteen yards seemed like a hundred, but then she was through the doors and confronting a sea of expectant faces.

Kate had looked at Boomer's photograph in the arrivals lounge. How old was it? Would she recognize him? She walked along the line, scanning male faces. Nothing registered. Then she saw the sign. A man was holding it like a taxi driver meeting someone from the flight. The sign said, "Darcy Roberts."

He looked at her and she nodded, serious. He started to walk towards the end of the barrier to meet her.

She headed in the same direction. At the end of the barrier she turned to meet him. What the...? Where had he gone?

She walked back, this time on the other side of the barrier. What was he wearing—grey top and jeans? Light brown hair and over six foot tall.

Just as despair began to tweak the edge of her thoughts, she spotted him. He stood by the washrooms, his hand on his brow, looking straight at her. He made a small motion, beckoning her.

As she approached, he turned his back to her but pushed a carrier bag into her hand.

"Put these on," he said.

She took the bag uncertainly and stepped into the washroom. In the bag was a black wig, baseball cap and a loose-fitting blue raincoat. She put them on and stepped outside once more.

He'd moved. Again she scanned for him and saw him by the exit door, again watching her.

As she approached, he walked away and she scurried to catch him. A pace behind, she said, "Where's Danny?"

"Not here," he said. "Just follow me. We'll talk in the car. I need to get you somewhere safe."

Reluctantly she let him guide her outside, across a road, towards a car park. At a silver-blue Volvo estate, he opened the rear door and helped her off with the bag. He threw it in then opened the passenger door for her.

She stood, hand on the door, and looked him in the eyes. "I'm not getting in until you tell me what's going on."

"Danny couldn't make it so he asked me to pick you up. I'm Matt. Now, can we get going?"

Kate didn't move. "How do I know I can trust you?"

"Who else are you going to trust?"

She shook her head, removed her hand from the door.

He put his hand on her back and pushed slightly. "Get in!"

She twisted away. "No!"

"Shit!" he said, "Look, Danny contacted you first via Facebook then through secure webmail. You both saved messages to the Drafts folder. I'd only know that if he had told me. Right?"

She shrugged, struggling.

He said, "Stop thinking and let's go!"

She climbed in, but there was still an uncomfortable gnawing in her gut. "So you are taking me to Danny?"

"Sure." Matt started up and reversed out of the parking space. "Let me get out of here and I'll tell you more. OK?"

She sat impatiently, her legs crossed, her right foot tapping. Matt left the car park, but instead of following signs to Washington and the Toll Road, he took another route. He followed Sully Road, eventually coming out on the Interstate.

When he headed east on the I-66 she said, "So where are we going? You're not taking me to Washington."

"No. We're going to a safe house near The Plains."

"And Danny'll be there?"

"Yes."

She sat in silence, studying the route. The gnawing in her stomach was still there but she was committed, and, as he'd pointed out, who else could she turn to?"

At exit ramp 31, he turned off and drove to The Plains. But he didn't stop there. He continued through a forest road, finally turning right and looping around until he reached a cabin by a green lake. A very remote spot, she decided. There was no sign of any other vehicle or anyone else around. The mouse in her stomach became a large rat. "When's Danny coming?" she asked as he parked under a lean-to.

He didn't respond but climbed out and pulled her bag from the back seat.

She followed him to the side door. It was unlocked and he walked inside. When she went in, Matt stood in a kitchen by a boiling kettle.

"Coffee?"

She struck what her sister would have called her petulant pose. "I'm not happy," she said.

"I realize that," he said. There was less abruptness in his voice now, less tension. "Let's have a cup of coffee and we can talk." He pointed to a room across the lounge. "There's a clean towel in the bathroom. Why don't you freshen up while I make the coffee? You must feel grubby after the flight."

She accepted his invitation. The bathroom was basic but clean. The towel smelled fresh. She removed the baseball cap, wig and coat. Then she splashed her face and neck, dried and retied her hair. When she came back into the lounge Matt was sitting in a chair. A large cafetiere was on a coffee table with two mugs. He pressed the plunger and served.

"No milk I'm afraid, but there's creamer. I have sweetener too if you need it."

"As it comes is fine." She dropped the disguise on the seat, sat down and blew on the steaming cup. She breathed in the aroma and took a careful sip. It helped. She began to feel a bit more calm. "So how long before Danny gets here?"

Matt picked up his own mug and took a gulp. He fixed Kate with a look that was somewhere between intrigue and sadness.

"Danny's not coming," he said.

She put her head in her hands. Somehow she had guessed. Her mouth finally started to articulate the thoughts running through her head. But Matt cut her off.

"I'm a friend," he said.

"You're still not telling me anything. What's your connection with Danny?"

Matt reclined on the sofa, looking relaxed for the first time. "It's complicated," he said. "And I'm not sure how much I should tell you, for your own good. I think it best that you tell me everything you know, everything that has happened, and I'll fill in the missing pieces."

Kate shook her head. "Why should I—"

"Because I'm here to help."

"All you've done so far is scare the life out of me with your cloak-and-dagger routine!"

Now it was Matt's turn to shake his head. "You told me you were in danger," he said. "Remember the email? You told me your friend and two others were dead. That you thought an Arab was the killer and I took that to mean you were afraid he was after you. And you mentioned the police. That all sounds pretty serious."

"Wait a minute. That was you emailing me—not Danny?"

"Yes. You hadn't heard of me, so I thought it wise to contact you using the name you knew."

"You lied!"

He held up his hands—guilty as charged. "And you're not really Darcy Roberts are you! Look, we do what we have to do. And you were in danger. I didn't want to take any chances."

"And I'm taking a huge chance on trusting you!"

"Look, I must be a friend. How else would I know the password numbers you found? Where were they by the way?"

"On my cat's name tag," she said uncertainly.

"Six... one... one... zero... eight... nine..." he began.

Kate had committed the number to memory in four groups of three. As Matt recited the code she played it back in her head. *Yes, that's it.* But then she realized something. "But of course you know them. You were accessing the website."

"True, but first of all it proves that it was me you were communicating with. And second of all I knew Joe had left you the numbers. I just didn't know where is all." He looked at her and she read honesty in his face.

"OK," she said. "So what do they mean?"

He smiled. "Tell me your story, and that's one of the pieces I can explain."

FIFTY

Thirty-one months earlier

Boomer removed Mirrorman's vest. Underneath was soaked. "I need a light here," he said. A torch came on and he tore the material away from the wound. "Hang in there, Mirrorman. It's just a flesh wound."

The truck continued to bounce and jolt over the stone-littered ground. Then suddenly there was a thump and it became smoother. They were on the road. It ran from the town of Rafha towards, but not all the way, to the border. "Just twenty-five klicks to Iraq," Boomer said to Mirrorman. "The other side is twenty-five klicks away." He tore open a pack of QuikClot and poured the powder over the wound.

Mirrorman jerked with the sharp pain.

Boomer checked for the exit hole and found none.

Mirrorman already knew: The bullet was still inside.

Boomer placed a pad over the wound and Mirrorman held it in place. Mirrorman said, "Feels real bad, Boomer."

Topcat held a satphone to his ear. "Cobra to Mongoose. Cobra to Mongoose. Break."

There was static on the line and then: "...Mongoose... status report."

"We have the package. Kilo Indigo Alpha Dogtag. Whisky Indigo Alpha Mirrorman. On way to extraction site. Break."

Static.

Topcat repeated the message three times.

Tinman said, "Jamming comms?"

"Or just interference. I'll try—"

But the command sergeant didn't finish his sentence. The truck's front right wheel hit a landmine, crumpling the cab and throwing the vehicle onto its side. Excruciating pain burned from Topcat's legs. They were trapped under the side of the truck. "Get this fucker off of me!" he growled. Four pairs of hands pushed at the truck and he dragged himself out.

Boomer said, "You OK, Boss?"

Topcat took a sharp intake of breath and felt below his knees. One leg shattered. The other badly damaged. "Shit!" he said. "Check everyone else."

"Hey," Mirrorman shouted. "The prisoner is running."

Tinman shone the torch into the desert and picked up a figure running. Boomer took off after him.

It didn't take long for Boomer to close the gap and tackle the man. They sprawled in the dust. Boomer got up and pulled the prisoner to his feet. The tape had come free from his mouth.

"You stupid Americans," the prisoner said, spitting his words. "You have no idea what is going on."

As Boomer dragged him back to the truck, the man said, "A landmine. Where do you think that came from? Do you think my people put landmines in our own roads? Ha!"

"Shut up," Boomer said, pushing him to the floor beside Topcat.

Topcat took out his Glock and pressed it into the prisoner's side, to make sure the man knew it was there, knew the implication.

"You may as well shoot me," the prisoner said.

Tinman was talking: "Gopher. Where's Gopher?"

"Here," Gopher called from the far side of the vehicle, his voice strained with effort. "I'm OK, just a bit dazed." He crawled around the back and squatted next to Topcat.

"Fuck!" he said, glancing down. "Can you walk, Boss?"

"Legs are fucked. We'll have to wait it out. I'll keep trying command. They'll be looking for us soon. We can be evac'd from here."

"We're still in Saudi," Tinman said. "So much for *Black in, Black out!*"

"Lights!" Boomer said. In the distance, from the direction of Iraq, a set of headlights bounced their way.

"Whoo hoo!" Tinman thumped his side. "Didn't take 'em long."

The prisoner said to Topcat, "Shoot me, you may as well. They don't want any of us alive."

Topcat prodded the man with the Glock. "What the fuck are you talking about?"

"That landmine was planted just for you. Who do you think put it there? Who knew you were coming for me?"

"Shut the fuck up!" Tinman said. "You ragheads are full of bullshit."

The headlights were two hundred yards away, the vehicle not slowing. Tinman stood up and moved around to the truck's cab. He flashed the torch in the direction of the oncoming vehicle. It flashed back, but still didn't slow.

"What the—" Tinman started but his final words gurgled in his throat. Automatic fire strafed the truck.

Mirrorman pulled himself up, Boomer beside him. Topcat rolled beside the tailgate. All three returned fire.

The vehicle didn't stop but continued past them, bullets spraying the air as it went.

Out of range, it stopped. The firing stopped.

"Sound off," Topcat called. Tinman didn't respond.

Boomer found Tinman collapsed, dead against the rear axle.

"They're back!" Mirrorman called, and they dived for cover as bullets fizzed around them.

Gopher shouted something above the noise, maybe that the prisoner was running.

"Leave him!" Topcat said, but Gopher was already up and after him. When the bullets stopped, Boomer found both men spreadeagled in the dirt. The prisoner moved. Gopher would never move himself again.

"Shit!" Boomer said, turning Gopher over and then pulling the prisoner out of the dust.

The man was muttering.

As Boomer brought him back, Topcat grabbed at the Arab and slammed him against the load bed. "Who the hell were they?" he barked. "Al-Qaeda?"

"They're yours," the prisoner said. "You really have no idea, do you?"

Topcat peeled off some tape and stuck it over the prisoner's mouth. "Enough of your crap," he grunted.

"They'll be coming back," Mirrorman said, "circling around."

Topcat: "Boomer, watch front. I'll cover the rear. Mirrorman, watch ahead."

They put on the night goggles.

Topcat picked up the satphone, listened. "Still too much noise."

After a few minutes of aching silence, Boomer said, "A bandit at five o'clock."

A few breaths later, Topcat said, "I've got two—forty yards out—both crawling, one directly behind. One at nine o'clock. On my mark." He counted three and both men fired and ducked back as the attackers responded.

"They're pulling back," Topcat said after the gunfire ended. He rolled over, ignoring the terrible pain in his legs. We're sitting ducks here and they're bound to come round and go for the fuel tank. We need to move. Mirrorman, can you walk?"

"I'll manage."

"Boomer, you'll have to help me. There are rocks—what, fifty yards out? We'll get to them."

Boomer took hold of a strip of tarpaulin. There was rope attached for tying it down to the truck sides. He helped Topcat onto the tarpaulin and then took hold of the ropes. Checking it was clear, he nodded to Mirrorman. "Let's go."

They were three-quarters of the way there when the gunfire started. The attackers were in the jeep again, heading straight for them as they struggled across the open desert. Dust began to kick-up all around and the soldiers threw themselves onto the ground. The prisoner dashed for the rocks. He screamed and fell just short.

"Keep going," Boomer said. All three returned fire. Mirrorman didn't move, but continued to train his fire on the approaching jeep. Topcat howled, his rifle dropped. At the same time, Boomer got to his feet. He cocked his arm and threw a grenade.

Mirrorman lost sight of it in the darkness and dust, but he imagined it sailing the incredible distance—the throw of a pro quarterback.

The jeep lit up and jumped a fraction before Mirrorman heard the explosion. When it landed it exploded again as the fuel ignited. The crash to the ground and double roll created the last noise. Silence flooded in. Then Mirrorman heard Boomer's moans.

He got up and moved over to his friend, the gun still aimed towards the burning jeep.

He was badly hit. Topcat lay close by, not moving. In the orange glow, Mirrorman could see immediately that the command sergeant was dead.

"I've still got it, Mirrorman," Boomer said, his voice far away.

"Hell of a throw, buddy," Mirrorman said. He cradled Boomer's head. Blood stuck his fingers to his friend's hair. Head wound. Mirrorman could see blood glisten like black gold on his friend's body. His own pain forgotten, he looked into Boomer's eyes. "I've got you buddy. Stay with me. Stay focused on my eyes."

Boomer coughed and took a ragged breath.

Mirrorman said, "Boomer, you aren't here. Remember your red Chevvy. We had great fun in that, didn't we? Remember those smart girls we met from ULA? You dog, took them both! I spent the night in that bar on my own. Remember that hike up to Machu Picchu? Think of that view when we finally got there, the beautiful jungle, the amazing temples, the exotic..." His voice snagged in his throat. He held back tears.

Boomer's eyes had frozen, his jagged breathing stopped.

Danny Guice was dead.

FIFTY-ONE

Present day

Detective Sergeant Littlewood stood outside Kate's maisonette as the uniformed police forced the door. It was almost 2pm, and she was hungry. She could smell food from a string of takeaways nearby. It didn't help the rumble in her stomach. In a sense she was hopeful the boss was right and this would be quick—that it was a wild goose chase. Maybe.

"Is there something wrong?" A voice from behind—an elderly lady with a stick.

"Police," Littlewood said in a monotone.

"I can see that," the lady said without any potential sarcasm. "I was just concerned there was a problem. Is Kate all right?"

"You're a neighbour?"

"I live downstairs—number nine."

"If you wouldn't mind..." Littlewood said with a nod towards the lady's front door. "Once we've taken a look around inside, I might come and ask you some questions."

The elderly lady pulled a concerned face but obliged by walking towards her door. Littlewood went into Kate Blakemore's apartment where the uniforms were already

245

searching. There wasn't much to go through on the first floor and, as the men progressed upstairs, Littlewood was about to follow when her phone rang.

Inspector Mather said, "Found anything incriminating?"

"Only just got in, sir. It's a small place though, so won't take us too long. Her car is here but there's no sign of her."

"I still think it's a long shot. She ran because she was spooked."

"Spooked because she was the last person to speak to Ms Harper and we matched her fingerprints to the glass in the victim's house. She might not be registered for a firearm but she said her ex was US military. If we find any evidence she has had a weapon here, I'd say she'll look very guilty."

"I'll eat my hat."

There was a noise from upstairs. Littlewood said, "Hang on a minute, sir. Looks like we may have found something." She looked up the second flight of stairs. One of the policemen was coming down a ladder from an attic. He held a pencil. From the pencil dangled a handgun.

"Sir, time to put some seasoning on your hat—there *is* a gun here."

Mather knocked on the window of the patrol car. The policeman at the wheel looked out, saw who it was, and opened the door.

Mather said, "Any sign of Kate Blakemore?"

"None, sir. Yesterday I followed the sister into Reading. When I returned there was the other car—the blue VW Touareg Ms Blakemore was last seen driving." He pointed to the car parked on the driveway of a house a little further along the street.

"The sister's car," Littlewood said as she stepped beside the inspector.

Mather said, "How did it get there?"

The policeman shrugged. "No idea—could have been dropped off or the husband could have collected it from somewhere."

"And what's happened today?"

"Mr Roberts left at 06:33 on his own in a grey BMW 530 estate." Again he quoted the registration plate. "Registered to a lease company. Company car. Mrs Roberts left at 08:21 with the two children. As instructed, I stayed here. Mrs Roberts returned at 17:40 this evening."

Mather looked at his watch. It was 6:13pm. "OK, Sergeant, let's go and speak to Mrs Roberts." He strode with a little more purpose than he felt, reached the front door of the modern detached four-bed. Nice house, nice village. He rang the bell.

A woman, who from her looks was clearly Kate's sister, answered the door. A young child clung to her leg. It had a snotty nose and had been crying. "Yes?"

"Mrs Darcy Roberts?" Mather asked. When Darcy confirmed who she was, Mather continued, "Police, madam." He held up his warrant card and introduced them. "Please can we come inside?"

The woman hesitated as though considering her options then stepped aside and opened the door further. She picked the child up and carried her into the kitchen. There she pointed to the aged pine chairs around a similarly styled table. She looked as though she hadn't slept, and when she said, "What's this about?" she failed to be convincing.

Mather said, "I think you know what it's about, Mrs Roberts. It's about your sister. Is she here?"

"No."

Littlewood tapped her pocket. "We need to take her in for questioning regarding the murder of Ms Stephanie Harper and the suspicious death of Kate's friend, Sarah Wishart."

Colour drained from Darcy's face. She put the child down. "Go and watch a DVD with India, please, Emmy." Then, turning back to the detectives, she said, "There's no way Kate had anything to do with the deaths of those women."

Mather cocked his head slightly then watched for Darcy's reaction. "The evidence suggests otherwise. Your sister lied to us about seeing Ms Wishart in Prague shortly before her death. She lied to us about knowing who Ms Harper was then she went to see her. And was again the last person to see her before she was murdered."

"But she never—"

Mather held up his hand. "We know she was in touch with Ms Harper. She called her first and then she was in her house. Her fingerprints were matched to a glass. The next day she returned to the scene—possibly to retrieve the incriminating evidence but she was too late. We were already there. We searched your sister's apartment in Windsor." He read Darcy's reaction and said, "Yes, we had a warrant to search it—and discovered a firearm."

Darcy stood up, shock, disbelief, indignation perhaps on her face. "No way did she have a gun. No way did she kill anyone."

Littlewood said, "Sit down, Mrs Roberts."

Darcy sat, but the expression remained.

"This afternoon, Ballistics confirmed that the gun found was the one used to shoot Miss Harper."

"Then it must have been planted!" Defiance now.

Mather said, "I haven't discounted that possibility— that's why she must come in for questioning. If she is innocent we can help. If she continues to evade us, it only serves to make her look guilty."

"She is innocent," Darcy said with total conviction.

"So where is she?"

Darcy said nothing but her face showed she knew.

"Of course, you realize that it is an offence to obstruct the course of justice. If you are harbouring or aiding a suspect you will be prosecuted."

The kitchen door opened and Tim Roberts stepped into the house. He showed no great surprise at the presence of two detectives in his kitchen. He put a laptop on the work surface and introduced himself.

Mather provided a quick run through of the situation and Mr Roberts looked at him impassively. However, when the detective mentioned Darcy accompanying them to the police station, Tim said, "Can I have a moment to talk to my wife in private?"

Darcy and Tim retreated to the hall and shut the door. A few minutes later Tim returned, closing the door and sitting down.

"Kate is in the States looking for Joe, her ex-boyfriend. You know about him?"

Mather said, "We do." He looked at the sergeant.

Littlewood said, "She has a friend looking after her cat and he told the old lady downstairs. So we already suspected she was heading for America, we just don't know where."

"She flew to Washington this morning on a BA flight from Heathrow."

"Which airport? What time?" Mather asked, urgency adding a catch to his voice for the first time.

"Dulles. Left at 10:50 and arrived 13:40 local time."

Mather checked his watch and snatched up his phone, made a call. He passed the information to the person on the other end. Still with the phone to his ear he spoke to Tim. "Was she travelling under her name?"

Tim hesitated then said, "No, my wife's."

Mather showed no surprise, just relayed the information. He waited, listening. Finally, he said, "All right, alert the authorities. And, Pete... get the description of the Arab guy over to Homeland Security too... yeah the one Ms Blakemore provided." He ended the call and looked back at Tim. "We were too late to pick her up at the airport. You did the right thing telling us. If she is innocent—"

"Oh, she is."

"As I said, then it's best for all that we clear this up and get the real criminal."

"The Arab."

Littlewood asked, "Did you or your wife see anyone that could have been this Arab person, the one Ms Blakemore believes broke into her house?"

Tim shook his head. "What about the airline ticket issue?"

Mather said, "Well, that is aiding and abetting a suspect, but for the moment we'll see how things develop. Let's hope for your sake that she is found and we can confirm her innocence."

"She is going to text us to let us know she's there safely."

"Is she using the same phone?"

"No. Well, maybe, but she took the SIM card out. It'll be a different number, if that's what you mean."

"Thank you." Mather reached forward and shook Tim's hand. "I know this must be very difficult for you. When she gets in touch tell her to contact me."

"I will."

Mather let go of Tim's hand, satisfied. "And if she suspects she is in danger she should hand herself into the police."

Security Officer Weaver sat at a bank of screens in his command centre in Dulles International Airport. Beside him, Special Agent Michelle Ramirez studied the screen showing the arrivals hall.

"OK, that's her—that's Kate Blakemore in arrivals."

"Early. Must have come straight through," Weaver said. "Look, only a backpack. No hold luggage." Then he stated the obvious: "Someone's here to meet her."

"She's looking along the line. Yes! Now she's spotted someone." They tracked Kate to the end of the barrier and saw the confusion on her face.

Weaver sniffed then said, "Mistake? Did she see someone or not?"

Ramirez said nothing but watched closely. Kate was seen to head back along the line, searching. Then she did a sudden turn and walked to the washrooms.

Women! Weaver smirked.

"Zoom in on the washroom and fast-forward until she comes out," Ramirez said.

They watched the tape at double speed. Weaver stopped it a couple of times by mistake then continued. After ten minutes Ramirez said, "Where the crap is she?"

"Shall I go back?"

"Yeah, let's go through, normal speed."

Weaver wiped his nose and restarted the clip. Ramirez leaned in and he was distracted for a moment by the line of her breast. *Nice figure under that suit.*

"There!" Ramirez said and pointed.

Weaver's attention snapped back. "I don't see her."

"Black wig and baggy blue coat. She's disguised herself. But she's still carrying the backpack."

Smart too, this special agent.

"Where's she gone?"

Weaver picked up the woman in a wig on another camera. *See, I'm not so dumb either.* "Camera eighteen covers exit C," he said, but was disappointed she didn't seem impressed as he reset the time and picked up the woman going through the door. "She's heading for the car park."

"Cameras there?"

"On it." He switched again and now they were looking at a bird's-eye view of a parking lot. Lots of movement, cars pulling in and out, people with luggage.

"What's going on there?" Ramirez asked, and he zoomed in, still too far out for detail. Two people seemed to be arguing. A woman with black hair had her hand on the doorframe of a silver car, but her posture said a refusal to get in. The other was a man, brown hair. Then confirmation. The man threw a bag on to the rear seat before they both got in.

The car, a station wagon, backed out.

"What sort of vehicle is that?"

"Volvo—XC model, I'd say." He gave the agent a smile as she glanced at him, impressed. "Hey, what can I say? I know my cars."

"Good. Now anything we can do to improve the quality. I need that plate."

Weaver flicked to another screen and set the time. The exit barriers. Within a few seconds the Volvo appeared, now clearly a silvery blue, the registration plate easy to read.

"Local car," Weaver said. "Probably not going far."

She patted his shoulder then held her phone to her ear. "And they won't get very far either."

FIFTY-TWO

As Kate told her story she paced the room, finally standing at the patio doors overlooking decking. At one time this might have been landscaped, but after a short patch of something akin to a garden it became wild, long grass and bushes. Beyond, the lake glinted in the afternoon sun. The woods on the far side, with their splash of autumn leaves, reminded her of the last day with Joe walking through Windsor Great Park. All of a sudden she felt drained.

Matt stood beside her. "Thank you," he said. "I needed to know the full picture. What I'm going to tell you may come as a shock, but the reality is that it changes nothing. You are looking for Joe and I can help you."

She turned to him and this time read concern in his eyes. "What is it?" A pain welled in her chest as she waited for Matt's response, time stretching. Was he going to say Joe was dead? Was that it? He could help find his grave?

Matt said something. It didn't register.

"What?"

"Danny Guice is dead. He has been for two years."

She staggered back to the sofa. She felt relief tinged with guilt. "So Joe's alive?"

"As far as I know."

"And your connection with Danny? You said he was your friend."

"No. I said I was *a friend*. I know Joe. I never really knew Danny."

"So Joe sent you?"

"In a manner of speaking. I was waiting for you to make contact with me."

Her head buzzed with a thousand questions, but she let Matt talk and bit her tongue.

He continued: "The document you found had my contact details not Danny's. I don't know why you received the photograph of Danny. Maybe, as you said, Peter Sikorski sent it from Prague. I don't know everything—just that I expected to hear from you. When you started posting messages about Danny, a search algorithm picked it up. Joe must have known you might try that. Maybe it was a backup plan in case you didn't find the document in the calendar."

"You still haven't explained the numbers."

"It has rotational symmetry."

"I don't understand."

"611089680119. Rotate the block and you get 611089680119. Use any combination of these numbers and then repeat them in reverse. Joe was into that sort of thing—cryptology, it's called. I think he liked it because it was a bit like reflectional symmetry, or mirror images. Also, reversing is an old trick. Did you know that in the Second World War British POWs used to write dates or phrases backwards in letters? It told the Intelligence Services—MI9—"

"MI9? Surely there's just MI5 and 6."

Matt shrugged. "The Brits used to have a whole bunch of departments—up to MI19, but you're right, it's just the two main ones nowadays. MI9 was disbanded after the Second World War, or got merged into another department. Point is, reversing something meant there was a coded message or other meaning. A reversed sequence of numbers therefore meant a code. He left you the document but it was encrypted. That won't be it. It's too blatant. There will have been another way to find him—a simpler message but less obvious unless you know where to look." He looked at her expectantly. "Can you think of anything?"

Kate pulled her handbag from the rucksack. "There's this photograph," she said, handing over the picture of her and Joe.

"Dare or truth. The expression is, usually, truth or dare, isn't it?"

"So there is a hidden message?"

"I hope so." He took it into the kitchen and she saw him take a bottle from a cupboard and put drops on the paper, then moved it to and fro, finally blowing on it. He then walked through the lounge into a bedroom and she heard a hairdryer for a few seconds. When Matt returned, there was a grin on his face.

"Success!" he said, handing the photograph back. On the reverse was a series of brown numbers. He was still grinning. "Did you know that the word 'cryptology' comes from Greek, meaning 'hidden writing'?"

The numbers were:
1 4 0 1 5 1 4 8 3 3 6 0 6 0 6 9 7 1 6 4 1 4 5 1 7 5 1 9 1 0 9 2 4 9 5 1

At the bottom of the page was a smiley.

"What does the code mean?"

"I have no idea." He went to a drawer and pulled out a pad of paper and a pencil. He wrote the numbers down then on a separate sheet wrote the numbers one to twenty-six in a column. Beside these he wrote the alphabet and then translated the numbers from the photograph. Having done this he wrote the numbers out in a square and stared at the letters. He said, "Sometimes

255

the letters aren't sequential. Since there are thirty-six it might be in blocks of six and then be read vertically." He shrugged. "But I can't see anything here." With that, he moved all the letters by one. Nothing sequential or vertically in the square.

By the time Matt had progressed through the whole alphabet in this fashion, Kate was finding it hard to concentrate.

"If you yawn one more time, I swear you'll put me to sleep," Matt said.

"Time difference is catching up with me. I'm struggling here."

He smiled. "Not the most exciting thing to watch. This could take hours so I suggest you get some sleep. Before you go, are there any words or phrases that he might have used. Cryptologists often use these first rather than have the sequential alphabet."

"*I dare you*, was a password he used. Maybe my name… or *Tolkien*, the name of my cat."

Matt wrote this down. "Both good, neither has repeated letters, which makes it simpler. What about a favourite book? Tolkien, that suggests *Lord of the Rings*."

"*Pride and Prejudice*."

"Hmm, OK, worth a go. Try and think of some more while you're resting."

"But you'll wake me if you crack it?"

"Sure. There're three bedrooms. Take your pick."

Kate chose a room with a vanity table and chair then quickly got ready. As she passed from the bathroom to the bedroom, she noted Matt had refilled the cafetiere and was frantically scribbling. Back in the room, she closed the door, moved the chair over to it and jammed the back under the handle. It wouldn't stop someone intent on getting in but it would at least wake her. Some comfort! She crashed on top of the covers and, within minutes, was fast asleep.

She awoke in the middle of the night with a start, her heart pounding. Bad dream or a noise? She lay hardly breathing, listening for something. It was so quiet. Living in Windsor, she was used to aircraft and the constant hum of the distant motorway. Here the silence was so absolute it made her uncomfortable. You can tune noise out but silence had a way of filling space, the way darkness seemed to fill space left by light.

Unable to relax, she decided to get up. The chair was still in place under the door handle and she removed it as quietly as possible then crept into the dark lounge. Turning on the light, she saw Matt had been through the whole pad. His early attempts were obvious—converting the digits into between one and twenty-six so that they could be converted into letters.

She stared at the results like she supposed Matt had. An anagram? Foreign words? Nothing obvious jumped out, and she noted the large number of awkward consonants.

He repeated this many painstaking times, staggering the conversion letters and circling any words that made sense. However it was only ever single words or abbreviations, no full sentence saying, "Here I am!"

What had started so clinically looked like it had degenerated into random guesses. Then he tried putting the numbers in a six by six square and began again with the conversion of numbers to letters, working his way through the alphabet. Then he seemed to transpose the square and start again.

On one page he had scrawled:

Why numbers not letters?

*

Keeping as quiet as possible, Kate showered and made herself a pot of coffee. Then she sat on the floor with all of Matt's attempts around her. When he'd found a word he'd circled it. Most were English, but occasionally there were other languages, mostly Spanish, she suspected. She knew Joe could speak Czech. Could he speak other languages too?

On a number of pages, Matt had scribbled notes.

Polybius Square—but not 1 to 5?

0 to 4 and 5 to 9 can't be right. Try double.

Then the numbers had been split halfway and the second half placed below the first and then he'd tried converting these into letters again. Nothing appeared to make any sense.

His notes said:

Problem with the Z's. Could this be a triple-level code?

There were a few pages of tables converting one letter to another, sequentially A becoming B, Z becoming A. Still making no real progress, he had written:

What's the key?!

This must be how the Enigma codebreakers at Bletchley felt before they got the captured machine, Kate thought. Surely Joe wouldn't make it so complicated would he? *I'm missing something obvious, I know it,* Kate kept saying to herself. Her eyes started to ache and she closed them for a while, wondering what the key word could be. And was there a significance to the numbers? Could it be something to do with symmetry? What was Joe telling her?

"Good morning."

Matt's voice jolted Kate from her sleep. She was slumped on the sofa, paper strewn all around. Her mouth felt and tasted like it was stuffed with sawdust and her head throbbed.

She forced her eyes open and groaned.

Matt handed her a glass of water. "Advil," he said. "May help with that headache."

Reflexively, she took the tablets and washed them down. Then in a moment of panic she wondered what the tablets really were.

Matt was studying her and shook his head, irony in his tight smile. "Still don't trust me, eh? I promise they were just Advil for your head. I *am* here to help. I promise."

After a hesitation, she nodded meekly. "Yeah, sorry. Did you have any luck making sense of the numbers?" she asked, pointing to the papers.

"No, I think we need two things. First of all a computer, and second of all someone who has the skill to use it." He read her next question before she articulated it. "Yes, I know someone who has both. Did you think of any other key words or phrases—anything at all, no matter how remote a possibility?"

"Well, you could try: Windsor, Laughing Train, possibly The Laughing Train. I don't know."

"Anything around about the time he knew he was going to have to leave the message?"

"Maybe: Windsor Great Park, parrots, deer, the Queen, Windsor Castle." She shrugged. "Changing the Guard, or Mounting the Guard, I suppose. Oh, the week before... Henley, Marlow. There is a pub in Henley called The Idle Hour. And there's my favourite pub, The Two Brewers, near the castle in Windsor."

Matt wrote all these words down and nodded, impressed. "Quite a bit to go on. I'm sure Myron will be able to run through these in no time."

"Sorry, who's Myron?"

"A cryptologist friend." He headed for the kitchen. "I'll fix up some breakfast and I'll go see him. Shouldn't be long. You all right with that as a plan?"

Kate stretched and shrugged. "It's better than anything I can come up with." Then, sounding serious, she added, "But I'm coming with you."

FIFTY-THREE

Thirty-one months earlier

Mirrorman held Boomer for a long time. Gradually he realized his lack of movement was due as much to his own weakness as it was his grief. His chest injury was bleeding again and the burn in his right leg told him of another wound. The flames from the jeep were fading and the faintest hint of pale blue appeared on the horizon. Maybe an hour to sunrise.

He tied a tourniquet on his right thigh then checked Boomer and the command sergeant for a Medikit, but found nothing. From the command sergeant he took the satphone.

"Cobra to Mongoose. Cobra to Mongoose." Noise. Mirrorman continued anyway. "Kilo Indigo Alpha Topcat, Dogtag, Tinman, Gopher, Boomer. Whisky Indigo Alpha Mirrorman. Repeat five Kilo Indigo Alpha. With the package. Emergency extraction requested. Break." He listened to the static and repeated the message before putting the phone away.

Struggling now, his fingers both trembling and stiff, he pulled out the codebook and checked for today's emergency extraction symbol. Then he gradually made something, using clothes and equipment, that he hoped would be picked up by the satellite—as long as they were looking.

When he had finished he took hold of Boomer and tugged him. Got to get him to the rocks, out of the sun, he told himself. Then come back for the command sergeant. He took four paces and stopped, two paces, stopped, then gasped for air as a searing pain shot through his chest. He gritted his teeth and looked at the rocks. Maybe twenty-five more paces. He began to walk again, two paces and rest. Soon he was taking one pace and rest.

By the time he reached the rocks, the sky had a gentle arc of morning light. There was blood on the rocks, lots of it. The prisoner. Then Mirrorman saw the Arab. He was sitting in a shallow cave watching.

"Help me," Mirrorman said with effort.

The prisoner didn't respond.

Mirrorman tried to pull Boomer through the rocks, but something snagged and the extra effort made him sink to his knees, coughing. Specks of blood appeared. He could pull Boomer no further without help. When he felt he could move again he crawled to the cave.

The prisoner hadn't moved, and although he watched, his eyes didn't move and his head hung, his posture limp. Even in the poor light, Mirrorman could see the man sat in a dark patch, his blood soaking into the sand.

Mirrorman crawled into the hole and finally the man's eyes shifted towards him but stayed strangely unfocused. When the Arab spoke, the tone was bitter, the voice a thousand miles away. "You are fools." A long pause. "You would never... get me back. Too much..." Again a long pause, and his head rocked back on an unsupportive neck, like a young baby's. The prisoner took a breath and refocused. "He wouldn't dare... risk it."

Mirrorman propped himself opposite. What was the prisoner talking about? He managed to pull water from a pack, took a sip. Then he reached out and poured some into the Arab's mouth.

The man nodded his gratitude. "We are... both dying, my friend... And for what?" Another long pause and a suggestion of a smile on the Arab's lips. "For who?"

Although Mirrorman's brain was fogged by pain and blood loss, he wanted the Arab to talk. He wanted to understand. And using his mind would keep him from slipping away, may keep him alive.

"Tell me," he said.

The Arab tried to shake his head. "You wouldn't... understand."

"Doesn't matter."

A real smile this time. "No it doesn't." A series of shallow breaths then: "I am a prince." He said a name, thick with Arabic that Mirrorman vaguely recognized.

"You are al-Qaeda." Intel confirmed the man organized attacks in Iraq.

The Arab shrugged ever so slightly. "Of course... your people have known... and do nothing... because..." The prince's eyes hardened. "...it is in his interest."

"Who?"

By the time the Arab prince drew his final breath, he hadn't told Mirrorman everything. But he'd told him enough.

FIFTY-FOUR

Present day

Matt removed the fake registration plate fixed over a genuine one.

Kate arched an eyebrow.

"Can't be too careful," he said. "The police might be looking for you—just in case they spotted me pick you up."

"I'm impressed, but please don't ask me to put on that itchy wig again."

"No, I think we should be fine now, so long as... we don't do something stupid." She noted that he almost said, *you* don't do something stupid.

He followed the lake road to the highway and then on to the I-66. For most of the journey she sat in silence watching the stream of cars, always amazed at how there could be so many cars on the road during the day. No wonder everywhere clogged up during rush hour.

Her mind kept going back to the numbers. She had kept the original photograph and pulled it from her handbag. Could staring at the numbers make the answer jump out? *Come on, Joe, what are you telling me?*

The smiley was a little odd. Joe wasn't one of those people that felt obliged to enliven their texts and emails with smiling or sad faces. It was out of character.

Eventually she said, "Where in Washington are we going?"

"Merrifield, not far from Arlington."

"There's bound to be an internet café somewhere near, isn't there? While you're with Myron, I'll go on the internet."

"I don't think that's wise."

"Why not? I won't use my name. No one can trace me. What's the risk?"

"I guess... Why do you need to get on the web?"

Kate waved the photograph. "Here's the thing: the message is for me. I'm no good with crypto-mathingy. Puzzles maybe, but the techniques you've been trying are totally alien to me. And I'm certainly no maths genius. Surely it's simple."

"But Joe wanted me to help and he knows I have friends who do this for a living. In fact, don't you know someone too?"

"Sort of, but not really. Maybe my friend Andrew could have cracked it. I don't know, I just feel the need to try."

Matt pursed his lips, thinking, clearly uncomfortable. However, by the time he parked he'd decided. "We just passed an internet café two blocks back. It's called *Cyber Ground.*" They got out. He locked the car and handed over the key. "I'll either meet you in there or, if you finish earlier, I'll meet you at the car."

"How long will you be?"

"I don't know, but let's say no more than an hour. If it looks like being longer, I'll come back and let you know."

★

Kate walked into *Cyber Ground* and was immediately taken by its size. In her UK experience, internet cafés were tiny, seedy joints with a handful of terminals. As she stood at reception ready to pay for an hour's access, she noticed there was a range of mobile phones with tariffs. The spotty young man behind the counter studied her. His name tag said *Harley*. If his face could say *it's-all-too-much-trouble* any more clearly, it would have been tattooed on his forehead.

Suddenly struck by the thought, she said, "Can I get a pay-as-you-go SIM for my mobile here?"

It's-all-too-much-trouble switched instantly to *what-are-you-talking-about?*

Then she twigged. She pulled out her phone. "My cell phone. Can I get a SIM for it?"

"Sure. Free with $20 airtime."

An hour on the internet was $3. She paid, inserted the SIM and sat in a booth. She logged on and immediately keyed the thirty-six-digit number into Google. At first she was excited by the large number of hits: YouTube; *Philosophical Magazine*: a journal of experimental and...; Hot Bird 6/8/9 at 13.0°E—LyngSat; DistroWatch.com; MBL—Los Angeles...; Arabic numbers—Wikipedia. The last one looked interesting. She clicked on the link and then realized it was just a page about numbers. Google was matching them in any order.

She went over to Harley. "Excuse me."

He looked up with that same *it's-all-too-much-trouble* expression.

She smiled. "I'm trying to do a search for a specific combination of numbers."

"What, like lottery numbers?" Hmm. At least there was a flicker of interest.

"Something like that. Google seems to match on any combination. Is there another search engine you'd recommend—one that looks for the specific sequence."

"No problemo. My best is *Alltheweb.com*. Just select *Exact phrase* from the *Advanced Search* options. That should match those lucky numbers." He brightened slightly. "Hey, but if you win, I want a commission."

Back in the booth she typed in the search engine, clicked on the option and entered the numbers.

No Web pages found that match your query

She tried putting spaces between the digits but it made no difference. She went back to Google and looked at the hits it had returned. Something made her suddenly remember to send a message. She switched on the iPhone to send a text to Darcy. What should she say? She typed:

Sorry I've taken so long to let you know all is OK. Being helped and making good progress. Pretty sure I'll find Joe! Hope you're OK. Love to the girls.

Then she deleted it. Tim had been insistent about a simple spam-like, coded message. If she used one of the twin's names it meant everything was fine. She typed:

Delays communicating. Use India mobile and all will be OK.

She sent it and returned her attention to the PC screen. The YouTube link was some Manchester United vs Sunderland football match statistics. The *Philosophical Magazine* was slow to load but just turned out to be statistical tables.

She thought *Hot Bird* sounded like it might be a porn site but turned out to be a satellite TV service. *DistroWatch.com* seemed to be a business card service. The very fact that she couldn't understand the page intrigued her. She searched it for a link to an address: business cards—business address? Nothing. The

MBL—Los Angeles link was similar to the YouTube one.

There were others but this approach seemed a waste of time and too random. She decided to go back to *Alltheweb.com* and try breaking up the numbers. Maybe into groups of six as Matt had done last night.

Her phone rang.

"Kate?" It was Tim.

"Probably best we don't talk," she said quietly, and immediately regretted being so brusque. After all, Tim and Darcy had gone through a lot to help her—probably were still going through it. "Sorry, Tim."

"It's OK. We need to talk."

Tim seemed to be ignoring his own advice. "What...?"

"The police have been here. They have a warrant for your arrest. It's been on the news too. They think you shot that Harper lady."

Kate started to say something but Tim continued.

"They found the gun in your flat."

It wasn't Joe's gun; he'd taken that away after she'd found it. It didn't make sense. "But I don't—"

"And your prints were on a glass at Ms Harper's. They know you were in her house."

"This is crazy. I've never been in her house!" Harley looked at her with disapproval. Kate held up her hand by way of apology and spoke quietly. "You've got to believe me. I'm being framed. I didn't go into her house and I certainly didn't kill her."

There was a pause then Tim said, "The US police will be looking for you." Another pause.

"It's all right. I suppose I knew you'd have to tell them I'd travelled here."

"Sorry, Kate, but they threatened to arrest Darcy. She's beside herself."

Kate was staring at the screen she'd started to put the first six numbers in. "I've gotta go."

"Call Inspector Mather. You can't go on the run over there. They shoot people in the States. Promise me you'll call him."

"OK, I'll call. Sorry, I've gotta go."

She ended the call and looked at the numbers she'd keyed in. Then she glanced at the code on the photograph, specifically the smiley face. *Oh my God!* She knew the meaning of the first part of the code.

FIFTY-FIVE

After leaving the airport, Ramirez had heard the All Points for the silver-blue Volvo. *May be armed, do not approach*, Dispatch had said. The voice also provided the vehicle's plate.

Idiots, Ramirez thought. The guy who met Kate Blakemore wouldn't have been so stupid as to use real plates. If he was really smart the silver-blue Volvo would be switched for another. But then again maybe he didn't know how close they were on Kate's tail.

Highways had confirmed that the car had not passed through the toll booths, so where had they gone? She'd called her partner and they'd agreed to split the search. She would cover the suburbs; he would cover the central area. Needle in a haystack, but her philosophy was: *hey, sometimes you just get lucky*.

It was 11am the next day, and after an uncomfortable night in the car, she was starting to think it was about time she got a new philosophy. She stopped in Woodbridge and got a vanilla skinny latte and bagel and enjoyed a break overlooking the state park.

She had barely started on the coffee when her phone rang. Her partner.

"Got them."

"Seriously?" She choked on her drink.

"Where?"

"Merrifield. The girl is in an internet café."

"I'll come to you."

"No. Sit tight. I'll update you." He ended the call.

Asshole! She took a final sip of coffee and tossed it into a trashcan. No way was she sitting tight. She jumped into the car and headed towards Merrifield.

The first four digits were 1401—the same number as *Runtime*—and then there was the smiley. Surely it wasn't a coincidence. It had to refer to the Laughing Train. But what was the meaning of the rest? On the Google search page she typed the next four numbers **5148**. Most of the hits seemed to relate to a chemical. Nothing attracted her attention. On the second page the words **Track flight status of 5148** looked interesting. The link took her to a flight status site. EV 5148 was an airline flight number. The flight left Atlanta bound for Tallahassee. It seemed reasonable that the code would relate to a location. Possibly implying that Joe was in either Atlanta or Tallahassee, but it was non-specific, and how did it relate to the Laughing Train?

She drummed her fingers on the desktop and decided to keep her promise to Tim while she waited for inspiration.

Inspector Mather answered on the second ring. "Where are you?" he said.

"Washington. But you knew that already, didn't you?"

"You could have travelled somewhere else, but I wanted to give you a chance to tell the truth..." He paused, and she wondered whether he'd stopped himself from saying "for a change!"

Mather continued in an earnest tone: "Kate, you need to hand yourself in. Go to the DC police station on

Indiana Avenue and ask for Detective Steve O'Donnell. He's responsible for your capture and I'll brief him that you made contact. If you can't get there then call him and he'll pick you up." He rattled off a 202 area code phone number.

"I'm innocent."

"Pardon? Can you speak up?"

"I'm in a public place—can't speak too loud. I said I am innocent."

"Then stop running and contact O'Donnell."

"But you found a gun in my apartment!" Kate looked around in case she'd been overheard but Harley wasn't paying her any attention. "Inspector, it must have been planted. I'm being framed."

She was surprised by Mather's next comment. He came back with, "I'm sure that's the case. You don't strike me as a murderer. Ballistics matched the bullet that killed Stephanie Harper to the gun. I've asked the Prague police to check the bullets found at the scene of Peter Sikorski's murder."

Hope swelled in Kate's chest. She saw her reflection in the PC screen. It was the first time she'd smiled for over a week. "And if they match then you know I'm telling the truth!"

"That's correct. We know you weren't in Prague when Sikorski was murdered."

The screen came into focus again. While she'd been talking she'd absently backtabbed until she was on the original search page. Mather was still speaking but her mind had tuned it out. A realization popped into her head: the link she'd thought would be a porn site—*Hot Bird 6/8/9 at 13.0°E*—ended with 13 degrees east. A direction. On the flight status site, she had been attracted by the locations. If Joe was sending her a simple message it would be a reference to a location. Like 1401, being Windsor. She googled **Windsor** and clicked on *Maps*.

"Kate?" Mather broke into her thoughts.

"Sorry, got distracted. I need to do something. I'll call back." At the other end the inspector said something else, but the phone was already away from her ear and then off.

Looking at the map of the city she knew well, she wondered where she could find map references, latitude and longitude. The session abruptly ended. The hour was up. She jumped up and handed Harley a five dollar bill. With no appreciation of the urgency, he ponderously gave her the change and a ticket with a new code for access.

She dashed back and opened Google Chrome. She typed: **search latitude and longitude**

A Google help link took her to Google Maps again, but this time there was an example in the search. So, if she knew the coordinates, it would identify the location. What about the other way around?

Kate remembered she used to use a site called Multimap.com. Didn't that have more search options? She went there and typed **Windsor** in the search box. Below the map was a grid reference: SU968768. Then: latitude 51:28:57N (51.48145). Below that: longitude 0:36:21W (-0.60596). 51.48145 was close to the fifth to eleventh digits of the code. 0.60596 looked remarkably similar to 060697.

She went back to Google Maps and keyed in: **51.48336, -0.60697**

Windsor central station. It made sense. The smiley related to the Laughing Train. The first four digits referred to the Laughing Train. The next thirteen digits were the map reference for its location, ignoring decimal points and signs.

Hands shaking, Kate counted thirteen back from the end. It left six digits. She clicked on Washington and noted the latitude started with -77. She counted back five digits after the decimal point. Latitude -09? That didn't make sense, so she included the prior digit. Latitude -109. That was better. Working back left only four digits. She ignored the 1641 based on the guess that they would be found at the location—like the first four digits were the train. She typed **45.17519, -109.24951**. The place: somewhere called Red Lodge, Montana.

Kate had no idea where Montana was, let alone a small town called Red Lodge, but she was sure about one thing. She now knew where Joe wanted her to go.

FIFTY-SIX

Patience was one of Amir's qualities. Delays at immigration had meant he had lost the girl at the airport. He hadn't been concerned about getting through, but he had no doubt that his Middle Eastern appearance had resulted in extra scrutiny. In Europe, Amir knew prejudice was there, but beneath the surface. Since 9/11, his experience of the US was of open racism. It was no longer targeted at the blacks, but the Arabs. Even with a Belgian name and passport, he looked like he could be Islamic and hence was more thoroughly checked.

The gun had been where he expected and there was a car available in the parking lot. However that was as much use as his contact in the US had been. As far as he was concerned it was enough. He didn't need help. If he could get this far, he could finish the job.

He didn't drive around looking for the girl. That would have been pointless. All he needed to do was prepare and wait. He drove to downtown Washington, found basic accommodation and paid in advance for the night. Immediately afterwards, he headed back to a RadioShack he'd passed and bought some equipment. From a convenience store he bought a large box of dates and mineral water. Then he set himself up in the room, listening to the police chatter, with a PDA by his side.

He heard the police discussing the need to look out for a silver-blue Volvo. They were looking for any silver-blue Volvo, guessing the plates would be false. However Amir figured that the car was either no longer in DC or would be ditched for another.

During the night he rested but, while half of his brain slept, the other half listened out for news from the police. By morning nothing had piqued his interest. He performed his ritual of isometric exercises for strength and conditioning, showered and dressed. Mid-morning, the PDA lit up. A map appeared on the screen and a blue dot flashed.

Amir smiled. The stupid girl had turned on her phone. He could track her again. Not only that, but she was in Washington on Lee Highway in Merrifield, not far away. He packed his carry-all and hurried to his car.

Kate wondered about searching for 1641—the four-digit code equivalent to 1401, the code for the Laughing Train. There would be somewhere in Red Lodge that the number related to. She was convinced that this was where or how she would find Joe.

She checked her watch. Where was Matt? He'd said an hour at the most. That had been almost an hour and a half ago. She headed out to the street, looked up and down and saw the Volvo parked beyond a set of lights.

Suddenly the doubts flooded back. He wasn't who he said he was. She'd felt tricked at first. Why hadn't he confessed upfront that he wasn't Danny? Would she still have come to the States? She thought so. He seemed to know everything. And yet, what had he really told her? She still didn't know why Joe had been taken away, why she had been misled by Detectives Hurwitz and Woodall? Perhaps she shouldn't just tell Matt that she knew where Joe was. After all, had she really needed him?

Kate looked across the road and saw Matt standing on the pavement, looking at her. His face spoke of frustration. Was it with her or the code, she wondered. She kept her face impassive so that he wouldn't guess she'd cracked Joe's message.

At a crossing, she looked left and right waiting for a gap in the traffic. Could she cross before it indicated if it was clear? She wasn't sure of the jaywalking rules. At that moment a car went past. An ordinary car. Nothing special except the driver looked right at her and then looked away. He was wearing a disguise, but Kate immediately recognized the face of the satellite installation man.

The Arab.

FIFTY-SEVEN

Thirty-one months earlier

Mirrorman's attention began to come and go in waves. The sun had risen and he managed to shift himself out of the direct light. An inconstant wind had started just before dawn and sand blew across the entrance. Outside, Boomer's body was already covered by a thin layer of grey dust. Mirrorman desperately wished he had the strength to crawl to Boomer and pull his buddy out of the sun.

He looked beyond his friend, across the desert speckled with rocks, and saw the air begin to shimmer as it heated up. Combined with the moving sand, he had the sense it was alive. Or was that his mind starting to play games?

His focus was on the horizon, willing a chopper to appear. Surely they were looking. Surely they had seen the emergency symbol. Or had that been covered by sand now? The other possibility, that the prisoner had been totally truthful, also worried him. Think, he told himself. Keep your mind active. You will survive.

Who had sanctioned the mission? Who knew about it? Mirrorman and the rest of the unit had been briefed by the command sergeant. Most missions were covert

278

and he was accustomed to the secrecy. Black Ops meant plausible deniability by the government. *Black in, Black out* had been the communication from Topcat. What did that mean really? Surely the CO ordered the mission. Who gave him the instructions?

They had been at Forward Base for five days before the signal was given: the package has arrived. The Arab, the man they had to extract and bring back alive, was at Rafha in his compound. Intel said that it wasn't heavily defended. The plan was to slip in, pick up the Arab and just walk out the main gates. A few casualties, but minimal force and subtle. But Tinman was covering the exit and realized there were far more armed men than expected. Plan B had worked; they'd gotten out, but Dogtag had been killed.

Mirrorman's mind went over this again and again. Dogtag had been killed. His unit had never lost anyone on a mission before. And now they were all dead. He forced himself to concentrate on his hand. In it he held the water bottle. Slowly, with no strength, he managed to raise it and pour water into his mouth. It dribbled over his chin as he tried to swallow. No point in saving it, he had lost a lot of blood. He wouldn't last much longer. He wanted desperately to write down what the Arab prince had told him. The link to the CIA. Politicians. Corruption. Was it true? He tried to write in the sand but his hand was too weak and the sand too fine.

The men in the jeep who had shot at them—the Arab had expected them. He said they were Americans or working for the Americans. Someone wanted them dead. Someone didn't want the Arab to be forced to say what he knew.

But he told me, Mirrorman thought. He knew he was dying and he told me. It must be true. He smiled. For a moment he was transported back to his eighth birthday.

His mother had made Superman-style outfits. A blue cape for him, a yellow cape for his brother—although they swapped depending who wanted the power of invisibility and who the super strength. Instead of Superman's "S" the tops had a giant "M" for Mirrormen. They'd worn those clothes to shreds until all that remained were the cloaks. He imagined wearing the yellow cape now. Imagined the power coursing into his arm. He moved his hand, then his arm, until the satphone was within reach. His fingers closed around its cold plastic and, slowly, he brought it up to his ear. He heard noise like a hundred voices speaking Arabic in a shredding machine. Was someone really jamming it? Why else would the signal be a problem?

He began to talk, although he didn't know if anyone could hear him.

Now and again he checked for a response but heard only static and the desiccated voices. He kept going, repeating himself, sometimes wondering whether he was speaking or just thinking the words. His voice was distant and detached, as if he were listening to himself in a dream. After a while he realized his hand had dropped and the phone was on the floor. He started to wonder whether he had ever held it. He could no longer think clearly. The words the Arab had said no longer made sense. They too became part of a terrible disjointed dream.

And in that dream he saw a speck in the distant haze. He struggled to see it but his eyes wouldn't open. Then it was back, larger this time.

It's a chopper, Mirrorman's addled mind told him. He blinked his eyes, focus coming and going. *Am I hallucinating?*

The thudding sound of chopper blades beating the hot air reached him.

He tried to move, to wave, to crawl. In his mind he did but in reality he sat and stared.

The dust swirled all around now and he could no longer see the helicopter. But it was there, the sound now thunderous in his ears like being by a giant speaker at a concert. Bon Jovi. He could see the band playing, almost hear their songs, but the bass was too loud, too pulsing, hurting his head. The dust was all around now. He couldn't see. It got darker and darker until finally all light was sucked from the cave and there was only silence.

FIFTY-EIGHT

Present day

Kate ran across the road screaming at Matt. Cars sounded their horns as she dodged through the traffic, finally reaching the Volvo.

Confusion distorted his face. "What's up? You're white as a—"

"The Arab!" she gasped. "I've just seen the Arab in a car! Get us out of here!"

Sudden understanding kicked Matt into action. He jerked open the driver's door and jumped in. As Kate dived in beside him, he gunned the engine. "Which way was he going?" he shouted.

Kate pointed out of town and the Volvo was immediately on the road heading in the opposite direction.

Matt stared in the rear-view mirror. "What make was he driving?" He sounded breathless.

"It was dark-blue. I've no idea what make. American." She opened her window and manually forced the side mirror so that she could see behind. "I don't see it."

Matt had accelerated and weaved between vehicles. Now he slowed to the speed limit and his voice was calmer. "Right, let's not draw attention to ourselves. Steady does it. We'll cut through and then loop back around." It was as if he were talking to himself. Then to Kate he said, "Keep looking out for him. If you see him, yell. We'll just have to take our chances with the law. OK?"

"Suits me!"

After a few blocks, Kate gave up trying to see through the side mirror and swivelled in her chair. The seatbelt was awkward so she took it off and set off the standard manufacturer's alarm when a seatbelt isn't buckled.

Matt waved at the seat. "Buckle it under you," he instructed.

With the seatbelt alarm silenced, Kate peered between the front seats and out through the rear window. Watching for blue cars. There were a few false alarms but no sign of the Arab.

They hit the I-66 but then Matt came off at the next ramp and slowed, watching who followed. No dark-blue cars. He rejoined the Interstate and seemed to relax. "Jeez!" he said, "I'd convinced myself it was the police we were worried about. This Arab guy scares the bejesus out of me!"

Kate kept her eyes on the vehicles behind, still watching for the dark-blue car and any unusual manoeuvres. She choked back an ironic laugh. "*You're* scared? Oh great! I've been petrified of this guy for over a week. He's following me and he's been killing people I know. Scared shitless doesn't begin to describe how I feel!"

"You're right... Sorry."

They left the I-66, and as they headed north, Kate wondered where they were going. This wasn't the route through The Plains. She swivelled back and faced forward, looked at Matt and asked, "Where are we going? This isn't the way we went yesterday."

Matt shrugged. "Just varying it. We're going back to the house. Myron will call if he gets something."

"So no luck so far?"

"No."

"You said no more than an hour. I expected you to come and find me at the internet café. What took you?" She tried to keep her voice flat but suspicion edged it nonetheless.

He shook his head slowly. "What can I say? I lost track of time. Myron was onto something. I wanted to see if he'd cracked it. He hadn't but he's got all the gear and I'm sure it's just a matter of time."

"But the code was a message for me. You said yourself that the message would be simpler. Dare or truth told you there was another message—one I should understand—not too difficult. But he still had to be careful. He must have realized someone with the skills could crack a standard code."

The car accelerated as he was distracted from maintaining a steady speed. At the same time, Matt looked at her. "You've solved it, haven't you?"

Kate said nothing. She stared ahead. They had been in a forest and now came out the other side.

"Come on, Kate. I'm risking my career—maybe my life—helping you."

"Your career? What is your job?"

"That is a classic misdirection. You're avoiding the question." He stole a critical glance at her. "Tell me. What have you worked out?"

Kate pursed her lips, deep in thought. She knew so little about this man. How trustworthy was he? What's his real involvement in this? But if she didn't trust him, then how would she get to Montana? She couldn't fly now the police were looking for her as Darcy. It would mean driving. She'd looked at the map and judged the distance at two thousand miles. God! She'd never driven more than about four hundred before. That could be four hard days driving on her own, possibly cut in half if she shared it.

They came to the side road that led to the lake house and Matt took it. When he reached the property, he parked under the lean-to and went in. She followed, her head still spinning with questions and issues.

He said, "I need a stiff drink. D'you want something?"

Kate declined and stood by the window, staring at the lake. How was she going to progress from this point? How was she going to trust this man?

When Matt appeared in the lounge with a tumbler of whiskey and ice, she decided it was time to talk. She said, "I need to know what's going on."

"I've told you." He sat, took a slug of whiskey and smacked his lips. "That's better."

Kate bristled. She stood with her hands on her hips and looked him in the eye. "No, you've told me precisely nothing. You've proved that you know as much as I do, that's all. You've tried to gain my trust, but the truth is there's so much I don't know and you aren't telling me."

Matt paused a long three seconds. A bird on the lake broke the silence with its shrill call as it took flight. When he spoke, Matt seemed genuinely concerned. "What like?"

"Well for starters, why Joe was abducted a year ago? What was going on? And why was I pointed to a fictitious internet story? Which, by the way, led me to someone in a prison for the criminally insane—oh, and it clearly wasn't Joe!"

285

Matt nodded and took another mouthful of whiskey. "OK," he said. "It's about time you knew." Then, like the click of a switch, his demeanour transformed from friend to aggressor. In a smooth motion, Matt reached under a trouser leg and drew a gun.

Special Agent Michelle Ramirez pulled onto Lexington and immediately spotted a commotion ahead. Cars sounded their horns and brakes squealed. *Jesus! There it is!* Just over a block away the silver-blue Volvo weaved dangerously between other vehicles. Ramirez put her own foot down, trying to keep the Volvo in her sights while at the same time not drawing attention to herself. But the whole thing only lasted seconds because, as suddenly as the excitement began, the Volvo slowed to normal speed.

Surprised though relieved, Ramirez got into the rhythm of covert pursuit. She tried calling her partner. No response.

The Volvo headed south and then picked up the Beltway, looping back. At the I-66 the driver headed west, out of town, then seemed to hesitate at off-ramp 57 before taking it. As Ramirez came off the Interstate she immediately saw the Volvo slowing and knew the driver was checking for a tail. Spontaneously she turned right onto Lee Jackson Memorial, drove past the I-66 on-ramp but then pulled into a parking lot and eased around. While she was certain the Volvo driver would go back onto the Interstate, she was prepared for almost anything. Within a minute the Volvo appeared and headed back onto the Interstate. Giving it a five-car head start, Ramirez resumed the tail.

At ramp 53 he repeated the manoeuvre but, instead of rejoining I-66, he picked up Lee Highway and headed through the state forest. There he turned right on a minor road. She dropped back further now, cautious not to be spotted.

The state forest ended and the trees started to thin out. Ramirez maintained her distance but patches of dense woodland, combined with a winding road, meant every now and again she would lose sight through a bend. She guessed they were heading for The Plains but, just as she decided to close the gap, she saw the Volvo turn off.

She drove past the lane, stopped and studied the satnav. The map showed the road led to a small house with a lake beyond.

One way in. One way out.

She took the next turn—a muddy track that tested her creaking suspension. At the end the track looped around, a short spur going to a cabin. According to the satnav she was now close to the other property, between them a copse and the lake.

Ramirez tried her partner again. His phone was now off. *What is he playing at?* Previous annoyance with him was on the verge of boiling over to anger. Well, fuck him, she was doing this alone then!

She got out, entered the wooded area and cut through undergrowth until she came out at the water's edge. To her left she could see a single-storey building with a decking, and on one side the Volvo was parked under a lean-to. Keeping close to the edge of the woods, Ramirez followed the lake towards the house. A coot made her jump as it skimmed away across the water, piping its panic as it fled.

Ramirez drew her gun and squatted. She could see the house clearly now, about eighty yards away. Large windows by the decking. Two people inside. One sitting, one standing. Definitely the blonde woman standing.

The other person was probably the man from the airport.

Then it all changed. The man jumped up with a gun in his hand.

"Get down!" Matt whispered urgently. "There's someone outside." Holding the gun ready, he edged into the kitchen. Moments later he rushed back. "Shit! There's someone around the front. Saw him checking out the car."

Matt moved through to Kate's bedroom. She followed.

A sharp knock on the door made her jump.

"Police!" A voice called.

Matt eased back the curtain. Kate peered over his shoulder and caught a glimpse of a man holding a gun.

"That's no trooper," Matt whispered.

Kate shrank back. "Oh my God, it's him! It's the Arab!"

"OK, back to the lounge—in the corner—out of sight of the kitchen door and window." He pushed her then, seeing fear starting to make her go rigid. As she went, he pulled the sofa round and flipped it over. They crouched behind it. Kate in the corner, Matt at the side, his gun aimed at the door.

The front door splintered open. A crash and then silence. Kate found herself looking at the window. She saw movement, a reflection. The Arab was at the lounge door. She found her voice, but when she spoke it had a strange gruff quality. More a growl than a whisper. "He's by the door."

Matt fired. Two shots in quick succession.

Shots responded, thudding into the sofa, tearing through it and striking the wall. Kate covered her ears.

Matt returned fire. "Keep low!" he shouted, barely audible above the shots and her pounding blood.

The window shattered, sending a thousand beads of safety glass skidding across the deck. Matt jerked backwards against her and yelled in pain. A rush of blood blossomed on his shoulder. Kate screamed. With Matt injured, the Arab rapid-fired, charging into the room.

Matt pulled himself around and resumed his position. His shots silenced the Arab's for a second and Kate heard a thud. Had the assailant been hit or had he dived for cover? Then intensive shooting began once more.

Kate curled into a ball, her whole body trembling with fear.

The Arab stopped firing again and the sudden silence was filled with dark anticipation.

Matt reached over and shook her. Kate looked at him, her eyes glassy with terror. Blood poured down his left arm, his face was drained.

He shook his head. "We've gotta get out. He'll come around." He nodded to the trees. "Can you run?"

Kate was unsure but she said, "Yes."

"Go when I say. Head for the trees, run in a crouch, head down, and don't look back. I'll draw his fire and cover you." Then he responded to her expression of concern. "I know what I'm doing. I'll be fine. Wait for me in the woods."

He checked for signs of the Arab then eased himself up, using the corner of the room as a partial shield and support. "Get ready." He edged into the room and checked through the kitchen window. He came back. "OK, I think he's behind the car, coming round that way. We'll both go onto the decking. I'll go right. Count to three and run." He touched her arm and forced a smile. Then a thought crossed his face and he said, "His real name was Cassano. Joe Cassano." He shrugged his eyebrows, forced the smile again. "OK... let's go."

He stepped onto the decking with Kate, still quaking, a shadow on his heel. He checked left and then hurried right. For a moment, exposed, she wanted to dart back inside. Then she steeled herself, counted and started to run. Her legs felt strange at first, heavy and disconnected, but the adrenaline drove her forward and she reached the first bushes before the gunfire began. Patches of ground were sodden and she slipped and fell. Immediately, she got up again and forced herself onward.

The gunfire stopped just as she fell again, lurching through reeds close to the green water. Had the gunfire ended because Matt or the Arab was dead? She squatted, looking back at the house. The Arab stood over Matt's body and fired. Then he started to run towards the lake.

Kate skidded to her feet, her legs moving too fast. Her mind screamed *No!* over and over.

She was almost at the treeline when the gunfire started again. She dived and started to rapid-crawl, scrambling over brackish, sodden ground before throwing herself behind a tree. She gulped for breath and looked towards the house.

No sign of the Arab.

Then a gunshot made her start with alarm. She spun around to see an Hispanic-looking woman, shielded behind a tree, her gun arm outstretched.

FIFTY-NINE

The woman wasn't aiming at Kate, but towards the bushes. "Over here!" she hissed and waved.

Kate scrabbled over and shrunk behind the woman. "Who the...?"

The woman ignored the question and pointed away from the lake. "I've a car back there. Not far. We're going to run for it." Then she paused and checked Kate out. "You're OK?"

Kate nodded.

"Right, let's go!" The woman fired three rounds at the bushes and, gripping Kate's arm, began to run through the trees. Within a few desperate moments they were beyond the trees and heading for a car. They both jumped in and the woman gunned the engine into life. A bullet pinged off metal.

"Head down!" the woman screamed as she pressed her foot to the floor, fishtailing the car around the muddy loop before jolting them towards the main road.

"Who the fuck was that?" The woman said, as her heavy breathing subsided.

Kate stared at the woman with eyes that were cold, beyond fear. She said, "Who are you?"

The woman held Kate's stare briefly but didn't respond. After a moment she picked up her phone, dialled and said, "Special Agent Ramirez reporting. I have the Blakemore woman... Yes, in my car. There was an incident at a lake house off the 234." She read off a grid reference. "Looks like the man from the airport is dead. There's another perp—armed—seems to be after the woman... Last seen by the lake." She listened for a while, glancing from the road to Kate. "All right. I'll stop in The Plains and find out what's going on." She ended the call and looked back at Kate with an ironic smile. "Honey, looks like it's your lucky day."

At a restaurant in The Plains, Ramirez tucked her car at the rear, out of sight, and nodded at the back door. "Let's go in and have lunch. I'm starving. Order some food and we can talk."

She led the way inside, the smell of pizza immediately making Kate's stomach rumble. People in diner-style booths turned and stared as the ladies passed. Ramirez nodded to the restrooms. "You better clean up first, honey. You look a mess." As Kate turned in the direction indicated, Ramirez growled through a smile. "Don't think about making a run for it."

Kate stood over the sink and saw the streaks of brown and green on her face and clothes. Not much she could do about the clothes, but she washed and tied her hair back, removing more forest debris from it than she would have thought possible.

When she came out, the agent waved from a booth.

"I ordered for us." Ramirez said. "By the way, you still look awful."

"Thanks."

"You're welcome. So you heard who I am. Special Agent Michelle Ramirez." She held out her hand and shook Kate's. "I've been looking for you. In fact a lot of people seem to have been looking for you, Kate."

Kate was still cautious, uncertain how to take this lady. The woman was toned, probably hard as nails, but there was a nice smile and friendliness, maybe humour behind those brown eyes. Kate shook her head as if to clear it. "Is it normal to arrest someone and take them to lunch?"

Now Ramirez gave a broader smile. "You aren't under arrest, honey. Looks like there have been some recent developments."

Kate waited. A waitress put down two large glasses of water and two equally large glasses of Coke. Both were filled with large chunks of ice.

Ramirez nodded at the drinks. "Diet, of course. So let me tell you what I know. There have been a few people murdered in the UK and Europe—people you know. The evidence seemed to point to you and you went on the run... to Washington. Why Washington?"

Kate said nothing.

"All right. So you travelled under your sister's ID and met a man at Dulles. He took you to the lake house and is now dead. The shooter is possibly the Arab who you reported to the British police. Right?"

"Yes," Kate said. "Why did you say it was my lucky day?"

"You mean other than me saving your life?" Ramirez chuckled and then more seriously said, "Looks like you're in the clear. The gun found in your apartment has been confirmed as the same one from the Czech Republic. You weren't there at the time. The British police know you didn't do it."

All the tension dropped from Kate's body then. Tears flowed freely. Ramirez reached out and put a hand on her arm and waved the waitress away. "Give us a minute," she said.

Kate dabbed away the tears and sucked pizza-air into her lungs. Suddenly a weight was lifted. She met the agent's eyes, smiled weakly and nodded. "Thanks... thanks for saving my life."

Responding to a wave from Ramirez, the waitress came back and deposited two bowls of penne pasta with chicken breast. Ramirez immediately took a mouthful. Between chews, she said, "Sorry, I really am starving."

Kate said, "So what now? Shouldn't you be going after the Arab?"

The agent gave a slight waggle of her head, an odd side to side movement. "Not my problem. Uniform have taken over. Me? I've been assigned to you."

"To get me back on a plane to England?"

"That's about it."

Kate ate thoughtfully for a while, and then she put down her fork. "Agent Ramirez... I'm in the States to find my boyfriend."

Ramirez raised an eyebrow, half interested. "Is that it?"

"Well if it makes it more interesting, I think the Arab was looking for him as well. I think people know something and the Arab wants that information, or..." the sudden thought struck her, "he doesn't want that information to get out."

Ramirez pouted, thinking. "What sort of information?

"I don't know but I'm sure my boyfriend is the key."

"So where is he?"

"Now there's the thing. He seems to be in hiding, maybe some sort of protection. I don't really know, but it's all I can guess. He's left me some clues that only I seem able to solve."

"Intriguing. What sort of clues?"

"Well the last one was a code. Twenty-six digits. The man who I met at the airport, Matt—the one shot at the house—was trying to solve it."

"Is that what you were doing in Merrifield?"

"Yes. He knew a cryptologist... Myron somebody. Anyway, Matt was sure he could solve it."

"And...?"

"I don't think he will have." Kate paused, enjoying teasing the agent. The sudden shift in tempo, the food, the relaxed atmosphere, everything was going to be all right. "No, I don't think he will have cracked it... but I have."

Ramirez laughed at the game Kate had played. She held up her hands. "Please don't tell me where he is, you might have to shoot me!" Then, more seriously, looking at Kate's expression. "What? You want me to help you? I'm supposed to put you on a plane and be done with you."

They ate in silence for a while. When they had finished, Kate looked into Ramirez's eyes. "Help me, Michelle."

Ramirez laughed. "Whoa, it's Michelle now is it?"

"Think about it. My boyfriend has information. There's been an international incident involving an Arab. Maybe, just maybe, this relates to national security. It could be really important. People don't get murdered for no reason..."

Ramirez held up a hand. "You had me there for a moment until you mentioned people not getting murdered for no reason. Welcome to America, honey!"

"Not like this though," Kate persisted. "If you were to find my boyfriend... Surely that could help your career."

Ramirez did the head wobble thing again and drummed her fingers. "Look, I'll tell you what. Tell me where he is. I'll have him picked up and then if he wants to meet you we'll get him brought here."

Kate shook her head.

Ramirez said, "Won't tell me where he is?"

"Ah... well, you see I only know approximately where. He's in Montana. Somewhere called Red Lodge. I won't be able to solve the last bit of the code until I'm there."

Ramirez squinted at Kate and said, "You're not shittin' me?"

Kate snorted a laugh and shook her head. "That's how the code worked. He wanted me to get there and solve it, to get in touch."

Ramirez thought and then nodded. "I can't do it without clearance, though." She got up and slowly paced towards the exit with her phone. She stepped outside and Kate could see her speaking animatedly. A moment later she was back inside, grinning. "You're on," she said. "Think I'll pack my skis."

SIXTY

Agent Ramirez took Kate to a WalMart after realizing she had no clean clothes to change into. Kate's bags were still at the lake house. "Get some clothes for now," Ramirez said. "Uncle Sam can pay, but I'm afraid he can only stretch to WalMart prices."

Kate was amazed at how cheap the clothes were. She bought underwear, jeans, a T-shirt and warm top. She put on the new clothes and dumped her dirty stuff. At the checkout, the over-friendly assistant found it very amusing. Kate handed over the tags and paid with the US government's cash.

While Kate was shopping, Ramirez was on the phone again. When Kate joined her she said, "I thought it a good idea to let you rest this afternoon rather than fly straight out." When Kate nodded gratefully, the agent continued, "There's an 8:50 Frontier flight from Reagan National. Changes at Denver and gets us into Billings, Montana at 14:57. I've sorted the seats and arranged for a car at the other end. Meanwhile, let's get you to a hotel so you can have a bath. You must be exhausted."

"That's the understatement of the year."

"Well, you relax for a bit. I'll arrange for your handbag and backpack to be collected from the lake

297

house and brought to the hotel. Hopefully by the morning, you'll be feeling half-human."

Kate had pictured something luxurious but realized that was unrealistic as Ramirez checked her into the Holiday Inn by Washington Reagan National airport.

Ramirez left her then, saying she had a report to write and promising to collect her from the room at 7:50. "No need to hang around. We'll just go straight on," she said. They also agreed a knock, three fast, three slow, so Kate knew it was all right.

The first thing Kate did as she was shown her room was double-lock the door. She ran the bath and stripped. As the bathroom filled with steam, she sat on the toilet seat and let the tears come. In the restaurant she had held back, or maybe it was too soon, but not now. The tears poured down her cheeks and continued to flow even after the sobs subsided.

Later, she lay in the bath, her head resting on the edge. She closed her eyes and breathed in the steam. She'd been aware of her heart rate—too high and under strain. The thought of how her new heart monitor would have coped made her smile. Now, for the first time that day, the stress began to release and her heart rate steadied.

After, she lay on the bed in a terrycloth dressing gown and watched TV. Six pm had just gone when a triple knock—fast and slow—on the door made her start. She looked through the peephole. "Yes?"

"Police, ma'am. I have your things."

Kate saw that the man did indeed look like a policeman and in his hands were her rucksack and handbag. She hesitated, uncertain, and then decided the man had done the correct knock so he must be all right. Mustn't he?

She opened the door.

He looked at her, uncertain of what to do.

Conscious of his gaze, she tightened the dressing gown. "Just leave the bags there, please," she said.

He placed them on the floor and backed away two steps, like a hostage negotiator would leave an offering for a terrorist. Then he turned and walked away.

Kate snatched up the bags, shut the door and double-locked it. Her heart was pounding again. "So jumpy!" she admonished herself. Would she ever be the same again? Ever stop being so nervous?

She climbed back on the bed and rummaged through her bag until she found her phone. She checked her watch—early hours of the morning in the UK, so better not call. She typed a message to Darcy:

Everything coming together. On my way to where Joe is! Did you hear they've cleared me? The gun they found was used to kill Peter. Now that they know I'm innocent, the FBI are helping me :). Will call very soon when I have more. Hope everyone is well. Thanks ever so for your support! Love you. Kate

In the browser she googled Joe Cassano. There were lots of hits and she tried a few pages before she edited the search and added US Army. That brought up only a couple of pages and it didn't take her long to find the relevant one from two and a half years ago.

BAGHDAD, Iraq (NewsNet)—Roadside bomb kills five U.S. soldiers Sunday in Iraq

"Five United States Special Operations soldiers were killed Sunday by a bomb explosion near Mosul, Iraq's third largest city. There were no enemy forces present, and no hostile fire was reported," U.S. military said in a statement issued on Monday.

The soldiers were assigned to operations in Northern Iraq. The location of the base and the soldiers' identities were withheld pending family notification.

The only survivor of the incident was Sergeant Joseph (Joe) Cassano. He is understood to be "very seriously injured," but assisting with investigations.

Recent attacks by insurgents have increased in the area of Mosul, 260 miles northwest of Baghdad. Some of Iraq's most feared terror groups—including the Ansar al-Sunnah Army and al-Qaeda in Iraq—operate in Mosul. On Thursday a bomber with explosives hidden under watermelons in a pickup truck slammed into a downtown police station near a market. U.S. Army Capt. Jack Saddler said 10 policemen and 2 civilians were killed. Less than two hours later, a bomber blew himself up outside an Iraqi army base on Mosul's outskirts, killing 16 people, Saddler said.

At least 18 people were killed in attacks elsewhere in Iraq on Sunday, including 4 Iraqi soldiers who were gunned down outside their base north of the capital.

The latest deaths raise to 7 the number of fatalities among American soldiers in war-ravaged Iraq during the month of December. So far this year, 302 U.S. soldiers have been killed in the country.

The US Army has lost 4,209 soldiers in Iraq so far.

SIXTY-ONE

Nineteen months earlier

Joe sat down opposite Woodall. "Thanks for meeting with me," he said. They were in a safe house in Smíchov, Prague 5: an imposing Baroque-style building, pale pink with white and brown finishes, shops below and four floors of apartments above.

As instructed, Joe had entered through the service yard at the rear and then a fire escape door that had been left ajar. He took the back stairs, found the apartment and spoke through an intercom. The door had clunked open and a voice said, "Room two."

The apartment had unadorned white walls and smelled of fresh paint. Room two was also stark, white shutters blocking the outside light. There were two leather chairs, a coffee table and a drinking water dispenser.

Woodall ran a hand through his sandy hair before looking up. His eyes narrowed but he still didn't speak.

Joe breathed out. "It's been a year."

"Eleven months, five days."

"Has anything happened?"

"You've been moved to Prague, changed identity, given a job."

"I mean is there any sign of progress. Has our guy made a move, followed a trail?"

"These things can take ages."

Joe shook his head, felt his hands damp on the black leather seat. "It sounded much quicker when you persuaded me to do this."

"I didn't say how long it would take. There's someone high up in the organization. They're careful. Catching them will take time."

Joe said, "I don't see why. If your guy is worried that Mirrorman has information and is still alive, then he would act. He wouldn't wait."

Woodall started to speak, but Joe cut him off. "I want out."

The other man snorted and looked away. When he looked back, he said, "It's about a girl isn't it."

Joe met Woodall's hard stare and said nothing.

Woodall said, "Of course we know about Kate Blakemore. We're watching you and you were warned about forming relationships. What does she know?"

"Nothing."

"Look, this is much bigger than a girlfriend. Much bigger than you. National security, corruption, maybe even links to al-Qaeda." He ran his hand through his hair again and looked down as if thinking.

Joe helped himself to a cup of water, took a sip and sat.

Woodall said, "I want you in the States. Maybe our man isn't making a move because he doesn't perceive the threat."

"No."

"You really can't say no." Woodall said this through clenched his teeth and then smiled. "You can't back out—there's too much at stake."

Joe put down his cup and stood. "You think I can't just walk away, then watch me." He took a step towards the door.

Woodall said, "OK."

"OK, what?"

"Where do you want to go?" Woodall pointed to the seat and Joe returned.

"England. Windsor."

Woodall tapped his fist on his lips, thinking. "Here's the deal. You get what you want, but at the first sign of a move—of a tripped tripwire—we move you to the States." He tapped again. "We treat this as part of the protection. You change your name—get a new ID and job. Hell, get a new life with your girlfriend if that's really what you want."

Woodall watched Joe's eyes. "Is the ID a problem? She can't know you've changed your name."

Joe thought about giving a longer answer but instead opted for a simple "No."

Woodall's eyes showed disapproval, although he said, "Fine, I'll get the paperwork sorted."

"And what about surveillance?"

"We'll keep that up—for your protection."

"I want Ben Hurwitz as my liaison."

Woodall relaxed, smiled properly for the first time. "Not a problem. You just uphold your part of the deal: if this kicks off, you're back to the States." He reached out a hand. "Look, it's tough on me too, OK? I know you have lost a brother and I know this has been a big ask for you to put your life on hold, but it means a lot."

Joe shook Woodall's hand. "Thanks."

Within a month he was living in Windsor, starting a new life and hoping to forget the past.

SIXTY-TWO

Present day

True to her word, at 7:50, Michelle Ramirez triple-knocked twice on the door.

"Have you breakfasted?"

"In my room." Kate was dressed and ready. She'd slept the sleep of the dead and, although still groggy from the deep sleep, the day was full of promise. She was on her way to Montana—and Joe. She slung her rucksack over her shoulder and they headed for the terminal.

Michelle said, "I presumed you didn't have any ID—except for your sister's."

"No. I thought it safer to just have Darcy's details."

"That's fine. You're officially UFS—under federal supervision."

At the airport she flashed her ID to security at the airport. The man made a quick call on his walkie-talkie before waving them through.

Ramirez said, "I'm going to have to cuff you and drag you on board. Do you want a bag over your head?"

Kate stopped mid pace. "Can't you…"

Michelle was smirking. "Sorry, honey, I couldn't resist it."

"I don't like you!" Kate said and they both laughed. When she sat on the plane and relaxed into her barely padded foam seat, Kate realized a tension in her shoulders had eased.

After the in-flight service, Michelle said, "You look a hell of a lot better today. Yesterday you looked like the little sister of Swamp Thing."

"Thanks!"

Michelle winked. "You're OK, y'know. You've been through a tough few days. Not many women could cope the way you have."

Kate sighed. "I guess it's survival instinct... that and adrenaline."

"I did fifteen months in Afghanistan. I know where you're comin' from, sister."

Ex-army. Kate nodded, piecing it together. That explained the tough-as-nails look the agent had.

She said, "What was it really like out there? In Afghanistan, I mean."

"A beach holiday, honey," Michelle snorted then bit her lower lip, a faraway look in her eyes. She shook her head as if to dispel bad thoughts. "Seriously though, it changes you. Being tense all the time, not sleeping, not knowing who's a friend and who's intending to blow you to bits..."

"Is that why you got out?"

"That and a desire to go back to college."

"You don't look old enough to have been in the army and college!"

Michelle laughed. "Well, that's not true but thanks anyway. Truth is I studied night classes to finish my degree. It's needed to join the FBI. Dumb rule if you ask me."

"You've done well it seems."

"I've done OK. Now tell me about England. I've never been, but I've seen pictures of Big Ben and Windsor Castle and Stonehenge."

"Now, Stonehenge isn't my specialty, apart from saying it was a Druid sacred site—something like 2,000 years old, used to tell the date and made of giant blocks from the Welsh mountains. It's a mystery how they were transported hundreds of miles. I'm much better on the subjects of London and Windsor mainly. The Queen is virtually my next-door neighbour!"

"Really?"

"No!" Kate grinned at getting revenge for the agent's earlier trick. "But I've seen her up close. She drives up a road we call The Long Walk. It's from the castle and through her grounds, The Great Park."

Michelle was on the edge of her seat, fascinated.

Kate continued: "I've seen her a few times, but this one time her Land Rover came right up behind me and made me jump out of the way. Actually, the Queen was in the passenger seat wearing a head scarf. Prince Philip was in the rear. They both looked grumpy, like they'd had a row. Because I'd been in the way, they both looked at me, the Queen said something and Philip laughed. At least it looked like she had said something about me. You know he's famous for shooting things he shouldn't? Well, I imagined she said something like: 'Philip, next time you're out shooting, clear this road of the bloody peasants, would you?'"

Michelle spluttered into her coffee. Then, once composed, she said, "You Brits crack me up. Surely the Queen wouldn't say *bloody*!" She tried to impersonate a British accent for the last word and failed terribly.

They both laughed and, on a roll, Kate continued to describe places in Jolly Ol' England and meaningless, but very British, anecdotes that Michelle found thoroughly amusing.

The four-hour flight was over before they knew it. In Denver they had a two-hour layover and Michelle was most concerned at finding somewhere reasonable to eat. They continued to talk and then headed for the gate for flight F1189 to Billings, Montana.

"You know it's Hicksville, right?"

"What, Billings?"

"Just about the whole of Montana. Country folk, I guess you'd say, but people use it to mean they're unsophisticated. Truth is I've never been there. Y'know it's a state the size of two UKs, I think, with a population of about a million. Of course, there are more horses than people!" Again she laughed. "I figure there are a lot more people in the UK?"

"There's often mention of about 64 million. But not that many horses."

The Billings plane was much smaller than the previous one, with three narrow seats either side of the aisle where two standard ones would normally fit. There were only thirty or so passengers so they spaced themselves out, everyone leaving the tiny middle seat vacant.

As they taxied along the runway, Kate got her first sense of what the flight would be like. The seats seemed to have a light aluminium frame, bolted to the floor. The padding under a colourful and deceptive material was the thickness of gnat's wing. With each bounce the seats rattled and vibrated and Kate felt every jolt. Once in the air, the seats continued to vibrate and move violently whenever the plane passed through turbulence. The closer they got, the more turbulence they encountered. A one hour forty-two minute flight felt longer than the first leg to Denver.

"Just in case we're about to die from... rattle death," Michelle said with a grin, "it's probably about time you started calling me Chelle."

Billings International Airport made Kate think of a bus terminal, only one with fewer people. They went down a flight of stairs straight into an arrivals hall along with baggage collection. Kate had her rucksack and Michelle pulled along a small carry case. As they passed the conveyors with bags on, it occurred to Kate that anyone could pick up the luggage.

Michelle must have read her thought because she said, "I guess that's one attraction of Hicksville—they ain't got much crime out here."

They walked through the terminal doors and to a strip of cars, herringbone parked and four deep. Michelle said, "Makes you wonder where the folks are."

Kate chortled, "Not here, that's for sure. Leave your car and get outta town."

"Now *you're* doing the terrible accent." Michelle held up her phone and stepped to one side to make a quick call. Then she waved Kate over to an information desk and collected an envelope before heading for the car park. Outside, she took a key fob out of the envelope and pressed a remote. "There's our ride," she said, pointing.

The ride turned out to be a compact Japanese car—a Honda Civic. Michelle opened the tiny boot, dropped in her bag and said, "Uncle Sam's generosity strikes again, honey."

Kate followed suit, putting the rucksack in the rear and closed the lid. Within minutes they were pulling out of the airport and heading down the steep road to Billings.

Michelle found an acceptable radio station and said, "Next stop Red Lodge."

SIXTY-THREE

Out of Billings, Michelle picked up the I-90 and headed west. She turned the heating up as they picked up highway 212, going south-west. They watched the outside temperature drop on the dashboard display. Ahead, Michelle pointed to the mountains pressing up towards the grey mantle of cloud. "Beartooth Mountains," she said. "Great skiing country, and beyond is Yellowstone National Park."

The snow started to fall, a light sprinkling at first but by the time they reached the town of Red Lodge, flakes the size of coins blotted the vision. The digital clock in the car showed a little after 4pm, but the combination of clouds and curtain of snowfall meant that Michelle needed to turn on the headlights. She also switched on the wipers but the reflected light became more of a problem than snow on the windscreen.

"So whereabouts in Red Lodge are we headed?" Michelle asked as they drove along Broadway aiming for the centre of town.

Kate had finally got her phone working. The mobile phone operators seemed to be different in Montana. Unused to scanning for an operator, it took her a while to figure out that she would never get a signal if she stuck with the one programmed in. Now she studied the

Google map and watched Michelle's satnav to determine their location. She said, "There's a right turn coming up. Goes off at a shallow angle. North Oakes Avenue."

Michelle slowed, spotted the turn and took the road that ran almost parallel with the main drag through the town. Main Street had a real frontier town feel to it, like something out of the late 1800s—hardware stores, clothing stores, inns and restaurants. This side road had larger lots and sheds giving the impression of a minor commercial strip. Kate was reminded of those western sets where from the street the properties looked real but from behind they were just façades with scaffolding. One side real, the other side not.

The road continued, changing its name to South Hauser Avenue. Properties became poorer and scruffier and then Kate said, "Stop, this is it." She looked hard, left and right, surprised at the area. Was Joe really here?

On one side of the road was a long uninviting post office that looked more like a depot. Opposite was a restaurant that had probably once been a row of connected residential properties. Then there was a parking lot with industrial units behind. A sign said *Do Not Enter*, so she supposed there was an entrance somewhere behind the buildings. In the parking lot were cars that could have been dumped for all Kate knew. Their condition was not good: rusty and damaged. The next property on the other side of the lot was a low rise, probably prefabricated.

They sat in the car looking up and down the street.

"What are you thinking?" Michelle asked.

Kate shook her head. "I don't know. Looks rather run-down I suppose, particularly on the left."

Michelle said, "I was expecting a hotel or lodge. I thought this was going to be straightforward." She turned and looked at Kate. "But didn't you say there was more to the clue?"

"Yes, a number: 1641. I found a link for Red Lodge Real Estate—a house for sale on 1641 Foothill Road."

"Should we try there?"

"I don't think so. The location we need is around here." She opened the car door, immediately caught snowflakes in her eyes and blinked them away. "Let's ask in the restaurant."

Michelle hung back to make a call as Kate went through the door, part sheltered by a small green-and-red-striped awning. The interior was no more tasteful but at least it was warm. A couple of early diners looked at her, smiled and said, "Howdy."

There was a rich aroma of baking and cooked meat. Kate could see someone in a kitchen at the rear and decided to wait. Michelle came in and picked up a menu.

"Where do you pack it all?" Kate asked. "Anyway, it's too early to eat."

Michelle looked like she was about to mention the two-hour time difference, when a middle-aged waiter wearing a baseball cap appeared. Kate figured him to be the owner—too small, too little custom to afford staff. He grinned broadly and also said, "Howdy." Then he spread his arms. "Take a seat, ladies, and tell me what I can get you."

Without preamble, Kate said, "I'm sorry, we're not here to eat. I just have a question, if you don't mind. Does the number 1641 mean anything to you?"

The waiter scratched his forehead under a baseball cap as though thinking hard, but there was something vacant in his eyes. He repeated the number slowly a few times. Eventually he shrugged and turned to one of the customers. "Lou, you know what 1641 means?"

"Nope," Lou said without the pretence at thought. But then he said something that made a lot of sense: "You should go ask over the road. Folks at the postal office may know."

It was a good idea. Kate and Michelle thanked them and headed out into what was fast becoming a blizzard. They found a public entrance on the right and went in, again grateful for the respite from the snow. Inside, they were welcomed by a large reception area and a long counter. Royal blue was the predominant colour, followed closely by dove grey. Blue floor, blue counter, blue units behind and grey walls. The walls were covered with posters and notices. Perhaps less welcome than functional then.

"Can I help you, ladies?" A voice said from beyond the blue counter. A head popped up. The man beneath was dressed in blue, although it was dark compared to the counter.

"We're looking for something with the number 1641," Michelle said. "Does 1641 mean anything to you, sir?"

"Can't say that it does," the postal worker said.

"What about mail boxes. Have you got one numbered 1641?"

"Nope, the mail boxes go up to three digits." He thought a moment and studied them with suspicion. "Can I ask what it's about?"

Michelle pulled her badge. "It's a federal matter," she said in such a serious voice that the man seemed startled.

"Oh, I... er... I could ask out back, see if anyone—"

"Please do that, Bob," Michelle said, reading his name tag. He disappeared.

Kate began to read the notices. She spotted a message board and read through the messages for anything that might be relevant. Michelle started doing the same from the opposite end.

Bob returned. "Nope. No one can help you there."

It took Kate ten minutes to work her way round to join Michelle. A lady with a young girl came in and shook the snow from her coat and hair, then brushed the girl before heading for the counter. "Hey, Bob. Howya doin' tonight?"

"It's a cold one," Bob said. "Not looking forward to the drive home."

The child distracted the lady for a moment and then she looked up. "Any mail in box LB-one-one-eight for me, Bob?"

Bob disappeared and came back with a handful of mail.

Kate stood with her mouth open for a second before the words came out. "Bob?" she said. "So you have letters before the digits on the mail boxes."

"Yes, ma'am."

LB—lowercase would look like a one and a six. Could it be? "There wouldn't be a mail box number LB-four-one would there?"

"Yes there would."

Kate couldn't believe it. Excitement coursed through her body. "Is there any mail in it?"

Bob eyed her sceptically. "You have ID?" He hit some keys on the keyboard and looked at the computer. "Hm... I doubt it."

Kate was sure he'd checked who the box was registered to. His reaction implied a man's name. *It'll be Joe. It just has to be.*

Michelle had her badge out again but Bob seemed to have predicted this and was already shaking his head. "I'm sorry, ma'am, but you know the law."

313

Kate was still excited. "It's OK. It's OK. Joe must want me to leave a message." There was paper and a pen on the counter. She picked up the pen and started writing:

Joe, I'm here. I followed your clues to find you. An FBI agent is helping me—

She stopped, unsure what to write next. Michelle looked over her shoulder. Kate said, "Where are we going to stay. Shall I give him an address?"

Michelle shook her head. "Ah, I haven't sorted that out yet. There's loads of places in town. Just put your cell number down and get him to ring."

Kate nodded and finished the note with: **God, I can't wait to see you—Kate**

She folded the note and handed it to Bob. "Box LB-four-one, please Bob."

Bob grinned and waved as they left. "Hope he calls you!"

Hardly aware of the snow, now starting to settle, Kate dashed back to the Honda. "I can't believe it," she said, laughing.

Michelle looked at her. "It wasn't confirmed. We don't know it was definitely his mail box."

"Oh it was. Did you see the look on Bob's face? He read my note. He saw Joe's name. He knew that box belonged to someone called Joe. I'm certain of it!"

"That's great," Michelle said, her tone a bit flat. Kate thought she could have been a bit more excited for her, but maybe she was starting to think about the consequences. Maybe she was wondering what would happen when Joe finally appeared.

After the two women had left, Bob picked up the phone and followed the instructions. He had given up the idea of earning an easy $100, but it had finally happened.

Someone had left a message for box LB41. He dialled the number on his screen. A man answered.

"Yes?"

"Is that Joe Conte?"

"Yes." Dull voice—no interest, but also no uncertainty.

"This is the post office on South Hauser, sir. Bob Turner, the assistant manager. You requested a call when a message arrived. Two ladies have just been in and written a note for you."

"Please describe the women."

"One white—British, I think. The other was Hispanic—a federal agent."

"What time do you close?"

"We're closing in a few minutes, sir."

"Bob... I want you to get me the message. I'll be there in fifty minutes."

"I can't—"

"Then let me in when I arrive."

Bob hesitated. Then the man said, "I'll double the money, Bob. I'm leaving now."

"Knock on the window at the side when you get here. Fifty minutes, Mr Conte."

Michelle drove carefully, leaning forward, squinting through the windscreen. She turned onto Main Street and headed out of town. The pewter sky was rapidly turning to night. Kate looked out of the side window to avoid the white flashes from the snow in the headlights.

"I thought we were going to check-in at one of the hotels in town," Kate said as they left Red Lodge.

"I know a nice place just outside. It's not far. You'll love the view in the morning."

She turned left into Bear Creek Hill and started a steady climb into the foothills of the mountains. They passed a few properties, but these thinned out quickly and when Michelle turned off down a lane, through the pine trees, Kate wondered why there hadn't been a sign outside.

Michelle seemed to read Kate's mind. "It's exclusive. They don't advertise. I came here with a rich boyfriend a few years back." She slowed as the little Honda Civic slipped on the thickening bed of snow. "First priority in the morning is to get some snow chains if this continues."

The road dropped and curved and after the trees diminished, Kate saw a large log cabin. The lights were on and welcoming. Beyond, Kate could just make out the impression of more trees and the mountains. There was a solitary car parked outside.

"Not many people staying," Kate said.

"Looks like we'll have no problem getting rooms then. It's early in the season so I was pretty sure there wouldn't be a problem."

She parked next to the other car and popped open the boot of the Civic. They grabbed their bags and dashed to the door under a sheltered porch. "After you," Michelle said, letting Kate lead the way. "First impressions are the best."

Kate smiled and opened the heavy wooden door into the cabin. And then she froze. A man sat in a chair facing the door, legs crossed and casual. Only the gun in his hand told a different story.

A smile snagged on one side of his mouth. "Hello, Kate," Amir said.

SIXTY-FOUR

A sharp pain in Kate's neck accompanied a burst of light in her head. She blacked out.

Somewhere an alarm was ringing. Her head hurt and a thousand thoughts and questions fired at once, vying for attention. What had happened? The Arab was in the lodge with a gun. Something had hit her on the back of the head. *Someone* had hit her. Had they been waiting behind the door? Was Michelle all right? Joe was so close. She'd come so far, tracked him down only to fall at the last hurdle. That damned alarm!

She realized she couldn't move. Her arms and legs were restricted. It wasn't an alarm she could hear, but ringing. The ringing was a phone—her phone.

Joe's calling! Answer it! She struggled against the restraints. Her eyes fluttered open. Blinding light forced her to close them again. With sheer determination she opened them again, trying desperately to see.

The phone stopped ringing and silence rushed in.

She was lying flat on a cold surface, arms and legs out wide and bound. Her legs were bent over the edge of whatever she was tied to. She tried to lift her head and turn it away from the light. Constriction around her throat and forehead made her stop. Her head and neck were bound too.

317

Her eyes started to compensate for the bright light. She was raised up off the ground, maybe waist height. She could see two vague images standing nearby, watching her. Where was Michelle? Was she bound in the same room?

"Chelle? Can you hear me?" Kate managed to say, her voice hoarse but loud in the quiet room. "Chelle, are you all right?"

A face loomed large over her. The Arab. A sneer puckered his face. "What do you know, Kate?"

She tried to spit but her mouth was dry.

The Arab laughed. "I like your spirit," he said. "You have a good deal of fortitude for a white woman."

Kate hissed, "Where's Michelle?"

"Let's forget the FBI agent, shall we?" Amir said. "Let's start by telling me how much you know."

Kate said nothing.

"Who is Mirrorman?" There was something in his eyes, a flash that meant he didn't expect the name to mean anything. Maybe.

Kate turned her face as far as the restriction allowed. Then she jolted, a sharp pain in her right nipple. The Arab pinched it between finger and thumb.

She looked back into his face, clenched her teeth.

He said, "A simple 'I don't know' is all I needed. Don't make me hurt you, Kate."

He removed his hand and then placed it close to her crotch, flat below her stomach over the zip on her jeans. "Now let's try again, shall we? Have you heard the name Mirrorman before?"

Kate took a couple of shallow breaths, trying not to breathe in his stink. "Yes."

"Who is he?"

"I don't know. I just heard the name, that's all. I don't know."

The Arab's eyes narrowed and he said nothing for a few beats. Then he said, "Who is Petr Sikorski?"

"Peter—you killed him!"

Amir moved his hand closer to Kate's crotch and grinned.

"OK, OK, Peter was engaged to my friend." She wanted to scream, *You killed Sarah too, you bastard!* Instead, she forced herself to feign calmness, her heart thudding against the cold surface beneath her.

"Mirrorman was Joe Cassano. You knew Joe Cassano as Joe Rossini. How did you meet Joe?"

"He worked with Peter. I met him at the party—at Peter and Sarah's engagement party."

"And you didn't know him before?"

"No."

"What about Petr... Peter. How well did you know him?"

"Not very."

"Were you aware that he was working part-time for the American government?"

"American government?"

"The CIA."

She swallowed. "No, I didn't."

"What about Stephanie Harper?"

"No."

He studied her face as if deciding whether she was telling the truth. Then he said, "Good. Peter sent you a photograph. Yes?"

"Yes."

"Why did he send you the photograph?"

"I... I don't know."

Amir's hand cupped Kate's crotch and squeezed, his fingers pushing inside her through the material to hold the pubis.

Kate screamed and fought against the restraints. She must have closed her eyes because when she opened them she had the impression of someone else there. She strained to see without pulling on the restraint but there was just the Arab and the light.

He grinned and moved his hand back to where it had been, flat but threatening more. "Try again, Kate."

Through ragged breath, she said, "It was a photo of two soldiers. On the back it said Boomer and Mirrorman. That's how I knew the name Mirrorman. Joe had told me Boomer was his buddy. I think Peter sent it so I would know Joe had told me the truth."

"He told you he and this Boomer were Special Forces, yes?"

She sucked in air and tried to control the shaking. "Yes."

"What do you know about the mission? What did he tell you?"

"Nothing..."

Amir's hand ran up the inside of Kate's leg, stopping just below her crotch.

"Nothing, honestly!" The light dimmed as though a shadow was close. She took a long slow breath, looked back into the Arab's dark eyes.

She said, "I read about it—the mission. They were in Northern Iraq. A car bomb, an accident killed everyone except for Joe."

"It wasn't Iraq," Amir said, studying Kate's eyes, moving closer. "It was in Saudi Arabia."

His thick coffee and vegetable-based stench became overpowering and made her breathe through her mouth, short and rapid. She returned his stare. "I didn't know."

"The Americans not only trespassed on an ally's sovereign land but kidnapped someone from the royal family. They had false intelligence that the prince was running an al-Qaeda cell." He snorted, and his spittle made Kate blink. "Ridiculous. But that is not the worst of it. Because of their incompetence, they all died except for your pretty boyfriend. They killed a crown prince."

Kate moved her head a fraction, side to side—a shake. "So this is all about revenge? You want to kill Joe for what happened to the prince."

The Arab pulled away from her face and she sucked in air again. There was no response and then there was another voice.

A woman said, "It's much more than that, Kate."

Kate stiffened, stunned like a poleaxed deer, her eyes wide and disbelieving. "Chelle?"

Michelle's face materialized over her. There was genuine sadness there as she said, "I'm sorry, Kate."

SIXTY-FIVE

Thirteen months earlier

The sun cracked a thin line against ash-grey clouds. As Joe pulled to the side of the road, he wondered what had brought him here, to the river. Climbing out, he stepped onto the verge. Behind him, business car parks were clogged with vehicles, offices blazed with lights and activity. A world away. A long stride and he was across a ditch. He covered the belt of common land, wet grass clawing at his work shoes, and stopped at the water's edge. He breathed in, long and hard; the smell of wet earth and the river filled his nostrils and pushed down into his lungs. He squatted, the fingers of one hand pressed into mud. This was real. This was certain.

The river was swollen and running fast. Brown eddies swirled on the far bank beneath sad trees that reached like long fingers as though trying to stir the water even more. Or perhaps to stop the turmoil that were the thoughts in his head: his dilemma. Who was more important, Kate or his brother? With his eyes closed, Joe pictured the river near his home where he and his brother used to play as kids. He saw the big sky and light dazzling off the ripples. He smiled, imagining his brother splashing to the other side, a rope around his waist.

Which year had that been? Yes, they had been twelve. Joe had tied the rope to a trunk on the far bank and that summer they had swung and dived and laughed more than he could ever remember. They were the Mirrormen—superheroes with secret powers they pretended to hide from the other kids. Superheroes had secret identities, although it never troubled them that their only heroic acts were play-acting: diving into the river to rescue a damsel or swinging into action and fighting the villain or alien or monster. The memories filled his chest with warmth. Joe opened his eyes, shook his head. And now his brother was dead. That was real too.

It was all about his brother. The man who lived life to the full. Would he understand the dilemma that Joe now faced? Would he tell his brother to move on, to live his own life?

More than a year and a half and nothing had happened. No sign of any pursuit. Why now? Just when he was getting his life back together, moving on. Damn it!

When Joe returned to the car, the sun had given up trying to break through and the dark sky pressed down. He listened to the tyres on the road, thoughts still spinning through his head. The working day was well underway when he arrived at the office and sat at his desk. His eyes barely focused as he opened the first report. He closed the file, took a slug of awful coffee and stared out of the window. He wondered how Kate's day was going. A grumpy regular with bad legs was her first patient of the day. She much preferred the sports injuries at the health club's physiotherapy unit, but that was only part-time. Perhaps he could earn enough so she didn't have to do the hospital work.

A junior interrupted his thoughts with a knock. "Stephanie's office, for the manager's meeting."

After an hour's tedious meeting and little contribution from Joe, Stephanie asked him to remain as everyone else filed out of her office.

"You look tired," Stephanie said, her dark eyes probing, trying to read his. Half-Chinese and with a small person's drive to prove herself, Joe found it difficult to see the human side of the woman he called his boss. He shrugged.

When it became clear he wasn't going to speak, her eyes narrowed. "You can't back out now."

"It's difficult. It's much harder now."

"Because of Kate." It wasn't a question. Stephanie read him and then shook her head. "I knew it. You can't mix business and love. And this is much more than business, Joe. What's Woodall said?"

Joe felt his lips tighten. "He's the one who told me. Said pretty much the same as you."

She raised her hands, "You need to get your priorities right. Remind yourself why you're doing this and commit."

He'd thought about asking for Stephanie's support but he could see now that he wouldn't get it. It was best that she wasn't involved.

"OK?" Stephanie prompted.

"Sure." Joe stood. "I just need to get my head straight."

He took a long walk beside the rail track and watched the Windsor train trundle away. He knew it made more sense for him to catch the train each day but he liked the freedom his car provided. A three-minute window before the London express roared past. He dialled a number from memory and, when it was answered, said, "I need your help," and then briefly explained his dilemma.

"Shit," the other person said, and then, after a pause, "Meet me Friday night. Usual place."

Scattered lights burned in the car park but Joe sat in almost total darkness under a railway arch. He wasn't far from home and Kate would be concerned he was working late. She'd noticed his tiredness and he'd explained it as stress at work. Could he tell her the truth?

He found himself thinking about the first time he'd seen her at the wedding, and their silly game of dare. The rollerblading and trip to Prague Zoo; with hindsight he could see he was in love right at the start. How could he have thought he could live a normal life in England as though nothing had happened?

A car scattered stones as it turned across the entrance and stopped next to Joe's but facing the opposite way: driver to driver. They buzzed their windows down, their faces hardly discernible in the blackness.

"I've spoken to W," Ben Hurwitz said, referring to Woodall. "It's happening."

"It can't. Not now."

"Seriously, buddy, there's no backing out."

Joe stared at nothing through the windscreen, breathed in, breathed out. "What did he say?"

"What you told me. That one of the tripwires has triggered. They've picked up on the trail."

"Some dodgy real-estate guy in Spain. Paid to leak my connection to Prague—to Peter."

"Paid with his life."

"Shit! W didn't tell me that." Joe watched as a figure moved through the car park. After a few minutes a car drove out and all was quiet again. Joe cut his eyes back to the silhouette of Hurwitz. "What did W say about Kate?"

"Nothing. You knew the risks when you involved her."

"Jeez..." Joe hissed and gripped the steering wheel hard. "Over a year I've been in hiding. Over a goddamn year. The trail had gotten cold."

"Apparently not."

"I can't risk Kate getting hurt, Ben, I just can't."

Neither man said anything for a while, and Joe realized he shouldn't have used Hurwitz's name. He was about to buzz the window back up, when his friend said, "You did a deal with W. Now you have to go to the States."

"What's that all about? Why back to the States?"

"Hey, I gave up trying to second guess the Agency years ago. But maybe they're worried you're unmanageable, and the closer to home... the easier to control."

Joe thought for a moment. "I should never have agreed. Now Kate's going to be part of the trail. She'd still be at risk."

"She won't know where you are."

Joe said nothing and eventually Hurwitz prompted: "So?"

"It's catch twenty-two. I stay and she's in danger. I go and she's in danger."

"Unless she's out of the picture."

"How would that work?"

Hurwitz blew air. "I don't know, buddy. Just thinking aloud. You agree to hide in the US and I'll get W to come up with—"

A scuffling noise made them hold their breaths. A cat, maybe, Joe told himself.

After a few minutes of silence, Hurwitz said, "We've been too long. Meet in a week. Same time at rendezvous three."

Joe watched Hurwitz leave and waited, window down, breathing the cool night air. How could they possibly get him away without leaving Kate in danger? No matter what the Agency came up with, Joe had to be sure she was going to be all right. Their objective was to get the man at the top of the tree, the one responsible for ambushing the Delta team in Saudi. Sure Joe wanted revenge for his brother's death, but he had found Kate and they had something special, something incredible. He'd discovered that love was more powerful than the need for revenge, for punishment, for death.

He was still thinking this when he arrived home. It was the night Kate lay on the sofa, cold and unwelcoming. The night she had found his gun.

SIXTY-SIX

Present day

Kate's phone rang again in Michelle's hand. She showed the display to her partner. "Should I answer?"

Amir grunted, "Wait."

When the phone pinged with a left voice message, he said, "Listen to it."

Michelle went into a bedroom and played the message.

It said, "Kate, it's Inspector Mathers from Thames Valley. You need to come back immediately. Stop running. I'm sure the ballistics will clear you, but I have to tell you you're a bit premature. The results haven't come back from Prague yet." A pause then: "Call me back."

Michelle shook her head in relief. That would have blown it. Kate would have known she'd lied about the bullet used in Prague.

She turned and jumped as the Arab came through the door.

"Was it him?"

"No, just the British police."

He took the phone off her, listened and nodded. About to hand it back, he stopped as the phone pinged with a message. He read it then showed Michelle.

OMG I can't believe you are here! Where are you? xx

"It's him," Amir said. He handed the phone back. "Find out where he is."

Michelle texted:

Not far from Red Lodge. Where are you? xx

The reply was:

A few hours away. Where exactly? I'll come to you, baby. Can't wait to see you xx

Michelle showed Amir before replying:

Checked in to a cabin off Bear Creek. There's a lane through the trees. I'm not sure of the address. Call me when you get to the two mile marker. I'll let you know the directions then. I love you!

Michelle said, "He won't make it tonight, the snow will be too deep."

"He'll come tonight," Amir said. "But we have some time. Some time to prepare—" He gave Michelle a twitch of a smile. "And some time to have a little fun."

Michelle tried to mask the horror she felt. This man made her skin crawl, but she hadn't anticipated depravity. She clenched her teeth and said, "You're not doing it."

"What are you saying?"

"You're not going to hurt her anymore."

Amir pulled his gun and jammed it onto Michelle's forehead. The move was so swift that she hadn't seen it coming. The force made her take a step back. Amir took a pace as well. Then they walked, Michelle backwards, Amir following, the gun pushing her head. They reached the door. "You will go outside," he growled, cold menace in his eyes almost willing her to defy him.

"Don't do this," she said. "This was not agreed."

He slashed her with the gun. "Just be grateful you don't have white skin. Now get out, before I change my mind."

Michelle twisted away and grabbed her coat hanging beside the door. She stepped out into the cold night and immediately pulled out her phone and dialled a number from memory. It rang for a long time and she climbed into the Honda and turned on the heating. She waited. When the phone was finally answered she said, "We're at the cabin in Red Lodge."

"Is everything all right? You sound different," the man said, his accent mostly Southern with a throaty grate underneath. He breathed like he was walking. Michelle also heard traffic noise in the background.

"No. It's not all right," she said.

"What is it? What's happened?"

Michelle tried to sound calm, rational. "That man you asked me to work with... We have a problem. He's a psychopath. I've just been threatened—a gun to my head—and God only knows what else he was thinking. He's got the girl right now. I think he's torturing her."

The man's voice remained impassive. "Does she know anything?"

"No, sir."

"How sure are you?"

"One hundred and ten per cent."

There was a long pause filled with crackles and the sound of distant traffic. "Have you located Mirrorman?"

"She left a message for him. Mirrorman's made contact."

"Good. So there's nothing more she can offer."

"She's a hostage." Michelle heard a touch of desperation in her own voice.

"Then make sure our Arab friend doesn't kill her."

"But—"

"This is war, soldier. Get over it and do your job." He paused then: "Are you good?"

She swallowed. "I'm good, sir."

The call ended. Michelle put the phone away and sat hunched in the driver's seat. She realized her hands were clenched in front of her, half in prayer, half ready to fight. She used the wipers to clear the screen then sat and stared at the flakes swirling in the porch light.

Amir slowly cut away parts of Kate's clothes. He had all night and he was going to enjoy the exquisite anticipation. As he cut, the knife ran along the girl's flesh causing it to prickle with goose bumps. He smiled. *She's excited!*

He removed the shirt and bra first then took the jeans away, working up from the bottom. When she had nothing on except for her panties, he stopped and admired her body. Not as fit as the Latino but that was better. Not too hard, not too soft—just as he'd thought. She had small circular scars on her stomach and a few on her chest. Chicken pox, probably from when she was young. He touched each one, delighting at her body's twitching response. The cluster close to her panty line made her arch as he stroked them.

"Easy," he said almost lovingly. "I won't hurt." A few of the scars on her legs caught his attention and he touched them, the final one on the inside thigh close to her pubic mound. He let his hand lightly touch the bulge and then continued and dragged the hand up to the side of her neck.

"I'm sorry I hurt you before. I didn't want to touch you like that, but you lied to me." His face was next to her ear now. He whispered, "You do understand."

SIXTY-SEVEN

Thirteen months earlier

Joe said, "I've had to tell Kate."

"Shit, Sc...! What have you told her?" Hurwitz choked. With the shock, he'd almost said Joe's real name.

They sat on a bench in the dark in Windsor Great Park, the orange glow of Windsor three miles beyond the trees.

"Joe, what did you say?"

"Don't worry. Nothing specific."

"What exactly?"

Joe shrugged, ignored the question. "Who's that guy you trust in Crypto?"

"What's he got to do with—?"

"I need his private email."

"Why?"

"I don't want to say—don't want to put you in an awkward position, but when the time comes, I want Kate to know the truth."

Hurwitz said nothing for a while and eventually shrugged. "So the extraction will be in about two weeks. The British National Crime Agency will arrest you—"

"Where?"

"The plan is to visit late at night."

332

"At Kate's apartment? Not going to happen." Before Hurwitz could argue, Joe continued: "And using the Brits won't work. Kate will want to know what's happened. She'll follow up."

"They've thought of that. They've created information about you—a backstory that'll convince her not to."

"She will and she'll still be the connection. When our guy comes after her—"

"It's the Saudis."

"What is?"

"The Saudis are the ones that picked up the information about Prague."

"Shit! So we don't even know if this is going to trap our guy!"

"W seems pretty confident."

Joe watched the dark shape of a couple of deer move out of the treeline. An owl called out. Joe groaned. "It's not going to work."

"It'll work."

"Kate will be at risk. She'll still be the connection."

"Stephanie will be the connection. Peter will lead to Stephanie, not Kate."

Joe shook his head. "This is shit. I'm out unless they come up with a better plan... one that doesn't involve the British police. When Kate investigates—and she will—the British police have to know nothing."

When they parted, Hurwitz agreed to persuade Woodall. Neither of them liked the Agency man, but he wanted Joe in the States. He'd find a way of covering the bases.

Two weeks and Joe had a lot to prepare. He needed a location so he could put the code on the photo and he needed a program for his *Trust Me* letter for Kate. Opening it with the passphrase *I dare you* wasn't enough. It should only be accessible at a specific time: 1401. Hurwitz's guy would be able to do that.

SIXTY-EIGHT

Present day

Michelle opened the cabin door and fought back the bile that rushed into her mouth. The Arab was naked and on the table with Kate. A memory of Afghanistan flashed into her mind causing her eyes to burn with tears and anger to flare in her chest. There was no doubt now, no hesitation. She took three paces forward, raised her gun and blasted a hole in the back of the man's head.

Kate screamed something guttural, animal—a sound that Michelle recognized from a thousand years ago, another world away. A sound she herself had made.

Michelle found a box cutter knife in the Arab's discarded trousers. She cut Kate's bonds and then dropped the knife as Kate grabbed her and clung on. Michelle put her arms under Kate and held her shaking body. After a long time, she eased Kate into a sitting position, still holding her, afraid that the British girl would collapse without support.

Kate's voice was coarse with strain and distress. "Thank... you."

Michelle eased her grip. "Let me get a blanket for you."

Kate let go and looked up searchingly into Michelle's eyes.

Michelle pulled away. When she returned, Kate sat gripping the edge of the stone table, her hands turning white with the effort. Then Kate started to shake her head slightly, repetitively.

In her hands, Michelle had a dusty-pink quilt which she wrapped around the other woman.

Kate pulled it tight and then tucked her knees up, hugging herself under the quilt. Her eyes searched Michelle's, full of confusion. "Why?" she finally croaked. "Why did you do it, Chelle? Why?"

Michelle stepped back slightly. "I'm sorry, Kate. It was my job... It still *is* my job."

"I don't understand. What is your job? Aren't you really FBI?"

Michelle did a subtle version of her head wobble. "Oh, I'm FBI all right. I just answer to a higher boss. My job was to lead the Arab to your boyfriend. But I didn't sign up to rape—and God knows what else."

"You saved me," Kate said. "That man murdered people I know—my friends. He would have killed me too." They both looked down at the naked body, crumpled face down, the back of his head a matted mess of hair, blood and brains.

Michelle put her arm around Kate and eased her forward. "Come on. Go and have a shower. Get the blood off you. Get his stink off you and get dressed. I'll clean up here and make some tea. Take as long as you need."

Kate's legs almost buckled beneath her but she found her balance and strength to stand. Hugging the quilt, she slowly walked to a bathroom pointed out by Michelle. Inside, she locked the door and turned on the shower, hot and powerful. She climbed under the scalding jet of water still wearing the quilt. The water pounded her head. She heard the roar echo through her skull but felt nothing. Then the strength evaporated and she sank to the base, resuming a foetal position, hugging her knees. Now she was aware of the cascading water burning her head and shoulders but she could do nothing about it. She just let it scald. She let it cleanse her body and mind of the horrors.

Although the whole ordeal had lasted no more than an hour, to Kate it had lasted an eternity. At that moment she knew the memory would scar her forever.

Gradually her strength and resolve returned. The quilt was a heavy, sodden mess and she pushed it aside. She stood, and using shower gel and a sisal mitt began to scour her skin, rubbing it raw. Finally, each drop of water began to sting and she felt as though the skin violated by the Arab had gone.

She stepped out, dried and dressed. She forced her mind to think of Joe. He was so close. Surely she would be in his arms soon and everything would be all right. Taking her time, she dried her hair and let it hang loose, as he liked it. She applied a small amount of make-up and, when she looked at herself and thought of him, she felt like a woman once more.

There was no sign of the dead man when Kate returned to the room of her torture. Michelle had cleaned away the blood and disposed of the body.

"Outside—at the back," Michelle said, reading Kate's expression. "How are you?"

Kate studied the special agent. "Confused... You were working with that... monster, weren't you?"

Michelle looked away as though the truth was difficult to admit. "Yes. Well, I was told to work with him. I had

337

no idea he was going to do that to you. I'm so sorry. Please believe me."

Kate said nothing.

Michelle moved from the kitchenette and handed Kate a mug of tea. "It's very sweet. I know you don't take sugar but it will help." She sat with a mug of something in her own hands. "I don't know everything, Kate, but the Arab has been following you for some time. You weren't really in danger from him because he wanted your boyfriend—wanted you to find Joe. But you needed help and that's where I came in."

"I should have guessed. You made a mistake, didn't you? You told me you'd never been to Red Lodge, but when we got here you said you'd been here with a boyfriend."

Michelle shrugged.

Kate said, "So when you saved me by the lake. What? That was set up—the Arab knew you were there."

"Kind of. He didn't want my help, but I knew he had seen you in Washington. I spotted the car too, and followed. If I hadn't found you, then I suspect he would have brought you here without me. Maybe he could have worked out how to contact Joe, but the plan was for me to gain your trust."

"I liked you!"

Michelle shrugged again. "I'm sorry."

"What changed?"

"Like I said before, I didn't sign up to rape."

"Matt—the man at the lake house was killed, wasn't he?"

"I guess."

"So then what?"

"That was different."

Kate shook her head. "All right. What was the plan once Joe got here?"

"The Arab wanted information. My boss wanted information."

Again Kate shook her head—too many questions still unasked and unanswered. "And then what? What would have happened to us?"

"I don't know. It wasn't up to me. It wasn't my concern."

"For God's sake. You must have realized he would have killed us. We couldn't live with what we know. You might have been a soldier once, but not now..." Kate saw a deep sadness in Michelle's eyes and, in that moment, knew why she'd done it, why she'd killed the Arab. She said, "You were attacked in the army, weren't you?—You were raped."

"A long time ago—another world." Now Michelle shook her head, full of sorrow. "But no matter how long or how far, there are some things that you can never recover from. I suspected it, but when I saw what he was doing, I flipped. I just reacted. I don't regret it."

"So what now? You should let me go."

After a long pause Michelle said, "I'm sorry, I can't do that. You don't know how powerful this man is. My life would be over if I defied him. He's on his way here. I called him and said the Arab had attacked me and I shot him in self-defence. He's coming to talk to Joe himself."

"Who is he?"

Michelle pulled a wan smile and shook her head. "You wouldn't know. But he's important and powerful and rich." She stood and walked over to Kate. "I can't risk you running off before my boss gets here. I'm in enough trouble already. I'm sorry about this, Kate, but I have to cuff you."

SIXTY-NINE

Kate's mobile phone rang. Michelle walked into another room and answered it.

"Joe?"

"Who is this?" Joe asked, his voice laced with suspicion.

"I'm Special Agent Ramirez. I'm with Kate."

"Then please put her on."

"She's sleeping. She's exhausted. There has been an Arab after her. He seems to have been responsible for a number of deaths. I gave her some pills to help her sleep. She's had a tough time this past week or so."

"Where's this Arab now?"

"He's dead. I shot him."

The line was silent for a while. Then Joe said, "I'm at the two mile marker. Where are you?"

Michelle gave him the directions.

"I'll be there as soon as I can—the roads are pretty bad." He ended the call.

Michelle returned to the room with Kate, drew her gun and went over to a window beside the door. She switched off the main light, pulled back the curtain and watched the drive that led up to the trees. She estimated no more than five minutes for Joe to find the snow-covered lane and navigate the track to the lodge.

340

Ten minutes passed. She called Joe's number and held the phone to her ear.

"Everything all right?" she asked.

"Missed the turning," he said. "Shouldn't be long now."

"OK, take it easy."

Michelle walked back to Kate and helped her to her feet. She led her into a bedroom and bound the cuffs to the bed so that Kate couldn't reach the window. "Not a sound, now," Michelle said. "I don't want us to get into a shootout."

"Your partner would have been happy with a shootout. I'm damn sure he didn't want us alive."

"The Arab had his own agenda. I just need Joe to talk to my boss."

"And you promise you're not here to kill him."

Michelle gave a Girl Guide's salute. "Promise."

Kate nodded. "I'm trusting you, Chelle. Don't let me down again. Remember what I've been through—what we've both been through."

"It'll be all right," Michelle said but, rather than return to the window, she stood thinking. When she did move it was to go into the kitchenette. A minute later she returned with a gag for Kate's mouth.

Kate struggled, alarm in her eyes.

"I can't risk it. I'm sorry." As Michelle said it, she realized just how often she'd apologized to this poor girl. She tried to smile reassuringly before leaving, turning off the light as she went. She stood at the window by the door and watched the track.

Lights appeared through the trees, sooner than she'd expected them, further down the track. Michelle's back brain wondered whether the headlights must have been off—wondered if something was wrong. Then the

341

vehicle was at the bend and heading towards the cabin, it's lights washing through the heavy falling snow. *He's going too fast! It didn't turn away.* The vehicle came straight for the front door. Michelle's front brain got the message. *Christ's sake, he's going to ram the cabin!* She prepared herself to leap out of the way but the Jeep slewed right, continuing the momentum of the bend and careened into the Arab's saloon. No dramatic explosion, just the crunch of metal giving way to metal and scraping as the Jeep dragged along the other car before shuddering to a halt.

Michelle aimed the gun, waiting for Joe to appear.

For a moment she could only hear her own breathing. And then a noise behind her made her spin, instinctively raising her gun. The Jeep had been a distraction. Before she completed the move, a sharp blow to her arm made her drop the gun. A man gripped her around the throat tightly, leaving no doubt that he could and would do damage.

With his other hand he reached past her and hit the light switch. He was dressed all in white, except for the hole in a balaclava around his eyes.

"Joe?" Her voice soft, her throat constricted under the pressure of his fingers.

He nodded. "Where's Kate?"

"She's safe."

"Where?"

"Close." Ramirez must have moved her eyes a fraction, because he guessed Kate was in the bedroom to the right.

Pain exploded in her head and her last sense was of the floor rushing up to meet her.

Joe picked up the fallen gun and pulled off the balaclava. He checked the agent—unconscious but otherwise fine—

and quickly moved to the bedroom door. He stood to one side as he opened it, unsure what he'd find. Kate grunted through the gag and jerked on the bed, sliding it from the wall. He rushed to her, removed the gag and then cut the ties.

She threw her arms around his neck and held him tight. "Oh my God, Joe!"

"It's all right," he said, reassuring in his tone. "Everything is going to be OK."

She gripped him hard for a moment, her tears of joy and relief wetting his neck.

"I've got you. You're safe now and I'm never letting go of you again."

She looked at him then and kissed him long and hard on the mouth. Then she held his face, staring deep into his eyes. "Oh, Joe, Joe. Life's been hell since you went. I never believed them. I couldn't believe it."

He kissed her tenderly.

She pulled away to look him in the eyes. "The news report about the attack in Iraq. Was that you? Are you really Joe?"

He kissed her again. "No, it was my brother. We'll talk—I'll explain later, baby. For now there are things I need to do."

"It's not over?"

"Not by a long way, I'm afraid."

SEVENTY

Joe slapped Ramirez's face until she stirred.

Her eyes sprang open, full of alarm and determination. Joe sat opposite her, a gun by his side. Kate sat on a stool near the door. He'd asked her to sit in the Jeep, check it would still start, but she had refused. Stockholm syndrome, Joe realized. Kate felt concern for the woman who had held her hostage. Or maybe there was more to it.

"The man out back—is that the Arab?"

"Yes," Ramirez said. Her eyes flicked between Joe and the gun, assessing her chances.

"I'm not going to shoot you unless I have to," Joe said. "You do what's right and you'll walk out of here." He could see her mind processing this, doubting his honesty and judging him by her own duplicity.

Joe said, "Did you kill the Arab?"

"Yes."

"Why? Weren't you working together?"

"That was the idea but he was a liability. He had his own agenda." She looked at Kate and Joe guessed the connection. "He attacked Kate, didn't he?"

Kate said quietly, "She saved me, Joe."

"Then one point to you," he said to Ramirez. "Let's see if you can earn another one." He paused and saw

344

anticipation on her face. How much did she know? He said, "Your boss wants to know what I know, right? Your job was to find that out and kill me..."

"Not kill you," she said, and he believed she'd somehow convinced herself that there could have been an alternative outcome. Maybe she was just a mere cog, a grunt. Maybe by killing the Arab she'd changed the game.

He said, "Well I have more than information. I have something that your boss will want. My deal is that he can have it but I want to be paid—I want compensation for what I've been through."

Ramirez didn't flinch. It was as though she already assumed it was all about money. She said, "I'll let him know."

Joe said, "Here's your deal: you put me through to discuss terms with your boss, you don't cause any problems and then—when it's all done—I let you go. Simple as that."

The agent looked at Kate. "Tell Kate you'll let me go afterwards."

"Kate, I guarantee it."

Ramirez did the slight head waggle and reached for her phone. It wasn't in her pocket. She looked at Joe and saw it in his hand. He tossed it over and she dialled. "Just so you know," she said, "he's already on his way."

"From?"

"Washington." She connected the call.

"Mirrorman is here," she said.

Joe couldn't hear the voice on the other end.

She said, "He wants to deal."

She listened and then stood slowly and walked to Joe. He met her halfway, took the phone and pointed to the seat. She retraced her steps and sat, her eyes fixed on Joe.

"I have something that you want," Joe said into the phone.

"Mirrorman?"

Joe thought the voice sounded Southern but it was distorted. There was also a background hum that suggested the man was in a plane.

"Yes. It's me." Then Joe used the code name he'd been told belonged to the traitor: "And you're Mustang?"

"I've used that name." The distorted voice came back. "And you—you've been very quiet for a long time."

"The line is bad. We can talk detail when you get here. I trust you can arrange a money transfer at any time because I want a million dollars in my bank account by the time we meet."

"All right." Easily answered, no negotiation.

"Then, when I give you what you want, then you can transfer another million."

"How do I know that will be the end of it?"

"That's detail. You will know when I show you. We'll meet at my cabin in the hills—it's remote." He provided the coordinates.

"Can I land a helicopter there? If so, I can be with you in about four hours."

"I'll mark a landing spot. I'll be close by." He listened to the man's breathing for a moment, wondering what he looked like, trying to picture the face. Then he said, "No guns. If at any time I think I'm in danger, then the deal is off."

"Sure." Again the easy, possibly too quick, answer.

Joe ended the call. He said, "Now, Special Agent Ramirez, we're going for a drive."

★

The snowfall had become a mere sprinkle and the drop in temperature had formed a light crust over six-inch-deep snow. Serious dents to the rear and side of the Arab's car made it look undriveable. The Jeep on the other hand, though badly scarred, started first time and drove without a problem.

Joe sat at the wheel with Kate and Ramirez in the rear. Ramirez's wrists were bound to the door handle with her own nylon ties. She provided no resistance, accepting her fate. He assumed it was because Kate wouldn't let him do anything bad to her.

He didn't trust Ramirez. He'd checked her credentials and she was genuine FBI—a trained agent. Her mind would be processing options and outcomes. For sure.

They drove in silence up Bear Creek Hill, switching back and forth up the steep sections. Ramirez was the first to speak. "Where are you taking me?"

"I'm taking you both somewhere safe," Joe said after a long pause. "We'll be in Wyoming soon. We're going to West Yellowstone. There's a quiet inn up here. You'll be fine until I return."

"How long?"

"When it's over and I come back."

"And what if you don't come back?" Ramirez asked.

Joe thought for a long time, concentrating on the icy road. Then he glanced at Kate in the mirror, directing his words at her. "It'll be over by morning. But just in case there's a problem, give me until 9am. I'll give you a phone number. If I'm not back ring the number—but only after nine."

Joe parked at the back of a place called Togwatee Lodge, by a small log cabin. When he opened the front door he handed Kate the key and a gun.

She looked shocked.

"I'm sure you won't need it," he said, "but I'll be happier knowing you can defend yourself."

While he lit a log fire, Ramirez leaned against a wall, watching. "So what's going to happen to me?"

"Let's see how this plays out shall we?" he said.

He was soon ready to leave and hugged Kate for a long time. "It will be all right. Unless I hear something that changes my mind, we'll let Agent Ramirez go when it's over." He took her hand. "See me to the Jeep."

They walked out and he held her face and kissed her. "I love you, Kate Blakemore."

"I love you, Joe..."

For a second, he looked uncharacteristically awkward. "Ah yes... there's something I need to explain, but not now." He slipped a piece of paper into her pocket. "That's the phone number just in case." He started to get in the Jeep but stopped before he closed the door. "About Ramirez... Just be careful. I can see you like her but remember she tricked you before and she might do it again. The reason you've got the gun is in case she tries anything. If she does... don't be afraid. Don't hesitate to use it."

SEVENTY-ONE

Joe stood in the open. He had made a giant "H" out of covers and blankets, black against the snow that was a couple of inches deep. He also stuck some oil-burning torches in the ground near to where he stood. The clearing was about half the size of a football pitch. Pine trees were all around, except for one side which dropped away to a small lake. The "H" was closer to the water than the trees.

Joe was still wearing the white ski gear but he'd been outside for over an hour and a half and was starting to feel the cold. Four and a half hours had passed since the phone conversation. Mustang was late. He took Ramirez's phone from a pocket and connected with the last call. When answered, thunderous noise in the background made it difficult to hear.

Joe said, "Mustang?"

"What?" Noise. "Say again."

"Where are you?" Joe shouted.

"On our way. Got a little delayed. Flew into the strip at Red Lodge and picked up the chopper. How's my landing?"

"It's marked. Look for the four torches." Joe listened to the helicopter noise for a moment then said, "How many are you?"

"Three. Pilot, me and my assistant."

"Why have you brought an assistant?"

"Say again."

Joe repeated the question.

"He'll operate the computer—check your information and do the transfer. Don't expect me to do the technical stuff."

It sounded reasonable.

The man continued. "I'll want assurance that you aren't armed."

"Not a problem," Joe said. Then: "How long will you be?"

"Soon."

Joe reckoned it would take under forty-five minutes to fly from Red Lodge to the site in the mountains. A hour passed before his phone rang.

"Mirrorman?"

Joe could barely hear the voice above the sound of rotor blades. "Yes."

"We're now on our way. You ready?"

"I'm here. Your landing is marked."

Mustang said something else but it was lost in the noise and the call ended.

There was no question, Mustang hadn't come direct. The delay was deliberate. Keep the other man waiting in the cold—a classic ploy. With the wind chill, the temperature was about five below. Low temperatures reduce brain function, blood flow, dexterity and muscle strength. But as a soldier, Joe was trained to deal with extreme environments, to wait for hours, barely moving. The trick was to ensure the core body temperature didn't drop, by keeping covered up, staying dry and moving. If necessary, using only small shifts in weight or flexing muscles. High temperatures were much more of a problem due to dehydration. He'd been outside for over two hours, preparing and waiting. Ice formed a thin crust in patches on his clothes. He wasn't too cold. His brain was working just fine. He'd been in worse than this, sometimes lying still for many hours. But then Mustang could be delaying for a different reason. Joe glanced at the black line of trees. Perhaps Mustang was allowing time for someone else to get there ahead of him—a sniper maybe, to take up position.

Joe spotted a searchlight in the distance, coming in low over the trees. The sound of the blades, first a whispering thump, gradually increased to a loud pulse, bouncing off the surrounding hills. The searchlight swept out across the lake and then back, fixing first on the torches and Joe, and then picking up the landing site.

The pilot took the helicopter wide, slightly over the lake before coming straight towards Joe. It hovered over the "H" for a second and Joe thought he could see a man leaning forward to talk to the pilot. Then the helicopter put down, the blades immediately slowing.

The door opened and a man stepped out. He crouched and fast-walked through the snow towards the torches.

"Hold your arms out," he shouted as he approached.

Joe took two paces forward and held his arms out, open and vulnerable. The man's face became clear, lit by the torches. Maybe early thirties, wearing an open coat over a suit, lean, round glasses, hard unfriendly features. This was not the man he expected. This was not Mustang. The assistant then. From the way he walked, Joe guessed the man was ex-military.

He man lifted a wand from his side, a small device in his other hand. "Need to check you first," he said, now close enough for Joe to see a ragged scar under the man's chin.

"Which force were you in?" Joe asked.

The assistant ignored him. He waved the wand over Joe's breast pocket twice. "Phone?"

Joe nodded.

The assistant held out his hand and took it then swept the wand over Joe's body again. "You're clean," he said.

"Ex-marine, maybe?"

Their eyes met and the assistant gave the hint of a headshake. His breath came out like a snort. "Wait here," he said. He stepped backwards, turned and ran to the helicopter. Joe also took two paces back to his previous spot, the torches between him and where he wanted Mustang, a clear demarcation line in the snow.

Another man appeared from the opposite side of the helicopter. He was wrapped up like a polar explorer with just an oval of his face exposed and too far away to recognize. While the second man waited, the assistant reached inside and got something, clipboard-like, from the seat. Then they walked towards Joe, the second man's face resolving as they approached the light.

"Mustang."

There was maybe a hesitation in his step before the man stopped four paces in front of Joe. He was large, six three or four, heavy build, but not yet gone to seed. The torchlight played tricks with his features, but Joe knew who it was. Spencer Kirkpatrick. A new senator rumoured to be on the fast track to high office. Also sat on the NSC—so that would be the connection to the mission in Saudi.

Kirkpatrick said, "Hello, Mirrorman."

Joe said, "You've done well, sir."

"And you survived. How's it been?"

Joe studied the man's easy smile and confidence and then said, "Let's cut the preamble, sir. Has the money been transferred into my Swiss account?"

"Simmons?"

The assistant stepped from behind Kirkpatrick and flipped round his clipboard. Only it wasn't a clipboard, it was an iPad. It showed details of the transfer of a million dollars to his account.

Joe nodded. He'd already had an automatic confirmation from the bank.

Kirkpatrick said, "Of course, you know the money cannot be traced back to me."

"Proceeds of crime?"

The senator didn't respond. Instead, he said, "What I don't understand is why you didn't just go public with who I was. But take it as a goodwill gesture that I have paid you the million before you tell me anything. I've come a long way tonight, I sincerely hope for both our sakes that it was worth it. I will also need to be convinced—one hundred per cent—that this is a one-time deal. If I'm paying for it now, it had better be something that once imparted cannot be reused. I won't tolerate blackmail."

"Nor would I expect you to. The information is on a secure server that can only be accessed by a passcode." The Agency had created the site and Woodall provided Joe with the code. Woodall hadn't known his whereabouts for the past year and was bound to be pissed, but the site was still there and the code still worked.

Joe continued: "Once in, the user cannot download or copy the information. This means that once you have access, you can change the passcode and prevent access by anyone else. I know what it proves but I will never be able to use the information."

"And," Kirkpatrick said, masking his eagerness to protect himself from whatever information was out there, "what does this information allegedly show?"

"It shows that you knew about the activities of bin Shahd's son. You must have known he was actively involved with al-Qaeda. You did nothing about it because you were—maybe you still are—in bed with bin Shahd. There are also documents relating to payments made to you by bin Shahd. It seems you were involved in fixing deals for him, with the US and in Iraq. You misused US personnel and information for personal gain."

"And you?"

"There's nothing about our mission in Saudi. I don't know how you knew about it, but I do know you were involved in stopping us, killing my team, killing bin Shahd's son."

Spencer Kirkpatrick said nothing.

Joe said, "The prince can't have been happy with that."

The senator's face barely moved as he said, "*You* killed him, son. That's the story he believes. But enough of this, let's get on and see what you've got." He waved to the assistant who handed the iPad to Joe.

Joe typed an address into the browser. A secure sign-in screen appeared and he entered a code. He flipped the screen around and handed it to Spencer Kirkpatrick. "That's *Read Only* for now."

The senator kept his face impassive as he scanned through some internet pages. Then he said, "What's the code?"

"Transfer the other million first," Joe said.

"That's not the deal, son."

Joe locked eyes with the big man and pretended to consider his options. He said, "Tell me what happened first, then I'll give you the code."

Kirkpatrick turned, took two steps towards the helicopter and beat his hands on his arms. "It's too God damn cold for this bull." He nodded to Simmons, the assistant, and then strode away from the flickering light.

Simmons stepped forward. "What do you want to know?"

"The black op to get bin Shahd junior wasn't communicated up, was it? The CIA didn't know about it until too late. Who were those guys who attacked us?"

Simmons stuck his hands in his pockets, looked like he was thinking. He said, "They were registered as Iraqi military actually. It's all pretty blurred out there. You know that." He shrugged. "It was a simple matter of telling them you'd gone rogue. There was no record of your mission—no approval. *Black in, Black out* has its own issues. Like your unit, the men who died were reported as lost in Iraq. You will have seen the official report. All tied up, no loose ends."

"And the jamming?"

"Yes. They'd heard enough to know someone called Mirrorman had been given information by the prince. As far as I can tell, you weren't expected to survive, but when you did, they lost you. The official line was you were in protection from the Saudis."

A gust swirled particles of ice around them. Joe looked towards the treeline to his right, looked back.

"You want the passcode."

Simmons said nothing then glanced towards the helicopter.

Joe said, "What?"

"There's a sniper out there. He made his own way from Red Lodge."

Joe nodded. That's why they had taken so long—to give the other guy the chance to get into position.

Simmons continued: "So no stupid, sudden moves, OK? This needs to look relaxed."

"What does?"

"You need to take the senator out. He can't get away with this. He's a traitor. Maybe not directly, but they were his orders. He killed your buddies."

For a second Joe was taken aback by the switch—Simmons, the assistant, didn't approve of the senator's actions.

Again the guy said, "He killed your buddies, Joe."

"I don't have a gun."

Simmons slid a hand from his coat. It held a revolver. He leaned forward. "Take it. We'll walk over to the chopper. I'll make the senator come out—tell him you have more information—and you can end it."

"Just like that?"

"Just like that. Then you walk away."

"No." Joe glanced to the trees again. "I give you the code and then we both walk away."

"Final answer?"

"Yes." Joe staggered. "What the—?"

Simmons pointed the gun and fired.

SEVENTY-TWO

Joe deflected the assistant's gun hand at the same time as a blow like a wrecking ball struck him between the shoulder blades. He pitched forward, hitting the icy ground hard. Snow kicked up close by—three rapid shots, inaudible above the helicopter noise. So there had been a sniper. His head stung like hell and he knew he'd been hit. He sucked in cold air, forcing the pain from his mind. What had his instructor once said? *Pain is just weakness leaving your body.* He repeated this like a mantra, gritting his teeth, scrabbling in the snow where he'd hidden a gun.

In a swift motion, he pulled an SIG from its pouch and swung it towards where the assistant had been standing. But the man was already down—a fatal head wound leaked black into the trampled snow.

The helicopter was already a few feet off the ground now, and Joe thought he could see Spencer Kirkpatrick screaming at the pilot. He aimed at the senator, the urge to pull the trigger strong. But he waited and then two short whistles stopped the myriad of conflicting thoughts. He dropped his aim. Stood and watched as the helicopter banked over the water and then up and round, heading for the faint line on the horizon. Daybreak was a few hours away. Snow began to fall again, and the few minutes of noise and chaos were transformed into a scene of peace and tranquillity.

Joe became aware of someone approaching. A man, also dressed in white, also wearing Kevlar under the ski clothes, stood beside him, looked at Joe's head.

Hurwitz said, "It's just a graze."

Joe wiped some snow over it. "You were late, this guy could've killed me." He bent down and confirmed that the assistant was dead. "And I need to get this vest off. I took a bullet in the back."

"Sorry. I just didn't..." Hurwitz stopped himself then said, "There were two snipers. I got one guy in the woods but didn't spot the second until he got the shot off that struck your back." He grinned. "It could have been worse."

"Great."

"So what happened?"

"Spencer Kirkpatrick—*the* senator—a key man on the NSC with connections in Saudi and Iraq; that's who it was. That's who we were after." As Joe said it, he felt something didn't add up.

"Joe?"

"Maybe it's the cold or the graze, but it didn't go down as we expected, and I'm damn sure it didn't go down as Kirkpatrick expected. When we met, it was like he thought I already knew he was Mustang—that I'd know his name. I was supposed to be flushing him out. Surely if I'd known who he was..."

Hurwitz said, "Doesn't matter. We know who he is now."

"Sure, but that's not what's troubling me the most. The assistant told me what had happened in Saudi, confirmed the senator was guilty and then wanted me to kill him."

358

Hurwitz squinted, confused. "But then he tried to kill you."

"Because I wouldn't do it. I damn well wanted to." Joe thought again about how close he had been to firing at the helicopter. It'd only been Hurwitz's signal that had stopped him.

Hurwitz gripped Joe's shoulder. "I know, buddy, but we've plenty of evidence against the senator and he's on film meeting you. And the pilot was probably innocent. If you'd taken out the helicopter it would have been both men."

"I don't like loose ends."

"I'll call him, send him what you've got. He's from a respected family. Maybe he'll take the honourable way out rather than let them suffer humiliation. It'll be best for everyone if this stays quiet. That's how these things normally go. Too much embarrassment for everyone otherwise."

Joe nodded. "Let's get this area tidied and pick up Kate.

"Sure. Then what?"

"Then we go to a safe house as per Woodall's original plan."

Joe packed a few things from the cabin where he'd lived for the past year. As he set the building alight he felt some sadness. While he'd been almost totally cut off from civilisation and desperately wanted it to be over and to find Kate, he had found living off the land, the hunting and fishing, spiritually rewarding. The year had changed him. He now knew exactly where he wanted to go, but Woodall's plan had always been to complete the job, regroup and debrief.

The flames licked up into the night sky as though trying to catch the snowflakes. Joe watched for a while, waiting for Hurwitz to dispose of the bodies: two snipers and the assistant.

It wasn't long before Hurwitz joined Joe by the Jeep and got in.

Joe drove them away from the secluded spot and located Hurwitz's BMW X5 hidden off-road.

"I'll be seeing you then," Hurwitz said.

"Whoa! You're not off just yet. I still need your help."

Hurwitz reversed the BMW back on to the road and followed Joe's Jeep into Yellowstone Park and to the inn where Kate was waiting.

When Joe opened the door, Kate threw her arms around him. After a long embrace she said, "You smell awful, Joe Cassano." She laughed and then looked concerned and touched his forehead. "What happened?"

"Nothing serious, just a burn and there's a bruise on my back from being shot through Kevlar. I'll tell you all about it but not yet. First off, how has Agent Ramirez been?"

Ramirez sat on a chair, her hands still tied, her eyes trying to interpret Joe's every move.

Kate said, "She's been fine. You will let her go, won't you?" Her eyes implored him until he nodded.

He walked over to the agent and cut the ties to the chair but kept her hands cuffed. He said, "Your boss is still alive... for now, but it's time you looked for a new career. I'm letting you go because you saved Kate but you've questions to answer first."

Ramirez started to say something but then looked at the door, which opened.

Hurwitz stepped inside and stamped snow from his boots.

Joe said, "Kate, I believe you've met Ben Hurwitz." Before Kate could say anything, he looked at Ramirez and said, "My friend here will debrief you. Then afterwards he'll be keeping an eye on you—he's just looking for the chance, so don't give it to him. Understand?"

"Thanks," Ramirez said.

Kate gave her a reassuring smile and then to Hurwitz, with eyes full of questions, said, "So... Agent Hurwitz, I didn't expect to see you."

Joe said, "Ben has some explaining to do, haven't you, buddy?"

SEVENTY-THREE

Hurwitz took Ramirez out to his car. When he returned he shook Kate's hand like a man half expecting it to be snapped off. He sighed, "So you remember me from Windsor? Sorry about that. I was responsible for getting Joe out and covering tracks. He wasn't really in witness protection. We wanted to lure someone out into the open, someone high up in the CIA or connected who may have sabotaged a mission—Joe's team's mission in Saudi."

Joe shook his head. "Only that isn't me. Joe was my brother."

Kate frowned. "Your brother?"

"He is—was—the real Joe Cassano. Joe died out there and I was supposed to pretend he didn't."

"So you were bait."

"I guess you'd call it that."

"So what do I call you?"

"If it's too confusing you can stick with Joe. After a couple of years I've almost grown used to it. But my real name's Scott."

"Scott... Joe?" Kate wondered if she'd get used to his real name, but then the enormity of the plan began to dawn on her. She frowned, real concern replacing confusion.

"Wait, does that make me part of it? Did you *want* the Arab to follow me?"

"No!" Scott put his arm around her.

Hurwitz said, "Joe... I mean Scott... wanted out because of you. He tried to quit, but Woodall—the other agent you met—wouldn't let him."

Scott added, "A year had gone by, I thought it'd never happen. And then—"

"He insisted we break the trail," Hurwitz cut in, "so that you wouldn't be involved."

Kate shook her head. "But I was connected to Sarah—and Peter sent me the photo of the real Joe with Boomer."

Now it was Scott's turn to be surprised. "What the hell? That wasn't agreed." He looked at Hurwitz.

The agent shrugged and shook his head. "Don't know anything about that. Peter agreed to be part of the trail and so was Stephanie Harper. They should have found Stephanie. Both of them were on our payroll—they provided a cover for Scott and enough information to provide the next link. From our target's high position and with his connections we thought this wouldn't be a problem."

Kate said, "So who was it?"

"The target? A senator on the National Security Council." Scott wondered again why Spencer Kirkpatrick thought he or his brother would know it was him and yet it took eighteen months for him to act. Or did he? Why had it taken another thirteen to find him? He shook his head, realizing he may never know all the facts. "Looks like the senator's motivation wasn't as high as we thought. It seems he was happy to wait, whereas the Saudis wanted to find me more."

"The Arab?" Kate asked.

"He'll have been acting for a Saudi prince."

Hurwitz said, "Somehow the Arab picked up the trail and found you."

"And Stephanie..." Kate tried to make sense of it all. "Why wouldn't she meet me?"

"I messaged her," Hurwitz said. "I told her to intervene. If you tried to meet her, she should have agreed. We knew the Arab was following you. We knew you'd left for the States and evaded the cops."

Kate said, "Sounds like you weren't in control."

Scott said, "No, and that's why I went off the CIA's radar. I trusted that you'd find me. No one else knew where I was."

"Until you got ahold of me today," Hurwitz agreed.

"So are you CIA or FBI or what?"

"NSA," the agent said. "I know it's confusing—all these acronyms—but these days it's more blurred, supposed to all be part of the same intel service."

"And were you really Special Forces, Scott?"

"Yes, though not Delta. That was my brother."

Kate started to ask more questions but Hurwitz said, "I really should get going." He stepped towards Kate, seemed a bit awkward and then held out his hand and shook hers. "Be seeing you," he said. Then he handed Scott his car keys. "You're taking the Beemer, buddy—Ramirez is in the Jeep." He winked at Kate. "And I know I don't need to say this, but take good care of your lovely lady."

When he'd gone, Kate said, "My God, the whole plan was a hell of a risk. People have been killed. You could have been killed. *I* could have been killed!"

Scott put his arms around her. "I know. If I'd known I'd meet you—if I'd known what you'd be put through, I would never have done it. I love you, Kate. I'm sorry."

Kate kissed him, pulled back just enough that their noses were still touching and smiled. "I reckon you've a hell of a lot of making up to do. It's a good job you're going to have a long time to do it."

Kate tended to the burn on Scott's head and winced at the size of the welt between his shoulder blades. A few inches higher, she guessed, and the outcome would have been very different.

They slept in each other's arms until late afternoon, ordered room service and left the lodge as it was starting to get dark.

"Where did you say we were going?" Kate asked as she relaxed into the big BMW's seat.

"Just outside Spokane."

"I have no idea where that is."

"It's in Washington—the state, that is. I'm afraid it'll take most of the night to get there. Once out of the mountains the roads are clear of snow but it's a ways from here."

"And what's there."

"A rendezvous after the mission. Maybe some answers."

Kate swivelled to look at Scott as he drove. "There's a lot I still don't really understand. Why were they after you when it was your brother's mission? What was the mission—and why Saudi Arabia? I thought they were a friendly country."

Scott nodded but said, "Hey don't ask me about politics. We've a long drive, so you tell me what you've been doing this past year. I know some stuff because I asked Ben to keep an eye on you and post updates to a secure site. And after that, I'll try and make sense of what happened in Saudi."

So Kate talked about her family, how quickly Darcy's twins were growing up and how different from each other they were. She mentioned her mum's new partner

365

Terry and that she found it hard to accept him. This prompted her to ask, "So what's the truth about your family? When we met, you said your brother had died. I read a report online that said you—I mean Joe—had been seriously injured in Iraq. Was that really in Saudi Arabia then?"

"Yes. They couldn't admit an incursion into Saudi. And the decision was to pretend Joe was still alive."

"And your family?"

"We lived in Virginia. Joe was my twin—identical, although we were pretty much what they call mirror twins. We both joined up, both Green Berets, although he'd moved into Delta Force for the last couple of years. I have an older brother too—by three years—Teddy. He was army but is something in insurance now. And I have a younger sister who sensibly kept out of the military."

"Her name?"

"Rebecca—Becky. She lives close to my folks in Palmyra."

Kate shrugged. "Sorry, another place I don't know."

"Charlottesville's not far. You may have heard of that. What about Richmond? That's where Teddy lives with his wife and two kids."

Kate shook her head. "My US geography really is pretty poor. What was it like—Palmyra?"

"Colonial South. Good country. Nice, God-fearing folk, but a place to leave rather than stay. Joe and I were inseparable, had fun as kids, but we were gone as soon as we could get out." He glanced over. "But you haven't talked about why you came before I was ready—before it was over. I told you in my letter that I would let you know when it was safe."

"Your *Trust Me* letter?" When Scott nodded, Kate continued, "I never read it. I don't know what happened.

I had it on a memory card. I had the password and time, but somehow lost it. But anyway, you left me clues."

They were out of the mountains, the headlights showing only fields to either side of a long straight road. Scott seemed awkward. "I just thought... if you tried to find me, it would prove we had a future. I don't know. It just seemed better than me turning up on your doorstep with a bunch of roses one day."

"A girl likes flowers."

"But anyway, you started looking too soon."

"It was the photograph of you and Boomer."

Scott shook his head. "That will have been Joe and Boomer. Odd though. I don't get why Peter would have sent it."

"Maybe he didn't."

"Then who?"

"Someone who wanted me to find you. I don't know. The Arab maybe?"

Scott was quiet for a while, staring out at the road. "It can't have been the Arab. He should have followed the lead to Stephanie Harper. If it wasn't Peter then it was someone else who knew about your involvement." He shook his head. "It must have been Peter, though I can't imagine what his motive would have been."

Kate thought about her friend Sarah and also Peter. So Peter was working for the CIA or NSA at some level, but did Sarah know? Was Sarah in on the whole thing? Did Sarah set her up with Joe/Scott?

Kate said, "Was it planned?"

"Right from the start. I was in Iraq and Woodall turned up, told me my brother was in hospital—"

"No, I mean meeting me. Was it planned? Was it somehow a set-up so that we could meet?"

"No!" Scott reached over and held her hand. "I had no idea who you were when I saw you at the party. Falling for you was definitely not part of the plan."

Kate leaned across and kissed Scott's cheek. "That's good to hear." She settled back and watched the road and must have fallen asleep because she jolted awake when the car stopped.

"Are we—?" she started to say in a groggy voice.

"Gas and coffee," Scott said with a stretch. "Sorry to wake you, hon. Want anything?"

She asked for tea and Scott was soon back in the car with drinks and doughnuts. After a few sips of the insipid milky drink, she poured it out of the window.

"About three hours to go," Scott said, munching on his Krispy Kreme.

Kate took a doughnut. "Tell me about the mission," she said.

"I only know what I've been told, but two years ago there was a mission to capture a Saudi who was believed to be actively involved with al-Qaeda. Trouble is, it was sensitive as hell. He was a prince or the son of a prince—though there seems to be hundreds of them. Anyway, the relationship with Saudi Arabia is... well, you know how important the oil is. A six-man Delta Force team went in and would have succeeded in the extraction if it hadn't been for Kirkpatrick finding out. He must have had a motive for preventing the prince's son from being interrogated. We think they arranged for the team to be killed—including the prince. They succeeded, but before the prince died he told one man about the agreements between the senior American and the Saudi prince's father. That man was my brother, code name *Mirrorman*."

"Ah, Mirrorman."

Scott said, "As kids, we called ourselves the Mirrormen. Joe kept it as a code name in the army. He tried to broadcast what he'd been told, apparently, but the comms were scrambled. A word they managed to decipher was *Mustang*—believed to be the traitor's name. A unit within the CIA was investigating them—Internal Affairs. They were investigating senior people and suspected Mustang was someone high up, maybe connected to the CIA. My brother died in the hospital before I got there, but not before Woodall turned up and got confirmation of the mole—Mustang. They didn't know who it was, but Joe's information was enough to try and flush him out. So Woodall asked me to take Joe's place—to pretend he hadn't died."

"Because you looked like him."

"That will have helped. I've known Ben Hurwitz since high school, knew he was NSA, knew I could trust him, so I insisted he was involved."

"But the CIA didn't know where you were in the States?"

"No. After I met you—and nothing had happened for so long—I wanted out. I wanted to be with you. The deal I made with Woodall was that I'd return to the States, but I never said I'd play by their rules."

"You didn't trust them?"

"One of their own was bad. No, I didn't totally trust them."

Kate held his hand and squeezed. "But it's over now."

He looked over and she was surprised by what he said next.

"I don't know, Kate. I hope it's over. I truly do."

SEVENTY-FOUR

Woodall came into the house smiling. "Well, it's good to see you. Must be good to be yourself again," he said, and shook Scott's hand.

The property was described as being one-and-a-half storeys. North of the city, it had a mesh fence and a yard that needed some attention. The mailbox had been lying in the grass. Scott hammered it in by the gate to signal his arrival and then waited. Woodall had taken two days.

The agent glanced around. "Settled in OK?" He sat on the sofa, placed his tan briefcase beside him and leaned forward. "Where's Kate? Upstairs?"

Scott said, "I expected you'd be cross."

"Cross?"

"Because I went off the radar—did my own thing for a year."

Woodall ran his hand through his sandy hair. "Hey, we were pretty pissed for a while, but it worked out— and here you are. Damn, I'd have been very pissed if you hadn't turned up for the debrief."

"So let's debrief," Scott said. "Was Spencer Kirkpatrick's assistant one of your men?"

"Who?" Again he ran his hand through his hair, and for the first time Scott wondered if it was to buy time. Woodall sat back and shook his head. "The assistant? I don't know who the guy was. Hey, I'm here to answer questions but mostly to hear what happened. So Kate made contact from Red Lodge. Had there been any contact prior to that? Did you know about the man following her?"

Scott told his story. He said he'd been hiding out in the Beartooth Mountains until the postal office worker had called him and described Kate and an FBI agent. Scott didn't mention contacting Hurwitz or his involvement in the Jeep crashing at the cabin.

Scott said, "I was suspicious when I couldn't speak to Kate. It was texting and then Ramirez. They were in a remote cabin. I created a distraction at the front before breaking in at the rear." Again he decided to bend the truth rather than discuss Ramirez. He said, "I killed the Arab and the FBI agent. Turns out, she'd gone rogue and was working for the senator."

"I see." Woodall nodded slowly. "So she got Kirkpatrick to meet with you?"

"Yes."

Woodall smiled slightly and Scott had the distinct impression he was missing something. "He's dead, you know? Took his own life. Looks like our website managed to convince him."

Scott said, "He thought I already knew who he was."

"Did he? Though maybe your brother did."

"I have two questions," Scott said.

"Fire away."

"Who sent Kate the photo?"

"I'm not aware of anyone sending any photograph. But if someone did, then I suspect it was Peter. He had photos of Boomer…"

Scott felt anger tighten his throat, tried to hide it and stood. "You said you didn't know."

"What are you talking about?"

"One second you don't know about a photo and then you know it had Boomer in it!"

"Scott, Scott..." Woodall started, his voice maintaining perfect control, "you didn't let me finish my sentence. I was about to say he had photos of people in the squad—like Boomer—as well as the connection to Stephanie Harper."

Scott sat. It sounded plausible, and a couple of minutes passed with the two men looking at each other until Woodall broke the silence. "Tell me about Spencer Kirkpatrick's assistant."

"That's my other question. Who was he? At first he was helping the senator and then the next thing he was encouraging me to execute him as a traitor."

Woodall looked like he was thinking then raised his hands, palms up. "Who knows? Maybe you convinced him. Did he see the website?"

"Yes."

"There you go." Woodall rested his hand on his briefcase and looked around again. "Where's Kate?"

"She's shopping—at the mall."

"NorthTown?"

"Yes."

"OK." Woodall smiled.

Scott said, "There were two snipers. Kirkpatrick delayed his arrival so snipers could get into place. Hurwitz got them both, though the second one only after I refused to kill the senator and had taken a shot to the back."

"So you think the plan was to kill you if you didn't agree and then take out Spencer Kirkpatrick? Then lay the blame on you?"

"Seems that way."

Woodall said nothing for a while and Scott prompted, "So where next? I presume we aren't staying here."

The agent's smile faded. "It's not as simple as that, I'm afraid. Although the senator is dead, we've got new intel—he wasn't the top man."

"Who then?"

"A congressman who was ex-CIA. Head of Mid East." Now Woodall opened his briefcase, removed a manila file and handed it to Scott.

There were photographs and transcripts of conversations. "Grant Hamilton?" Scott asked. "Wasn't he also onetime a Marines Corp colonel?"

Woodall nodded.

Placing the folder beside him, Scott said, "But you have a name. You can go after him."

"Too sensitive—and we don't have enough hard evidence."

"So you want me to flush him out?"

"Something like that."

Scott picked up the folder, held it as though looking right through it then held it out to Woodall.

"No."

Woodall cleared his throat and gave a wan smile. "You can't say no, I'm afraid."

"I can and I have."

"It's too dangerous—for you and Kate. You can't walk away until this is over."

Scott said, "You can leave now. If you won't help us, we'll find our own way from here."

Woodall put the folder in his briefcase, but, when he stood, he had a snub-nosed gun in his hand.

"You'll do it," he said.

Scott shook his head.

Woodall removed a phone from his jacket and pressed a button, the whole time keeping the snub-nose trained on Scott. When the call was answered, he said, "Do it. She's in NorthTown Mall."

"You bastard!" Scott started to rise but Woodall prodded him with the gun, forcing him down.

Woodall sat. There was a glint in his eye and a brief smile flickered on his face. "So this is what you will do. The congressman is a traitor. Not only is he behind the funding of the so-called friendly tribes in Iraq, he's also involved in selling them arms."

"What about the senator?"

"He made sure the money went to the right tribes. He doesn't care that these guys are Sunni militants and supporting an Islamic state. But the senator is just in it for the money. The congressman is ex-CIA with the connections in Iraq. They were his men who attacked the mission. They were his men who killed your brother."

Scott shook his head. "I was suspicious."

"What of?"

"You. I suspected something was up when I called Kirkpatrick *Mustang*. The first time I said it, he ignored me. He was in a helicopter so I put it down to the noise. But when he approached on the ground, he definitely heard me use the name and it made him hesitate for a second." Scott watched Woodall's eyes as he spoke. The senator's assistant had tried to get Scott to execute Spencer Kirkpatrick. Woodall had known about the assistant—in fact, he gave it away when he said he didn't know him but talked about him in the past tense. No one had told Woodall that the assistant had been killed.

Scott said, "You also gave it away that you knew about the FBI agent—Ramirez. I said I'd killed her and the Arab. She made a call for me and has since spoken to no one. The only way you know about that is if she called you." In that moment, Scott put it together. He continued: "She called you. It was you who I spoke with on the phone. You pretended to be Mustang. You put on a Southern accent so I wouldn't recognize you."

Woodall said nothing.

"And that means you knew who Kirkpatrick was. So you called him. Kirkpatrick wasn't even looking for me, was he? He wasn't Mustang. And the Arab finding the clue and tracking me to Prague. I should have guessed it was a coincidence, happening shortly after I agreed to go back to the States. God, I bet you sent the photo to Kate to help things along. Weren't things progressing fast enough?"

Woodall said nothing and then clapped his hands slowly.

Scott said, "This was all a set-up for me to assassinate the senator. It was about making amends for the death of the Saudi prince."

Almost imperceptibly, Woodall inclined his head.

"But what I don't get," Scott said, "is who you're working for. I would have guessed the congressman, but now you want him dead too."

"He likes to think he's in control."

"So who is?"

Woodall didn't answer. Instead he dialled on his phone again.

Scott said, "It's the Saudi prince, isn't it? He wants a US soldier to assassinate a senior politician with links to the Iraq conflict."

Woodall said nothing, listened to his phone go to voicemail.

Scott scoffed. "Jesus, is this an al-Qaeda plot?"

Woodall dialled again, shaking his head in a you-can't-begin-to-understand kind of way. "It's much more complicated than that. You see, we are arrogant enough to think we understand the Middle East, with its thousands of years' history, with its religions and factions

375

and tribes, with its arbitrary borders drawn up by the Brits and the French a hundred years ago. You can't turn a hornet's nest into a beehive—and poking a stick in it can only make it worse. Look what's happened to the rise of Islamic State. This isn't as simple as al-Qaeda. It's not IS or al-Shabaab or any other nice little enemy the West would like to label." He shook his head, put the phone in his pocket and sat back on the sofa. An expression of superiority played across his face.

With the gun still trained on Scott, he opened the briefcase again and took out a blue folder. "These are your instructions," he said.

Scott's phone rang. Both men glanced at it, listened for two seconds until the ringing stopped.

Woodall waggled the gun, sounding unsure for the first time. "Are you expecting someone?"

It had been the signal Scott had been praying for. Kate wasn't at the mall. She was in a safe place with Ben Hurwitz. The NSA were listening in and will have picked up the guy Woodall would have sent to get Kate.

But all Scott said was, "No."

He saw something change in Woodall's eyes then. Realization. Before the agent could pull the trigger, Scott pushed off, overturning his chair. Woodall fired into the underside as Scott rolled backwards. At the same instant he heard the door burst open and the room filled with the sound of running boots and the commands: "DOWN!

"GET DOWN!

"ON THE GROUND NOW!"

SEVENTY-FIVE

Six weeks later

Scott drove his GMC four-by-four under cover and unclipped the rear. He stamped the remaining snow from his boots and dusted off his jacket. A deer was strapped to the flat bed. He hoisted it over his shoulders and carried it into the house.

Kate met him in the kitchen. "A deer!"

"Venison for dinner." Scott grinned disarmingly and dumped the carcass on a bench. "Special occasion."

Kate pouted. "Look, I know I agreed to do this living off the land, back to nature thing out here in the wilds of Canada, but I'm not so sure about shooting deer. And I have no idea about how to cook it."

"I'm joking about venison tonight. It'll need to be hung for at least a week... outside."

Kate studied his face when he returned from hanging the deer. "Were you also joking about a special occasion?"

"We have visitors this afternoon."

"Oh? Is that safe? I thought we were supposed to be low profile. I'm not even allowed to tell my family where we are!"

He held up his hands in defeat. "You're right, but this is different. Can't tell you now, wait and see."

"You are such a tease!" She handed him a cup of coffee and they sat in the lounge and looked out of the window at the snow-covered Rockies. The peaks dazzled like diamonds in the light.

Scott put some logs on the fire and put his feet up. "This is the life."

She snuggled next to him. "I'm very happy."

He smiled. "I couldn't be happier." He saw something cross her face. "What is it?"

"The money. The only thing I'm unhappy about is the million dollars you extorted from the senator."

"I've a confession to make," Scott said. "We haven't touched a bean of that money—and never will, I'm afraid. All the money went to establish a charity for the families of soldiers killed in action."

"I'm pleased."

"But we're pretty broke."

"We have each other—that's the main thing."

Scott gave his best Hollywood smile. "Yes it is."

Kate and Scott prepared dinner in the kitchen. All afternoon he'd refused to tell her who was coming. When she needed to know how many guests for dinner, he said it could be one or two.

A little before 4pm a black SUV parked outside and Hurwitz got out. Scott opened the door for him and pumped his gloved hand.

"Hi, Ben," Kate said. She wiped her hands and gave him a kiss and hug. "Scott implied there was more than one visitor." She looked over his shoulder with raised eyebrows. "Oh God, you haven't brought Agent Woodall along, have you? Whenever I've seen you, he hasn't been far behind!"

Hurwitz laughed. "No, ma'am, just me."

Kate exchanged glances with Scott and could read something in his face. There was something she wasn't being told.

Scott led him to the fire in the lounge so he could warm up. Kate took his coat and gloves.

"Snow's not as bad as I expected," Hurwitz said.

"Not had a fall for a few days. It's expected tonight though," Kate said. "Are you hungry?"

"Always," Hurwitz said. "A quick tour of your homestead, and beer though, if I may?"

Scott whizzed him around their lodge and guided him back to the lounge by the fire.

"Cosy lodge." Hurwitz said. "You've made a fine home here."

Kate passed Hurwitz and Scott a beer and they chinked bottles.

After a long slug, the agent wanted to know what life was like without being connected to the world and Scott described how he loved it and how they spent their days. When he was done, Scott asked, "So what's the news? On the outside."

"Oh the usual world crises," Hurwitz said with a grin, "but nothing important. Of course, you know Kirkpatrick killed himself a day after we sent him the recording. We've not been able to get the congressman yet, but he's resigned and it should only be a matter of time. Woodall has offered to turn state's evidence. One piece we have confirmed is that the senator had personal information on a number of people and was effectively blackmailing them. You'll never guess. One of them was—"

"Michelle Ramirez?" Kate guessed.

Hurwitz was impressed. "Right! It seems that she was raped in Afghanistan—in the army. She reported the soldier, nothing was proved, no action taken, so she paid someone to take care of matters for her. A contract killing made to look like an accident. She'd have gotten away with it if it weren't for the fact that the assassin she hired knew Kirkpatrick. Senator Kirkpatrick used that information to make Ramirez work for him. By the way, she's now living in Mexico and working for a legitimate security firm."

Kate said she was happy for her.

Hurwitz looked at Kate. "Before my other news, how do you feel about being out here in the wilds?"

A little uncertain, Kate said, "It's OK I guess. I'm getting used to it."

"Perhaps there's something or someone who would make it better?" He finished his beer and took a glance outside.

Kate was intrigued. "Have you brought someone with you, Ben? Surely you've not left them waiting in the car this whole time?"

Hurwitz grinned. "No, ma'am. Well, I've not brought another person." Retreating to the SUV, he returned with a carrier. A cat carrier.

"Tolkien!" Kate was beside herself with joy. She took her bemused cat from the box and hugged him tightly.

"Took some organizing, I can tell you," Hurwitz said. "But I guess he's family."

Kate buried her face in his chocolate fur. After a while she said, "That seals it. He's the guard-cat." She placed an arm around Scott's waist and hugged. "We're staying here—at least for a while."

"Another surprise," Hurwitz said, and handed her a bundle of envelopes. "Letters from your family back home."

During dinner, Hurwitz agreed a secure way Kate could get messages to her family. Then he said, "You know, by conservative estimates, the war in Iraq has cost over $2 trillion? The funding for so called *tribal security forces* is around $25 million a year. It's just a drop in the ocean, but that literally means handing over suitcases of cash to the tribal leaders. This whole ISIS thing has kicked it back up the priorities. The Senate Select Committee on Intelligence wants to support another Sunni Awakening. Someone decides who gets the money and someone executes delivery. We think Prince bin Shahd was pulling the strings. Kirkpatrick got approval and Hamilton made sure the money went the intended way."

Scott said, "And what about the ghost soldiers—the ones paid for who didn't exist?"

"A sign of the institutionalised corruption. Through extortion and abuse of power we think there are people making hundreds of millions of bucks a year from the investments in Iraqi security. Whether this was going directly to the likes of Hamilton and the senator, we don't know, but it's easy to believe. Even if they were just skimming off the top, it's a hell of a lot of money over the years."

"OK but what was in it for the prince? Surely he didn't need the money."

"Kingmaker, I guess. When this shit settles—and eventually it will—the landscape will have changed. The theory is that bin Shahd will never rule Saudi, but he could create a new kingdom."

"But bin Shahd junior was al Qaeda..."

"And the biggest recipient of US funds has been a tribal leader called al Suleiman. He's now believed to be supplying weapons to ISIS. Allegiances are as definitive as a game of poker. It's all about politics and positioning."

"And money... especially for Hamilton and Kirkpatrick."

"As I said, we don't know what they were doing, how they were on the take, but have you heard about the Mossack Fonseca leaks? Well, we now have evidence against the senator for syphoning money through Panama and off-shore accounts. Maybe it's just a matter of time before we can find the money trail left by Hamilton."

"I get all that but, personally, what has this been all about? Why have I really been on the run as Joe?"

"My view? Bin Shahd wanted revenge for the death of his son."

"That's nothing new," Kate said.

Hurwitz raised his eyebrows. "The SSCI have Intel that suggests the Saudi's knew Joe died in Iraq. Bin Shahd was never after Joe, he was after the man who didn't want the prince's son interrogated. Hamilton sent in the team to stop Joe's Delta Force. But the real mission was to kill the son."

Scott nodded. "So our friend, Woodall, lied about that. He said Joe had confirmed Mustang's role. He was in on it from the get go."

"Yes, we think Woodall was ultimately working for bin Shahd."

"They wanted to flush out Mustang and have me kill him. But Hamilton offered up Kirkpatrick who, like a fool, fell for it."

"And it almost worked. We believe it was as much about revenge as getting the man responsible. The prince wanted to wound the US. Embarrass a superpower by a simple act. Just like 9/11 demonstrated how weak we are, having a US soldier execute either the senator or congressman would demonstrate our corruption or failings. The ultimate insult: to be killed by one of your own. Hamilton had a man on the inside who was willing to execute Kirkpatrick if you failed to."

"Simmons—the senator's assistant."

"Yes."

Then Scott realised the connection. "Simmons was an ex-marine wasn't he?"

"Served under Hamilton for thirteen years."

"Everyone seems to have had their own agenda." Kate shook her head. "It was a set-up by the Saudi prince and Woodall for you to execute the senator or congressman. So where does that awful Arab fit in?"

Hurwitz said, "We think he was helped to follow the trail to Scott acting as Joe. Hamilton didn't react so the Arab came into play to make the threat seem genuine. Woodall had to get Scott running and connect the dots for the Arab."

Kate said, "If Woodall is that involved, you won't let him turn state's evidence and get away with it, will you?"

"To get the congressman?" Hurwitz asked, raising an eyebrow. "Sure we will. Whether we like it or not, it's always the bigger fish we want to fry." He shrugged. "Anyway, the upshot is, no one—not the Hamilton, not Woodall, not the Saudis—has anything to gain and no further incentive to go after you guys."

Scott knew it would be a long time before he could truly relax. Something still didn't feel right. If the congressman was so smart, would he have trusted Woodall? Wouldn't he also have a backup plan? Maybe it was just paranoia. Scott resolved to keep his concerns to himself.

Hurwitz was still talking. With one eyebrow raised, he said "So, we're pretty sure you don't really need to be in protection anymore."

Kate exchanged glances with Scott. "But only pretty sure?"

"We're staying put for the time being," Scott said, "Until we're at least a hundred percent convinced."

It was dark when they finished and the agent said it was time to get back.

He handed Scott a phone. "Look, as I said, we think you're safe but just in case if you want to make a onetime call to me, my number's on this."

Kate picked up Tolkien and they waved Hurwitz off. She ran her hand round his collar, causing the tag to clink. She smiled, contented.

"When did you engrave Tolkien's tag?"

"Sorry, hon?"

"The code on the tag. When did you do that?"

Scott shook his head confused. "I don't know what you are..." His heart began to race. "What's the relevance of the code?"

Now it was Kate's turn to look uncertain. "It was the code you left to get into Danny's email... that proved I could trust Matt."

"I only left you the code on the photo. If you'd read my letter you'd have understood it. You shouldn't have needed anyone else's help."

"So you didn't arrange for Matt—?"

"That's what I'm saying. Did you see him die?" Scott ran to the door as he spoke.

"He was shot in the arm...The Arab. He was standing over him. I heard him shoot... Oh my God, you don't think...?"

"I need to tell Ben."

Scott snatched open the door. The SUV had gone. Hurwitz would be well into the forest by now. Could Scott catch up? Maybe. Shouting to Kate to lock the door, he ran for his four-by-four. As he reached the GMC's door, he froze. He heard something he hadn't heard for a few years. Since his time in the army. Not much louder than a bird call but distinctive.

The sound of a suppressed gunshot.

SEVENTY-SIX

The worst-case scenario had happened. The man known as the Janitor stopped his Nissan pickup before the forest ended and watched. The road dipped for about two miles. Through binoculars he could see a stream and a lodge just beyond. The black SUV he'd been tailing pulled up next to the lodge. Hurwitz got out.

The Janitor turned and found a side track that would both provide cover and give him a line of sight to the property. It also gave him options depending on what happened. If Hurwitz left fairly soon, the Janitor would get back on the road, drive through the forest and pretend to break down. The Janitor's disguise made him look elderly. With no other traffic around, the agent was bound to stop and offer assistance.

The Janitor popped a stick of gum in his mouth and settled down to wait.

It wasn't long before Hurwitz re-emerged. The Janitor started the Nissan, prepared. But instead of driving off, the agent collected something from the SUV. A pet carrier maybe. The Janitor settled down to watch again. He opened another gum and started to play with the wrapper.

Mustang hadn't explained the issue but it was easy to establish. The congressman had panicked when he heard of the raid to capture the Saudi prince's son. Congressman Hamilton's men had failed to stop it, failed to save the son. Bin Shahd would want revenge and the first contingency was to let Kirkpatrick become the target. Ensure the Arab didn't kill Cassano and convince him that Kirkpatrick was Mustang.

The congressman was under house arrest but he would never be indicted. The state's evidence would never happen. Dead men can't give evidence. The Janitor would see to that. Woodall would be dead before anyone knew about Hurwitz and Cassano.

The air was still and smelled like maybe it would snow again. The Janitor much preferred the heat of Panama to this. A small herd of white-tail deer came close, looped around his pickup as though he wasn't there.

He would take out Hurwitz and then move and dispatch Scott Cassano and the girl. Quick and easy. They thought they were safe but Hurwitz had led him straight here. All he needed to do was bide his time. Just like he had for Senator Kirkpatrick, making it look like suicide. It could have ended there if Woodall hadn't been captured. So this was the worst-case scenario. The second contingency. A fallback. The main reason the Janitor had been appointed.

The light began to fade and the Janitor decided to change his plan. If it was dark when Hurwitz came across the broken-down pickup, he was less likely to stop. Then it could get messy.

He started the engine and slowly manoeuvred the Nissan until the rear of the pickup pointed to the target area. Clambering into the back, the Janitor dropped the tailgate and spread out his mat. He took his rifle—an M2010 ESR—from his kitbag and adjusted it. He fixed a suppressor and night scope and set the focus for 100 yards. Well within the range of the magnum round. He could put a round between a man's eyes at almost ten times that. Only, the forest restricted the line of sight. Any nearer and there'd be no sport in it.

Although there was snow on the ground, the road was clear. If Hurwitz was doing sixty miles an hour, he'd see the SUV for about five seconds before he'd take the shot.

He lay down, popped another stick of gum in his mouth and looked through the scope at the lodge. Lights came on inside and seemed like bright green flares in the twilight.

He filled the time by counting his heart rate. Relaxing, getting it sub-fifty. Waiting was good. He'd been waiting for almost two years. He'd followed events and his people had given him control. He'd used the hapless Matt but the genius had been getting Cassano's girlfriend to contact him. To trust Matt. He'd managed to get someone close to her, to be her friend. She'd gained access to the photos and the cat's name tag. He'd used Lisa—the stewardess. An easy conquest and an easy pawn.

The Arab had killed Matt. One less problem to worry about. Once the Janitor had removed Cassano, his girlfriend and Woodall, there was just one more thing to tidy up. Invite Lisa to stay, meet in Chicago where she used to work. She'd come. No doubt about it. And disposal stateside was definitely the easiest option.

It was full dark when the front door opened to a burst of light. He watched Hurwitz wave and get into the SUV, turn onto the road and head towards him.

He switched the scope back to 800 yards and aimed at the gap in the trees. He began to count. A white-tail raised its head and looked about as though it sensed him watching.

An urgent vibration and beeping of his phone broke his concentration momentarily. He judged he had twenty seconds. A quick glance told him he needed to read the message. He could hear the SUV almost at the forest edge. But his heart rate was no longer slow, no longer under control. He read the headline, breathed in and breathed out.

Hamilton's Dead

There would be no big payday. It was over. Always a possibility that the final instalment wouldn't be made. He wouldn't be able to buy that island paradise but there was still plenty of the advance left.

The Janitor looked through the scope. Panama wasn't too bad. At least it was warm. And there was plenty of work if he wanted it.

The SUV's lights flared briefly and were gone. The white-tail deer had probably bolted. Then he saw it again, moving back to the spot by the road. It stopped, turned its head and stared back at him.

He calmed his heart rate, breathed in, and fired. Time to go home.

The gunshot had coincided with Hurwitz's SUV disappearing into the forest. Fear gripped Scot's guts. He had one hand on the shotgun beside him. He dialled and jammed the phone under his chin. The line was engaged. He tried again.

Come on, Ben, answer.

Scott tore up the hill and passed the treeline. After a short distance, his headlights picked up something lying in the drift alongside the road. He slewed the vehicle to a halt.

Even as he was stepping out of the cab he saw it was just a deer. Heat rose from the body; a recent kill. The back of the head was a mess of freshly poured blood. At first he didn't spot the entry point and then saw the shot was cleanly through the right eye.

The crunch of compacted snow made Scott look around.

A vehicle moved out of the woods from a side track less than fifty yards ahead. A dark, flatbed four-by-four. Foreign, probably Japanese. Its lights were off. It lumbered through the drift into the road, almost like it had a problem.

The man at the wheel turned towards him. Hard to see in the dark, but the guy was definitely looking. The guy's hand came up and touched the brim of his cap.

And then, breaking the spell, the vehicle's headlights burst into life and it took off down the road, into the forest.

Scott watched it go, his breath steaming in his own vehicle's headlights.

When the taillights were gone, he walked back to the deer trying to make sense of it. Why had the hunter had just shot the deer and left it? From the damage it looked like an over-specced high velocity round. Nothing unusual there, but why use a suppressor? And was the shot through the eye a lucky one or precision?

Intrigued, he swung into the GMC and headed to where the other vehicle had come out. Bumping over the drift, across the other's ruts, he edged down the track.

The mobile rang.

Hurwitz said, "You OK, buddy? Didn't expect you to call so soon."

"I couldn't get through. I heard a shot, thought—"

Hurwitz laughed. "I'm fine."

"Yeah, I know that now."

"Not like you to be jittery. In fact I was on another call and would then have called you anyway. News about

Congressman Hamilton: He died an hour ago. Massive heart attack. Some guys have all the luck, eh?"

Scott stopped and climbed out of the GMC. There was something in the compacted snow, glinting in his headlights.

"I guess. Take care, Ben."

He ended the call and picked up the object: a folded, silver chewing gum paper. Made up of three pieces. An animal of some kind, maybe a deer.

This is where the hunter had positioned his vehicle. There was a good line of sight to where the deer lay. To his right he could see the lights of his lodge. Kate was in there, doors locked, waiting.

Scott looked at the folded wrappers again and thought about the deer. No genuine hunter would shoot a deer and immediately leave it.

Unless, of course, he had some news that changed the game.

And then Scott got it. The origami animal wasn't a deer. It was a kind of message: a horse. That had been no ordinary hunter. The guy had been there to clean up Hamilton's mess; to remove the witnesses. Hurwitz first, so there would be no warning, then Scott and Kate, and then Woodall.

But he hadn't carried it through.

It was over. Really over.

Scott flicked the paper horse away and jumped into the four-by-four. He K-turned, jounced down the track and pulled onto the road.

He paused by the deer and saw a brief flash of what had come so close.

Snow began to fall. The flakes danced in his headlights then, moments later, heavier ones hit the windscreen. He put his foot down and headed for home.

Acknowledgements

There are many ups and downs in writing—especially a book that took six years to go from the first draft to something I was happy with. I am grateful to my family for their cajoling and general encouragement—and finally insistence that I Dare You be published. Thank you to Robert Barrington and Tobias Block of Transparency International for your information on corruption in Iraq. Thank you to my family and friends for their reviews of early drafts. To John Christiansen for research and for being my tour guide in Prague. To Pete Tonkin whose comments helped shape this final version. I am grateful to the Barbara Levy Literary Agency especially to Mike Bailey (no relation) for his review of an early version. Hopefully you'll approve of the changes I've made. A final mention should go to my editor, Richard Sheehan, who did an excellent job. As always though, any mistakes are my own.

Author's note

The "ghost soldiers" of Iraq has been widely covered in the media and is the reason Islamic State fighters found little resistance when they took Mosul from Iraqi forces in 2014. Military commanders had 50,000 soldiers on their books—the equivalent to four battalions—receiving salaries without showing up for work. In reality the commanders were pocketing the money. They paid $1 million for the position of military commander which resulted in extortion and the abuse of power on a staggering, institutionalised scale. Transparency International report that at each year least $380 million of international funds intended for defence and security goes to corrupt officials.

If you would like to know more about the corruption associated with the defence and security of Iraq, the most comprehensive available source of information is Transparency International's "Government Defence Anti-Corruption Index":

http://government.defenceindex.org/countries/iraq/

The "personnel section" is of greatest interest.

There is no evidence that the US were directly or indirectly involved in the corruption. However the expression "the buck stops here" seems apt. Where did the aspiring military commanders and other corrupt officials get the $1 million each to fund their roles. And who did they pay this to?